ARABA

LET'S SEPARATE

The Story of the Nigerian Civil War

Ayuba Mshelia

authorHOUSE®

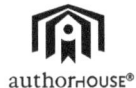

AuthorHouse™
1663 Liberty Drive
Bloomington, IN 47403
www.authorhouse.com
Phone: 1-800-839-8640

© 2012 Ayuba Mshelia. All rights reserved.

No part of this book may be reproduced, stored in a retrieval system, or transmitted by any means without the written permission of the author.

Published by AuthorHouse 4/24/2012

ISBN: 978-1-4685-2427-7 (sc)
ISBN: 978-1-4685-2426-0 (hc)
ISBN: 978-1-4685-2972-2 (e)

Library of Congress Control Number: 2011962561

Any people depicted in stock imagery provided by Thinkstock are models, and such images are being used for illustrative purposes only.
Certain stock imagery © Thinkstock.

This book is printed on acid-free paper.

Because of the dynamic nature of the Internet, any web addresses or links contained in this book may have changed since publication and may no longer be valid. The views expressed in this work are solely those of the author and do not necessarily reflect the views of the publisher, and the publisher hereby disclaims any responsibility for them.

This Book is dedicated to the men and women who fought on both sides of the Nigerian civil war. Their gallantry and ultimate sacrifice will never be forgotten by their compatriots. It is because of them that Nigeria is still an indivisible and better polity today. We hope to never have to revisit that sordid and terrible experience again.

Contents

Araba – Preface ix

Prologue xiii

Chapter One The Prophetic Dream 1

Chapter Two Sir Ahmadu Bello 13

Chapter Three January 15, 1966 *Death comes at Night: The Night Marauders* 25

Chapter Four *The Calm before the Storm* The Northern Poets/Praise-Singers and the Sardauna 33

Chapter Five Decree No 34, Gossips, Innuendoes and Riots. 57

Chapter Six The Counter-Coup d'état 65

Chapter Seven *Araba/Aware-To separate- and the Aburi Accord* 80

Chapter Eight Declaration of Hostilities 101

Chapter Nine Selected Battle Scenes 123

Chapter Ten *Bugile Wallace Gwor and Marianne Rabi Sambo Wedding* 171

Chapter Eleven *The Southern theatre* 211

Chapter Twelve Light at the End of the Tunnel The Marine Commandos 218

Chapter Thirteen *Lessons of the War* 257

References 267

ARABA Figures

Fig.1: Nigeria's Regional Structure prior to May 1967 5

Fig.2: The Twelve-state structure announced by Gowon on May27, 1967 103

Fig. 3: Liberation of Mid-west 107

Fig.4: Operation OAU 117

Fig. 5: Retreat 216

Fig. 6: Front line in Mid-1969 232

Fig. 7: Final Offensive 240

The infamous mobile 'Voice of 'Biafra' Radio Station at Obodo Ukwu... 246

Araba – Preface

The impetus for writing this story was conceived and begun immediately at the end of the last chapter of my book *Suksuku* (2009). The feat of documenting the story of political strife in Nigeria, comprehensively, in a single book, such as this proposes to be is quite plausibly a herculean task. In view of such difficulty this book *Araba—separation/division*—limits its scope to one single but important event in the life of the nation (that occurred in 1966). This was the January 15 *coup d'état* that led to the massacre of mostly prominent northern politicians including the then-Prime Minister of Nigeria, Sir Abubakar Tafawa Balewa, and the indefeasible Premier of the North, Sir Ahmadu Bello, the Sardauna of Sokoto.

The Northern elite, including those serving in the army felt the need to do something to ameliorate the imbalance of the disproportional amount of killing that had occurred on January 15. Such need was further made evident by some of the Hausa praise-singers, but, most especially, by the promulgation of the obnoxious "decree No 34", by the head of state and commander-in-chief at the time, General Ironsi. This decree abrogated the federal structure of Nigeria and replaced it with a unitary system of government.

This was the catalyst the North had been waiting for to bring about some sanity to the system introduced by Ironsi. Ironsi's regime didn't last long after the promulgation of decree No 34; he was overthrown by the military led, among others, by Murtala Mohammed, a Northern officer from Kano.

Gowon was chosen to replace General Ironsi as head of state and commander-in-chief of the armed forces. The first official action taken by Gowon was the abrogation of the obnoxious "decree No 34", and the creation of a twelve-state structure for Nigeria. The effects of Gowon's actions and the rampant killings of Igbos that were taking place in the

North and Northerners in the East led Ojukwu to declare the secession of the Eastern state, where he was the military governor. He called his dream republic "Biafra". The seeds of civil war were thus planted - with untold consequences for all Nigerians, but most especially the Igbos of the East.

It took the Nigerian army, under such distinguished officers as, M. Mohammed, M. Shuwa, Adekunle ("the black scorpion"), and A. O. Obasanjo, to mention just a few, four years to bring an end to the bloody, internecine civil war. The general and magnanimous amnesty given to those who fought against their fatherland by, General Yakubu Gowon went a long way towards soothing wounds of the civil war and permitting the re-entrance of the Igbos, without bias or acrimony, into the economic and political life of the country.

In writing this story about the Nigerian civil war, numerous sources and individuals have been contacted to gain its balanced perspective and to help the story reach a final completion. These sources include the article, *Citizen for Nigeria-Northern Nigerian Military Counter-Rebellion of July, 1966* by Dr. Nowa Omoigui originally published and posted on the website: *www.citizensfornigeria.com*. Also consulted were *My Command*, (1980) by General Olusegun Obasanjo (the final draft of this manuscript was shown the General who recommended the title *"araba"* instead of the option *" aware"* which the author was also contemplating; and he expressed his profound appreciation of the author's efforts. I'm grateful and indebted to him for allowing me to use some images from his book, **My Command**); *Nigeria: The Challenge of Biafra* (1980), by Arthur A. Nwankwo; *The Man Kaduna Nzeogwu & Ojukwu*, (2006) by Prof. Tom Forsyth, and, finally, *The Nigerian Civil War and its Aftermath: Views from Within*, (2001) by Gen.(Dr) Yakubu Gowon, GCFR and Obong (Gen.) Philip Efiong (rtd).

For advertent and inadvertent comments and discussions which have helped in writing the story I'm grateful to my brother, Colonel Markus Y. Mshelia (rtd), who's input about military culture and behavior, especially in a war time, was invaluable. Of equal importance were the comments and encouragements I received from my son, Bilar A. Mshelia (Esq.) from the start to the end. For this I'm indebted to him. I'm also indebted to my friend, Dr.Lawrence Nii Nartey and Ms. Xin Gong, who, without any foot-dragging, offered me his expertise in computer technology and photo scanning and transposition. Last but not the least is the contribution made by Mr. Simon Pettet who, single-handedly, edited the whole manuscript and collated the book with literate intelligence and uncanny sensitivity. His experience in such endeavor made the story succinct and pleasurable to read. For this I'm eternally grateful to him.

Writing a book can be a lonely and miserable business, not only for the writer, but for all those in his immediate orbit. It leads to obsessive behavior of many sorts by the author and a selfish protection of his every waking moment, with the resultant inattention to personal relationships and basic natural sympathies and care. In spite of all of these shortcomings, my wife Wahir and my son Bilar have sustained me with love and unfailing encouragement, helpful criticisms and characteristically stylish down-to-earth suggestions. For past neglect I owe my family a sincere apology and promise to make it up to them in due time.

Finally, this book is not about the history of the Nigerian civil war, but an attempt to present history in a fictional form for an easy and interesting reading for the general public. However, in some instances actual full names or first names of some historical figures have been used to reflect their historical role in the war. Otherwise all the characters and the battle scenes are fictional and have no direct reference to any living or dead person.

At the time of going to press with the book, on November 26, 2011; it was announced that the former secessionist and rebel leader, Ojukwu had passed away in a London hospital, England, at 2:30Am. He was 78 years old.

AYM
New York, 2011

Prologue

The Northern city of Kaduna, where the events of January 15, 1966 took place, leading subsequently to the internecine civil war, is located on the Kaduna River in the central plains of Northern Nigeria, only 100 miles from the present Federal capital Abuja, which, at the time, was a mere wild open virgin land with scattered Gwari villages and hamlets. The river is a tributary of the Niger River, the longest river in West Africa (4180km/2600mls). Other tributaries of the Niger River in Nigeria are the Sokoto, Benue, Anambra, Forcados and the Nun Rivers. The source of River Niger is Tembakounda in the Guinean highlands of Fouta Djallon. The river flows through five West African countries (Guinea, Mali, Niger, Benin and Nigeria) and nine major cities, which include Siguir (Guinea), Bamako, Segou, Mupti, Timbuktu and Gao (all in Mali), Niamey (Niger) and Lokoja and Onitsha (Nigeria).

The city of Kaduna was founded in 1913 by the British colonial traders and became the Northern Nigerian capital in 1917, until 1967. The city derives its name from the *"kada"*—-a word in the Hausa dialect which means 'crocodiles'— crocodiles infested the river and its surrounds. The city became the Northern Nigerian seat of Government because of its central location in the lush northern plain with major hubs of transportation and a river that provides a rich fertile settlement and abundant farming land.

The cosmopolitan nature of the city is reflected in the number of ethnic groups represented, which include; Gbegyi (Gwari or Gbari), Hausa, Yoruba and Igbo. Kaduna is now the capital of Kaduna State, comprising of twenty-three Local Government Areas, with over six million people. The state was created in 1976 from the former North-Central state. The population of the city is about one and-a-half million people. As mentioned earlier, prior to its present status as the capital of Kaduna state, it had served as the capital of Northern Nigeria (1917-1967), and, more recently, that of the North-Central state, from 1967-1976. At the time of our story, in 1966, the city was the seat of the Northern Nigeria Regional Government.

Kaduna city has three distinctive architectures reflecting itsdiverse and multifaceted influences of historic times. Some settlement areas have dome-shaped buildings reflecting its Arab influence, in others there are two- and three- storey buildings and structures reminiscent of buildings you might see in any major western cosmopolitan city; still others, in some quarters, mostly on the outskirts, are local ramshackle structures of mud houses with triangular thatched roofs, reflecting a local indigenous development or culture. Despite these different influences and the variety of settlement zones, the City enjoys a burst and bustle of activity in direct proportion and magnitude to its status as a seat of three different Northern Governments and home to the two major religions;Christianity and Islam.

In the South-western part of the city are a wide variety of a number of factories and for organizations such as the Northern Nigeria Petroleum Corporation (NNPC), producing predominantly petroleum products, breweries; the home of the *Star beer* and *Fanta*, and numerous other industries of manufacturing including facilities for textiles, steel, aluminum and pottery. In the center is the popular Central Kaduna Market, which was recently rebuilt after fire destroyed it in the late 1990s. The market is the nerve center of all local trades and business transactions. There are numerous mega-stores as well, such as the Kingsway and Leventis, which grace the all-important Ahmadu Bello Way. Other important buildings include the *Hamdala* Hotel and the Lugard Hall (Northern seat of the House of Representatives and Emirs). There are numerous large and small retail stores and foreign Consulate buildings embracing and hugging the *Ahmadu Bello* Way on both sides along the Kaduna-Zaria road.

All of these places form the major nexus of human interaction and business during the restless, relentless, and ever- busy daily life of the city, with pedestrians, cyclists, *amalanke* pushers, *mai moya,* and motorists, all juggling for the rite of passage, along most of the city's arteries of communication, but, most especially, the *Ahmadu Bello* Way.

Night-life however is the polar opposite of the hurried bustle of the day-time. It is practically a lock-down, controlled and patrolled by ruthless, sinister and malign night-marauders, armed with machetes, knives and in some instances, yes, guns. These pernicious and evil men who hover on the fringe of society cause untold havoc on property and on the lives of the residents.

On the night of January 15, 1966, amongst those mean and dangerous rag- tag night-marauders might be heard the sound of the melancholic ill-conceived Regimen of an organized group of unsuspected soldiers under the command of the myopic and self-righteous Major *Kaduna* marching in cadence in purposeful and deliberate formation along the Kaduna-Zaria road, where the Premier of the Northern Region, Sir Ahmadu Bello, Sardauna of Sokoto and some of his high-ranking ministers lived. The nocturnal armed brigands (and thieves) heard the marching boots along the Zaria road but thought it was merely the careless maneuvers of other marauders like themselves, and did nothing to interfere or check them out. Many of the soldiers it turned out were oblivious, unaware of the malevolent and machinate intentions or mission of their commanding officer, or indeed even of the purpose of their nocturnal march, other than as a normal military night training. Little did they know that their perilous mission that fateful, gloomy, dark and moon-less night under the ambitious and self-righteous Major *Kaduna* would; forever change the political, economic and social life of the people of the Federal Republic of Nigeria.

January 15, 1966, let me hasten to say, and remind my readers, was exceptional in the annals of Nigerian history; an event which was almost impossible to comprehend or objectively contemplate at the time. All words, my avid readers, are finally inadequate and must be discarded with respect to the shocking facts of that extraordinary barbaric massacre in the dark and lull of the pre-dawn hours of that fateful day. As you now know or perhaps might have already known, the momentous events of January 1966 embodied all the smoldering angst, apprehensions and malaise of the Nigerian public but, most specifically, in the North, where those killings had the greatest impact and acrimony.

No individual ever arose from the Nigerian political scene with equal dedication to his peoples' welfare as the Sardauna. In fact, ever so in his time up to today, the word "northerner" has always come to represent or evoke a "tribe" instead of a diverse collection of the more than two hundred tribes in the north."Oh you're a northerner? Then you must be a Fulani/hausa", is an inept question always asked. When you answer that "yes I'm a northerner, but I'm", say Angas, Bura, Kanuri, Birom or Kanuri to mention a few, most people are mesmerized and shocked; because they've always thought of the "north" as a tribe, such as Yoruba or Igbo.

The massacre that took place that day when most honest Nigerians were safe at home huddled under their blankets; was therefore viewed by many patriotic Nigerians as an attack on the very foundation of the

Republic and its unity. This was especially true in the then-Northern Nigeria —now composed of nineteen states and Abuja the federal capital. It was viewed in some isolated quarters as a paltry sentimental or tribal plot by a few misguided dissident officers against the Northern leadership, most specifically Sir Ahmadu Bello, the Sardauna of Sokoto and the then-Premier of the North, and Sir Abubakar Tafawa Balewa, the Prime Minister of the Federal Republic at that sorry moment. There were those who hailed it as a god send to cleanse the sins of nepotism and religious fanaticism. Zeal needed to be met with zeal But whichever side of the fence you were on, the fact remains a disproportionate cadre of Northern leaders was selectively murdered, and for no other obvious reason as far as the common man was concerned than their ethnic identity and religious beliefs as Northerners. To quote an old adage: "To die is nothing, but it is terrible not to live"; as was true with those who died that day, including not only the political leaderships, but the military as well, perishing for no other reason, in most cases, other than that they were first and foremost Nigerians, and only secondarily spokespersons for a region, Northerners representing the interests of their diverse and particular peoples.

One of the traits that had endeared the Sardauna to the people of the North but were regarded by his enemies as a catalyst for his downfall and contributing factors to his eventual death, included his unique ability to pay personal attention and interest to all individuals, regardless of their tribe, religion or party affiliation. One example of this was on the occasion when he noticed a particular student from Plateau state had scored the highest on the Higher School Certificate (HSC) results for that year. It was his habit to personally go through and review the results as soon as they were released. He immediately ordered the boy to Kaduna. The boy's father became scared fearing the worst because it wasn't normal or expected that the premier of the Northern region would invite you to come over for a visit. He therefore showed his premonitions and misgivings by asking if he could come along and accompany his son. His request was granted, and he joined his son on the long five-day journey by lorry/truck traversing through the peaked and meandering dirt roads that characterize the Plateau Mountains and valleys, forests and plains to Kaduna. When they finally arrived at Kaduna, they found the Sardauna having his lunch and he invited them to come in and share it with him, but the father absolutely refused, declaring, "We don't deserve such honor. We're just peasants and local villagers". The Sardauna gave them his broad and infectious smile to put them at ease and continued to insist that they join him, but the father stuck to his guns though gave in to some degree by saying they would eat whatever was left over after he was finished. But the Sardauna would hear none of this. He stood up brusquely and pushed away the plate of food in front of him and declared in his deep voice "then this means all of us will go without". On hearing this, father and son succumbed to the premier's entreaty and they joined him. After the meal, he confided in them that he had invited them to Kaduna because the boy was an example of the kind of people the North was going to have to depend upon "in order to close the educational gap". As such, the boy had been secured admission to a prestigious educational establishment overseas and was going for further preparations in England! "So, congratulations, on behalf of myself and the people of the North". Both father and son were stunned and shocked, and remained speechless for quite a long while. When the father finally came out of his stupor, he fell on his knees in gratitude, but the Sardauna picked him up and assured him that this was unnecessary. He wasn't doing them any favors, but merely dutifully rewarding meritocracy which the boy clearly had "in abundance". They were understandably completely taken aback, in part because they hadn't heard of the results yet — nobody had. But most perplexing to them was that they were Christians and didn't think, in their wildest dreams, that it was possible. This wasn't an isolated incident. The Sardauna had acted this way on hundreds of occasions, towards a diverse number of minorities from all over the Northern region, people who had the least expectation of receiving such a magnanimous gesture.

Another example known to this writer was the case of a grade-two teacher who was teaching in a missionary school in the former North-East State. For reasons unknown to the (missionary indigene) teacher, the Sardauna had heard about his diligence and dedication to education. Unexpectedly, one rainy day, as he sat with his wife and friends on his porch, a telegram came to him from Kaduna requesting him to make urgent arrangements to go there immediately, with a caveat that he should "put his house in order" because he "might not be back soon". He followed the telegram to the letter before embarking on his journey. It would be another fifteen years before he would set his foot on that soil again.

When he arrived in Kaduna everything had been done for him; his first-ever passport was ready and already stamped with a visa to England; ticket, admission letter, a contact address for when he arrived and three months' advance allowance for books and clothing including a special allowance for his winter clothing. On arrival he started work on his General Certificate of Education (GCE) Ordinary Level papers first, followed by the requisite Advanced Level papers. After meeting the legibility requirements for a degree admission, he enrolled in a degree-course at the London School of Economics. He earned his BSc. in Economics three years later. All in all he was away for more than fifteen years, on a full scholarship that he had never applied for. When he came back there was no demand made on him by the Sardauna to join the Civil Service or the public secondary school systems, instead he went back to his former Missionary school where the missionaries themselves decided to have him replace the outgoing expatriate Principal whose contract had expired. He thus became the first indigenous Principal of the College.

There was the instance of some students from Kabba Division, now in Kogi state, who took the exam for the military school and shared the top three scores on the exam, their dilemma was that they were all from the same school and weren't sure that they would all be allowed admission, having come from a non-Hausa/ Fulani and non-Muslim enclave in the North. But to their amazement, and everyone else's great surprise, they were the ones the Sardauna selected and recommended for admission. All of them, in particular Major General Jemibewon, went on subsequently to serve the country with distinction. The other two served the Federal republic with equal distinction in various capacities.

The Sardauna saw everyone as a human being and a "Northerner", and not as Birom, Kanuri, Yoruba, Bura, Higgi or Hausa. Of course the Hausas' might have expected to have gained more of such privileges because of their sheer numbers but the Sardauna didn't discriminate.

Also the Sardauna had launched a massive campaign against illiteracy in the region, which his enemies didn't appreciate. His success in creating unity among the North's two hundred diverse tribes was repugnant to some, especially the pre-eminence given to Hausa as the unifying language, which some Regional authorities bitterly opposed and despised.

The 1952-1953 crash programs at the Kano Medical Corps to produce indigenous doctors for the North was a rarity and a perfect example of his passion for promoting and "bringing up" the North in all spheres of human endeavor, and was one typically looked upon with resigned anger and indignation by his enemies.

The democratization of the Native Authorities from Emirs-in-Council to Emirs-and- Council, where some members were elected by the people, was frowned upon by his enemies as well. The enthusiasm he displayed in the creation of the crash programs in Law and Accountancy, and the introduction of Assistant District Officers (ADO's) training programs at the Institute of Administration, Zaria, wasn't shared by everyone. There were many who didn't want to see the North "rise" from the ashes of ignorance to close the so-called "educational gap". The creation of ABU, Zaria, and the Northern Regional Development Corporation (NRDC) that later became Northern Nigeria Development Corporation (NNDC), weren't popular at the time either. And finally the creation and establishment of the Bank of the North, the Broadcasting Company of Northern Nigeria (BCNN) and the Nigerian Citizen Newspapers sealed the considerable resentment and execrable hatred some of his critics had.

People who knew the Sardauna close-up said that one of the achievements that he was most proud of was his creation of the most able and most efficient civil service in the country, which he continued to insist was based solely on merit and above petty political and tribal quarrels and corruptions. Its success was in its transcendence of sub-regional interests and its ability to incorporate inter-generational cohorts into a cohesive whole. It's worth mentioning perhaps the significant and professional role the Northern civil service continued to play even after the death of the Sardauna.

Another milestone achievement of the Sardauna, which no doubt was acknowledged as the most significant of his numerous unparalleled achievements was the establishment of Ahmadu Bello University, Zaria. He was vehemently opposed by the Southern politicians when he first broached the idea, because, as they claimed, the North "hadn't the needed students for admission" into a University. The Sardauna barked back declaring in his booming voice, that it would be "good for students from the South to come over en masse so they that they will understand our culture and promote national unity". He added, prophetically, "In the next ten years, we'll need more Universities to accommodate students from the region". How right he was! When we look at the expansion of the number of Universities in the region, between the periods of October 4, 1962 when ABU was established and the present, we note that there is an increase by a factor of almost 1000 percent!

In terms of politics, one of the major political successes that the Sardauna achieved and cherished more than anything else was the incorporation of northern Cameroon into northern Nigeria. Northern Cameroon was a German colony, but after the war—World War II— it became a protectorate under the joint supervision of England and France. The British northern section became a Trust Territory and was attached to Northern Nigeria. In November 7, 1959 a plebiscite was conducted to decide whether it remains with Nigeria or join Southern Cameroon under the French influence. The vote was lopsided against Nigeria - the result was 42,979 for Northern Nigeria and 70,041 against. The Sardauna was infuriated and flushed with anger, but he wasn't going to take no for an answer. First, he lobbied the powers-to-be for a repeat plebiscite "because the people weren't adequately educated about what was at stake". He was granted his request, and immediately appointed Mr. D.J.M .Muffett as Resident General for Northern Cameroon to be in charge of the new 1961 plebiscite. Mr. Muffett was no stranger to the hard politics of the Sardauna, because he had been the Chief Electoral Officer for the North in the 1959 general election where the NPC had won an outright majority. In his efforts to turn the results of the second plebiscite around, he interviewed a large segment of the populace and was informed that in many cases they hadn't voted for Nigeria because of the color of the ballot box! In the first plebiscite, a red ballot box stood for Nigeria and a blue box for Southern Cameroon. However, unbeknownst to the Sardauna and indeed for many others involved, the locals had erroneously associated the red box with "the white man" and, since they had suffered a lot under the Germans, they refused to cast a vote for what in their minds, represented colonialism and a return to the German era of intimidation and suffering. The Sardauna in his ingenious way immediately changed the Nigeria's ballot box color to black after hearing this, subliminally invoking "the black man". In his campaign for political education for Northern Cameroon during the subsequent plebiscite he coined the following slogan:"*Mutanen Kamaroon ta Arewa, ku zabi bakin akwati mai fiter da farin tuwo*". This translates as: "People of Northern Cameroon you better choose the black box that brings out good benefits. The result was never in doubt when the votes were counted: 146,296 for Northern Nigeria and 97,659 against. In appreciation of his efforts and dedication during the campaign that turned the results around, thereby incorporating the Northern Cameroon in Nigeria, permanently, he was honored by having the province named after him; Sardauna Province, with headquarters at Mubi, now in Adamawa state. The incorporation of Northern Cameroon into Northern Nigeria reinforced for him his own sense of destiny.

The Sardauna was consciously aware of the sensitivity of the non-Muslim Northern tribes, not to mention Borno, with regard to the Sokoto caliphate and its influence. To counter these sensitivities he embarked on constant touring, using jokes to make those around him feel more at ease and with his easy, friendly manner, he was able to co-opt local tribal leaders. But above all these charms was his humanism, his absolute respect for the integrity of all, and his ability to disarm his opponents through direct personal relations. He never regarded his political opponents as his enemies, but, rather, as dedicated Northerners or as fellow Nigerians that just happened to be in a different camp.

His style of "winning people over" contrasted sharply with the firebrand nationalist rhetoric of the Southern politicians. His style of building bridges and winning people over, instead of creating divisiveness and confrontation served him well, as shown by his circle of friends including many those who were from different political camps. Such Inner circle included the Northern Elements Progressive Union (NEPU) leader, Mallam Aminu Kano, who, it was said, could walk into the Sardauna's living quarters without any appointments at any time any day. Others were a mix of both Muslim and Christian politicians; Awoniyi; Michel A. Buba; E. Mamiso; J. Tanko Yusuf; P. Achimugu, and J. Tarka, even as he was leading the Tiv uprising against the premier's legitimization.

In short, the Sardauna never stopped building bridges of unity all across the country, but most specifically amongst northerners which he always referred to as "my people". His worthy philosophical legacy of "One North, One People, One Destiny" stood for some short while, even after his death, but seems now to be somewhat submerged under the mighty weight of international globalization -or not?

However, before I delve into a full narration of the catastrophic events of January 15 and its consequent impact on individual lives and on the society at large; I'll like to introduce you to the main characters, the people from whose perspectives and aggregate memories this story is being told.

The Monte Sophia Residents

The *Monte Sophia quarter* (another appropriate name for this residential quarter is *Monte Logos*, but in order to avoid confusing it with our dear commercial city Lagos, "Sophia" is adopted and will be used instead) is a small exclusive, hilly, lush residential enclave that forms part of the larger Government Residential Area (the GRA). This quarter, like the GRA itself, was settled some forty years ago. At present, it forms the hub or nucleus of one of the most intellectually stimulating, most prestigious and rigorously sought -after residential settlements in town. It is an area of magnificent scenery— the massive central mosque within the city wall is clearly visible, especially the tall towering spire of the minaret to the south-west and the modern spiral dome of the airport to the north-east —and a treasured oasis for abstract rational thought —both scientific and religious— and pragmatic innovations in industry and the arts. Most of the houses in this quarter were constructed during the early colonial era and still bear some of the vestiges of that period, for example, well-laid cobbled stone streets, with the corner stone's cut with impeccable accuracy.

The trees that adorn the houses and streets include the eucalyptus, neem, acacia, palm and, yes, the *gamji*. They look as if they have been meticulously arranged by the most accomplished artist in town. The canopy, if viewed from above, seems to blanket the entire quarter like a luminous green tent. Most of the houses on *Monte Sophia* are massive and heavily-walled with meshed security wires or mud and stone walls "*katanga*". It was said that house **No** 93 between Hunt road and Aminu street was once occupied by the first Principal (Sir G.A.J. Bieneman,) of the famous Katsina College (a.k.a Barewa College), which most of the cadre of the immanent Northern leadership of the time attended. The college (founded in 1922) was initially staffed mainly by stiff-upper-lip colonial British graduates, for whom language (diction and oratory) was a sacred art, to be pursued and perfected at all costs. Thus nothing was spared in the process of language instruction, to ensure that the students of the college spoke "proper" English; that is English with all the diction and intonation of the proper British accent.

The interior antique furniture and murals of the residencies of *Monte Sophia*, and the palpable artistic displays of picturesque artifacts found in most of the old houses, have drawn the attention of coterie film directors, actors and archival-preservation buffs, for example Kasimu Yero's "Uncle Gaga" a sitcom shown on the NTA; the "Cockcrow at Dawn" series by the same actor/producer shown again on NTA in the 1980s. Most recently Kasimu Yero's "Kasarmu ce" produced by Matthew Rose and much other comedy sitcom series. The surroundings of the *Monte Sophia residential* quarter are always impeccably spotless and free from the ubiquitous street hawkers that patrol and populate our other streets at all and odd hours, for instance the newspaper-boys thrusting their commodity through your open window, and jogging alongside as you drive to collect their fee; the *maimoya,*people who sell water in kerosene cans on their shoulders, the two cans joined together on each shoulder by a rod or stick tied with rope at both ends; pan-handlers; simple beggars and squeegee (window-washers). Unlike most of our inner-city neighborhood quarters, the garbage is collected, religiously, every other day. Nothing is left to chance or unwanted predators. Sometimes you wonder why this isn't the norm everywhere in the country!

Above the high decorative *Katanga* (mud walls), meshed security-wires and the evergreens, such as the eucalyptus, are huge and towering antennas. These ubiquitous towering antennas, as a rule, hug the high *Katanga* walls in a conspicuous manner, as if to announce to a visitor the owners' status his capability for international Cable-reception and thus international contacts. In addition to these symbols of leisure and bourgeois mentality, behind each house stand inevitably humongous gray tanks, like barren ant-hills, for capturing rain water for storage, and a generator to supply electricity instantly if there is any outage—there are more outages than you can ever imagine, in spite of the politicians' lip-service of providing a sustainable and uninterrupted supply of electricity, in spite of all of the privileges and prestige of the residents, water shortages and electricity outages are still rampant. The elegance and prestige of *Monte Sophia* for all its singularity doesn't absolve it from the vagaries of the Water and Electricity Commission.

The setting for our story is thus the august and prestigious enclave of *Monte Sophia*, where seven families banded together and formed a **Local HistoricalSociety Study Group** (LHSSG) which met regularly every weekend to discuss events of great importance to one and all. At the time of writing the present story, the topic they were reviewing is the causes of the Nigerian civil war and its subsequent consequences, and whether or not the country is any better today. In short, has anything been learnt as a result?

As part of their bye-laws, it was agreed that the person leading the discussion of any particular topic at any time automatically assumes the role of President or Chairman. Thence, at the time of our present story, this role was fulfilled by Professor Balarabe Usman Yousef.

Among the residents of *Monte Sophia* were a good number of representatives of our diverse ethnic or tribal *melting pot*. They differed however from the general population in that most were more upwardly-mobile middle-class—if there is such a class categorization in our society—and in a way more educated than the typical Nigerian.

It was through their rigorous discussions and wise insights into the events of January 15, that this story is based. More often than not, the events of January 15, the life of the Sardauna and the eventual *"Aware/ Araba"* movement (to separate) and its consequent metamorphosis into civil war, are presented here through the *'eye'* of the *Monte Sophia member*—residents of the Local Historical Society Study Group.

The Chairman leading a discussion and analysis of the events, that had occurred more than forty years ago for the residents, was retired Professor Balarabe Usman Yousef; simply referred to as "the *Prof*" by the Historical study group. Professor Balarabe was a six-foot tall lanky gawky-looking sixty-five- year old Hausa man with thin gray and receding hair. He was originally from Wusasa Zaria, but now resided in our town at *Monte Sophia*. He often seemed off balance and absent-minded, which many of his friends attributed wittily to too much *reading* in conjunction with old age! He's still very handsome now, almost as when he was a young man growing up, in spite of his now advanced age, as is often heard whispered by members of the opposite sex. Even though most of the hair from his forehead has gone, he has a full and heavily-grayed beard in the form of a goatee. He still looks attractive and full of stamina and vitality. Professor Balarabe was retired from the University, but he still remained obsessed with history and politics. He remained an avid reader of history and historical novels and a great story-teller. As a young man, he had won his district's competition as the best oral story-teller and debater of his generation., He went on to win the Northern Regional award in his final year of Secondary School in that category, and since that time had never relented. The Prof had tried his hand or fortune in party politics, but had given up because, "my passion for storytelling and debate led me to be a teacher… I believe an effective teacher must be able to intellectually argue both sides of his propositions as well as being able to get over his points in a dramatic manner, bringing his characters to life so that his students, or listeners, can identify with them".

Balarabe saw himself as an innovator and thought hard over that for which he was responsible in creating, be it a story or argument. At times he perhaps seemed too energetic for the task at hand, but more often than not he might be, or appear lethargic and more laid back. Balarabe was often most active in the morning hours, but, as the sun moved across the tropical sky, he slowed down very precipitously, as if the sun were sucking his energy every time it disappeared behind the golden western horizon.

Professor Balarabe Musa Yousef and his wife Mariayamu (aka *Mamu*) occupied the house next to the one once occupied by the first Principal of Katsina College - House No87 Hunt Road and Kaita Street. Being retired, his main preoccupation now as he sees it is "the adoration and care" of his beautiful wife Mariayamu Aishatu Lamido, who was the daughter of the most distinguished Mallam Haruna Lamido, originally from Adamawa. *Mamu* has four older siblings which include the now-retired Colonel Haruna Buhari, Dr. Shuaibu of the University of Maiduguri, Alhaji Sanusi Bako the popular and distinguished Parliamentarian, and Drs. Kubili Binta Shehu of the Department of Pharmacology, Bukar Abba Ibrahim Damaturu University, Damaturu, Yobe state.

More than anything else, the Professor loves to enthrall and entertain any of his visitors who will listen with narratives recounting many aspects of pre-Colonial Nigerian history, the subsequent struggle for Independence, and, most specifically, the more recent history of the January 15, 1966 coup and its consequent role in leading to the civil war.

Professor Balarabe confessed to me that when he first set his eyes on his wife more than three decades ago, it was as if he had met his soul-mate love at first sight. "Those sweet innocent piercing eyes" he said "cut my heart like a dagger". And since that day, he confesses, he has never looked back or regretted his "divine" love-union with her. Balarabe is such a devout Muslim so much so that to him everything comes from the "divine", hence his reference to his marriage as a "divine" union.

He was an avid consumer of political intrigues and scandal magazine or newspaper gossip scandal-sheets. He was also a fanatic when it comes to the game of football, especially the Green Eagles, Plateau United FC, Jos (formerly JIB Strikers, FC); the Kano Pillars FC, and the Enugu Rangers.

Mariayamu or *Mamu* his wife was a very beautiful and energetic now fifty-five-year-old lady, whose beauty was well-known around Wusasa when she was growing up. She went to Wusasa Federal Government Girls' Queen Amina College before going on to major in English at one of the prestigious Universities in the West, Ibadan. She also attended a one-year course at Oxford University in London before joining the Federal Civil Service as a Principal of one of the few Federal Girls' Colleges at the time. She is now semi-retired but still active in the States' branch of the Parent Association Council (PAC), of which she is a founding member.

Adjacent to House No87 is House No56 on Dan Gote Street and

Maitama. This house was occupied by Mr. James Dong and his most lovely wife, Jamima Idakoji. James was a forty-year-old good-looking and good-natured fellow, originally from Makurdi but now living in our town. He claimed the same lineage as Joseph Tarka, that invincible, popular and prolific politician who had passed away some years previously. James was of a medium height, only five- foot seven inches tall, and more on the overweight side of the scale. He was always gentlemanly and had a fresh face and a clean hair-cut all the time, courtesy of his loving wife. He was by training a mechanic, who hadn't been born at the time the events under review took place, and was thus keen on knowing "what actually happened?" as he was in the habit of saying. After attending Makurdi Boys' Federal College, James went to Bukuru Technical University College where he majored in Engineering and Metal Sheet and business. He now owns his own transport business, the ubiquitous and there-in-all-season *JJ &Dong Associates Transport*. He's also an export-import agent for Mercedes and Volvo cars.

Jamima Idakoji, James' beautiful and fashion-conscious lady, was by profession a nurse. Jamima Idakoji was originally from Numan and attended Federal Government College Waka before going on to major in Nursing at ABU, Zaria. Jamima was selected the home-coming queen at her prom in the final year of secondary school. Those who knew her when she was growing up swore they had never seen such a "black beauty", with long wavy black hair hanging on her beautiful upright shoulders. Her large, sparkling, and beautiful brown eyes seem to penetrate the soul of her admirers when she looks or gives them one of her cordial, knowing and infectious smiles. Besides her beauty and intellect, Jamima also excelled as an athlete. She was a strong willed girl. Her records in the 200- and 400- meters at her secondary school still stand today and with no attendant loss of her femininity. Nobody has ever doubted or suspected her gender!

James first met Jamima at a church (Christ Benevolent Church) in Bukuru where she was spending one of her summer holidays with a relative. At the time James was still a student at Bukuru Technical University. He was instantly enraptured and charmed by her palpable exquisite ravishing beauty combined with a deep religious fervor during the *long* service. At the end of the service, after what seemed like an eternity, he approached her and introduced himself. At first the reception was cool and nonchalant, but, being a business-man cum student, James had learnt never to give up, that the greater the investment and patience, the greater the profit. This is how he had approached most important events in his life and this is how he approached this one. Hence after concerted and relentless efforts of rabid and fervid displays of passion and devotion to her, he eventually won her heart. They were happily married in the same church nine months later.

At thirty-three, Jamima is still a beautiful, plump, and still fervently religious woman; who continues to wear her long wavy black hair in a knot protruding from the middle of her skull just like she did when she was a much younger woman in the University. Although she has slowed down a little bit and hardly remembers any of the details of her triumphant and dominant athletic days let alone those records that still stand, she stays active and busy in different ways. In spite of, at times, feeling breathless, due in part to asthmatic and febrile episodes, she takes uncomplaining her children's education and church attendance as non-negotiable responsibilities and obligations. She has two children with her husband, a boy and a girl, Peter and Juliet respectively. Peter has expressed a strong interest in medicine and seems inclined to pursue his interest with vigor, while Juliet shows some predictable and impressive flashes of lawyer-like qualities— a quick tongue, fluent language (diction and oratory) and the ability to argue and convince her parents about anything, literally anything she deems, or perceives to be, paramount for her maximum comfort and survival!

James and his family moved to *Monte Sophia* quarters more than eight years ago and have since been singularly active in community programs and philanthropy.

In House No 80 on Dungu Road and Ahmadu Bello Way lived Aminu Kaita and his beautiful wife AiShetu Bilkisu Ibrahim. Mallam Aminu was a Hausa man from Kano but now lives in the **Monte Sophia** enclave. Mallam Aminu was six-months-old when the events under their consideration for discussion were taking place. He is of medium height, weighing about 175 pounds. He went to the famous Kano Boys' Federal Government College, which lies south-west and opposite of *Kofar* (Gate) Nasarawa and the Emir's Palace, within the old city walls. To the north of the College is the GRA proper, and to the north-east is *KofarMata* and to the north-west is the popular Magwam Water restaurant. After the completion of his secondary school education he went to Bayero University, Kano, and earned his MBA after a BA in business. He worked in Kano in the office of the Federal Ministry of Trade & and Investment as a Director, before moving to our town as a retiree. Mallam Aminu's hair had started graying around the edges—he sported side-burns and a well-kept goatee.

His wife the beautiful Hajiya AiShetu Bilkisu is Aluor Khan's cousin. She is a teacher by profession and has recently been promoted to Assistant Principal at Wambai Girls Federal Secondary School. She was originally from Yola and of Fulani ancestry. She met her husband at the University in a Social Science 102 class and immediately fell in love with him. Six months later they were married, according to their Islamic faith. They have three children, a boy, Mohammed Abubakar and two girls, Adama and Fadimatu. Mohammed is married with two children, so is Adama. Fadimatu is just completing her university education and aspires to work in the Federal Ministry of External Affairs, where she hopes one day to be the first female Foreign Minister.

House No 73 on the *Monte Sophia* was occupied by Golu Bunzu, a sometimes gruff private gentleman and his beautiful inspirational wife Francisca Janet, whom he first met at a friend's wedding, where he had been the best man. He always likes to tell those who would listen how on that occasion he had to hire a bicycle and ride forty miles, arriving in the village the night of the wedding, because the truck he was travelling in broke down and there was no other means of transport available to the village other than a bicycle! He confessed it was love at first sight when he spotted Francisca at a pew during the service and how he dutifully asked for her friendship after the service was over. Unfortunately they never hooked up again after the wedding ceremony. Francisca returned to her parents in Kano, to the home where they have lived since they emigrated from the Caribbean, more than forty years ago, and Golu went back to Toro Federal Government Secondary School, where he was an Assistant Principal. Two years later, however, as if by fate, they met again overseas, and happily renewed their acquaintance and commitment to each other. Mr. Bunzu had gone for his Master's degree in Public Administration with emphasis on Contract and Financial Management. Francisca was there on a special course for university teaching-hospitals' senior matrons. "I fell for her again instantly, but she was still not very receptive at the beginning. However, I gradually lured her to a study-group of two in Financial Management — her and me! From then on it was a smooth ride with no stormy episodes. We got married eighteen months later after our return home to Nigeria", he narrated to the writer.

Golu is now retired at the age of sixty-four, after having put in more than thirty-five years of public service in different positions and departments. He retired in 2004 as a Federal Permanent Secretary in the Ministry of Education.

Golu, by nature, was taciturn, except in the company of his cronies, like Dr. Aluor Khan and Bello Kabiru. Even though retired, he maintained his well-groomed habits —— a regular clean fresh face and hair-cut, exquisite immaculate tailoring, courtesy of his wife, who wouldn't allow him to go to the barbershop! Recently he has immersed himself in and dedicated himself to the creation of an association for retired workers, similar to the AARP (American Association of Retired People) in America. His initial efforts were rebuffed and scorned, but attitudes are changing and his efforts are now beginning to pay off through the more positive responses that he's been starting to get from the retired people he's been contacting all over the country.

Francisca is still with the University of Jos teaching hospital as a senior matron, but is already thinking of a second career as perhaps a member of the clergy. She's been taking part-time courses for **the robe** at Gindiri Seminary. For those who know her this shouldn't come as much of a surprise because she has always been a devout believer, a born-again Christian like her late parents. Most of Mr. Bunzu's friends and relations believe that marrying Francisca was one of the greatest blessings to ever come his way. She completely turned his life around at a time when he very much needed it and offered him a sanctuary of undiminished constant love and care.

They have four children, three boys and a girl. They are Julius, Dauda, Suleiman and Ngwakat, respectively. Julius and Suleiman have already completed their University education, and Suleiman now works at the Federal Ministry of External Affairs with the prospect of representing his country overseas some day as a Foreign Service career officer, or maybe even as an Ambassador. Julius works in the Federal Ministry of Finance as a Director. Dauda is now a successful mechanic after completing his Highest National Diploma (HND) at Bukuru Technical College of Education. Ngwakat is in her final year of medicine at the University of Jos, Plateau State, but has recently shown real talent in singing and acting. For instance at the most recent inter-universities talent completion, she came in first in solo folklore singing (the song is available on tape and CD) and her team came in second in the category of drama with her as the star actress.

Mr. Golu Bunzu and his wife are good friends of the Khan family because Francisca had her roots in the Caribbean and, additionally, Mr. Bunzu and Aluor were classmates in HSC at Kano Boys' Federal College, in the 'sixties. Mr. Bunzu was originally from Plateau State. He and his lovely wife moved to the *MonteSophia* enclave about fifteen years ago.

Owoleye Jide occupied House N̲o̲102 between Sophia Avenue and Logos Street. Owoleye was a short and stout thirty-five- year-old gentleman with dark, cropped hair. He sometimes wore side-burns and a goatee. He was one of the pastors required for the growing number of ubiquitous *mega*-churches that were spreading throughout the country; which gain their popularity by showering their patrons with the church's leisurely holiday hot-spots and special privileges, such as private quarters and meals at their monthly or annual awakenings.

Owoleye Jide was endowed with a booming and shrill voice which at times caused his congregation to put cotton in their ears when attending service. He was married to the beautiful and exquisite Fumilayo Afolabi. Owoleye and Fumilayo (aka Fumi) were high school sweethearts who first met at a **Fellowshipof Christian Students Association** (FCSA) meeting when both were in the final year of their **Higher School Certificate** (HSC) at Oyo in the West. After HSC both Owoleye and Fumilayo went to the University of Ibadan where he majored in Religious Studies and Fumilayo majored in English and Education. After they graduated, Owoleye answered the call of the cloth and worked as an outreach young pastor at the Evangelical Ebeneza Trinity Church of the Savior in Africa, Abeokuta, and Fumilayo taught chemistry at St Mary's Girls' Secondary School in a small town outside Abeokuta. They got married in the Evangelical Ebeneza Trinity Church in Africa, eighteen months later. Immediately thereafter, they moved to our town, more than twenty years ago, where they established a branch of the Evangelical Ebeneza Trinity Church where, at the time of writing, he is Senior Pastor. Both Pastor Owoleye and his wife Fumi have been active in outreach programs to the youth and the poor in the town and the villages around it.

They have four children, Samuel, Olumuyiwa, Omotayo and Bukola. Olumuyiwa has expressed an avid interest in medicine and Omotayo wants to be a lawyer. Samuel hasn't made a career choice yet—he's always admired his father's clerical attire and the whisper going around is that he may follow the father and wear the cloth. This is indeed most likely to come to fruition, given the lucrative nature of running a church in this country. It's becoming, if it hasn't already become, a huge and profitable business, as it is in the West. An allusion has been made by Pastor Lote of Christ Church with regard to the similarity between the mega-churches in

Nigeria and those in the West, especially those in the United States. Many of these churches now provide their elders with special privileges, especially during the monthly three-day **revivals**. Such privileges may include free personal lodgings for all three days of the revival or for the one-day weekly prayer *awakenings*, or it may involve a personal visit to one's suite by the Bishop for special prayer requests, promotion in place of work, good health, the ability to buy that extra house you've always wanted... At the end of these revivals or *awakenings*, patrons are expected and obligated to leave behind hefty checks for the church collected by the "**Ma**"or "**Madame**". *Ma* is a reverential title of the senior Bishop's wife.

Bukola isn't so sure of what she wants to become, but recently she has shown some interest in political science and economics. If my guess is right, I think she is leaning toward law as a profession because of the special skills she seems to possess in convincing people around her to respond to her needs and comforts without complaint or a second thought. Both Olumuyiwa and Omotayo attend Gwagwalawa University, while Bukola attends ABU, Zaria, and Samuel attends the University of Lagos. Fumilayo is now the Principal of Federal Girls' Ukpan College (in honor of the late political activist and philanthropist) conveniently located between the intersection of Tafawa and Maitama streets.

Alhaji Abba Habib and his wife Hajia Jummai Miriam Bukar hailed from Borno State, and they occupied House N̲o̲85 between Lamido and Kashim Ibrahim Streets, opposite the Garki Conference Center, not far from the Peoples' Parliament. Alhaji Abba is a tall and lanky thirty-eight-year-old dude who, by nature, is quiet and hardly speaks unless spoken to. However, he can spring into life when it comes to football and politics. He is an avid consumer of football statistics, and is good at it. He can recite off his head, the winners of the World Cup and the man of the match for each final, (the "Golden Boots" winners) and, in some cases, the margin of winning goals from the inception of the games in 1930, right up to the present —the cup wasn't held in 1942 and 1946 because of the war (World War II). By profession, however, he is a pharmacist, and, as it happens, a very successful one.

Alhaji Abba met Jummai while he was in his second year at Maiduguri University and she was entering her fourth year in Federal Girls' College Potiskum in Yobe State. The Alhaji expressed his sentiments to the author in the following words, "the moment I saw her, I knew it was her or nobody. I was knocked off my feet. Her big, beautiful and piercing sparkling eyes penetrated my soul and I instantly fell in love, never to look back". They got married at the end of her secondary school attendance.

Jummai went on to earn a degree in economics from the University of Maiduguri, in spite of family demands and commitments. She now works as an economist in the Federal Ministry of Trade as a Deputy Director. Alhaji Abba's lucrative private pharmacy is located at the Queen Amina commercial and residential quarters on the Kano-Garki-Wambai road. Both moved to *Monte Sophia* quarters ten years ago.

They have three children a boy and two girls, Sanusi, Hadizatu and Amina respectively. Hadizatu completed her law degree at the Bauchi Technical University and went overseas for a Masters degree. She now works in the Federal Capital as a Consultant to Hawul Ltd., a subsidiary of *Bal4Kwaya* Inc. the British export & importing company. She is still single and waiting patiently for Mr. Right. Amina graduated from Jos University and now works in the National Planning and Census Bureau office. She wants to get married but tradition dictates that she wait until Hadizatu is well ensconced in *her* matrimonial home before she takes the step. And so she keeps on waiting for the coast to clear! Sanusi is in his second year at Birmingham University, in England. He's planning on majoring in mechanical engineering and printing technology.

The last of our **Monte Sophia** neighbors is Dr. Aluor S. Khan and his most beautiful and genial wife Veronica Tyra. They occupied House No 93 between Hunt Road and Aminu Kano Street. Dr. Khan is a fifty-five-year-old retired mathematics professor who spends most of his time writing and reading political journals. He is an avid consumer of political gossip and innuendoes. Aluor Khan is a quiet and deliberative gentleman who harbors his emotions and privacy with great restraint. However while amongst friends and cronies he is vivacious, cunning and full of humor. During his youthful secondary school days he was popular on campus because of his athletic prowess. At present, however, all that remain are the memories and an abiding vanity.

Aluor Khan attended a Baptist Missionary Secondary School in Akwanga, Benue State, after which he gained admission to Ahmadu Bello University, Zaria. After graduation, he taught for few years and went to Cambridge, England for his doctorate. It was there he met Veronica Tyra, his wife.

Veronica is now fifty and is the Principal of the prestigious Queen Amina Girls' Federal College, Garki. "When I first saw her", Dr. Khan said, "My soul cringed, and almost stopped. I felt like a baby listening to a lullaby, and was almost knocked off my feet. I was mesmerized by her beauty and poise. It was as if she was a being from another planet. My heart melted and sank under the spell of her adorable brown eyes. Although she gave me a cold shoulder to begin with my persistent display of show of love and passion won her over time. I tell you it was love at first sight, and I've never once looked back or ever regretted it. And Veronica, since then, has never equivocated in her love for me. She has always adored and respected my hard work, diligence and intelligence. We got married two years later at Akwanga Church of the Nazarene", Dr. Khan recalled tepidly.

Veronica Tyra has black wavy hair, which she constantly wears in knots. She is often seen wearing a splendid gold chain around her right ankle."Her energy level and sweetness have always infected those around her", remarks her friend Sharon Williams. She radiates exuberance and confidence wherever she goes. Veronica Khan's life had been occupied by acts of selfless devotion performing good works with the under-privileged deaf and blind children, and these noble gestures have endowed her with a kind of personal luminosity and earned her respect and adoration from her colleagues. As she grew older she acquired what one might call, "the beauty of goodness", and, as she matured further, she developed a quality of unique transparency, through which her palpable saintly nature could be seen to sparkle and shine.

The Khans have four children, three boys and a girl, Jonathan, Blair, Samuel and Jimbala Ngozi Khan respectively. All the boys have completed their university education and are working. Jonathan is married to the beautiful Debra Sanusi and works as a lawyer in the Federal Ministry of Oil Resources and Export as a Director. They have two children, a boy and girl, Dicca and Qwatir. Blair is a corporate lawyer and a senior partner with the *Blair, Anderson & Williamson Export-Import Security* firm (LLP). He is married to the popular singer and dancer, Ms. Henrriett Daso. They have three children, a boy and two girls; Ibrahim, Quamtin and Carru, respectively. Samuel majored in Economics and political science and works in the *National Security and Homeland Protection Administration Agency* (NSHPAA) office branch in Lagos as an Assistant Director. He is still single, waiting for Miss Right! Jimbala is the youngest and is in her final year at Columbia University, New York, and aspires to be an astrophysicist-cosmologist! "I want to contribute to our knowledge of the beginning of the Universe, the Cosmic Dark Ages; the Cosmic Expansion-Inflation; Singularity, Dark Matter, DarkEnergy, Black Holes, the Cosmic

Microwave Background Radiation (CMBR)"—discovered, accidentally in 1965 by two Bell Laboratory scientists—the radiation left over from the very hot and dense early Universe that resulted or would have existed for 380,000 years after the big bang, a term pejoratively coined by a Cambridge astrophysicist named Fred Hoyle. The CMBR reflects the time when the expanding fireball from the big bang became diffuse enough that light could travel freely, which establishes the moment the universe became transparent to light; in short it's a frozen fingerprint of the big bang fireball — not to mention "hosts of other topics including Interstellar Exploration", she recently proudly exclaimed.

Dr. Khan was originally from Otukpo, Benue State and his wife Veronica Tyra came from the Caribbean, specifically, from St Martin Island. They have been in the *MonteSophia* enclave for the last twenty years.

The most recent addition to the **Local Historical Society study group** at *Monte Sophia* settlement was a retired banker, a gentleman by the name of Dr. Ahua J. Kasimu. He lives in House number 5 on Broad Street and Row Avenue. Dr. Kasimu is a quiet, taciturn sixty-three-year old single gentleman, with gray hair and plenty of facial hair including an impressive goatee and beard. His sideburns are always neat and low trimmed. In short, he's what you might call 'a dapper dresser'. He has a handsome and elegant physique which secured him beautiful women in his youth. He was married to his college sweetheart, Mariayamu (aka Mairam/Mairo), for more than three decades; until she succumbed to ovarian cancer at the still-youthful age of fifty-seven, some five years ago. They have three surviving children, AiShatu (aka Ai), Billa and Nani (one passed away in miscarriage). At the time the physician, Dr. Tukur expressed the opinion that the miscarriage happened possiblyeither because Mairam was malnourished or had above normal blood pressure; this in addition to her being a sickle cell carrier.

Dr.Ahua J. Kasimu (aka "Kas") came from Canada (he has dual citizenship, because he never relinquished his Nigerian citizenship). He arrived from Toronto, where he had lived and worked as a banker for more than three decades. Dr. Kasimu was originally from Kwande local government area in Benue state before he won a Federal Scholarship to the University of Toronto to study mathematics. His wife Marriayamu was also from Benue state. She was born at Garki in Kwande local government area. After earning his first PhD in Mathematics, he started to work on a part-time basis whilst pursuing another PhD in economics majoring as an econometrist, specializing as an actuary.

After completing his second PhD degree, Dr. Kasimu ingenuously figured that, with his PhDs secured under his belt, and without any contractual obligation or serious demand by the Nigerian Federal Government for him to return, he could pursue further work. He started to work for a branch of the famous Wall Street bankers *Goldmann Sucks*, after intense competition from *Modicum Stately*, *Towngroup* and *HMBC* Banks for his services. To be fair to Dr. Kasimu, after his first Ph.D. he'd written the Federal Scholarship Board, informing them of the completion of his studies and of his desire to return to the country. He then requested them to send him a return ticket. He waited and waited for a long time, but in vain, nothing happened, and nobody ever tried to get in contact with him. "With my PhDs in mathematics and economics I should be able to find a niche somewhere in the Ministry of Finance or the Central Bank where I can be of some service to my country", he reasoned, and contacted the Federal Civil Service Commission for a job in either the Federal Ministry of Finance, the Central Bank or the Ministry of Trade. But, boy, how wrong was he in his reasoning! All of his pleas fell on deaf ears, and he had the same result as with the Scholarship Board, immutable dead silence. He even tried to reason cogently and asked himself how a government could send you overseas for a study, and yet stubbornly refuse to show any interest in having you back to contribute your bit to the development of the country! It was after his every effort to return failed, that he started to work for Goldmann Sucks in earnest.

As fortune or fate would have it, depending on whom you talk to, Dr. Kasimu was one of the first PhDs on Wall Street to come up with the concept of *credit default swaps* (CDS), a bilateral contract in which the protection buyer of the CDS makes premium payments—called *the spread*— to the protection seller, and, in exchange, receives a *par value* or pay-off if the credit instrument or loan goes into default. It is a *zero-sum* game, which means you either win or lose. Originally it was used as a tool for *hedging*. The innovation and introduction of the CDS and its effective performance in raising the *return on equity* (ROE) to its corporate investment bankers served as a precursor to the introduction of *collaterized debt obligations*—CDOs (the collaterized debt obligation was first used by bankers at the now-defunct Drexel, Burnham & Lambert Inc. in 1987. It is a type of structured asset-backed security whose value and payments are derived from a portfolio of fixed income. These are securities backed by a pool of bonds, loans and other assets; and can be sold as alternatives to conventional bonds.). But after three or four decades of productive innovation and successful trade in mortgage-backed securities, in the form of highly structured, *collaterized mortgage obligation* (CMO), *collaterized debt obligations* (CDOs), subprime CDOs, CDOs squared, *collateralized loan obligation* (CLO) and *underwriting (*helping a company go public, raising capital or selling debt), he rose to the position of Chief Financial Officer (CFO), and, with the future of his children secured, he decided it was now time to retire and return home, he could now certainly afford his return ticket!

Dr. Kasimu now works on a part-time basis as a consultant to the Canadian consortium firm *Yamta-Rawala Financial Products and Assets Management* LLC, (YFPAM), with their headquarters at Suleiman Tukur and Tafawa Balewa Square in the Federal capital, as well as overseeing the management of a hedge fund he had personally established—*Kasimu Capital Innovation Investment*, LLP (KCII). He left the daily running and management of the *Kasimu Capital Innovation Investment* hedge fund to his cousin Alhaji Manga Alagali, the former Managing Director of the North Capitalzone Bank.

Dr. Kasimu had vowed not to remarry because as he grandly put it, "no woman can fill the humungous empty spot left by my youthful sweetheart". His wife, the late Mrs. Mariayamu Kasimu, had indeed been a very beautiful, elegant andfair-skinned lady with long hair which she usually tied in a web-like style or let loosely hanging on her shoulders. Both Dr. Kasimu and his wife were from Benue state. They met at a public lecture by Professor Patrice Wilmont, titled: "Nigerians Must Throw out Bad and Corrupt Leaders" at Ahmadu Bello University, Zaria, and instantly fell "head over heels"— as he called it—, in love. He was, at that time, a graduate assistant in the mathematics department while she was a second-year student majoring in history and English. Mariayamu had attended the now-famous J. Tarka Federal Girls' College in Makurdi before gaining admission into ABU, while Kasimu had attended Gindiri Boys' College. After their vicarious memorable encounter and a brief period of courtship, they got married two years later, after her graduation. Two further years later they moved to the University of Toronto, Canada, where Dr. Kasimu pursued a PhD degree in mathematics. Mariayamu had always been a teacher, all her life, first as an elementary school teacher, and later, secondary school, "because of my deep and abiding love of children", she used to say. They stayed married together for more than thirty-five years until her untimely death in 2000 to ovarian cancer. She was survived by her three children beside her husband.

"My wife's memory", Kas confessed recently, "continues to haunt me and always paralyzes any thoughts…. of another relationship. Having stayed together for more than thirty years, in spite of the ups and downs of marriage, and all the hassles that are involved in combining academic work and bringing up children at the same time, it's so difficult to start all over again. I loved her very, very much, and I know she loved me more than anything in her life. There's just no way can Ilove another woman with the same, or anything near the same intensity, complete devotion and commitment of purpose. I know that, even if I tried, I wouldn't be true to her, or to myself, so why try? My only consolation and the sole reason for my existence at present are my children, and the fact that, before her passing, we had both discussed and agreed upon what each wanted to happen in the event of death. We had carefully documented and planned everything in detail, including; for instance, whether to have the traditional open or closed casket?, cremation or burial?, we made a list of the friends and relatives we each wanted to see and have dinner with before we die. And my wife was able to have all the people she wanted to see visit her, including our children, her friends and our parents. I vividly remember the emotional meal we had with all our children and parents which consisted of my wife's favorite dishes of rice pudding, *tuwon shinkafa*, sorghum pudding, *tuwon dawa*, pounded yam and bitter leaf, *ukazi* and stock fish and *kuka* sauces (*miya*), which unfortunately turned out to be the last one that we ever had as a family. Every time I look at my children's faces it reminds me of her"; Dr.Kasimu broke down and wiped a tear from his glistening face.

Part of the reason Dr. Kasimu is haunted and obsessed by his wife's demise, a friend explained, is that she died while he was away. He knew she was suffering from cancer, but didn't, in his wildest imagination or dreams, suspect that her death was imminent or that it would come to her so suddenly, so he had travelled in late October to the United States to attend the Annual Fiduciary Management Conference of the Goldmann Suck's Senior Alpha Team, when death struck. His guilt was therefore very palpable, and immense, and, indeed, weighed heavily upon him, like a ton of bricks every waking moment. He would have hoped to have been able to cuddle her and hold her tightly to his bosom, as she took her last failing breath, or at least to have been able to feel her last pulse with his own warmcomforting hands, but fate dictated otherwise. For this reason, he remains always in a constant state of guilt and melancholia. To avert some of his vile feelings about himself, his nagging feeling that he'd deserted her, he immersed himself, in a profound way, in philanthropic work, particularly in funding the quest to help find a cure for cancer. He is active on several boards and a founding member and life-time member of WORCEC, the *World's Organization for Research, Cure and Eradication of Cance*r. He made sure every year of her death anniversary; he published a memoriam for her in the national papers, Daily news and New Nigeria.

Chapter One
The Prophetic Dream

Now that we have been introduced to this cast of immanent members of the *Monte Sophia* discussion group, who will help us navigate the catastrophic events that took place in our country, Nigeria almost half a century ago, with the ultimate consequence of a bloody and brutal civil war we shall next proceed to report, and in some instances try to analyze, the discussions and seminars they conducted and left us, as a record, now housed in the University Political Historical Archives, located in the Federal National Archives at Abuja. The narrations here presented, including the war reports and the battle preparations and dispositions, are, in most instances, verbatim, as it happened amongst them, or, as they say, *"as it is"*.

It was very early in the morning on that fateful day in January 15, 1966 that Professor Balarabe Musa Yousef, because he could no longer sleep, came out to his front porch to bathe in the early-morning sun and enjoy the cool morning breeze that streamed through the clear-blue tropical sky. He was out unusually early this Saturday morning because he had had a dream which had kept him petrified and sleepless all night. When he awoke he grabbed a pen and swiftly jotted it down before the details vanished from his memory. It was only later that he settled down looking over his notes and wrote it up in full. Both the initial draft and the actual manuscript of the dream account are currently kept in the basement of the city's archives - for posterity, and also for all who might be interested in, and attach some metaphysical importance to, dreams to go and peruse. "This is what I remembered", he calmly states:

"At about 3:00 a.m after my *nafila* prayer (a prayer of commitment to Allah), I was still pacing my room up and down because I couldn't sleep (Mariayamu, my wife, has her own room on the upper level of the duplex). After pacing like this for several hours, I finally sank down on the burgundy sofa in the middle of my room and nodded off, exhausted. When I slept I had a dream. Like most dreams, mine was related of course to my immediate circumstances that is, my concern with living and retirement. Nevertheless, this dream disturbed me. It made so great an impact on me that I have documented it now for posterity. Here is my recall of the substance of that dream:

I am in the country/village, a vast and barren landscape where there seems to be neither day nor night. Everything is blurred and indiscriminate.

I am walking along with my childhood brother who died many years ago, when I was just a small child. I never thought I would ever dream about him, indeed I'd almost forgotten about him. We're talking and people are passing us by in utter silence and with seemingly no substance, as if they were just mere silhouettes of themselves. We were, I think, discussing some acquaintance of ours, either a man or a woman obviously remembering when they were living in the old neighborhood, how they were always leaving their windows wide open, regardless of the season, or whatever it was that they happened to be doing.

There were no trees or grass to be seen. Then, suddenly, a man appears, who was butt-naked and the color of ashes, pallid and gaunt, and the animal — I couldn't tell if it was a horse or donkey, maybe a mule? — He was riding was dun-colored, the color of the earth. The man was hairless and we could see his bare elongated skull, and even the criss-crossed veins on his jutting out curiously prominent forehead. In his hand was what appeared to be a magic wand, which seemed too heavy a burden for him to bear, but he did, and he passed us by in absolute silence.

Then my brother suggests we go in the direction of a sunken road to the left. The road is bare and everything around it reflecting, the colors of the earth— brown, gray, green. When I make some passing comments with regard to the now-dried *fadama* (wetland) expecting my brother to say something or respond, nobody answers, so I turn look around, and realize he's disappeared, like a phantom, just as he came.

I continue on my lone, scary, sojourn and come to a town whose streets are completely deserted. I head on then to the next town with the same result. However, right at the meeting-point of the two streets there is a man who is standing, holding in his right hand what looked like some kind of weapon. He has his back facing the town and he faces the vast expanse of the wetland farm fields. "What is this place? Where am I?" I ask him, but he doesn't answer or show any sign that he understands my question. Then, suddenly, as if by some spell or apparition, I see a house, which I swiftly enter because the door has been left open.

Once inside the house I see what looks to me like a small garden in the courtyard, but I'm not sure. However I enter in. It is as silent as a graveyard, and there is no sign of life, but then a man in his early thirties, malnourished and as bald as eagle appears behind one of the leafless trees and I approach him and ask him; "What kind of garden is this?" He doesn't answer. "Where am I?" Still he doesn't answer. I tried to open my eyes to see if I was dreaming, but could not.

The next thing I know I am walking through a village, which, to my utter amazement, was completely deserted as well, all the doors of the houses open but no human soul outmoving or walking in the open spaces or deserted gardens, no signs of life, except for a horde of vultures flying low overhead in splendidly sinister formation.

But, you know what? On closer inspection at every street corner and behind every door beside these dry trees, a lean man in his forties with shining bare skull was standing at attention, with sword in his hand, but as silent as a door-bell or a nail. There was never more than one man at what seemed like a designated post, and they were all watching me with stern implacable faces as I passed along in fear and solitude. There were dogs all over the place too I remember that well but none barked or moved. They too were as silent as a graveyard.

In the dream about an hour later I left the village and walked back through the now-dried wetlands. After some time has elapsed, roughly about fifteen minutes, I saw a crowd pursuing me from behind. I recognized at once that it was all the men and dogs that I'd seen in the village threatening. They were on my trails.

Without saying a word or seeming to be in any hurry, they caught up with me and encircled me. They were all the color of the earth, including even the dogs. Then the first man that I'd seen when I had first entered the town (I recognized the open veins pulsing on his bald skull), opened his mouth and spoke to me: "Where are you going? Don't you know that you've been dead for a very long time?"

Again I tried to open my mouth to say something or answer him, but I found that no words would come out. When, eventually, I opened my eyes, I discovered that the mirage had disappeared and I was all alone, in my bed, soaking-wet, drenched in a cold sweat. I was scared to death.

After the Professor awoke from this strange and disturbing, scary dream, he looked through his window and noticed that it was still dark out but there were glimpses of light and life showing through the veneer of the thin *harmattan* dust. He surmised that it must be somewhere around five o'clock, and decided to check his prayer-kettle to make sure that he had sufficient water before he performed his *Subhi/fajr sallah* (*asuba sallah* in Hausa—early Morning prayer). After his *subhi* he began to reminiscent on the dream he had that night. "That wasn't a dream. No I swear it wasn't a dream!" He declared," It all happened!" He ran out onto the porch through his bed room on the second floor of the duplex building; where we now find him meditating, calmly counting his prayer beads. "No, that was not a dream", he said quietly to himself.

The question that you, my readers, are doubtless pondering at the moment is whether this was precognition, and that Professor Balarabe foresaw the death of the Sardauna on the eve of January 14th and the early hours of January 15th? Or is it just the random apparitions of an old mind struggling to make some sense in his remaining days? I'll leave it to you to work out the probabilities of the imagination of such a scenario, of the appearance of such a dream right at the very moment when the Sardauna was being attacked and murdered in cold blood, when all around him was dark and silent. There are some who see dreams as the transcendence of the mind to a different plane of consciousness, one where the ego thinks, acts and fleetingly remembers, independently events and has a temporary, sporadic illusive existence. The planes of consciousness and the dream state, of course differ in their portrayal of objective and subjective realities, perhaps calling into question the very definition of such reality. Certainly to those who have some sympathy towards the more abstruse metaphysical beliefs, the more esoteric appearances phenomena the apparitions of the mind, the answer to the question posed above will very likely be a *slam-dunk* positive. Yes! (But isn't also true that, not withstanding highly suggestive evidence and an obvious desire for conviction, that nothing is ever a slam-dunk as long as it remains a mystery?)

Fig.1: Nigeria's Regional Structure prior to May 1967

The Prof. has come out onto his porch to ponder and to turn the dream over in his head when, all of a sudden, he remembered a second dream that he'd had that night, although be it a shorter one. That dream was blurred now, but he remembered seeing his father holding onto a scrap of white cloth, and beckoning him to come. In normal waking life Balarabe didn't have a particularly good image of his father, because he'd passed away when Balarabe was still young. Consequently, most of his memory of him had come from his mother, who had told him everything she could about him. Prof. Balarabe clasped his hands and raised them to the heavens in praise and offered a silent meditative prayer to Allah, then sitting down, silently reviewed his life and considered what forces were at work here and what the two dreams might portend. Professor Balarabe always prayed whenever things did not seem clear to him, and today was one of those days.

"Allahu Akbar (God is great*), innalallahi wa inna illaihirraji un* (from Allah we are and we shall return to him).

"He's dead!" shouted Bashir Musa Katam in the Professor's ears.

"Whom are you referring to", Balarabe inquired, in brusque, intense but nevertheless subdued and controlled voice.

"Why, you didn't hear? They've killed him!"

"Killed whom?" He asked agitated

"The Sardauna", Bashir responded, wiping his tear-soaked face.

"Bashir, it's too early in the morning for such expensive and unfunny sick jokes", the Prof. enjoined, with fear spreading over his increasingly sullen frightened face.

"It's all over the radio, why, you didn't listen to the news this morning before you came out?

This was one of the exceptional days that the Professor hadn't turned on his short-wave radio to listen to the BBC or the Voice of America before coming out to enjoy the sunny Saturday week-end morning.

"Of all days; why must it be today?" He lamented ruefully and rushed in to hear the news for himself. "Could it be that I foresaw the Premier's death in my dream?"

"*Mamu*! Did you hear the news, did you hear what happened?" Balarabe shouted out the questions to his wife.

"Hear what?' she responded

"That the Sardauna is dead", he answered

"How is this possible?" She asked frenziedly and obviously rhetorically because she didn't expect her husband to have the answer.

"Well they have gone and done it!" He answered.

"Who are the "*they*" that have the nerve and the audacity to kill the Sardauna? Don't they know they cannot possibly get away with it? The spirit of our great leader and the symbol of hope and aspiration that he represents for the North will never permit them to get away with it. They will pay with their blood some day. Indeed, not only them, but those of their kin and kith. Allah will avenge this inhuman and barbarous act of cold-blooded massacre".

She broke down, sobbing.

The Professor and his wife were still listening to the radio when the newscaster paused momentarily and said in a sorrowful yet unwavering voice, that, the same fate had befallen the Prime Minister, Sir Abubakar Tafawa Balewa in Lagos. As the news kept trickling in, it was also announced that Brigadier Maimalari (Brigade Commander- Lagos), Colonel Mohammed

(Chief of Staff, Army Headquarters Lagos) Lieutenant Colonel Pam ('A' Branch-Army headquarters Lagos); Alhaji Shettima Kamsalem (Inspector General of the Police) and Lieutenant Colonel Largema (Commander 4 Battalion Army-Ibadan) had also all been killed. The cream of the North in Lagos had been wiped-out in a single night.

In the immediate days following, there were wild rumors flying around that the soldiers had not found themselves able to shoot Tafawa Balewa or Brigadier Maimalari, even as they stood in front of them. What they did, after their guns kept on misfiring, according to this account, was to try and murder them by twisting their necks, but that didn't work either; so they hung them on a tree on the Lagos-Ibadan road. The rumor was that they had had a tougher time with Maimalari because his head kept on turning around, as if it were a wheel. It was only when he, momentarily, took out something from his pocket and bit into it, that they were able to snap his neck. But what was especially shocking about the death of Brigadier Maimalari was that he was killed by one of the chief architects of the coup, Efejuna who had hitherto respected him and considered him as a mentor. Such betrayal is like modern-day Shakespeare - Caesar and Brutus. It must have made Shakespeare turn in his grave! In the Western Region the news came in that Chief Akintola had also been killed, but he too didn't go quietly. He wreaked havoc on those evil men who went to kill him, even after they were able to subdue his cadre of security guards. He killed several of his attackers, and, true to his words, he always said he would die fighting for his life, a life he had built up, from humble beginnings as a poor farmer's son, through sweat and hard work. He hadn't been born with a "silver spoon in his mouth" -unlike some of his contemporaries.

"What is happening to this country?" Both Alhaji Haliru and his wife Hassana asked in chorus on hearing the news.

"May *Allah* save us and grant them everlasting peace", Haliru declared, with a stoic solemnity, after gathering his inner strength.

"It would seem the only region that was left unscathed and safe was the East", Dr. Khan whispered to Veronica, who had come out of the kitchen to hear the news for herself.

"It's a weekend so the children don't have to go out", Veronica replied. Unconsciously or so it seemed, everyone in the neighborhood, indeed in the whole region, started speaking in whispers. The whole country was operating with hushed voices and discreet hand signals. My dear readers, this is hardly a normal way to function day to day, let alone to run a country. It was atangible manifestation of the fear and sign of the demonic slaughter to come. It was imperative that something needed be done, but first what? And by who?

Golu had travelled to the village to take medicine to his sick old mother who lived with her older son. On his way back he had stopped at the *Shagalinku* restaurant on Jos road to eat, but the place, which was normally bustling with people and music, was now solemn and deserted, as if the specter of death itself had recently visited it. He had a sense something terrible had occurred but he had no idea what it was and didn't have the presumption or nerve to ask anyone. He eventually gathered up his courage and asked one of the attendants, but the attendant just continued silently serving him, then retired to a corner and sat down, without uttering even a single word. Golu sputtered something to himself but that didn't help either. He observed the robotic behavior of the attendants and he hated it. Confused and frustrated, he rushed through his meal, paid the clerk at the counter and ambled out quietly, without saying anything more. "Why on earth are the attendants acting in this strange robotic manner?" He wondered, "Why won't they speak to me"? He sighed and exhaled as he madehis way back to his old 504 Peugeot car.

Golu was ignorant and blithely unaware of the news of the death of the Sardauna and the Prime Minister, because, as most of us know, or *should* know that at time radio technology had not yet reached the outer reaches ofthe villages. He kept on driving, driving in solitude, only on occasions to be brought to life by the blasting horn of an on-coming vehicle. As he approached town, he became more and more agitated and uneasy because everything seemed far too quiet and still and the streets were unusually desolate and deserted. The few people that he did observe all walked with their heads and shoulders down. The *Monte Sophia* quarter wasn't any better, if anything, it was worse. It was preternaturally quiet and deserted, and nothing seemed to have any life or reason at all. Normally on a weekend around this time, the open streets and courtyards would be infested with kids who would be out playing a game of football with their tennis balls or with a locally-stitched rag-like ball— a home-made equivalent, made out of stitched rags — but not today. He turned some hypothetical scenarios around in his head, but failed to come up with a reasonable explanation. "For goodness sake, what awful tragedy has occurred that is *so* important as to immobilize and force everyone to speak in whispers and communicate only in signals? I know that when I left two days ago everyone was fine, except perhaps for Owoleye's younger son, Ade, who was febrile and in the hospital, but the doctors said it wasn't serious Malaria; his temperature wasn't that high, they kept him in merely for 'observation'. Is it possible that the malaria had turned for the worst? But why would this affect people in the other surrounding towns and villages"? When Golu came up to his house he noticed that none of his children came out to meet him— usually they would dash out shouting *"o ye ye, o ye ye"*—, but of course today was not an ordinary day. The symbol of hope and aspiration for the North has been untimely vanquished and untimely slaughtered like a hapless dog.

"*Uhmm, sannu da zuwa* dear, *yaya hanya?Ka dawo lafiya?*How was the trip? I was worried about your safety because of the armed robbers on the highway. Is mamafeeling better? You know being old is kind of a disease in its self"

Francisca shot this series of questions at him, but her eyes were glued to the screen of the black-and-white television in the corner of their small sparsely-furnished sitting-room. (Color television had not yet become commonplace in town.)

"Francisca, what's going on? You don't seem to have noticed my presence at all. It's very unlike you. Everything you have said seems distant. Normally you would rush to the door and hug me and immediately fetch me some cold water or juice to drink. But today I notice that, instead, you're sitting here glued to the tele', even as you try to ask me about the trip and about mama. Is something wrong?"

Golu angrily and exasperatedly spat out these questions, partly because he felt insulted that Francisca didn't even bother to get up to welcome him the way she usually did every time he came back from the village, or any trip for that matter. Furthermore, she didn't even bother to go to the kitchen to get him something to eat or drink. Indeed he had reasons to conclude clearly today was not normal, something was very much amiss.

"Why, you didn't hear what happened, dear?" She asked in a whisper.

"No, what happened?" he answered, holding back his confusion and frustration.

Francisca was flustered and kept silent for a moment before running to him grabbing him, and giving him a formidable hug, squeezing him really hard around the chest (to tell you the truth, Golu was a bit surprised with the strength of her grip! He didn't think his wife still had that bear-hug in her; the same strength and passion she had possessed when they were newly-married many years back).

She was sobbing with tears streaming down her fluffy cheeks.

"Ok, for goodness sake, tell me what happened", he said in a patient calm reassuring voice.

"They have killed him, in cold blood, like a dog! He didn't have the security we all thought he would have to fight them back. He didn't stand a chance against a trained killer. I assumed that the Premier would have a heavy security detail to protect him", she responded, with some venom and more than a little anger in her voice.

"Who killed who?" Golu asked, agitated

"The Sardauna was killed this morning by some dissident military officers. The news-casters kept on naming a "Major Kaduna"asthe nominal leader of the coup".

She replied in a sad and heavy voice.

"The who? The Sar…What"?

"The Sardauna of Sokoto, of course, the Premier of the Northern region!" She answered in a high-pitched Voice and sobbing.

"They're still talking about it on both the television and the radio, blanket coverage.The Prime Minister, Sir Abubakar Tafawa Balewa, has also been killed, and, according to the news reports, Brigadier Maimalari and Colonels Pam and Mohammed Kuru are also dead.

Golu was beside himself in utter shock and delirium, and went and sat down on the sofa-chair next to the black and white TV and turned up the volume. They were still narrating and trying to explain how the Premier of the North had been brutally killed, in cold blood, with his prayer-beads in his hands and his senior wife, Hadsatu beside him similarly riddled with gun-shot wounds (the Sardauna was shot multiple times, his body, when it was found was almost unrecognizable.

Golu was disturbed because he had known Colonel Pam's family. He had gone to the same secondary school with Pam's younger sister, Verera Sue Pam.

He ventured to ask himself a flurry of questions and posited few possible scenarios quietly.

"This country is in trouble, ooh! I fear we're heading for a bloody and prolonged civil unrest. It also seems that only the Northern and Western leaders were killed. Nobody has been saying anything about the East. Who is this Major Kaduna? Where is he from? Could he be a Northern officer? Or is it just a pseudonym that somebody adopted to conceal his true identity? From the information coming through, it seems, undoubtedly, that the Igbos planned and executed this heinous crime. I don't think the North, specifically the Hausas, will take this, sitting down. We should all I fear prepare for a bloodbath, there's going to be unimaginable slaughter, including of innocent ones. Blood's going to flow freely everywhere", he surmised.

Of course these were all rhetorical speculations and projections which at the moment nobody could even attempt to answer.

"Oh my goodness, it's true, and, even worse than what we expected", Golu further observed after listening to the stream of bad news coming from the black- and- white television.

"One really has to wonder about that country" Dr. Kasimu declared, in exasperation, to his wife, Mariayamu (aka Mairam/Mairo), in his typically gentle sympathetic voice, (notwithstanding the enormity of the news), after reading a letter which he had just received from his cousin in Nigeria, Alhaji Manga Alagali, a branch manager in the North Capitalzone Bank.

"What's the matter this time", Mairam asked in an excitedly shrilly voice.

"Oh, the manner in which they killed the Sardauna and the other high- ranking members of the Northern delegation in Lagos. According to this letter, and some of the newspaper clips that he sent, several Northern Permanent Secretaries and senior military officers were massacred as well. The Prime Minister, Sir Abubakar Tafawa Balewa, the Inspector General of Police, Alhaji Kamsalem, Brig. Z. Maimalari, commander of the Second Brigade, Apapa Lagos and Col. Kur Mohammed, Army Chief of Staff were all brutally murdered. The *New Nigerian* alleges that Maimalari's neck was twisted and snapped and that the Prime Minister was hung upside down",

Dr. Kas continued in a mournful and bewildered tone. Bewildered, because he couldn't believe that these leaders, no matter what they were allegedly accused of doing, deserved such inhuman barbaric deaths; and indeed, if the allegations, such as they were, had any validity at all.

"Who are the 'they' that you refer to? Who would dare kill the Sardauna and expect to get away with it? I've long suspected his feverous, evangelical, almost fanatical, devotion to Islam would be a problem to some, but that doesn't seem enough of a reason to kill the man! As a human being, he's clearly not infallible, but, hey, he's still the hope of the North. He's frankly all we've got! It's my belief that without his strong belief in the *Northernization* policy, many Northerners, including ourselves, wouldn't stand a chance of procuring a federal scholarship, despite your stellar first-class honors degree " Mariam declared.

"And yours too. Indeed, you're right, it's almost like you were picking my thoughts, because those are the reasons that most of the newspapers are alleging that those who killed him gave"; Dr. Kas concluded in a hushed voice.

"They accused him of corruption and nepotism with this *Northernization* policy, which he initiated in order to bring the north on par with the rest of the other regions in terms of education and opportunities in the federal civil service, and they were indeed troubled by his religious fervor, according to Alhaji", he stopped to seep his green tea.

"This letter and these newspaper clippings seem to confirm what the Voice of Canada (radio) and the BBC have reported, except in more detail. The television newscasters just gave it a perfunctory report in their regular "breaking news "segment because they didn't think it's all that important and were not helpful at all. However, according to Alhaji Manga and these newspaper clippings, the main culprit, as reported by the BBC, was an Igbo major, nick-named 'Kaduna', because he was said to have been born and grew up in Kaduna. His father was a postal worker, who moved to the North many years ago" Kasimu concluded cautiously.

"I feel sorry for Nigeria, because, even though you may hate some of the Sardauna's admittedly zealous religious fervor, as we said earlier, he's still a true Nigerian or maybe not, but certainly a true Northerner", Mairam declared.

"Well, I'll write Manga asking him to keep us abreast of events in the old country", Dr. Kasimu replied, in a terse, abrupt and clearly emotional voice, which was curiously uncharacteristic of him.

Chapter Two
Sir Ahmadu Bello

It now seems appropriate for me to diverge a little bit, in order to introduce to you, my avid readers, Sir Ahmadu Bello, the *Sardauna* (senior advisor to the Sultan) of Sokoto, who was killed in cold blood and is the subject of our story.

The title *Sardauna* in this narrative refers to Sir Ahmadu Bello of Sokoto. He was born in 1909 in Rabah (in Sokoto Province, now State) to Ibrahim and Mariayamu (*Mamu*) as member of the Dan Fodio royal family. Ibrahim was the son of Sultan Abubakar Atiku and was District Head of Rabah when the Sardauna was born. He had thirteen daughters and twelve sons, of which Ahmadu was the eleventh. It was alleged, but never proven, that Ahmadu's mother was a concubine who had come as a gift from the Lamido of Adamawa. There were various claims to her ethnicity, some thought she was Fulani but this seemed rather unlikely; rather, most probably, she was a Jidiga. No matter what her ethnicity, we do know that she was a beautiful, tall elegant slim lady, dark in complexion. It was also said that she was well-versed in Qur'anic learning.

Legend has it that on the day that he was born there was a total eclipse of the sun in Rabah, the day turned into night. This exceptional occurrence has been conjured up by his admirers as a divine indication of his eminence within the lineage of Shehu Uthman Dan Fodio founder of the Fulani empire/dynasty or caliphate, of which he was a direct descendent great-great-grandson.

Let me make it abundantly clear from the on-set to you, my readers, that the Sardauna, from his infancy, was observed to be a special soul, a precocious lover of humanity and, if it appeared that he had taken up areligious life early, this it was because of his upbringing and the values instilled in him as a member of a respected royal dynasty. As it transpired these early religious orientations served him as an ideal avenue of escape as he struggled to emerge from the darkness and the world's pernicious wickedness or worldly corruption. Some of you my readers might think that he was arrogant and elitist and eccentric, but, indeed, on the contrary, in real life, he was, what you might call a populist, a humble 'man of the people'.

The Sardauna was a tall six-three or six-five, handsome, noble gentleman and as mentioned earlier, from the line of Shehu Dan Fodio, the founder of the Sokoto dynasty, and a gentleman indeed (*Dadtijo ne kwarai!*); with thick black hair and conspicuous well-groomed sideburns and whiskers. All in all he was a perfect expression of all that is implied by that word "perfect" model of respectability. He looked very thoughtful and certainly very self-composed. As far as I can relate to you, he was a realist, more so than anyone of his generation. He was futuristic in outlook and remarkably prescient, a man less concerned with philosophical *finesse* but, rather a pragmatist, committed to practical actions. Even as a young man he believed in fate, and, it's my opinion that, fate will never confound a realist, because he is always aware of his mission. Contrary to the popular belief, that a true realist will always find the strength and the tenacity *not* to believe in fate, and, if faced with fate as an undeniable fact, will sooner rather than later disbelieve his own senses rather than admit that fact. On the contrary, the Sardauna had always admitted the reality of fate. His religion so demanded it. His death, then, was a "manifest destiny". When all is said and done, he was a man living out the seasons of his life (like most of us, my readers), hoping for a son he never got, fighting fatigue and preparing to die. He was married five times, and went through two divorces.

Education and Work

He attended Sokoto Province government secondary school before entering Katsina College (No. 87, this means he was the eighty-seventh student at the college since its inception) from 1926 to 1931 before qualifying as a teacher. After his graduation, he was posted to Rabah middle school, Sokoto, where Sani Dingyadi was headmaster (*wakilin makaranta*), later he was given the title "*makama*" by Sultan Hassan.

His students at Rabah still remember him as the most brilliant and dedicated teacher they ever had. He shared his meals with the students and with the other teachers as well, especially the Sunday "main meal" and took genuine interest in each of them and in their academic and social life. It wasn't like he was rich at this time (if he ever was, at the time of his death he didn't have any bank account or savings), but he borrowed heavily from merchants or traders, or some would give, *gratis*, as a gift because he was a descendent of the Shehu (it's a tradition to shower gifts (*garawa*) to the descendents of Shehu Usman dan Fodio in the hopes that you might partake of some of their blessings in this life and the hereafter).

He often, as part of their social studies, took trips with his students to visit the tombs of his ancestors There was for example the occasion when they travelled from Sokoto to Wurno on foot to visit the tombs of Sultan Bello and Sultan Abubakar Atiku. From there they went on to Degel, where Shehu Usman and his father had once lived. That wasn't all, after some respite, they continued to Gwadabawa, and rested again before proceeding to Kware to visit the tomb of Isa, Shehu's son. After which they walked back to Sokoto to pay respects to the tomb of the Shehu himself. On this occasion there were thirty boys in the senior class, and they all travelled with him without any complaints, protests or permission-slips from their parents! Several of Ahmadu's students later became distinguished leaders in their own right. These included such prominent men as Aliyu (later, Magajin Garin Sokoto), Abdu Gusau (later, a renowned engineer), Maitambari (later, Madakin Gwandu), Umaru (later Wazirin Gwandu), Sambo Wadi of Birnin Kebbi, Garba Gorawa, and a host of others who became prominent in the services of their people in the North and, by implication, the whole of Nigeria.

According to records left in the Northern library archives these former students uniformly agreed that Ahmadu was always punctual for class and demanded the same punctuality in his students. They all said he worked very, very hard, till late in the night, with the blurred light of a candle or a kerosene lamp, long after everyone else had retired. He was also very meticulous with assignments and grading of the exam papers. He was sympathetic, but insisted on high standards. He later encouraged, indeed, almost forced, some of his students to attend his *alma mater*, Katsina College. The habits he acquired as a teacher served him well later in life as Premier of the North. It was alleged he was never once late for any function or debate.

Katsina College opened in the winter of 1921, and when, five years later, the Sardauna joined, along with sixteen others—it was still in its infancy—, there had only been eighty-four boys who had preceded them and two boys preceded the Sardauna for registration when they entered (No 85 was Shehu Ahmadu, Kano; No 86 Jima from Ilorin and No 87 Ahmadu, Sokoto...). At Katsina College he excelled as a student both academically and socially — seventy-five percent of the final grade at the time was based on character assessment—he was immensely popular. He was the one who had the other students in his room entertained till lights-out time. He also excelled as one of the best squash players in the college, a game he continued playing throughout all his life. Some of his schoolmates at the Katsina College included Sir Kashim Ibrahim (Borno, No 73, Class of 1925) ; Abba Habib (also from Borno, No, 122, Class of 1928); Abubakar Tafawa Balewa (Bauchi, No. 145, Class of 1928); Mallam Aminu Kano (Kano, No. 317, Class of 1927) and Isa Kaita (Katsina, No., 111 Class of 1927).

Katsina College moved to Kaduna as Kaduna College in 1938, and eleven years later, in 1949, moved to Zaria as Government College, which later became Barewa College. All graduates from these various different colleges are known as "Barewa Old Boys".

From records available in the archives, Ahmadu Bello became the tenth and youngest (twenty-four years old) District Head of Rabah as was his father Ibrahim,(the sixth District Head), between (1934-1938); and was appointed the Sardauna of Sokoto at the end of his District headship in 1938 a title he held until his death in January 1966. As District Head he brought unparalleled development to his district. He built schools and expanded free education to all eligible school-age children. His attention to details and his skills at philanthropy won him the admiration of the people, and they elected him to the Northern House of Assembly in 1949. It was rumored he was one of the best campaigners of his time. His diction and eloquence were unmatched, either in Hausa or English. These leadership qualities showed up at the regional level and he was rewarded, in 1954, when he became the President General of the Northern Peoples' Congress *(NPC)* of which he was a founding member, thus becoming the first Premier of the Northern Region. According to records in the northern archives and confirmed by Nuhu Bamali the formation of the NPC started in 1948 as a cultural group in Zaria as *Jam'iyyar Mutanen Arewa* by Dr. R. B. Dikko (first northern indigenous doctor) and at the same time in Kaduna *Mutanen Arewa a Yau* was formed by Mallam Rafi. The two cultural groups merged in the same year as *Jam'iyyar Mutanen Arewa* (Northern Peoples' Congress; NPC) with Dr. Dikko as its first President and Mallam Rafi as Vice-President. It was however declared a 'party' in a meeting in Jos in 1951 before the first election to the newly formed Northern House of Assembly with Alhaji Sanda as its President. It was at this time that both the Sardauna and Abubakar Tafawa Balewa joined as members. NPC did very well in that first election. In 1952 the house elected Ibrahim Imam as Secretary General of the party. The Sardauna took over the realm of the party at a convention meeting held in Jos in April 1954, replacing Alhaji Sanda as President and Inuwa Wada became Secretary General after the resignation of Ibrahim Imam.

The Sardauna wisely and deliberately guided the Northern Region's self-government in 1959, and became President of the Executive Council. Even though his party dominated the 1960 elections at both the federal and regional levels he chose to remain in the north as Premier. "I need to be with my people in the North. He once declared. It was his assassination, by some crazed dissident, ambition-fueled, rogue military officers that the Professor and his neighbors were crying over and lamenting in the previous section.

"Did the Sardauna leave any surviving heirs"? Aminu asked the Alhaji Wada (Alhaji Wada lives in the GRA but not the exclusive enclave of *Monte Sophia* however, as their representative on the Emir's local council and a man knowledgeable about the events under their purview he'd joined them to enrich the discussions).

"Of course, he left behind two wives and three daughters one of whom was born posthumously", Alhaji Wada said and stopped to sip some water.

Wives and children

For us to fully understand the Sardauna, we turn our focus to his three wives and his life-time desire for a male heir. These wives devoted themselves, and subordinated their actions, thoughts, even timorous feminine instincts, to the servicing of his habits, mission and purpose, as they understood it, by their Islamic faith, without his needing to express himself explicitly in words. They too were indeed martyrs.

The Sardauna's first wife, according to available information from friends, relatives, mere acquaintances and from the marriage records stored in the archives at Rabah, Sokoto State, and also the former regional archives now under the custodianship of Ahmadu Bello University Zaria, ABU, was Hafsatu/Hadsatu*(Goggon Kurya*, he called her with the nickname

Manga*). They were married in 1932 through "arranged" marriage, but had no children from this marriage, despite doing everything humanly possible to get a child, especially a boy. She was killed together with him on January 15th 1966. The second wife was Kande, they got married in 1934 but were divorced in 1938 due to irreconcilable differences, there was a son (Muhammad Tambari) but he died after weaning at the age of two. Cause of death wasn't known. The third spouse was Amiru (aka Fadima) whose marriage date is uncertain but seems to be around 1934, at the same time he married Kande, (and, incidentally, divorced her, also in the same year, in 1938). The reason for this divorce was not made public, but, again, there was no child from the marriage; which makes it likely that this was very much at the root of it all, that the Sardauna was doing all he could to get a male inheritor. The fourth wife was Amina (*Goggon Kano*), they got married in 1940, and she had three children however they were all girls! Inno, born in 1942; Aisha, born three years later in 1945 and Lubabatuwere born posthumously in 1966 after the Sardauna had been murdered. The fifth was Jabbo (*Goggon Jabbo*). They got married in 1952, had a son who tragically died when he was only five days old. Again the cause of death was never made public. Both Amina and Jabbo returned to Sokoto after the events of January 1966. Amina remains unmarried as of the time our tale, but there were rumors that Jabbo married one Ibrahim Dasuki in 1968. And, from what we know, they had three children. Interestingly, as some of you may remember, Dasuki was once the Sardauna's Private Secretary.

From what we have gathered from friends and have been shown by verifiable marriage records available to all who might be interested Inno, the elder daughter married Abubakar, Wamban Kano in 1956. They had two girls, Hadiza, who married Sani Kangiwa, and Balarabiya, (aka Fadima) who married Usman Dantata, from one of those iconic business families in Kano. Hadiza had one child, Ahmadu, and Balarabiya had Farida.

The second daughter, Aisha, married Ahmad Marafan Sokoto, according to available registry records. They had seven children, Nana, Abdulkadir who died, Safiya, Hadizatu, Hassan, Hussaini also deceased, Mai Raimu and Aisha.

The youngest daughter, Lubabatu, was fostered by the Emir of Daura, Muhammadu Bashir, after the age of two. Lubabatu got married to Umaru Shinkafi in 1984. At the time of our tale there is no record available of any children having been born in this marriage.

All in all, the Sardauna didn't do that bad at all in terms of gene-pool- continuation-through-posterity; he had three children, admittedly, all girls, ten grandchildren (two of whom died) and five great-grandchildren!

While the assassination of the Sardauna caused panic throughout the country, sending shivers and uncertainty into every nook and cranny, and, most especially, in the North, the rebels and murderers seemed almost to be gloating over what they had done, (unrepentant), even with a tinge of pride. Some of the criticisms that were leveled against the Sardauna, especially by 'Major Kaduna' were that he had shifted the center of political power and activity from the coastal areas (where Europeans had first settled and thus instilled their values) to the interior. "Kaduna" also complained about the Sardauna's *Northernization* policy, which the Premier had implemented with a fundamentalist, almost religious fervor. The essence of the policy was that if there was a Northerner available who was qualified for a certain position in the (Northern) Government, he should be given priority over people from any of the other regions of the country.

Although it might not have been obvious or directly linked to the coup, there were at the time a number of rumors and his juncture I gossips circulating about the Sardauna as he became a powerful symbol of the political and cultural life of the North. For, indeed, what is reported of men, whether or not it be true, may yet play as large a part in their lives, and, above all, in their destiny, as the things that they do. One such piece of gossip circulating was that the Sardauna intended to make Nigeria an Islamic Republic and was intending to impose *jihad* or *sharia* on all of the country. This and all such accusations as these I can assure you were false mere fabrications of an ill- conceived mind, and had not the slightest grain of truth in them.

It was a common knowledge at the time that, after his death, there was a massive and unprecedented destruction of files and photographs in order to obliterate as much as possible the memory of Sir Ahmadu Bello from all future political discourse to expunge him and his achievements from the record. But, as you can see, this abhorrent machination, and execrable plan absolutely failed. As the Professor told his younger audience, forty years after the fact, (and fifteen after his retirement), the soldiers even went to the *New Nigerian* newspaper offices and attempted to destroy thousands of photographs and documents. After the break-up of the North, Professor Balarabe contends, even the files of the *Gaskiya* Corporation, (dealing with the 1950's and 1960's), were ordered to be burned. Some records were re-located from Kaduna to the other provinces of origin. The *Arewa* House(Northern House) located at No 1 Rabah Road, was the official residence of the Sardauna, however as of 1970 serves multiple purposes—library, study-center—contemporary studies on policy, Peace and Leadership— archives and the documentation of the northern peoples' cultures, under the jurisdiction of Ahmadu Bello University, Zaria.

"Why was the Sardauna killed by this barbaric gang of dissidents?" Abba asked the Professor.

"To put his death in perspective" the Professor replied, "we need to review the contemporary events of the time. The purported "national crisis" of the time, and the escalating violence in the Western region, following the allegedly rigged elections of 1964 made the Sardauna a symbol and target of assaults and threats. But, above and beyond all of these, was his being a Northern symbol, the embodiment of all of its values and aspirations. In spite of, or maybe because of, his beliefs in the will of God and fate, he wasn't blind to the immanent dangers that confronted him"." I can tell you", he continued, "many of those close to him at the time observed the premonitions and brooding moods weighing heavily on his shoulders. There were some signs, (for instance when he cried at the grave of Sultan Atiku when visiting) of withdrawal from the mundane day to day issues of life as if those things were somehow increasingly less important. In short, he appeared to have a feeling of what would happen to him and he seemed to have resigned himself to his fate". "For example", the Professor continued, "even though in 1964 he was advised to cancel his farewell-tour in Sokoto, prior to his plan of attending the *umra*(the lesser pilgrimage) because of the distinct possibility of being waylaid and killed, he refused to return to Kaduna, and instead he continued brazenly with the tour.

"At Wurno", the Professor said, in a hushed voice as if he was whispering to a child, "as if prescient to his death, coming close to the grave of Abubakar Atiku (his grandfather), he spotted an empty space in the ground, and pleaded with those with him to "bury me here, please do me the favor. You see, gentlemen", he explained; "as I listen to you, I seem haunted by a dream… a curious kind of dream…. I often dream it and it keeps recurring… that someone is chasing me… but I am never afraid and he chases me in the dark, at night… intensely looking for me, even though he knows perfectly well where I am. He never finds me - until I avail myself to him". He concluded with a burst of laughter, but was it really laughter? No it was tears and sobbing. On another occasion during another premonition of his own death he told one Alhaji Ibrahim from Biu, Borno that "if the Premier dies tomorrow, none of you ministers will be here" (sounds similar to a saying of more than two thousand years ago, and from another faith; "you will deny me three times".

"Indeed"the Prof. told his captive and attentive audience, at this time the Sardauna was exposed to mallams who engaged in a variety of fortune telling from *Masu Bugun Kasa* (fortune tellers) to *Masu Duba* (the lookers) to the *istiharahMallams* (learned Islamic scholars who devote their time praying about specific important things they desire). All had told the Sardauna that he would not live longer than Muhammad Bello and that he would die on the same day with Abubakar and he believed them"(at first he thought the prophecy refers to Abubakar the reigning sultan of Sokoto, which means he will never become a sultan, a life-long ambition he harbors. It was later understood however to refer to his simultaneous death and Abubakar Tafawa Balewa, not sultan Abubakar) "Thus, for him", Professor Balarabe continued,"Time, fate and destiny appear to be coming together. When in Medina for the *umra*," Balarabe continued, "the Sardauna pleaded with his entourage to leave him to die there, but they refused".

According to the Premier's closest and most intimate colleagues, he wanted to return to Wurno (Sokoto) after the early Independence period, but he was persuaded by delegation after delegation to stay. Between January 11th and the 14th, the Western crisis spilled over to Lagos and the Commonwealth of Prime Ministers Conference , where it engaged the attention of the Prime Minister Sir Abubakar Tafawa Balewa. The British Prime Minister, Harold Wilson, had reliable intelligence about the impending coup and had passed it on to Tafawa who, it was said, passed it on to the Sardauna. However, it seemed both Tafawa and the Sardauna were fatalistic and did not act on the intelligence. But the Premier of the Western Region, Chief Akintola *was* concerned. He believed that there was going to be a bloody coup that could change the face of Nigeria's political landscape forever, and he flew up to Kaduna on Friday January 14, to remonstrate with the Sardauna kneeling down and pleading with him to do something, "for Allah's sake" — but he did nothing. As a matter of fact, the Chief tried to convince the Sardauna, using all the persuasive tactics he could muster, to fly with him to Niger, to prepare for a counter-coup, but again the Sardauna rebuffed him and politely declined. Chief Akintola tried again, pleading with him to, please, have the Prime Minister, Sir

Abubakar Tafawa Balewa intervenes with troops, or otherwise "we're all going to die". The Sardauna just smirked gently and promised him he would to talk to the Prime Minister in Lagos and impress on him the urgency. But, of course, he did nothing instead he went into his private room and prayed before joining his other guests in the spacious *Arewa* House living room. According to those present he appeared to them "as if he had been infused with some angelic shine and smile upon his face", the likes of which they had never seen before.

Chief Akintola left Kaduna at six o'clock on Friday evening and prophetically declared that he would return to Ibadan, to face his death if nothing was done urgently by the Sardauna and the Prime Minister in Lagos. Before leaving, he expressed his solidarity with the Sardauna that he would not wish to be alive if the Sardauna died.

The Yugoslavian Ambassador came to the Sardauna panting and wheezing, (he was said to be chronically asthmatic) and, also, hinted at the possibility of an impending coup, and pleaded with him to ask the British to bring troops in, by air, at night, in order to forestall it, but, again, he declined to take action, instead thanking the diplomat, and telling him that, if Allah has willed this to be his last day, then no human intervention could forestall it.

"Is it possible, then, that he willed his death?" Both Aminu and Veronica asked Professor Balarabe, simultaneously.

Veronica was accompanying her husband, because, after this discussion they planned to go on to the Wadilh village market, some twenty miles away, to buy a live goat to slaughter—the meat would provide, if properly stored, sustenance for their family for a whole month. Mariayamu, Balarabe's wife, intended to follow them to the village to buy a ram for the same purpose. It was a common practice amongst many of the residents, once they were paid, to go to the different surrounding village markets at the end of each month to buy foodstuffs which were relatively cheaper as compared to the city. Livestock — goat, sheep, or cow—was one of the more common things they would usually go to buy because meat was expensive in town. When they bought the animals they would have them slaughtered and the hair on the outside of the carcass burnt, instead of simply having them skinned, before the animal was cut into pieces with the skin, for storage placed in a refrigerator—in the absence of a refrigerator, the meat would be hung to dry. Sometimes two or three friends would pool together their resources to buy a cow and communally share the meat.

"I wouldn't say it in exactly those words", Balarabe replied, "because in Kaduna at the time people generally didn't even believe a coup was possible, and so this, in a way, reinforced that sense of fate on the part of the Sardauna".

"At a meeting with Sam, the Brigade Commander of the First Brigade, in charge of all troops in the North, including two battalions in Kaduna, one battalion in Kano, and some units in Zaria and Benue", Professor Balarabe continued, "the Sardauna was given the assurance that nothing could happen. "They would have to kill me first" he had declared — and this they had, together with his wife, butt-naked in bed. Sam was also overheard telling Dr. Atta, the Premier's personal physician that he had had a premonition 'I'll probably not be alive, and you probably will not be alive, however, the difference between us is that I intend to cause havoc when I go'".

Some credible reports have claimed that Sam had wanted to talk to the Premier directly about the impending coup, but had never had the opportunity to do so. However, according to the Sardauna's personal physician, Sam apparently told him he *had* informed the Premier of the coup but that he-—the Sardauna — didn't seem to be taking it seriously, and so he, had asked him, to inform the Premier again about the gravity of the situation, which he believed the civil service was incapable of handling. Furthermore, according to this view of events, Sam stressed to Dr. Atta that all he required was the designation of authority so he could arrest the plotters;"We know the boys responsible. Give us permission and we'll round them up. It will be serious. You know…we….will be consumed by this". It was never entirely certain whether Dr. Atta was able to inform the Premier of this version of events. Regardless, it would seem on the surface an abdication of duty as brigade commander *not* to take the initiative of arresting disgruntled soldiers that you knew were planning a coup! Did Sam inform the Sardauna about his requirement for permission to "arrest the boys"when he first met with the Premier? One wonders if, at that time, he had remembered or himself taken it seriously. Anyway, as it turned out, both the Sardauna and Sam, the brigade commander were brutally silenced by the events of that night — they both got killed.

Sam, however, unfortunately wasn't able to cause any "havoc", as he'd promised. Both he and his wife were summarily and brutally killed, in cold blood, without being given the slightest chance of firing back a single shot, even though he had his gun beside him, by his bedside, loaded.

"You see", Balarabe continued, "some of the Sardauna's guests stayed up with him that night but only until midnight. It has been recounted by many close friends, and, even, for that matter, family members, that the Sardauna would typically keep his guests entertained into the wee hours of the morning but not the morning of the 15th! However that day he asked everybody to leave early, sometime around midnight. This prescient action has convinced some of his more devout followers, leading them to assert that the Sardauna knew exactly what was afoot that night, and consciously refused to abdicate or take shelter somewhere else to protect his life.

His generosity to people around him and to those whom he came in contact with was legendary and is reflected in the following statement which he was once overheard saying "Do not ask the name of the person who seeks a bed for the night. He who is reluctant to give you his name is the one who is most in need of shelter".

Chapter Three
January 15, 1966
Death comes at Night: The Night Marauders

"So how did the Sardauna die?" Owoleye asked the narrator.

"Aye, tou yaya aka kashe shi?"(Yes, so how was he killed?)AiShetu interjected, in Hausa.

"The attack on the Sardauna's official residence at *Arewa* House, along the Zaria road", the Professor began, "started, we now know, in the early wee hours of January 15, 1966. According to available historical and archival records, the chief instructor of army training at the Nigerian Military Training Center (NMTC), Kaduna, Major Patrick Charles, (aka "Kaduna"), gathered some soldiers that he had been training —for nocturnal warfare exercise — that night and marched them along the Zaria road. Many of them had no idea of what was afoot. They just obeyed orders and did as they were instructed. They had assumed it was their regular nocturnal drill exercise. When they were commanded to move toward the *Arewa* Houseon the Zaria road and attack it, they became disillusioned and conflicted angst pervaded over their most basic instincts of right and wrong. The centrality of the instinct of self- preservation became overwhelming and took control over their feelings of honor and rational thought—two soldiers were summarily shot by the major for openly expressing their misgivings and disobedience to the order. "You either follow my orders or face instantcoward's death", he thundered fuming. Immediately the fear of death and the loss of their own lives clouded any human qualitiesthatthey might have otherwise possessed, consequently they started firing, at first, randomly, and later with some precise focus. Police guards on duty were, at first, stripped of their guns, before being gunned down. It was then that "Major Kaduna" moved up the stairs behind the house, cut the security wire-fence, and moved inside to the main household, armed to the teeth with a bullet-belt around his waist and grenades in his right hand, as if he were some Special Forces operator, bravely corralling a dangerous serial killer.

"Then what did he do? How dare he try to assassinate the Northern Premier?" Golu queried contemptuously, not addressing any one person in particular.

"First he shot the gate-keeper or the protector (*Zarumin*) who didn't even have a gun at his disposal, only a sword, shield and knife; and then the Senior Assistant Secretary for Security, Audu Yaro, who still had his gun in his left hand. Neither of the two had a chance against this Sandhurst weapons-trained officer. Even if the *Zarumin* had little more than the sword he had, he didn't stand a chance. Major Patrick (a.k.a. "Kaduna") then set the house on fire, as a result of which there was pandemonium, but he didn't find the Sardauna. He searched the quarters frantically but there was no sign of him. He became agitated and started shouting vehemently and cursing, fearing that the Sardauna had somehow escaped, which would have meant that hisplot had failed. He started to ponder now about how *he* would be killed — "hung or shot?" But he tried not to dwell too much on the form of death that he might face; instead, he found himself fantasizing a sexual orgy with Ngozi Bassey his girl friend, and past sexual engagements, all the wonderful rhythmic sexual movements and bed-sheet conversations that they had had. He agonized over fondly-recalled caresses and thegentle feel of her erogenous chest, abdomen and the soft flesh between the legs, that bliss, which he would have to leave behind if he were to die. "Of course she is no longer a virgin, but, all the same, I'm going to miss the ecstasy, the voluptuous unparalleled love-making that we have enjoyed together", he found himself murmuring, — but of course it wasn't loud enough for whoever might be listening to hear. "But what the heck", he continued, "she'll certainly find another man to fulfill her sexual desires and fantasies and, after all, she has declined my marriage proposals twice already because so she says, she wants to complete her education".

Preoccupied with his past sexual conquests and regrets if, indeed given, that the *coup* failed, he soon realized where he was and why he was there. As soon as he came out of his stupor, he remonstrated with himself "Oh my god! What am I doing thinking of sex, while I'm here to save Nigeria from the evils of imminent *jihad*, religious fanaticism and corruption of the grandson of the founder of the Sokoto caliphate, Usman dan Fodio, the future heir of the Sokoto dynasty, in short, the most powerful and evil person in the country?" Suddenly, as if by divine plan, the Sardauna appeared in front of him (legend has it that, he was standing next to Major Patrick, all this time, counting his prayer-beads, but Patrick wasn't able to see him until he *allowed* himself to be seen). There he was, seated on his multi-colored *darduma* (rug) made from camel hide and embossed with both the Northern and Nigerian coat of arms and flag as calm as a baby feeding at its mother's breast, serenely counting his prayer-beads. Beside him, sitting down and watching, was his senior wife, Hafsatu (aka Habsatu), and the other two wives, Amina and Jabbo some distance away. When Patrick and the Sardauna encountered each other in the family quarters, the Sardauna stood up and begged him"for Allah's sake to "spare the women and allow them to go", because, "I know it's me you want, and I've been preparing or getting ready for this day all my life. *Allahu Akbar*(Allah is great) *innalallahi wainna illaihirraji un*"(From Allah we are and we are going back to him). At that moment he was instantly shot, as was Hafsatu, his senior wife, even though he had pleaded with the Major to spare her. Amina and Jabbo were in the shadows and escaped to safety.

Although the Sardauna had known a coup was afoot, he never wavered in his belief, he never ran away, as was proposed to him by men like Chief Akintola. He would often say in that fatalistic way *"alhamdu lillahi"*—all praise and thanks be *to Allah,* only he can protect me", and "if I should be killed in the service of the North, so be it".

After some prolonged silence, Aminu broke the ice by saying it was his belief that "the Premier is so virtuous and noble that the most benevolent and merciful Allah will not forsake him… indeed, will help us crush this execrable criminal act… We alone as a people must expiate the blood of the righteous".

He paused and then continued on. "The perpetrators of these heinous crimes do not understand, they are incapable of understanding, the self-abnegation of the Premier, who wants nothing for himself, but desires everything good for this country, and most especially for the North".

He stopped abruptly, wiping his face with back of his left hand.

The room fell into complete silence again, until Abba asked;

"What did they do with the body?"

That's a very good question", the Professor said.

"At around seven in the morning, the Sardauna was certified dead by Doctor Atta, his personal physician who had been previously summoned, and his body, alongside those of Hafsatu, and the *Zarumi,* was patched, cleaned up, then removed, and taken, by, amongst others, Mallam Abubakar (a friend who had spent the night in the guest house). It was taken to the Sultan's Kaduna house, which was in the same quarter, just a few meters away.

The Sultan's residence in Kaduna served as the focal point that day for all sorts of people. Conspicuously absent, however, just as the Sardauna had predicted to Alhaji Ibrahim, were the ministers.

When the Sultan was contacted about the death of the Sardauna, and was asked for instructions as to where the body should be taken, he responded by saying, "Take him to Wurno". However, it became physically and strategically impossible to get a plane to take him there that day, because of the numerous check-points around Kaduna and around the whole of the North for that matter! Consequently, when the Sultan and other close relatives of the Premier's were told of the difficulty of getting out of Kaduna with the body that day, the Alkalin Alkalai of Sokoto stepped in and declared: "It was the Sardauna's wish to be buried in Sokoto, not Allah's wish. He is to be buried here. He died in Kaduna and will be buried in Kaduna". So it was that the Sardauna was buried at Kaduna, in the Sultan's house, in the same vicinity as the Arewa House where the massacre took place. Present at the burial were Aliyu, *Magajin garin* Sokoto (Prince-in-waiting of Sokoto); Ibrahim Gashash, U. Baki and Dr. Dikko. Aliyu gave up his own personal clothing for the occasion. "It was a simple, typical Islamic burial conducted by Imam, Grand khadi Abubakar. Gummi", Dr. Atta recalled.

"It was obvious", the Professor continued, "that the Sardauna has known all along that there was going to be a coup, and that is why that evening he sent most of his guests away early, in order to minimize casualties, and to have enough prayer and meditation time with his maker, because he knew that it was him alone that they were after".

"Throughout Kaduna that day as you can imagine", Dr. Khan broke in and volunteered his thoughts on the subject, "there was general confusion bordering on malaise, confusion, hopelessness and uncertainty".

Brigadier Nam, as we saw earlier in the narrative didn't fare any better either. The Governor of the North, Sir Kashim Ibrahim, was taken but was not killed. In short, even though several people, including, it was said President Nasser of Egypt knew about the coup and had advised the Sardauna to act he didn't take any additional precautions. He simply accepted the verdict of fate and history and prophetically said, "You can't run away from a fate"— a reference to the 19th century imperialist notion of "manifest destiny".

"Dr. K", Veronica addressed her husband as others often did, and in the same coquettish tone she used with everyone, "what did you discuss with the Professor today"?

"Ah the usual stuff" the retired Professor of mathematics replied, except, as I pointed out the Premier's concern toward the end of his life over not having a male child".

"He didn't have a male child?" Veronica asked putting the emphasis on the adjective, "male".

"No he didn't. He had three girls", Dr. K retorted calmly.

Dr. Khan (aka, Dr. K) kept his thoughts to himself for a moment and contemplated how lucky he was to have three boys and a girl. He searched deep into his soul and thanked Allah for all his blessings, most especially for fulfilling his tribe's unapologetic expectations of leaving behind a number of male children who would perpetuate the family's gene-pool, onward through eternity, long after he himself had joined his ancestors. If he had been in the Premier's position, his tribe would have shunned him and declared him "weak between his legs" and incapable of earning tribal title, no matter what good he had done. He then paused and wondered out loud how good fortune came to some but not others, that he "didn't deserve this", having a male child and an inheritor, "any more than the most powerful man in the country at the time, but again, it's fate, and one doesn't run away from fate", he concluded somberly.

Later in the day, "Major Patrick Kaduna" announced the overthrow of the Government, and immediately imposed Martial Law. In his broadcast after the coup he said, in part, that they had staged the coup to end corruption, inefficiency and anarchy, this latter, in reference to the riots in the Western state following the 1964 election. "The military has taken over", he said "to bring an end to gangsterism and disorder, despotism and corruption. My compatriots, you will no longer be ashamed to be Nigerians", ah say what?

What an idealistic, self-serving, foolhardy and bitterly ironic pronouncement! All the ills that he listed are still prevalent, if not more prevalent, today than they were on the day of the coup in 1966. Societal values and mores aren't forced upon the people through the barrel of a gun;

they're accomplished through a vicarious, gradual and mutually-respectful learning process.

In Lagos the Prime Minister, Sir Abubakar Tafawa Balewa, was reported missing and presumed dead.

Major Patrick *Kaduna* gave the impression to those who went to see him that he was a hero, but, indeed, the Northern leadership and the people certainly didn't see him in that way. They saw him for what he was a mean, cold-blooded murderer and opportunistic ambitious officer. Some of the senior Northern ministers gathered around him that day, heard him murmur under his breath that he "didn't like the feeling that a Nigerian was a foreigner in his own country", and that the Sardauna was killed, in part, because of, as we have said earlier, his provocative *"Northernization"* policy.

Whilst most of the Northern leaders in Kaduna and Lagos were barbarically and selectively eliminated, there in the Western Region, Chief Akintola was killed, though it was said that he gave them the fight of his life with his pistol drawn, taking several soldiers with him before they subdued him. The only region that was unscathed or untouched was the East. Apparently there were no corrupt politicians or inefficiency there!

From the rapid succession of events it would seem the planners of *code damisa* (code leopard) failed because Major Kaduna was quickly outmaneuvered by his senior officers and was forced to hand over the Government to senior rather than junior officers, that is a less easily manipulated men, while most of the plotters were rounded up. In the North, Major Hassan Katsina was appointed Military Governor, and Major-General Aguiyi Ironsi was appointedSupreme Commander and Head of the Federal Military Government. Major Patrick was lured to Lagos and was sent straight to *kirikiri* prison. However, when Ojukwu became Governor of the Eastern region, he engineered the transfer of the conspirators to the East, to his jurisdiction where they were astonishingly released, and at the very beginning of hostilities. Ojukwu was quoted saying that, the officers in Lagos were understandably "dead-scared of the release of the detainees". Major Patrick Kadunawas eventually killed in battle in the Nsukka sector during the civil war, fighting for Biafra, even though he was never formally incorporated into the Biafran army.

The passing away of the Premier, the Sardauna of Sokoto,*"aka gamji"* (a large fig tree) was the end of an era, for many Nigerians. For many in the country, it was the occasion for a time of prayer.

"But if prayer works, the Sardauna, and all the rest of those who died, really should not have died" wryly observed Dr. Khan. "Why wasn't God listening to the prayers of the millions, who were praying to him daily? I've always held the view that no one really listens to prayers. I know the Sardauna was a man of faith and hope. But is it even remotely possible that Baruch Spinoza might be right when he says "all things are determined by the necessity of divine nature", that is, our lives, thoughts, actions, successes and failures are all predetermined, just as the rising and the setting of the sun. This means, all events in our lives are predetermined. The statement poignantly makes us question the premise of free will. According to Spinoza, free will itself is predetermined! Our behavior, like the orbits of the planets, is determined by the laws of physics and chemistry. This argument about the 'delusion of free will' can be explained by a recognition of the evolutionary adaptation of natural selection, thus free will as an illusion is brought to us by through evolution. "God", Einstein once said "did not play dice by allowing any events to be random or undetermined. I am a determinist", he went on, "I do not believe in free will, prayer… I reject that doctrine". Human beings in their thinking, feelings and active states are *not* free, but are as "causally bound as the stars in their motions", declared Einstein. You might not believe me if I tell you that a recent book I was reading, **The Evolution of God**, claimed that the concept of 'God' first arose as an illusion amongst our ancestors as part of the process of natural selection, and that the subsequent history of this idea' is, in a very real sense, merely the evolution of an illusion. However, Mr. Robert Wright continues, that "as humans become more rational about such evolution, the illusion itself has gotten less and less illusory". I'm not vouching for everything he's saying, but there's some truth to some of it, is there not, at least tangentially", observed Dr. Khan. Everybody kept quiet and the silence was only broken when Professor Balarabe murmured almost inaudibly under his breath, "alright, enough already, let's move on with our narrative".

"Dr. Khan, I don't subscribe to your pontifications, God, the creator, is a spirit and does not evolve. He was there at the beginning, and will be there at the end. Where do you think you're going when you die?" Mr. Owoleye Jide entered the debate with something like vehemence in his voice.

"I have a poem here and I want you to read it", he added somewhat sarcastically.

"Oh, well certainly, thanks", Khan replied.

This is the poem Pastor Jide gave Dr. Khan to read from *The Brothers Karamazov* by Fyodor Dostoyevsky, Volume 1

> *The Soul of all creation*
> *Blessed joy eternal fills,*
> *The secret force of fermentation*
> *With fire the cup of life instills,*
> *It lures sweet grasses to the light,*
> *And from the far-off outer spaces,*
> *Beyond the ken of furthest sight,*
> *Suns come out and take their places.*
> *At the breast of bounteous Nature*
> *Everything that breathes is glad;*
> *All nations, all creatures seek her pleasure,*
> *She gives the juice of grapes and garlands,*
> *And lust in lowly insect fires,*
> *But up above the angel stands*
> *In sight of God- his joy admires*

"Alright enough of poetry, *dun Allah*", Jummai pleaded.

"Let's continue with our discussion of the events of January 15, 1966", Veronica declared emphatically.

It was a time of sober reflection, when the destiny of the individual, and, so it seemed, perhaps the very nation, had been fulfilled. So, as the events of January 15 sank in, anger, seething anguish and indignation took over, replacing hope, most especially in the North. Throughout the North, prayers were offered up in mosques and churches; and you could feel in some sense, the thick air of morbid and pernicious explosion of a catastrophic event waiting to happen. There was no doubt an imminent resolve to do 'something', to appease the atrocities but do what?

The Northern poets/praise singers — these are traditional Hausa singers who have beenwith the Sardauna in better times and were in turn generously remunerated—openly provided a platform of resolve and a forum for hope through their songs of praise and adoration for the late Sardauna and his fellow Northern martyrs.

"Suffice it is to say that, at that moment in the North, there was a malaise and a general wait-and-see attitude. Everybody wanted to see significantly what Ironsi was going to do.

Chapter Four
The Calm before the Storm
The Northern Poets/Praise-Singers and the Sardauna

According to the first law of thermodynamics as postulated by Isaac Newton or was it Einstein —nature abhors entropy so that a vacuum or empty space does not actually exist in real life. The preponderance of scientific postulations asserts that there is nothing like an empty space or void. The leadership massacre of all those elite northerners — the Sardauna of Sokoto; Tafawa Balewa the Prime Minister; Brigadier Maimalari Commander, 2nd Brigade Apapa, the highest decorated Northern military officer at the time, Kamsalem, Inspector-General of Police, Colonel Kur Mohammed, Chief of Staff, Army Headquarters, Lagos, and Lieutenant Colonel Pam—which was supposed to create a leadership vacuum or entropy was, in this regard, unsuccessful. The vacuum didn't materialize. The vacuum that was supposed to be created was, to the chagrin of the plotters, filled instantly with anger, melancholy, malaise, gossip, innuendo and the urge to wreak revenge at all costs.

In Lagos the situation wasn't any better. All the northerners yearned to come up north. They were worried about the future, scared of what might happen.

The vacuum thus created during the mourning period was filled up now by the Northern poets or praise-singers.

"Who were these poets that whipped up the spirits of the North? Including those of the Emirs and Chiefs, and galvanized them into wanting to do something?"

Abba asked with a rhetorical flourish

"You really want to know?" the Professor inquired.

"Yes" Abba answered

One of the first of such poets/praise-singers whom we might sensibly note is Adamu Dan Maraya (the orphan) of Jos. Adamu Dan Maraya (a.k.a Maraya) of Jos was born in Bukuru in 1946, where his father, Mallam Wayya, had migrated from Sokoto. He was orphaned at age two and was brought up by the District Head of Bukuru. He titled his tribute to the Sardauna "*Ta'aziya Ahmadu Bello'* (Tribute to Ahmadu Bello). Mamman Shata (a.k.a. Shata) was born in 1923 in Rugar Dan' Malam, Musawa village in Katsina province (now State). He died on June 9, 1999. He didn't attend any western school, but did go through Islamic training. He was one of the most popular poets/singers associated with Northern Elements Progressive Union (NEPU) which was led by Mallam Aminu Kano, an opponent of the Sardauna's NPC. But at the Sardauna's death he paid him a tribute entitled: '*Mallam Ahmadu Bello*'. There were many Sokoto poets/singers who sand the leadership qualities of the Sadauna, but we would only listen to few. Prominent amongst those we would listen to their poets/songs areAlhaji Musa DanKwairo (a.k.a.Dan Kwairo). Dan Kwairo was born in 1910 in Dankad, Bakura District in Sokoto province (now state). Dan Kwairo had written many poems/songs in praise of the Sardauna's leadership qualities and heritage, but the one we would listen to was titled his tributes '*Wakar Sardauna*" (Sardauna's praise song) and "***Ya wuce Raini***" (He is Above Disrespect), respectively. The other Sokoto poets/singers we would listen to are Salihu Jankidi, Aliyu Dandawo and Garba Dan Kyana. These poets galvanized an already angry and suspicious Northern population ready to avenge the sudden deaths of a cadre of their brightest hopes, the cream of their leadership.

"Oh, I know the song Dan Maraya sang to the Sardauna by heart", Abba proudly interjected and began reciting the words.

"Alright, we should perhaps go through each of them, one by one, and analyze what each is saying", James suggested.

"Well let's look at Dan Maraya's tribute: *Ta'aziyar Ahmadu Bello*,which is still popular today on both flat disc and tape".

Veronica jumped in and declared proudly "we have both the disc and the tape; it's a moving song, you should pay close attention and listen".

Ta'aziyar Ahmadu Bello by **Alhaji Adamu Dan Maraya**
1. *L'llaha Illalla/yau dada ba gwani sai Allah*
2. *Amma La'Ilaha Illalla/ba gwani sai Allah/Allah jikan maza sum fadi/Allah jikan Sa Ahmadu Bello.*

3. *Tun rasuwan Sa Ahmadu Bello/Kowa ka gani fa babba da yaro/ ba wani hankali a jikinsa.*
4. *Amma La'Ilaha Illala/abin da ke maku zafi/ni ma ya kam mani zafi/abin da ke maku ciwo/ni ma yak am mani ciwo/abin day a cuce ku/Wallahi ya cuce ni/Allah jikan Sa Ahmadu Bello/Allah jikan Firayim Minista*
5. *Sa Ahmadu Bello ya yi Kayinji/sannan kuma ya yi Unibasti/yai Ahmadu Bello Situdiyo namu/babban ko wajen kwallo/nan a Kaduna can aka yi shi.*
6. *To Allah jikan Firayam Minista/babba Tafawa Balewa/ga ilimi kuma ga hakuri/to ai ga adalci wajen Tafawa Balewa.*
7. *Amerika suna mani tadin/Rasha suna mani tadin/Laberiya na man tadin/Afirka suna mani tadin/har Legas suna mani tadin/ wajen hakurinsa har adalci.*
8. *To/don haka nan mutanen ame/kuma ku rike mu amana/kamar Tafawa Balewa.*
9. *Allah ya riga Ya rantse/duk mutumin da ci amana/ka ga amana sai ta ci shi/mai hakuri yak an dafa dutse/amma har ya sha romonshi.*
10. *Yaro bay a daukan yaro/sai dai rungumanni mu fadi/dole ruwa ba zai ci gwani ba/sai kwanan gwani ya kare.*
11. *Sa Ahmadu Bello bawan Allah/wanda ya zagi bawan Allah/ sanyi rike masa gwiwa/tunjere rike masa mara/in ya yi tsugunne ya gaza tashi/sai sababi da yara kanana.*

Transcribing this tribute in English, the Professor went onin this manner:

"The song begins", he said:

*There's no other God except God and only God is great

    *May the souls of the fallen heroes rest in peace. May the souls of Sir Ahmadu Bello rest in peace
    *Since the death of Sir Ahmadu Bello, whoever you see, young and old, /none are in his normal sense(s).
    *But there's no other God but God. What is hurting you/is also hurting me/What pains you/is also paining me/What cheated

you/ I swear also cheated me/May Sir Ahmadu Bello's soul rest in peace/ May the Prime Minister's soul rest in peace.

*Sir Ahmadu Bello built the Kainji/and then built a University/ And our Ahmadu Bello Stadium/The big football playground/ which is built in Kaduna.

*May the Prime Minister's soul rest in peace/the honorable Tafawa Balewa/There's calmness [patience] and education/and there's fairness [fair play] with Tafawa Balewa.

*Americans are telling me/Russians are telling me/Liberians are telling me/Africans are telling me/Even Lagosians are telling/About his patience and justice.

*So/because of this, military man/you should also take care of us as a trust/As did Tafawa Balewa.

*God has already sworn/that whoever dishonors a trust/will pay for his dishonor/whoever has patience will succeed/and even be the happiest.

*A child cannot carry a child/It can only be seen as attempting and failing/A good swimmer cannot be drowned unless it happens to be his last day.

*Sir Ahmadu Bello, God's servant/Who would cheat God's servant?, Whoever cheats God's servant/may cold lock on his leg joint(s)/may he have abdominal trouble(s)/So that when he bends down, he can't rise up again/May he also be having trouble with little children.

"What an inspiring song" Aminu observed.

"You know I've listened to this song more than a hundred times, but I've never understood its implications until today", Owoleye chimed in.

Before anybody could say anything they heard soft steps approaching, the curtain parted gently, and a feminine voice called out almost in whispers;"You guys are not going to be leaving this house at all today? It's already high noon! You've all been sitting on that couch now for hours on end. It was Balarabe's wife, Hajiya Mariyamu, who, once she'd announced herself, immediately disappeared, unobtrusively just like the way she had sneaked in on them.

"Oh Indeed time *has* passed quickly without our noticing it. Won't your young wives worry about your whereabouts?" Balarabe inquired of Aminu

Araba Let's Separate

"I told her I was coming to see you, so at least she knows where I'm at", interjected Aminu.

"You're right we have an appointment this afternoon to see Dr. Khalib, because my cousin, Pettte Dong has a high fever. I need to go home before Jamima starts making trouble for me", James commented;

"What kind of trouble? Just tell her you are with the Professor. Maybe you should bring her along next time. They, like everyone else need to know what actually happened to the Sardauna, and to the country as a whole, now more than forty years ago", Golu said, getting to his feet. He needed to drop off Francisca, his wife, at the hospital, where her shift starts at two o'clock; it was already half past twelve.

"Well, I have to rush home now to take Tanimu to the clinic, because yesterday he didn't sleep at all during the night. He has this boil on his backside which was throbbing and hurting him all night", Abba declared.

"I must also go home to take AiShetu to the market", Mallam Aminu said.

"Yesterday she was complaining about the fridge being empty. Everything is gone! We have no food. The fridge, she said, is as empty as a pauper's purse!"

"Well, then we'll call it a day. Tomorrow, what time would you guys like to come around, so we can listen to the other Hausa poets' tributes?" The Professor asked.

They all paused momentarily and then in chorus said, how about *asubar (*two in the afternoon)

"Well then, I'll see all of you tomorrow at *asubar"* Balarabe concurred.

AiShetu and her husband didn't go home directly, they stopped at the store on their way home to buy some few household items—soap, salt, magi, canned milk, Lipton tea-bags, bread and other essentials. Thirty minutes later after they had finally returned home, her close friend, Roslyn, sent on one of her house boys to tell her that she would be on her way to see her (phones weren't a common feature of the community as yet). Within fifteen minutes, Roslyn was there and the two friends prattled on about the weather and the new hair salon that had just opened around the corner on Balewa and Aminu streets. After some further small talk, Roslyn told her friend the main purpose of her visit. She had heard about what was going on between AiShetu's sister, Hajara, and her husband, Alhaji Ibrahim Tafawa.

"Surely you don't believe that divorce is impossible. I was told — I won't tell you by whom — that her husband has already consented to it", she stated somewhat matter-of-factly.

"Rosy dear, I don't want us to talk about this", AiShetu responded.

"Oh, then we won't", Roslyn declared, immediately noticing the expression of deep pain and suffering on AiShetu's face.

"All I can see is that you take far too gloomy a view of things. It may in fact be better for her".

"I? Not at all! I'm always positive and optimistic toward everything. I have positive *karma*, AiShetu assured her friend.

"Yes, to tell you the truth, I didn't like your husband's tone when he was talking to you a moment ago", Roslyn observed.

"Oh, that's nonsense! He just amuses me dear Rosy, that's all; he's just a boy and, in a way, feels under my control. You know, I turn him and do with him as I please. It's just as it might be with your ……!" She halted in mid-sentence and abruptly changed the subject.

"You say I take too gloomy a view of things, but you just can't or won't understand. It's awful. I'm trying not to take any side at all in this matter".

"But I think you ought to, you ought to, and should do, all that you can to help them settle it amicably", Roslyn said.

"But what can I do if they can't live together in harmony? Nothing!" She exclaimed in frustration. "Do you know that for months now they haven't been talking to each other? Imagine two people sharing a space who won't converse with one another! For them, speech and discussion have no purpose at all in marriage!"

She got up, straightened her chest and sighed deeply and heavily. She started pacing up and down the room, stopping now and then to express her regrets, strong negative emotions and considerable misgivings about her younger sister's marriage.

"You have to make a serious concerted attempt at reconciliation, you have to try", Roslyn said with effort, getting up to face AiShetu.

"Suppose I make all the attempts I can, and nothing happens, what then does that mean?" She declared, evidently having given plenty of thought to the suggestion.

"Well, suppose I make the effort, I guess there are only two outcomes; either I receive a humiliating rebuff or, in the most unlikely circumstances, reconciliation, which I really don't expect, because they have allowed the venom and acrimony between them to fester for too long", she concluded, walking out to the main sitting room and again facing Roslyn, who had come out to the sitting room herself because it was getting dark and hot in the bedroom where they had been.

"These are two creatures that I really, really love, but I can't have the two of them together. Oh, I'm sorry. I really don't like to talk to them about such personal issues. Rosy dear, please don't judge me or blame me. It will end one way or the other, so please withhold your judgment or blame at least for the time being. You don't, and can't, properly understand the suffering I feel in my heart"; she went back into the bedroom and began sobbing. Roslyn peeped in, feeling a little tinge of guilt for perhaps having pushed the matter a little too far and having said too much. She went in and held her friend's head on her lap and silently comforted her. Tears welled in her eyes. Both women started to cry.

When AiShetu saw her friend Roslyn off, she went back into her bedroom and served herself a good shot of some strong drink. After drinking it, she sat still for a short while on the edge of the bed, and eventually was able to doze off in a more cheerful and clear frame of mind. Within a few moments she'd fallen into a deep reverie. In her sleep she dreamt of what she had been discussing with her friend especially that utterance about her role as a reconciler between her baby sister and her husband. In the dream she saw them all at a dinner table, with her and her husband cheerfully sharing conversations and making jokes. She saw the resolution of the issues between the two of them, resolved amicably with candor, honesty and simple common sense. She was able, with the help of her husband, to fend off each of the challenges the couple presented her successfully. In the end, she saw all four of them, walking out holding hands and hugging, under the intense light of the stars and the moon. She woke instantly opened her eyes and shouted, "It worked, it worked!" sitting up with a broad smile all over her face. Only then did the truth dawn on her. It had been a dream. But she consoled herself with the outcome, because her dreams often turned out exactly as she saw them. This knowledge of the possibility of success nudged her on to take the first and appropriate effort at reconciliation that very day by calling on her sister later in the evening.

Ayuba Mshelia

All the neighbors and their wives were there at Professor and Mariayamu's quarters at *asubar,* as agreed to the previous day.

"Well, let's go through Mallam Mamman Shata's tribute to Sir Ahmadu Bello, the Sardauna of Sokoto", Balarabe said.

He cocked his head to one side cleared his throat and then remarked: "You know, Mallam Mamman Shata's politics were more akin to those of Mallam AminuKano (a.k.a. Mallam) than the Sardauna's.

It was this perspective that his tribute meant so much to his Northern listeners.

To add even more importance to what Shata did (he was very much honoring Mallam Aminu Kano's request); Mallam Aminu Kano, the leader of the Northern Elements Progressive Union (NEPU) had sternly instructed his followers "to be nice and respectful of the Sardauna in death. He died for all of our cause. He died because he loved the North. We had our differences but they were more about process than substance".

It was thus comforting that Mamman Shata felt moved to pay this tribute to the Sardauna. It is entitled "Mallam Ahmadu Bello" and, in short, goes something like this:

1. *Mallam Ahmadu Bello.*
2. *Mallam Ahmadu Bello.*
3. *Allah jikan Ahmadu gamji/dan kwarai Ahmadu gamji.*
4. *Rabona da ganin mutsa-mutsa in ga wata kura/tun zamanin Ahmadu Bello.*
5. *Allah jikan Ahmadu gamji.*
6. *Allah jikan Ahmadu gamji.*
7. *Shi ya fada ma damgi yace da gudun kahuri Ahmadu gwan-da shahada.*
8. *Ya ce da gudun kahuri Ahmadu gwan da shahada.*
9. *Dan kwarai Ahmadu gamji.*
10. *Dan kwarai Ahmadu gamji.*

The English transcription reads as follows:

  *Mallam Ahmadu Bello
  *Mallam Ahmadu Bello

*May Ahmadu Gamji's Soul rest in peace/The good son, Ahmadu Gamji

*I haven't seen a large congestion of cars with dust-rising/Since the time of Ahmadu Bello

*May Ahmadu Gamji's Soul/rest in peace

*May Ahmadu Gamji's Soul/rest in peace

*It is he that informs relatives/that to run from pagans [accept defeat from pagans /Ahmadu prefers dying a martyr.

*He said rather than running from a pagan/it is better to die a martyr.

*The good son, Ahmadu Bello/Ahmadu Gamji/Ahmadu Gamji the good son

*The good son, Ahmadu Bello (Ahmadu Gamji). Ahmadu Gamji the good son.

"That's Shata's tribute", Professor Balarabe concluded.

"We'll discuss the last of the three poets in a short while. Meanwhile, does anybody have any personal observation or comments about this tribute?"

"Yes", James piped up.

"I think it addresses the general acceptability of the Sardauna by the Northern public. It was very generous of Shata to compose such a moving tribute to his political foe. Furthermore, I would sincerely congratulate Mallam Aminu Kano, the leader of NEPU, who, in spite of the fact that he had been at logger-heads with the Sardauna over all those many years, threw in his support and his sympathy for him at the time of his death and encouraged his supporters to do the same."

The first of the Sokoto poets/singers who was amongst the Northern poets whose actions seemed to have spurred sympathy and action was Alhaji Musa Dan Kwairo of Sokoto. Kwairo was very prolific in his production of songs lamenting the demise of the Sardauna. In one of his "Elegy for the Sardauna" (*Wakar Sardauna*) he starts by praising his magnanimity and generosity to all. He then goes on to recount the unforgettable events of that fatal early Friday morning.

"He titled one of his elegy tributes as *Yaki ya ci Ahmadu* (The Battle defeated Ahmadu)", professor Balarabe observed.

"Of all of the Dan Kwairo songs about our fallen leader, the Sardauna of Sokoto, this one is the best of them all; I've listened to it more than I can count", Golu observed.

After nobody made any further comments, the Professor stood up to go to bathroom. While he was away, some of the other guests also stood up to straighten their legs. Several of the women present ran in to Mamu's kitchen to see if they could find something perhaps to munch at or eat. After ten or fifteen minutes, everybody was back and ready to continue.

The Professor gathered everyone together, "Alright, let's start listening to Dan Kwairo's tribute".

The Professor acknowledged the excellent work the scholar John Paden had done withhis translation and transcription of these songs. He advised those who might be interested to look them up in *John Paden: Ahmadu Bello Sardauna of Sokoto: Values and Leadership in Nigeria* (1986). After his acknowledgement of Paden's work he said, "alright, *bari mu fara jinta* (let's start listening to it). *Yaki ya ci Ahmadu* (The Battle-defeated Ahmadu) by Dan Kwairo".

Professor Balarabe drew the tape recorder close to him, slipped in the tape and started playing, "oops! It is the wrong tape! I'm sorry I must have left it in the old car" (the house boy has gone out looking for gas around town in the car). So instead he just red them the English transcription which reads as follow:

"When he (the Sardauna) lost the war, he (the singer) cried and lamented and became sad. Later he was consoled when he realized that, rather than aMuslim be disgraced by an unbeliever (*kafiri*), he [Ahmadu] would rather die. He [the singer] then felt happy for what had happened, for God had made it so, in that God had taken him [Ahmadu] to be with him. It is better to die with honor, than to be disgraced he surmised… Ahmadu was beyond being looked-down-upon. No one could look down on him. A fixed pole is difficult to uproot…The father of Sir Kashim…the master of Zagge, Bello dan Hassan [i.e. Ahmadu Bello] has the blessings and dignity of Mamman Bello, Abdullahi, Shehu Usman Dan Fodio, Attahiru, Umar Daji, Nana [Asma'u], Isan Kwari…

Son of elephant, you cannot be faced, son of Alu the Sultan, is beyond being looked-down-upon. East, West, North, and South, everyone knows you are the Sardauna. You spend the whole day distributing gifts. Because of your generosity and good deeds, people had to surrender. Premier of the Northern Region, for what you did for us, up to the end of the world, you will be remembered. Well-born child [gamji dan kwarai], up to the end of the world, you will be remembered. Premier, person with the mind of a saint, evil will be done to you, but you will respond only with good. This is the habit of the Shehu Usman. The back-biters, the enemies, these are the ones who worry themselves… As for Ahmadu, he doesn't care … The past has become past, it is now the future that we are looking to. The future is not bright, in that there is no one up to his standards. Our concern is where to get one who might be equal to him. Ahmadu is not afraid. He doesn't shake. He thinks straight and acts immediately. He shows that he is the son of the Shehu. He has the world. He embraces all the children, and the children's children, all subjects alike … I cry and lament and cry and cry. Then I remember that it is a disgrace for a Muslim, that it is better to die with faith, than to die at the hands of an enemy and a non-believer (*kafiri*)".

"What a song!" Both Jamima and Owoleye commented (Jamima had come with her husband that day because she wanted to see Mamu, whom she hadn't seen in a very long time).

"It's the ultimate tribute, all that one could ever hope for", James agreed.

"Well, wait until you hear the second song, entitled *"Ya wuce Raini"* ("He is Above Disrespect) which is another variation of the theme above by Dan Kwairo I hope I have the correct tape", the professor declared.

Ya Wuce Raini

1. *Ya wuce raini/Ba a yi mai shi/Ahmadu jikan Garba Sadauki.*
2. *Kai Alhaji Musa Dankwairo/ Ka taba wakar Ahmadu Bello/ Mu yi sujuda don kowa/kasan kowa baif furce lokaci nai.*
3. *Shi Ahmadu sanda ya yi mulki/ Ya rike jama'a tai zak kyawo/ Na tare da kai bai lallace ba/Har yanzu na tare da kai/Ko gobe na tare da kai bai lallace ba.*
4. *Firimiyar jihar Arewa, Ahmadu/ Abinda kai ma Nijeriya/Har kasa ta nade ana tuna ka/Ahmadu jikan bawan Allah/Gamji dan kwarai, gamji dan kwarai/Gohe Allah gafarta ma/Mallam Ahmadu Allah dai ya ji kai nai.*
5. *Gaba ta wuce/Baya ad da saura/Yanzu ku samo wani kama tai/ Ba tsoro ba karayar zucci/Ya gwada jikan Shehu/Ahmadu ya gwada jikan Shehu ne shi.*
6. *Ya samu duniya/ya ko gwada ya samu duniya/Yai alheri, ya rika*

*kannai, ya rika ya'ya/Ya rika bayi, ya rika barwa da talak-kawa/
Ran Juma'a da karfe biyu/Rannan yaki yac ci Ahmadu/Niy kuka,
niy bakin rai/Nit tuna Allah, niy mashi murna/Da wulakanci
gara shahada ga musulmi/Don ba illa ne ba.*

7. *Ya wuce raini/Ba a yi mai shi.*
8. *Firmiya mai halin waliyai/Sui maka sheri ka rama hairi/Wanga halin Bello ya gado/Mahassada nai na ta jidali/Ahmadu dan' Iro ba ruwa nai.*
9. *Ya wuce raini/Ba a yi mai shi/Ahmadu jikan Garba, Sadauki.*
10. *Gungurun kashin giwa na Alu ba ka haduwa/Kowah hade ka sai ya fasa Makosi.*
11. *Ya wuce raini/Ba a yi mai shi/Ahmadu jikan Garba, Sadauki.*
12. *12.Alhaji Abubakar Jibrin/Dankwairo bai raina mai ba.*
13. *13.Ya wuce raini, ba a yi mai shi/Ahmadu jikan Garba, Sadauki.*
14. *Turakin Zazzau na kirki/Na gode maka dan Tijjani.*
15. *Ya wuce raini/Ba a yi mai shi/Ahmadu jikan Garba, Sadauki.*
16. *Gargarau barkan ka da yaki na Madawaki/Ki sake barkan ka da yaki na Madawaki.*
17. *Ya wuce raini/Ba a yi mai shi/Ahmadu jikan Garba adauki.*
18. *Dankwairo mu yi godiya ga masu yi man domin Sardauna/ Alhajiya Yar'tsohuwa Dankwairo bai raina ta ba/Ta ba Dankwairo kudi fan saba'in/t ace man domin Sardauna/Alhaji Sarkin kaya Maradun/Ya ba ni kudi ya ba ni kaya/Sai yac ce man domin Sardauna/Ya rike amanar da anka bar mai/Mamman ya rike amarar da anka bar mai/Sarkin daura Mamman Bashiri/ Ya kaini makka/Yace man domin Sardauna/Ya rike amanar da anka bar mai/mamman ya rike amanar da an ka bar mai.*
19. *Ya wuce raini/ba a yi mai shi.*
20. *Tijjani Hashim/Dankwairo bai raina mai ba/Ga sutura ya ba mu kudi/y ace man domin Sardauna/Kuma ga mota ya bai wa Kwairo/y ace man domin Sardauna/Ya rike amanar da anka bar mai/Ahmadu ya rike amanar da anka bar mai.*
21. *Abdu Keftin Sokoto/Allah ya taimaka ma/Ya ganni ya yi kirana/ Ya ban*
22. *riga, ya ban wando, ga taguwa/Dankwairo, ya ban fan hamsin*

23. *baki dai/Y ace domin Sardauna/Ya rike amanar da anka bar mai/Shi ma ya rike amanar da anka bar mai.*
23. *Manjo-Janar dan Shehu na kirki/Dubu tara ya ba Kwairo/Y ace man, saiya ce mun domin Sardauna.*
24. *Fan goma sha biyar/Ya ba ni gaba dai/Na ji dadin Alhaji Dabo.*
25. *Ya wuce raini/Ba a yi mai shi.*
26. *Gagarau dan Maihano Zaki/Ki-sake dan Maihano zaki/Na Madawaki.*
27. *Sakkwato nis san Alhaji Garba/Sakkwato nis san Alhaji Ali.*
28. *Ya wuce raini/Ba a yi mai shi/Ahmadu jikan Garba Sadauki.*

The following is English transcription of the song:

*He's above disrespect/It is not taken [done] to him/Ahmadu grandson of Garba, gifted one.
*Alhaji Musa Dan Kwairo/Sing for the Ahmadu Bello, so that we are sober, because no one/you know, no one would exceed his time.
*Ahmadu, when he governed/, he ruled his people very well/ whoever was with you would never go astray. /Up to date Up to now, the person with you didn't go astray. /Even tomorrow the one with you won't go astray.
*Ahmadu, Northern Regional Premier/What you did for Nigeria/You will be remembered till the last./Ahmadu, the grandson of God's servant/Gamji the good son, Gmaji the good son/May God forgive you/Mallam Ahmadu, May your soul rest in peace.
*The past has passed/It remains the present/Now to get another replacement. Without fear and a weak mind/He has shown that he's Shehu's grandson. /Ahmadu has shown that he's Shehu's grandson.
*He has got the world/has shown that he gets the world. /He was generous, he takes care of his brothers and sons/Looks after servants and the masses./On Friday, at two o'clock,/ That day Ahmadu meets his death./I cry and became sad/I remember God and congratulate him./Rather than being disgraced, it is better to die a martyr/Because it isn't wrong.

*He's above disrespect/It is not taken [done] to him

* Our Premier who has the character of a saint,/They did bad to him and he repaid them with good./This is the character of Bello that he inherited/His enemies are worried/Ahmadu, son of Iro doesn't care.

*The big bone of the Elephant that's unswallowable/Whoever swallows it, it will break his throat

*Alhaji Abubakar Jibril/Dan Kwairo is grateful to you.

*The Turaki of Zaria, good one/I thank you, the son of Tyra.

*The warrior thanks you for your effort, Madawaki's associate/ The unreluctant thanks you for your effort, Madawaki's associate

*Dan Kwairo, let me be grateful/ to those helping me because of the Sardauna/ Alhaji Yar'tsohuwa, /Dan Kwairo is grateful to you/She gave seventy pounds to Dan Kwairo, and said "because of Sardauna. /Alhaji Sarkin Kaya of Maradun/he gave me clothes and money"/Andsaid, "because of the Sardauna. He holds the trust left to him". Mamman took the trust left to him/Mamman Basher, the Emir of Daura/Took me on pilgrimage/ and said "because of Sardauna. He holds the trust left to him, /Mamman holds the trust left to him"

*Tijjani Hashim/Dan Kwairo is grateful./He gave me clothes and money/And said "because of the Sardauna"/and he gave a car to Dan Kwairo and said "because of the Sardauna./He holds the trust left to him,/Ahmadu holds the trust left to him".

*Captain Abdu Sokoto/May God help you/He saw and called me and gave me fifty pounds/And "because of the Sardauna/ He holds the trust left to him". /He also "holds the trust left to him".

*Major-general, son of Shehu [Hassan Usman Katsina] the good one/He gave nine thousand to Dan Kwairo/and said "because of the Sardauna.

*He gave me fifteen pounds/In a whole/I am grateful to Alhaji Dabo.

*The hero son of Maihono lion/Unreluctant son of Maihano lion/Associate of Madawaki.

*It was at Sokoto I know Alhaji Garba; /Sokoto is where I know Alhaji Garba.

"Again, what a song this is!" Francisca observed

"It is amazing that all the poets we have perused so far saw the Sardauna's death as his destiny and the will of God", the Professor observed.

"Yes, but even more than this, they clearly respected his dignity and bravery in choosing death rather than to be disgraced by a *kafiri*(a non-Moslem*)*. However, nowhere in these songs did the singers call for revenge, the fact that they focused, instead, on those positive qualities and virtues which endeared him to the public, is an indication of their deep feelings of respect.

The *Gamji* tree was sadly no longer there to provide protection and shade or to guide his followers", Veronica evoked the familiar metaphor.

"You know, I have had the privilege of listening to this song on several occasions now, and every time I hear it played, it still sounds fresh and new ", James said.

Just as they were about to get involved in the discussion; Hassana, Maryam's house helper walked in with a full tray; while Maryam tagged behind.

"What do you have for us?" Her husband, the Professor, asked politely.

"Oh it's the *fura* that you brought over yesterday when you went over to the stadium to watch the game of football game between Ghana and Nigeria. I feel sorry for those poor Ghanaians they got beat bad, three -nil?" She said.

"*To sannu mun gode*", Balarabe replied in response to his wife's considerate attention to his well-being.

The women immediately stood up and followed *Mamu* to the kitchen for their own share. In our culture men and women still do not mix freely. A large section of our women folks believe it's improper for them to share meals with men in public other than their husbands while at home. There's nothing wrong with this at all, it's just a convention and tradition, even though the wind of change is blowing the other direction!

The gentlemen sat on the *darduma*(a velvet carpet) and shared the *fura*. They all thanked Mamu, through her husband, for her kindness and consideration.

Among the poems/songs written earlier during the late 'fifties and early 'sixties in praise of the Sardauna, and before the events of January, 1966, but which became popular during the January 15 episode was, Salihu Jankidi's *Sassalar Ahmadu Bello*. Jankidi was born in Gusau (Sokoto) and was said to be a close associate of the then Sultan, Abubakar III.

Sassalar Ahmadu Bello ("The Origins of Ahmadu Bello"). The *amshi* (chorus) is *Ahmadu Kara Shirin Duniya; Allah Shi Ya yi ma Daukaka* ("Ahmadu, Prepare for the World, God made you great").

As the Professor played the tape cassette, those present listened intensely.

Salsalar Ahmadu Bello by Salihu Jankidi

1. *Ahmadu kara shirin duniya/Allah shi yai ma daukaka.*
2. *Ahmadu kara shirin duniya/Allah shi yai ma daukaka.*
3. *Ku sauraramaganar mai girma/Jikan Mu'azu dan Ibrahim/ Komai y ace dauka akai(repeat)*
4. *Ahmadu kara shirin duniya/Allah shi yai ma daukaka (repeat).*
5. *Aikinka na wuyar koyo/Maza sun gane ka sun hirgita/Ai tun da fari tun fil azal/Hali nai halin Alu Babba ne.*
6. *Ahmadu kara shirin duniya/Allah shi yai ma daukaka.*
7. *Zaki ya yi karo da giwa/Mun ga jikinai ya hurhura (repeat).*
8. *Ahmadu kara shirin duniya/Allah shi yi ma daukaka*
9. *Su wadanga masu son sui turi/Tunkurdarsu me take kan dutse/ Aikin banza shina sukai (repeat).*
10. *Asalin Ahmadu Sardauna Bello/Tun daga ya Rasulillahi (repeat).*
11. *Har bias Fatsima har Ahmadu/Shehu Muzamilu kuma da Sanusi, Mustapha/da Hayatu hard a Musa, Tukur Hukuba/ Ibrahimu, Abdulahi, Sinkiyu Abdul' Samadu,/Nasiru, Sirajo, Haruna, Ahmadu, Salisu,/Usumanu, Muhammadu Fodio, Shehu Usumanu,/Mamman Bello, Abubakar Mai Rabah Ibrahimu, kun ji sal'salar Ahmadu Bello/Sardauna dan' Hassan.*
12. *Ahmadu kara shirin duniya/Allah shi yai ma daukaka.*
13. *Annabi shi ya haifi Fatsima/Fatsima ita tah haifi Hassan/Hassan kuma shi ya haifi Mamman/Mamman shi ya haifi Isa/Isa kuma ya haifi Mamman/Mamman shi ya haifi Tanimu Mukari'u/*

Tanimu shi ya haifi Ahmadu/ Ahmadu shi ya haifi Attahiru/ Attahiru shi ya haifi Audu/Audu shi ya haifi Yusha'u/Yusha'u shi ya haifi Hussaini/Hussaini shi ya haifi Hashimu/Hashimu shi ya haifi Halmasu/Halmasu shi ya haifi Abdul Razaki/Abdul Razaki shi ya haifi Abdullahi/Abdullahi shi ya haifi Abdul Hamadu Attahiru/Abdul Hamidu shi ya haifi Ahmadu/Ahmadu shi ya haifi Hasamatu/Hasamatu shi ya haifi Salihu/Salihu shi ya haifi Abdul Razaku/Abdul Razaku shi yahaifi Aliyu Rabbiku/Aliyu Rabbiku shi ya haifi Sa'idu Ahmadu/Sa'idu Ahmadu shi ya haifi Muhammadu/Muhammadu shi ya haifi Hauwa'u/Hawau'u ita ta haifi Shehu Usumanu/Shehu Usumanu shi ya haifi Mamman Bello/Mamman Bello shi ya haifi Abubakar/Abubakar shi ya haifi Ibrahim/Ibrahim shi ya haifi Sardauna Ahmadu.

14. *Duk wanda ad da asala hakanga/Duk duniyagga wai gabanai/ Ko Lahira ina za su ma (repeat).*
15. *Ahmadu kara shirin duniya/Allah shi yai ma daukaka.*
16. *Ku saurara maganar Mai girma/Jikan Mu'azu dan Ibrahim/ Kome yac ce dauka akai.*
17. *Ahmadu kara shirin duniya/Allah shi yai ma daukaka.*
18. *Asalin Ahmadu Sardauna Bello/Tun daga Ya Rasulullahi (repeat)*
19. *Har bias Fatsima har Ahmadu/Shehu Mubari'u kuma da Sanusi, Mustapha/da Hayatu hard a Musa, Hakubu/Ibrahim, Abdulkadir, Sulmiyu, Abdul' Samadu/Sirajo, haruna, Hamza, Usumanu/Muhammadu Fodio, Shehu Usumanu/Mamman Bello, Abubakar Mai Rabah/Ibrahimu/Kun ji salsalar Ahmadu Bello/Sardauna dan' Hassan.*
20. *Ahmadu kara shirin duniya/Allah shi yai ma daukaka (repeat).*
21. *Zaki ya yi karo da giwa/Mun ga jikinai ya hurhura(repeat)*
22. *Ahmadu kara shirin duniya/Allah shi yai ma daukaka (repeat).*

The following English transcription was made, some years later by the previously-mentioned John Paden.

The Origins of Ahmadu Bello by Salihu Jankidi

*Ahmadu prepare for the world/God made you great.
* Ahmadu prepare for the world/God made you great.

*Listen to the talk of His Highness/Mu'azu's grandson, son of Ibrahim/whatever he says is accepted

*Listen to the talk of His Highness/Mu'azu's grandson, son of Ibrahim/whatever he says is accepted

*Ahmadu prepares again for the world/ It's God that uplifts you.

*Your work is hard to learn/Men saw you and become afraid, /because in the first place/your character is like that of Alu Babba.

*Your work is hard to learn/Men saw you and become afraid, /because in the first place/your character is like that of Alu Babba.

*A lion collided with an elephant/we noticed the effect on its body

*A lion collided with an elephant/we noticed the effect on its body

*Those wanting to put pressure (push), their pressure won't affect the mountain/It a useless thing that they're doing.

*The origin of Ahmadu Sardauna Bello/is traceable to the Holy Prophet/

*The origin of Ahmadu Sardauna Bello/is traceable to the Holy Prophet/

*Coming down from Fatsima and up to Ahmadu,/Shehu Muzamilu and also Sanusi, Mustapha, Sinkiyu,/Abdul Samadu/ Nasiru, Sirajo, Haruna, Ahmadu, Salisu/Usumanu, Muhammadu Fodio,/Shehu Usumanu, Mamman Bello, Abubakar Mai Rabah/to Ibrahim/You have heard the origin of Ahmadu Bello/Sardauna son of Hassan.

*The Prophet begat Fatsima, /Fatsima begat Hassan, /and Hassan begat Mamman, /Mamman begat Isa, /Isa begat Mamman, /Mamman begat Tanimu Mukari'u, /Tanimu begat Ahmadu, /Ahmadu begat Attahiru, /Attahiru begatAudu,/ Audu begat Yusha'u,/Yusha'u begat Hussani,/Hussani begat Hashimu,/Hashimu begat Halmusu,/Halmusu begat Abdul Razaku,/Abdul Razaku begat Abdullahi,/Abdullahi begat Abdul Hamadu Attahiru,/ Abdul Hamadu begat Ahmadu,/ Ahmadu begat Hasamatu,/Hasamatu begat Salihu,/Salihu begat Abdul Razzaku,/Abdul Razzaku begat Aliyu Rabbiku,/ Aliyu Rabbiku begat Sa'idu Ahmadu,/Sa'idu Ahmadu begat

Muhammadu,/Muhaamadu begat Hauwa'u,/ Hauwa'u begat Shehu Usumanu,/Shehu Usumanu begat Mamman Bello,/ Mamman Bello begat Abubakar,/ Abubakar begat Ibrahim,/ Ibrahim is the father of Ahmadu Sardauna.
*Whoever has this type of background/who would ever supersede him in the whole world, /even in the Hereafter, won't reach you
Whoever has this type of background/who would ever supersede him in the whole world, /even in the Hereafter, won't reach you
*Listen to the words of His Highness/Mu'azu's grandson, son of Ibrahim, /whatever he says is accepted.
*The background of Ahmadu Sardauna Bello/is right from the Holy Prophet.
The background of Ahmadu Sardauna Bello/is right from the Holy Prophet.
*Down from Fatsima and Ahmadu/Shehu, Mustapha and Sanusi, Mustapha/with Hayatu and Musa, Hukubu/Ibrahim, Abdulkadir, Sulmiyu, Abdul Samadu/Sirajo, Haruna, Hamza, Usumanu, /Muhammadu Fodio, Shehu Usmanu/Mamman Bello, Abubakar mai Rabah, /Ibrahim/You heard the origin of Ahmadu Bello/Sardauna, son of Hassan
*A lion collided with an elephant/we notice the effect on his body/
A lion collided with an elephant/we notice the effect on his body/

"This is a wonderful praise song", James observed

"Yes, it's amazing how Jankidi could recall all the names of the Sardauna's ancestors in a song this long", Veronica commented and Mariyamu concurred.

"These poets seem to have a special ability for songs, such as these. Such people are commonly called savants", Francisca observed.

The Professor continued, "In this poem, Jankidi is trying to urge the Sardauna to take on the responsibilities of the world. Whoever wishes to be great must be willing to face insurmountable challenges. He was linked to Sultan Mu'azu and Hassan, which put him in a direct line of succession to the Sultan-ship. The reference to him as a mountain means that those who want to oppose him have a herculean task — imagine removing a mountain! The allusion to/ analogy with the Prophet endows the Sardauna with special qualities of leadership, blessings and charismatic prowess.

The early fifties songs/poems praising the Sardauna's traditional leadership qualities created a tremendous pressure on the Sardauna to live up to their expectations. There were two other song writers in the same category with Salihu Jankidi in praising the traditional leadership qualities of the Sardauna; Aliyu Fodio Dandawo and Garba Dan Kyana. Dandawo was born in Shuni, Sokoto. He died in 1973. The nickname 'Dandawo' was given him because he sold forage (dawo) as a child. He had two major songs about the Sardauna, but we have time only for the first. The songs are: *Ahmadu Bello Sardaunan Sakkwato* (Ahmadu Bello the Sardauna of Sokoto) and *Sardaunan Sakkwato* (Sardauna of Sokoto). The professor slipped the tape into the cassette player and pressed the play button as the group waited.

Ahmadu Bello, Sardaunan Sakkwato by Aliyu Dandawo

1. *Ya rinjayi maza tu azal/Na Dan Hodiyo mai babban rabo/ Ahmadu mai karhin arziki/Mu hanzarta mu bi Bello dan'Shehu kada/jirgi shi yi nuta da mu.*

2. *Musulmi kada Shedan shi yake mu/kwak ki biyaj jikan ShehuLahira/Allah na banza das hi/Mu hanzarta mu bi Bello dan Shehu kada/jirgi shi yi nuta da mu.*

3. *Musulmi kada Shedan shi yake mu/kwak ki biyaj jikan Shehu, Lahira/Allah na banza das hi.*

4. *Suna na ad dai arziki daban shike/Yanzu bani Shehu duk azurhwa nag a zinariya/Suna na ad dai arziki daban shike/ Yanzu bani Shehu duk azurhwa nag a zinariya.*

5. *Abubakar Mai Rabah dan Bello, /Shugaban jama'a na Magajin Gari, Alu Gumbi,/Yadda ka samu duniya, ana damma ka gobe lahira/Ka ga Shehu Mujaddadi/Inda Annabi al'ummarka duk tana tare,/Ahmadu don Shehu Annabin Allah shi yi ma azrziki.*

6. *Watan Sallah mai dadin gani,/Ganin kowa kak kwan yag gane ka/ Yay ta mubari'a Usumanu na Ahmadu yardarm Allah/ gareka, tabbata Allah yai ma rabo.*

7. *Watan Sallah mai dadin gani/Ganin kowa kak kwan yag gane ka/Yai ta mubari'a, Usumanu na Ahmadu yardarm Allah/ gareka, tabbata Allah yai ma rabo.*

8. *Da Ikko da Gwalkwas duk inda kan nuhwa/Ahmadu tahi kai ad das u/Garin kowa kak kwan ba ka taka oda, /Kowa kai ad das hi.*

9. *Da Ikko da Gwalkwas duk inda kan nuhwa/Ahmadu tahi kai ad das u/Garin kowa kak kwan ba ka taka oda/Kowa kai ad da shi*

10. *Ina rokonka inai ma tuni/Batun alkawari wanda munka kulla, in Sarki ya nuhwa.*

11. *Ina rokonka inai ma tuni/Batun alkawari wanda munka kulla, in Sarki ya nuhwa.*

The English transcription reads as follows:

1. *Originally he won men over, /Dan Hodio's descendent of great luck, /Ahmadu of formidable riches/We should hurry and follow Bello, son of Shehu before the train leaves us behind.*

2. *Muslims, don't allow Sartan to deceive us/Whoever disobeys Shehu's grandson,/would face God's wrath in the hereafter/We should hurry and follow Bello, son of Shehu/before the train leaves us behind.*

3. *Muslims, don't allow Satan to lead us astray/ whoever disobeys Shehu's grandson/God will forget him on Judgment day.*

4. *The name may be the same, but the blessing differs/Now all of Shehu's descendents are silver, / but here is the Gold/ The name may be the same, but the blessing differs/Now all of Shehu's descendents are silver/but here is the Gold.*

5. *Abubakar Mai Rabah, son of Bello,/ people's leader of Magajin Gari, Alu Gumbi,/ as you get the world, you are honored/later in the hereafter,/ to see Shehu, the Reformer,/with the Prophet, with all your community together/ Ahmadu, may the Holy Prophet bless you because of Shehu.*

6. *The moon of Sallah night is nice to sight/ the sighting keeps all throughout the night/ to continue mentioning, Usmanu of Ahmadu/ of God's will, no doubt God has blessed you fully.*

7. *Repeat 6*

8. *Both Lagos and Gold Coast, wherever you intend going/ you*

should, Ahmadu own theme/ In whatever town you spend a night, / you don't break any order/ You own each and everybody.

9. Repeat 8
10. *I am beginning and reminding you/ about a promise we made/ if God allows.*
11. Repeat 10.

The last of our poets to be considered was Garba Dan Kyana of Sokoto. Like Salihu Jankidi and Aliyu Dandawo, his poems/songs inspired positive feelings for the Sardauna after the events of January 15. We'll listen to only one of his three major songs about the Sardauna.

Gagarau Namijin Duniya Uban Jakada: The Unbeatable Hero, Father of the Emir's Messenger; by Garba Dan Kyana.

1. *Gagarau namijin duniya uban Jakada/Babu mai kabra da kai Ahmadu toron giwa.*
2. *Gagarau namijin duniya uban Jakada/Babu mai kabra da kai Ahmadu toron giwa.*
3. *Gangaho namijin duniya uban Jakada/Babu mai kabra da kai Ahmadu toron giwa.*
4. *Gagarau namijin duniya uban Jakada/ Babu mai kabra da kai Ahmadu toron giwa.*

   Giwa mai ban tsoro dan Ibrahim/

   Garzazo fiyi mashigi dan Ibrahim/

   Ture mai shige gabanka giwa.
5. *Gagarau namijin duniya uban Jakada/ Babu mai kabra da kai Ahmadu toron giwa.*
6. *Da lahiya ya kawo/ Kuma da lahiya yad dawo (repeat)*

   Giwa mai ban tsoro dan Ibrahim/

   Toya matsafa na Garba.
7. *Gagarau namijin duniya uban Jakada/ Babu mai kabra da kai Ahamdu toron giwa (repeat).*
8. *Da lahiya yah hau (repeat)/ Kuma da lahiya yad dawo (repeat).*
9. *Gagarau namijin duniya uban Jakada/ Babu mai kabra da kai Ahmadu toron giwa.*
10. *Ya farke gummi nai dai/ Dan Hassan madaukin fansa/ inda ta*

Araba Let's Separate

sha sai ya sha/ Ya maida gura nai nai/ Dan Hassan madaukin fansa/Inda ta sha sai ya sha.

11. *Gagarau namijin duniya uban Jakada/ Babu mai kabra da kai Ahmadu toron giwa.*
12. *Ya maid a filatai nai/ Dan Hassan madaukin fansa/ Inda fada sai ya ja.*
13. *Gagarau namijin duniya uban Jakada/ Babu mai kabra da kai Ahmadu toron giwa.*
14. *Komai anka ce mai/ Kyalewa ya kai kamar bai jib a/ Ya jiya fasawa yay yi (repeat)*
15. *Gagarau namijin duniya uban Jakada/ Babu mai kabra da kai Ahmadu toron giwa (repeat).*

The English transcription by Paden reads as follows:

1. *The unbeatable hero, father of the Emir's Messenger (Jakada),/ No one confronts you. Ahmadu the bull elephant (toron elephant)*
2. *Repeat 1.*
3. *The greatest hero, Jakada's father, / No one confronts you, / Ahmadu the elephant.*
4. *Unbeatable hero, Jakada's father/ No one confronts you, / Ahmadu the elephant, /elephant, the fearful son of Ibrahim, / big thing above entry, son of Ibrahim, / push whoever stands in your way, elephant.*
5. *Repeat 1.*
6. *He went safely/and returned safely/ (repeat)/ Elephant that is fierce, son of Ibrahim/ Destroyer of shrine, of Abubakar (Garba).*
7. *Repeat 1.*
8. *He went safely/ and returned safely (repeat).*
9. *Repeat 1.*
10. *He realized his objective/ Hassan's son the avenger/ If there is anything/ you would make it/ Hassan's son the avenger/ If there is anything you would make it.*
11. *Repeat 1.*
12. *You make your things/ Hassan's son the avenger/ If there is a fight, he would do it.*

13. *Repeat 1.*
14. *Whatever is said to him/ he leaves as if he didn't hear it; / He just leaves (repeat).*
15. *Repeat 1.*

Aminu commented that, although the tributes did not in themselves amount to an explicit encouragement for an uprising or a counter-coup, they surely added fire to the heap of simmering ashes, which was waiting to explode in an uncontrollable dangerous conflagration.

"The central symbolism of Shehu Usman and Hassan's son provided the basic legitimacy for leadership, but within that lineage group, some are more worthy (gold) and others silver. The reference to Lagos and Gold Coast (now Ghana) implies the wide range of the Sardauna's influence and power. The overall impact of the poem is to link the Sardauna religiously and politically with his ancestors and to God's blessing. In Garba Kyana's poem the constant reference to words like 'gargarau' symbolized the Sardauna as "the unbeatable hero". The continual reference to him as a bull elephant, *toron giwa*, was intended to instill fear in the minds of his opponents either real or imagined. Lastly the reference to him by the poet as "Hassan's son, the avenger", *Dan Hassan madaukin fansa*; leaves the listener to presume what is being avenged, or it may be a general warning to opponents to think twice, before they try to harm him", the Professor declared.

Chapter Five
Decree No 34, Gossips, Innuendoes and Riots.

One of the episodes that helped ignite that wait-and-see attitude or posture at that time was the now-infamous "decree number 34" that Major-General Ironsi promulgated and signed into law on May 24, 1966, which has far reaching consequences for our story as we continue our march to*"Araba/Aware"*. The decree that Major-General Ironsi signed stipulated that: *(1) Nigeria had ceased to be a Federal Republic, (2) Regions were abolished, to be replaced by Groups of Provinces, (3) the National Military Government would legislate for the whole of Nigeria* and *(4) the Public Services would be unified under a National Public Service Commission, and, finally, (5) that all political parties and tribal associations or affiliations and unions were now listed and banned.*

The effect of this "Unity Decree" was profound and had a sobering effect on the general public, especially on the Northern Civil Service. Not only had the region been disintegrated, but the *Northernization* policy which had been conceived as the vehicle of equity, for level playing-fields between the regions' services appointments to the federal Government, was over. Hence, while there was jubilation in some parts of the country, in the North, as you can well imagine, there was a state of shock, it was like a sudden and untimely death in the family.

"Today we're going to discuss the so called "Unity Decree", right? But how could the Federal Government abolish the regions, and, at the same time, force a Unity Civil Service on the population without a referendum"? Francisca whispered to Veronica. She had come to the meeting today because they were going to have their hair done later.

"Do you think our people should have swallowed all of these sudden and suicidal changes? Given the simmering anger over what happened on January 15?", Hajia Jummai lamented to her husband, on their way to the General Hospital, next to the old market, to see his nephew, Yaquab

Musa, who'd just had a prostate operation earlier in the day, before their planned visit to the Professor's house for that day's meeting about the now-infamous decree.

"It's hard to envisage how or what our people could do, other than a direct public uprising. What options were there?" Her husband responded in his usual calm, measured manner, in spite of the gravity of the situation; revealing hardly no emotion at all, almost as if he didn't care.

Professor Balarabe and his wife Mariayamu were also discussing the same decree when James and his wife walked in. The couples had planned to visit Mr. & Mrs. Owoleye, because the Owoleyes had paid each couple several visits in the past, but neither of them had visited *them* even once, as yet.

When all had gathered, the Professor opened the discussion by thanking everyone for coming. "Our main discussion today will deal with the signing of the now-infamous decree 34 and its after-effects". He paused for comments, but, noticing there was none, continued:

"Hence while there was jubilation in some parts of the country, in the North it was a somber mood, as if a death had occurred in the family. When the Federal Government drew up the list of seniority the Northern civil servants were shocked. They were all at the bottom—far down—on the seniority order, because the region was not only educationally disadvantaged at this time, but, traditionally, paid the lowest salaries in the Federation to its civil servants—this, in line with the Sardauna's slogan of "One North, one people, one destiny and sacrifice by one for all and all for one"— thus relegating them to the bottom of the Unified Civil Service. To add salt to the wound, there were rumors rampant that Ironsi *knew* about the Prime Minister's death—that, in fact, he had personally tried to interrogate the Prime Minister, but the Prime Minister had refused to answer any of the questions he posed to him, and thus, so the rumor goes, he was summarily handed to the soldiers to be killed. To make matters worse still, there were no denials. You can imagine what combined effect these two facts had on the Northern civil servants. As a matter of fact, A. Richard, the then Attorney General of the federation under Tafawa Balewa, in part declared in July 2000 when launching a book that he was amazed that the "GOC Major-general Ironsi was going all over Lagos unarmed at the time, in spite of the fact that the coup has not been quelled".

"It was also learned or asserted" the professor continued "that as a matter of fact, the Cabinet *didn't* voluntarily hand over power to Ironsi as

Araba Let's Separate

was first announced. Richard observed in the speech referred to that; "we did not hand-over. Ironsi told us 'you either hand over as gentlemen or you hand-over by force'. Those were his words. Is that voluntary hand over? So we did not hand over. Rather, he kind of usurped it through machination and intrigues". What happened was this, because the NPC was the senior partner in the coalition with the NCNC, the Cabinet selected the most senior NPC minister, the eloquent and dynamic Zanna Bukar Dipcharima from Borno to be the acting Prime Minister until things got a little bit more settled. But when they approached Dr. Orzu an Easterner and as the Acting President, to swear him in, he refused after he had had a prolonged discussion with Ironsi (a fellow Easterner). This conspiracy was not lost on the senior Northern representatives in Lagos", he concluded.

As a digression, my readers, I'll like to acquaint you with all circumstances and the information floating around at this time that made the January 15 plot look like an Eastern affair. Can you believe that the then-President of the Federal Republic of Nigeria, Dr. Azikiwe, had conveniently been out of the country since 1965, first to Europe, and then, on what was called a '*health cruise*' in the Caribbean, after it was alleged his cousin, one of the chief plotters, Efejuna, had tipped him off about the coup. In fact, his personal physician, Dr. Humphrey so bitterly inveighed about his constant change of itineraries that he had abandoned him and returned to Nigeria because his wife had had a baby more than a year previously while he had been away with the President and he had never seen the child who was now already walking.

"Mr. President, Sir, I ask your honor and indulgence to permit me to travel back home. We have been away for too long and I fear that my baby son, Christopher may not even recognize me when he sees me!" He pleaded.

As for the President himself, not even the Commonwealth Leaders Conference, being held in Lagos at the time, was enough of an incentive to induce him to return to the Federal Republic of Nigeria. It was also noted by keen followers of events at the time, and there were many of them, that, during a press conference he held in London on January 16, he never, in a real sense, condemned the coup plotters *per se*". As a matter of fact, he referred to them almost indulgently as "our Young Turks"! Whatever this meant in the present circumstances of Nigeria, no-one could tell. And to tell you the truth, nobody has properly divine its meaning, even to today!

"Now back to the power grab by Ironsi. Dr. Orzu told the senior Northern politicians that the NCNC had selected Dr. Mbadiwe (an Easterner). This, naturally, was unacceptable to the NPC Ministers because the NCNC was the junior party in the coalition and there was no chance, come hell or high water; that they would acquiesce and allow this dastardly sequence of events to happen; an open and unambiguous grab of power. Later, in a room full of soldiers wielding their semi-automatic rifles and strapped with magazines of grenades around their waists, however, Ironsi boldly told the Ministers that, since he wasn't able to suppress the coup quite yet, it was "in your best interests", and, indeed, in the interests of the country, that they should defer to him - or else! Silence fell upon the room, nobody said anything. With soldiers wielding guns in your face, there's little one can do, other than hope for the best. Eventually, it was decided that he could have his wish, and they all returned to their residences to await the news, some were more than happy to speedily get out of the situation with their lives intact! To their chagrin and shock at ten minutes before midnight, Dr. Orzu made a tense sober nationwide broadcast, announcing that the cabinet had as of this moment *voluntarily* transferred power to the armed forces, with Ironsi as both Head of State and Commander in Chief of the Armed Forces.

"Not long after, it was rumored that Ironsi had plans to kill all of the Emirs and the first-class (senior) Chiefs from the North when they attended a conference which he had called for in Ibadan in a fortnight's time. Also circulating was the rumor that he had abolished the compulsory Hausa language test requirement for entry into the Northern Civil Service, which had an appeal to some non-Hausa Northerners, but most specifically to the Southerners who were already eyeing future employment in the Northern Civil Service as a possible career move. These rumors and the appearance of a photo of the Sardauna in a *Drum* feature story, portraying him seemingly floating in limbo, and surrounded by the gloating smirks of Igbo officers and the rank-and-file helped ignite the fire that had been dormant up until this time", the Professor explained.

"I heard that, at this time, even within the army, there were tensions which were created because some Igbo officers and NCOs openly teased the Northern officers", Owoleye said, "accusing them of cowardice."

"Yes indeed", Alhaji Musa Wada concurred (he'd joined them in the discussions at the *Monte Sophia,* even though, as already mentioned he didn't live in the enclave. He'd come in late because previously he had had to see the district head of the whole GRA about collection of garbage and the appointment of a new headmaster for the public school in the GRA, two important matters to the residents; "Some Igbo officers deliberately tried to create unnecessary provocations in the barracks. Northern officers and NCOs had complained that some Igbo colleagues deliberately and insultingly invited them to come celebrate the January 15 event! A photograph of 'Kaduna' standing atop the late Sardauna appeared in the "Drum" magazine portraying him as if he was begging for forgiveness from the writer Idapoh, was being openly distributed in both the barracks and the market place. Some Igbo officers wore sticker reproductions of this picture, pointing out 'Kaduna' and proclaiming "*Shi ne maganinku*" (that's what you deserve/he's your boss). Records were released with gunshot sounds mimicking real shots to remind Northerners of the bullets that had felled their leader. Derogatory remarks were made about Northerners—they were even referred to as "women" in some barracks (at the time women weren't allowed in battlefield combat). All of the above provocations, in one way or the other, didn't help quench the thirst for revenge, in fact, if anything, they exacerbated and intensified it, bringing things to the boiling point", the Alhaji paused to take a sip of water.

"Just as Shakespeare said in *Macbeth*", Veronica reminded the group,

"And they say blood will have blood", it was approaching that boiling point.

The group agreed that they would have stop there for today, because some of them had errands to run. As for the planned visit to the Owoleyes, it was decided that it had to be postponed, because the heated discussion about the signing of decree No 34 had so engaged their time that, by the time they all agreed that the North must do something, it was already dark outside.

The May Riots

"What were the causes of the riots in Kano?" Francisca asked James, who had been commenting about the factors leading up to the riots. James said he would defer to Alhaji Wada to answer (the Professor had left to go answer the entrance door).

"The crux of the matter", Alhaji Wada began, "was the May 24 broadcast which made Nigeria a Unitary State. Initially, there were sporadic peaceful demonstrations, by students and the civil service alike. Then, on May 28, (four days on) copies of the June edition of *'Drum'* magazine arrived in the North, containing two provocative articles: 'Why Nigeria Exploded', by Ottakah, which derided Northern leaders; and another, entitled 'Sir Ahmadu Rose In His Shrouds And Spoke From The Dead', by Idapoh, which, allegedly, featured the Premier of the North begging for forgiveness from Idopoh. Many have cited these articles as incendiary indeed, and contributing to the subsequent outbreak of wanton violence which began on May 29th and continued through until June 5.

During this mass killing, inflamed and assisted, by the unnecessary provocation of the articles, more than 600 Igbo deaths were reported in the Northern provinces of Kano (the 5th battalion garrisoned near the airport under M. Shuwa was featured prominently in this act; Bauchi where the words *A ware/Araba*—let's undo it/let's separate—were first uttered—later became a popular slogan—; Sokoto (mostly in Gusau), Katsina, and Zaria. In Sokoto township, because of an intervention by the Sultan, and the fact that, a fortnight earlier, there had been a deployment of a police unit consisting predominantly of Igbos, which helped, temporarily, calm the volatile environment there, the killings were minimized.

Immediately thereafter however, an army company was deployed to Sokoto, also under the command of an Igbo officer. This latter action, intended supposedly for internal security, caused shivers, melancholy and not the least pandemonium up in the North because this was something new — they had no precedents for this, going right back to the *Satiru* rebellion under the British. The rebellion which had challenged the established authority and occupation of the British was began by the Islamic Mahadists' movement in French Niger and swept through the Sokoto caliphate to the village of *Satiru*.

Satiru was brutally crushed and razed by the British police and soldiers on March 10, 1906. The situation was made even worse because Ironsi had issued an order earlier, prohibiting the issue of ammunition, even for target practice. However, in the North, because of the dominance of Northerners in the Officer Corps and NCOs in the infantry units, such orders were disregarded. There was one Northern officer who was almost killed because he was suspected of harboring or protecting some Igbo officers.

The failure to prosecute the January 15 plotters in accordance with, and following the manner of, military law was palpable to some and an indication of the misgivings they had against Ironsi — they held him thus partially responsible for igniting the barbarity. Ironsi had also, in the eyes of the Northerners, become a hostage to the Southern press corps, who had hailed the plotters as heroes. In addition, in spite of police reports and other investigations which recommended that the plotters be charged and prosecuted, nothing happened. In his book: "*Why We Struck*", Ademoga eloquently states that "each time the matter was brought up for discussion at the Supreme Military Council (SMC) Fajuyi …was opposed to any trial". It is not surprising the Colonel was hunted, tortured and brutally killed by an angry mob of Northern soldiers after being abducted from Danjuma. There were rumors floating around, which were never denied, that the plotters were getting their salaries in prison in addition to prison allowances, that they were also not only getting their normal promotions but had unfettered access to their families, including "all conjugal rights"! Some of these allegations and innuendoes have since been proven false, but, at the time, they were rampant, and that, and the fact that nobody denied them, perpetrated them as unassailable facts in the psyche of the people. In his book *"Revolution in Nigeria; Another View"*, the late soldier-cum-diplomat Garba explains how some Northern members of the Federal Guard in Lagos broke down in tears when they heard the album 'Machine Gun'. The record was to be released to remind northerners of the bullets that felled their leaders in January. Ulowu a popular Igbo musician was alleged to have released another record titled *"Ewu Ne Ba Akwa"* (Goats are crying) in Igbo—it was later said the song originated from a non-Igbo artist from Rivers. It was also alleged that even Igbo soldiers' wives were involved in teasing their Northern counterparts in the barracks and at the market. "In the final analysis", the Alhaji continued, "many events and rumors conspired to push the Northern troops to the precipice or edge".

"But one of the main brunts at this time were the riots and killings which were going on in the Western region as a result of the 1965 elections, which were considered rigged by almost everybody, altho', of course, nothing ever happened"

"In that sense, nothing has really changed, because we're still experiencing the same phenomenon today — election-rigging, corruption and religious fanaticism. The only difference is that Nigerians have perhaps now learned *not* to give their lives for any "orange", "jasmine "or "velvet" revolutions. Aminu made these observations with the present events in Nigeria in mind.

"It was so chaotic at that time, almost to the point of anarchy, especially in the West", the Professor jumped into the discussion, "so much so that the civil unrest had started spreading to Lagos, and apparently nothing was being done, or very little, by the police force. Soldiers were sent out to augment the efforts of the police but, by that time, it was too late, the riots had developed and taken on a life of their own. The skirmishes in Kano were thus a direct result of what was going on in the Western region. This, in part, was because prices of foodstuffs were raised astronomically high, due to fears of instability, but which some people interpreted and alleged had been done deliberately, by the Igbos, solely for profit. As a result the rioters ran amok; and it resulted in more than 600 Igbo deaths in the North. In addition, miraculously the riots seemed to occur simultaneously near public institutions felt as dominated by Igbos, such as the Sabon Gari market in Kano, as well as local post-offices and railway-stations. The levels of violence were so sudden and so intense that some Igbos in the North began retreating to the Eastern Region, where they were promised protection by the then-Military Governor of the Region, Ojukwu", the professor paused to take a sip of his tea.

Professor Balarabe stopped and advised the group they suspend their discussion of the events of January 15, 1966 and the civil war until next week-end. Those in attendance thought that was a prudent thing to do, to pause, because some did indeed have errands to run. For example, Golu and his wife Francisca planned to visit a relative at the Murtala General Hospital and then proceed on to the central market to pick up some, yams, meat , rice and *acha* (similar to millet). Pastor Owoleye had to attend a meeting, as well as choir practice with his congregation before morning service the next day. Moreover, he had to prepare his sermon for the Sunday service, which was to be titled *"ChristianTolerance and Forgiveness in the Global Society"*.

Chapter Six
The Counter-Coup d'état

"Active planning of the coup to overthrow the Ironsi regime began in earnest immediately after the promulgation of the "Unification Decree No. 34", the Professor began." Prior to this time, some relatively senior officers (Shellang, Jega, Abacha, Hannaniya, Sali and Dambo) from Kaduna wrote a letter to Yakubu then Army Chief of Staff openly stating that, if the Northern officers didn't take action within a certain date, of say six weeks, they would themselves take matters into their own hands, and that the senior Northern officers would have only themselves to blame for the catastrophe that might ensue. They were angry that, so far, only lip-service had been rendered with regard to the fate of the plotters of the coup, who some believed were currently ensconced in Kirikiri prison in Lagos. The chief architects of the counter-coup plan were Muhammed (Inspector of Military Signals), Danjuma (General Staff Officer 11, SHQ) and Martin (2nd Battalion, Ikeja), but the overall leader of the coup was Muhammed. It was alleged that, very often, he would drive to Ibadan to pick up some of his Southern fellow-conspirators (e.g. Ibrahim, and Abdulahi) at some pre-arranged spot, and then drive around the city, continuously, in circles, without stopping, in order to avoid any suspicion or clandestine recording of whatever was being discussed as he briefed them on the most current plan.

In the South, the leaders included such people as Garba (later turned diplomat), Walbe and Tarfa (Federal Guards), Buhari and Longboem (2nd Battalion), Nwatkon (Abeokuta Garrison, Recce); Useni, Bako and Garba (4th Battalion Ibadan) and Yar'adua (Adjutant 1st Battalion, Enugu).

There were at least four dates set and subsequently cancelled for the purported, counter-coup. The first was an attempt to seize Ironsi at the State House in Lagos, but Muhammed later decided that would likely entail a blood bath with the Federal Guard unit, and this was unacceptable because, as he put it "enough blood has been shed already". In addition, one never knew when Ironsi was around, because he had formed the habit of sometimes sleeping in a boat alongside the Marina. Another plan was to take place when the first battalion at Enugu would be exchanged with the one in Ibadan. According to this scenario, Yar'adua would be the coordinator, creating some sort of diversion and confusion as a signal announcement for the coup. This plan was scrapped however, because of the continued delay in the implementation of the exchange by the battalions involved. The third was to have taken place in the North on July 19. In this scenario, Ironsi would be abducted, in the North, during his tour of the regions however, this idea was later dropped, in deference to the Northern traditional Emirs and Chiefs, some of whom had good relationships with the GOC. It was, at the time, reliably alleged that Ironsi had good personal rapport with a number of the Northern Emirs, especially the Emir of Kano. As a matter of fact, it was alleged that the Emir of Kano had given Ironsi a wand that enabled him to disappear at will when he was in the Congo as the United Nations' General Officer Commanding (GOC)!). Others, however, contended that it was aborted more because of the logistics inherent in its implementation. Finally, even the one that eventually took place on July 28 and 29 was, initially, supposed to have been scrapped, because Muhammed suspected it had been penetrated and become fatally compromised.

"On Friday July 28, Ironsi opened the conference of Emirs and Chiefs in Ibadan, discussing, that first day, the importance of the Flag and the National Anthem".Many of the Emirs became suspicious right from the beginning, because "you don't invite Emirs and Chiefs from the North to Ibadan and allocate the whole day to such a discussion of the Nigerian flag and national anthem", one of those in attendance pointed out.

"He called them to come to Ibadan to discuss the importance of the National Anthem? That's weird and patently absurd. It must have been a diversion for some more execrable and devious intentions", Abba observed, to the chagrin of Veronica, who had felt the exact same thing and had wanted to speak up but had deferred to Alhaji Abba as her elder.

Conspicuously absent was Dr. Khan. He had travelled to the village to be with his dying father. As fate would have it, he never made it to the village in time to see the old man. He, who'd passed away before his arrival, and had even already been buried. He was merely shown the grave, on a hill-side overlooking the village where most of his elders, including his grandparents, had been buried. Dr Khan had only been able to kneel down and pray for a few moments, for the safe passage of his father's soul as he sojourned in the spirit world to join those ancestors who preceded him. However, he remained in the village for a protracted period of time for the *sadaka* and *kuri tuwa* (a mourning period, during which it is believed that the spirits of the dead continue to hover around in different forms before joining the dead ancestors). At the end of the *sadaka,* which often lasts as long as seven days, the diseased property will be dispensed with, and his wives—if it's a man—may decide to stay in the old house or, if they are young, wish to be married to any of the man's male relatives, preferably his brother, in order to maintain the woman's reproductive potential right within the clan. Also, at this time, some animals would be slaughtered and the meat distributed to each household in the village as a kind of send-off to the man's/woman's spirits. K*uri tuwa* period is, traditionally, longer and may take up to a full year. It is believed that, by this time, the dead man's spirit has already departed and this ceremony is meant as a ritual send-off to the spirit world. It's instructive to note that only the Doctor himself had made this journey. Veronica, his wife, stayed behind with the children, and didn't make the trip with him.

"However", Balarabe continued, " even that July 29 coup almost never happened, because, on the eve of the fourth planned coup attempt", the professor resumed, "Anwunah, a General Staff Officer for Intelligence at Army HQ,Lagos had intercepted Muhammed on a street in Lagos and challenged him as being in charge; the ring-leader of the planned coup. The people who witnessed the encounter unanimously claimed an intense violent and mean-spiritedexchange took place between the two, until they were separated by a force of not less than ten men! Thus, from this encounter, Muhammed knew that his plan had been infiltrated and compromised. In view of this he instructed his co-plotters to send out signals that the coup had been cancelled. But, as fate would dictate otherwise, signal-failure occurred, to ensure that not all of those involved in the coup were aware of the cancellation. The information could not get to all the Northern conspirators.

It was a mixture of fate, panic and incidental happenstances that finally forced the July 29 date, when a handful of Northern NCOs in Abeokuta mistakenly took matters into their own hands. This was especially in regard to Sergeant Koleh (a NCO from the Bachama tribe, from Adamawa) who was alerted by an Igbo NCO, waking soldiers to, "come out, come out, there is trouble… come collect your armor". The Sergeant thought he was dreaming because he had drunk more than his share of palm wine that night and was nauseous, and his head was kind of turning, when he'd been in bed some moments earlier. Now, when sleep was beginning to come to him, all of a sudden he was woken up with such obscene and frightful message! When the Sergeant from Adamawa heard this nocturnal call, he sat up quickly to clear his head and to ascertain that he wasn't dreaming, while seated idly thus, a thought came to him: "This is it, the Igbo Plan 15 or the final solution, code named Operation *Kura* (hyena)". At the time there was rumor circulating that the Igbos were planning "Plan 15" to complete what they'd started on January 15, which was the liquidation of all Northern military officers, emirs, chiefs and senior civil servants", the Professor stopped abruptly as he was interrupted by a knock on the door by a friend, Dr. Usman who had dropped in to say hi.

"The Bachamas are a tough bunch, they are nuts of a clan", interjected Abba!

"Indeed, they are not only firkin' tough, but brave as well!" James retorted.

"In retrospect" the professor resumed, "this is what actually happened. After the encounter with Muhammed, Anwunah was satisfied that, since he had exposed the ring-leader, there wasn't now going to be any coup. However he was prepped by Officer Madiebo not to take anything for granted, but, on the contrary, to do something. After a brief contemplation, following his discussion with Modiebo, he decided to alert some unit commanders about his encounter with Muhammed and advised them to "be on the look-out for any suspicious movements".

It was on receiving Anwunah's alert that Akonweze of the Abeokuta garrison decided to call a meeting of the officers in the mess.

"Gentlemen I've just been informed that there was going to be a coup tonight", he thundered.

"Any of you who know about it should please tell us. I'm not an ambitious officer, my only ambition is to become a full colonel" and then I'll retire, honorably, to the village, as yam or chicken farmer." He sighed and stopped. "I'm not going to report any one, however, as you know, or *ought* to know, in a coup, you know the beginning but you never know the end", Akonweze somberly concluded, especially since nobody was really acknowledging any prior knowledge of an impending coup.

It was from this background that an Igbo NCO went around waking soldiers excitedly "to come out, come out, there is trouble; go to the

Araba Let's Separate

armory and collect your arms". This was the alert that Sergeant Koleh Sabo— a Bachama tribesman from Adamawa province, now State, heard and misinterpreted as an attempt by Igbo NCOs to selectively wake up only Igbo soldiers.

After hearing the alert, Sergeant Koleh then woke up quietly and dressed up before tip-toeing to his neighbor and kinsman, Corporal Maje Maisamari to wake him up (Maisamari was the Corporal in charge of the Unit Armory). Maisamari himself had just begun to fall asleep, because he'd been out together with Koleh, the night before and had had more than enough of his share of the palm wine. His head was still heavy with the drink. "Listen", Koleh whispered, as softly as he could, "They have launched "Plan 15 final solution", please get up quickly and get ready to go the armory and ensure that only our Northern brothers receive weapons." Maisamari didn't react as he should; he was delirious and didn't comprehend the gravity of the situation. Koleh had to nudge him hard on the shoulders, hard enough to force him to wake up and open his eyes. Koleh then helped dress him and managed to squeeze him out of his room quietly and discretely, because he was rooming with a non-Northerner. With the help of the likes of Maisamari, he —Koleh— mobilized a small guard of Northern soldiers, including Corporal Inua Sarah and Shagayaya to protect the armory against any attempt by any other group to dislodge them.

After they had secured the armory and were well-armed, they marched to the officers' mess under the direction of the duty officer, Pam, the younger brother of the Colonel who became a victim in the January coup.

"All stand up and raise your hands! "Be quick!" Thundered Pam to Colonel Okonwuze, and when Okonwuze did not respond with the urgency expected of him under these indisputably tense conditions, he was summarily ordered shot! It was Koleh who did him the honor. This was followed immediately, in succession, by Obienu and Oroko being shot at point-blank range by Pam himself. "The July 29 counter-coup is on"! The Professor stopped to sip some herb tea.

They heard an old car screeching to a stop outside the house, and when The Professor looked through the curtains he recognized the Alhaji.

"Sala mala ikum", the Alhaji knocked gently on the gate, and a house boy opened the gate.

"Mala ikum Salam alhaji"; the Professor answered. "We are talking about the counter-coup staged by the Northern soldiers".

"Oh, the second coup, it almost never happened, if it were not for the Northern NCOs at Abeokuta", Alhaji Wada calmly surmised.

"After the attack on the officers' mess", the Professor resumed; "A frantic call was placed by Pam to Paiko, the adjutant of the Fourth battalion in Ibadan. This is the message Pam relayed to Garba:

"Look man, we have done our own, ooh! If you people just siddon down there, we have fucking finished our own…We have finished and eliminated the Igbo officers here in our garrison. We have liberated our unit! It's now your turn to do your fucking part man".

But wait, not yet, unbeknownst to Pam, an Igbo officer named Ogboona was alive, as well as Okoli. As soon as Ogboona was out of danger and safely ensconced, he relayed an urgent signal to Lagos that the Northern coup was on, in full swing, and that most Igbo officers at Abeokuta garrison had been shot! Unfortunately for Ogboona, or, as some persons would surmise, since fate dictated it; the persons who initially received the message in Lagos were Northerners, Nuhum Nathan, the duty officer, and Malami Nasarawa. Nahum, whom Muhammed had earlier contacted with regard to the postponement of the planned coup because of his spirited encounter with Anwunah of military intelligence, as a matter of utmost urgency, immediately alerted Muhammed, with regard to Ogbona's frantic signal reporting what had already taken place at the Abeokuta military garrison. The Colonel quickly went into action realizing that events were moving faster than he'd thought, and maybe even faster than he wanted, and now he was frigginbehind, far behind, in executing his long planned *Operation Aure (*Marriage*)*. Not to be outdone, he immediately ordered Nuhu Nathane and Malami to mobilize all Northern troops at Ikeja in order to prevent any efforts by the military establishment to regain control of an already dicey situation. Meanwhile, some Northern soldiers were quickly dispatched to round off some Igbo officers especially 'the jubilators and those who had been teasing and calling the Northern soldiers names, (like "women," or "cowards"), or also those who deliberately wore a sticker or the buttons with the Sardauna shown prostrating at the feet of an Igbo officer".

The Professor stopped abruptly because Alhaji Wada has cleared his throat and was now eager to jump in.

"You see the Northern NCOs and ordinary soldiers went berserk in

Lagos, hunting down and killing any Igbo soldiers they could round up, and sometimes not even using their guns but butcher knives, swords, and all manner of weapons they could lay their hands on. When they were asked by an officer that they didn't have orders to kill, their answer was always; "accidental discharge *Sah*". It wasn't a nice situation being an Igbo at this time in Lagos, or indeed for that matter anywhere else in the country, other than probably in the East",

Alhaji summarized his thoughts.

"You see", he resumed, "The actual drama took full swing or place in Ibadan, when Danjuma got the news that *"Operation Aure"*— Operation Marriage— was in operation full throttle! In the South the Northern soldiers there nick-named it *"Auren Paiko"*. This was the code word used for this operation. It seems all military operations must have code words, *Operation Damisa, Operation Torch (World War II), Operation Overlord (World War II), Operation Barbarossa (World War II), Operation Desert Storm* and *Operation Shock & Awe!*

"Danjuma didn't have his military combat dress so he borrowed a mis-sized and mis-matched one from a colleague and wore it over his pajamas. The American-type of camouflage uniform didn't fit him that well, he looked clumsy in it, but who cared? His main concern was winning the support of the Fourth battalion, because they didn't as yet know him. He was not one of them. However, this he was able to do through their adjutant, Garba Paiko. Danjuma asked the adjutant to issue a *legitimate* order to all his soldiers on duty to be disarmed. He got the Northern soldiers in the Fourth battalion and supplemented them with the ones he and James Onojah had brought with them from the barracks to be armed. All others he ordered disarmed. In order to get the cooperation of the Federal National Guard commander guarding the building where Ironsi was staying, he confronted Walbe directly and secured his unflagging and unflinching support. This wasn't difficult at all because Walbe was in the picture, he had attended meetings in Lagos with Garba about *Operation Aure;* it was just that he didn't know the coup was taking place that very night. The soldiers surrounded the rest house where Ironsi was staying with his host, Fajuyi. One important factor overlooked by the coup plotters, but very important in this sort of business, was the fact that no effort was made to cut off the phone-lines.

While there, Danjuma accidently intercepted a call from Yakubu Gowon from Army Headquarters, Lagos which was meant for Njoku who was staying at the Rest House and this because he could not reach Ironsi's ADC, Sani Bello. Njoku meanwhile had just escaped from the rest house and barely avoided having been shot. The following is an edited and modified transcription of a conversation that transpired between Danjuma and Yakubu. Again, my readers this is a modified version and not verbatim conversation:

Danjuma: "hello who's there?"

Yakubu:" Hi, hello, who is it? I want to speak to the Brigade Commander. …I want to speak to Njoku!

Danjuma:"Again, May I ask who is speaking? Please identify yourself"

Yakubu: "My name is Gowon, Colo…Yakubu Gowon- Army headquarters",

Danjuma: "Oh, *To kai ne Ranka ya dade*! This is Yakubu Danjuma".

Yakubu: "Yakubu Danjuma! What are you doing there? That's not your order, oh, excuse me, or your assignment"?

Danjuma: "No Sir, I am in the State house here".

Yakubu: "I know that! So where is the Brigade Commander? Can you put me in touch with him immediately?"

Danjuma: "*Ranka dade*, he is not around; and, you know what? To tell you the truth, I don't give a hoot where he is right now (*To gaskiya oga ban ma damu a wurin da yake ba a yanzu)*".

Yakubu: "Danjuma, have you heard, or have any knowledge of, what has happened?"

Danjuma: "Yes, I have heard and that is why I'm here. We are about to arrest or blow up the Supreme Commander and his host. If we don't, the alternative is that the Igbo boys who carried out the atrocious January coup will be released and will seek vengeance, *tit for tat,* since we have already killed their officers. Besides, our officers' lives are already at risk given the gruesome events in the Abeokuta Garrison".

Yakubu: (after a long period of silence) "What do you mean? However do you think you can do it without any further bloodshed?"

Danjuma: "Yes *Sah*, we have merely got the place surrounded so far".

Yakubu: "But for goodness sake, Danjuma! We have had enough bloodshed already. Please, there must no be any further bloodshed".

Danjuma: "No, we are only going to arrest the two of them, him and his host, so long as they don't try any tricks or offer any resistance, and court-martial them at the appropriate date and time", he answered tersely

Danjuma put down the phone after this comically brief conversation, and faced the soldiers, who were getting restless because they were eager for him to blow up the building. They became more and more agitated and impatient with Danjuma for not allowing them to blow up the Residence with grenade. With Onuga gone (he ran away when Danjuma and the Northern troops surrounded the building, and, I understand, he was later captured) and with no other duty officer on the ground or from the Fourth battalion whom they knew, the NCOs began to wonder if they should perhaps just take matters into their own hands? After all, they asked themselves, who *is* this strange *Major* in an over-sized American camouflage uniform? They even began to wonder if Danjuma himself might, in fact, be an Igbo officer, given his physique and bearing. Just as all this was going on, Shalleng returned from his check-point along the Abeokuta road. He was able to calm and persuade the Northern NCOs that "yes the Major is a Northerner and you should obey him, and do whatever he tells you; this is an order"! Paiko (the Fourth battalion Adjutant) himself returned, and the soldiers appealed to him again, almost pleading with him, to blow up the building and its occupants inside, but he refused to do so, unless he told them Danjuma gave the order. It was tense and already early-morning; but Danjuma chose to maintain the siege, waiting for the occupants to one-by-one emerge.

At about six-thirty in the morning, however, Ironsi's ADC, Sani Bello, emerged from the building and was immediately arrested and disarmed. He was forced to remove his shoes and sit on the ground. As some of the Head of States' entourages arrived for the programs of the day, they faced the same fate as Bello, and this included Olou Tomas (a physician), Lawson (Secretary to the Western Government) and a host of others. At about seven-thirty, Fajuyi emerged to see for himself what was going on. According to archival records, this is what transpired between Danjuma and Fajuyi:

Fajuyi:" Oh Danjuma, come. Why are you here? What do you want?"

Danjuma: "I want to speak to the Supreme Commander."

Fajuyi: "Ok, please promise me that no harm will come to him."

Danjuma: I'll try, but can't give you a solemn commitment or guarantee that no harm will come to him. However, we are here only to put him under arrest".

Fajuyi:"Let me go upstairs and call him."

Chorus of the Northern NCOs: No! Sir! Don't allow him to go! OOh!"

Danjuma turns and shows Fajuyi, who has turned to go upstairs what he has: "*Sah*, you see what I have? This is a grenade. If there is any false move from you the two of us will go together."

At this juncture, the Colonel slowly led the way upstairs closely followed by Danjuma, and five fierce-looking armed Northern soldiers these included Walbe just a few inches behind, as they entered the room where Ironsi was.

Ironsi:"Hi young man, what can I do for you?"

Danjuma: "Nothing, *Sah*, but you're under arrest."

Ironsi: looking at Danjuma askance "What is the matter with you, young man? What crime did I commit?"

Danjuma:"The matter is you *Sah*. You told us in January, when we supported you to quell the mutiny, that all the dissident elements that took part in the mutiny would be court-martialed. It's July now. You have done nothing. You kept these bastards in prison that's all and the rumors are now that they will soon be released because they have become national heroes. All we have been given or promised are asinine excuses, like the English say "All mouth and no trousers"! or the Texans' "all hat and no cattle"! Now we are demanding our pound of flesh."

Ironsi: "Look, What do you mean, my man? It's not true. The document is on my desk in Lagos. As soon as I return I'll sign it and they will all be court-martialed instantly."

Danjuma:"Again, words, words, words and no action! All hat and no cattle. As far as we are concerned, it's over. We're no longer interested in listening to mere words and empty fuckin' promises, the chickens have now come home to roost."

At this point according to published accounts Danjuma and Ironsi began heatedly arguing, with Fajuyi intervening, reminding Danjuma of his promise that no harm would come to Ironsi.

Danjuma: "Fajuyi! Get out of my way! I'll get to you later. Now! You, Ironsi, just come down!" He commanded Ironsi the Commander- in- Chief.

Danjuma: (to Ironsi) "… You organized the killings of our Northern brother officers in January and you did nothing to bring the so-called

Araba Let's Separate

"dissident" elements to justice, because you are part and parcel of the whole scheme. All we get is procrastination and false empty promises. You also were fully aware of the torture and of the death of the Prime Minister; in fact you ordered it, when you could not get him to say what you wanted him to say."

Ironsi: (smirking) "Who told you all of these stories, my man? You know it's not true!"

Danjuma: (grimacing and foaming)"You're lying! That's your chief foible! You've been fooling us for too long. I ran around risking my fuckin' neck, trying to calm the restive ranks, and in February you told us that they would be tried! This is July and nothing has been done! You will answer for your negligence"

At this juncture, Irons's Air force ADC, Andrew Nwankwu jumped forward and faced off Danjuma with fierce mean-spirited verbal exchange of counter- accusations and threats of court-martial when this is all over; he, holding a pistol and Danjuma, holding a grenade with the pin pulled, and, to make a bad situation really worse for the ADC, as he calculated very quickly, all the odds stacked very much against him, because, beside the grenade there were five fierce-looking Northern soldiers, armed to teeth with their fingers on the triggers of their automatic rifles, just in case he made the wrong move, in fact, if he dared to make any move at all!

With Ironsi, the Commander-in-Chief and Fajuyi arrested by one of his own Majors and a bunch of NCOs, and without any further incidents, they were all brought downstairs. At this juncture Danjuma promptly instructed the Fourth battalion adjutant, Garba (Paiko) to take the Commander-in-Chief and Fajuyi to the rest-house on the cattle-ranch in Mokwa. Paiko, however, had his own plans and he reminded Danjuma that he was not a party to the commitment he'd made to Fajuyi or Yakubu that no harm would come Ironsi's way. He'd made no such pact he pointed out and therefore, by implication, he was free to act in any way he sees fit. Serious emotional argument ensued between the two and the other northern NCOs' anxiously standing-by waiting for orders. The Commander-in-Chief meanwhile just listened in silence and awaited his fate with humility not seen before at the hands of these Northern NCOs, he knew, at this point, that his time has come. He felt like a cat on a hot tin roof. How he wished he had "court-martialed those January 15 bastards!" Now he was in this fix because of them! But also, Fajuyi, he reasoned to himself, had to bear the blame for his unflinching support, sometimes bordering on insanity, for the bastards at Supreme Military Council (SMC) meetings, where he always argued that the boys did not deserve a court-martial, instead they should be seen as "national heroes", because they've saved Nigeria from imminent jihad, sharia, corruption and tribalism! Basically he often just reiterated a catalogue of the plotters' announced objectives. Just as these thoughts were percolating Ironsi's seemingly serene but actually convulsive mind, one of the Northern soldiers tapped Danjuma on the shoulder with the butt of his loaded rifle and said, speaking in Hausa, but translated in English, thus;

"These foolish young boys; that is the kind of leadership you have given us — and you're messing us up. They killed all your elders, both civilians and your fellow officers, and you're *still* fooling around here, arguing on saving these monsters' lives? The man you are fooling around with here will disappear right here, right now, before your eyes, before you even know it." (There had been rumors circulating at the time that Ironsi had '*juju*', certain magical powers, in the form of a baton with twin heads given to him by one of the Northern Emirs when he was in command of the United Nations forces in Katanga (now DRC) which would permit him to disappear instantly so the rumor went if faced with a life-or-death threatening situation).

With this dire warning the other soldiers pounced upon Ironsi and Fajuyi wrestling them to the ground and restraining any further movement. Danjuma had lost control, and he just looked the other way. "You gave us your assurance', Fajuyi shouted, as he was being led away, "Yes, *Sah*, I am sure you will be alright, you are in good hands!" Danjuma was either being sarcastic or indeed *misjudged* the whole situation, but he couldn't have been naïve about the outcome. Ironsi and Fajuyi were taken to a remote area where they were ruthlessly interrogated for their role in the January massacre and tortured before being shot. Sah", one of the NCOs blurted out before shooting his erstwhile Commander-in-Chief, "today the chickens have come home to roost".

Immediately thereafter, both men became mere asterisks in a heap of history", the Alhaji declared, and then paused.

"There are now some historical revisionists" he resumed, "who want to claim that Fajuyi offered to die rather than 'abandon' his guest, but that is far from the truth. As a matter of fact Walbe S. stated"; he paused, "… We arrested him just as we arrested Ironsi, no difference between the two. In our view, he is just as guilty. We suspected him of being party to the

January coup. You remember the Battle Group Course which was held at Abeokuta?... Fajuyi was the commander of the Battle Group Course... All those who took part in the January coup were those who had taken part in that Course. We even had the impression that the Battle Course was arranged for the January coup by Fajuyi, so he had to suffer it too. We also believe he played a significant role in delaying or stopping the January 15 dissidents from being properly court-martialed. We know of his staunch support for them in the SMC meetings. I am sorry about that, but that is the truth, and consequently the nature, of the life of a military man..."

As to who actually pulled the trigger that killed Ironsi and Fajuyi, the facts are murky and fluid but some have suspected Tijjani".

"Why didn't they kill him on the fuckin' spot?" Golu asked

"Oh my guess is because he Danjuma had given his words of honor to Yakubu and Fajuyi that Ironsi would not be hurt", the Alhaji straightforwardly surmised.

"But do you know what"? The Alhaji began with a rhetorical question, "The irony of the whole thing is that the original intention of Muhammed was to cede the North from the Federal Republic of Nigeria. He was very vehement and forceful about this. "I insist the North go it alone. We don't need the South", he was heard shouting out in grave anger at a meeting of both senior Northern officers and civil servants and politicians in Lagos after Ironsi had been disposed off and a new Commander-of-Chief and head of state had to be selected. However, cooler heads later prevailed and he was persuaded by his advisors, including, Ayida the Permanent Secretary of Economic Development and some of the senior judges, but, most importantly, by the agents of the British and American Governments who had vested interest in the Nigerian polity. You see, initially, everybody deferred to Muhammed. He was the leading 'personality' in the room they were having one of the first of what was to become numerous meetings; he was the one doing most of the talking. He turned suddenly to Gowon (Northern political leaders, Ministers and Permanent Secretaries, had advised Muhammed earlier to defer to Gowon as the most senior Northern officer present, even though in the beginning, he had initially been with the establishment), saying, "You're the senior, go ahead".

Even after his acquiescence, he continued to interrupt and dominate the discussion, until Gowon mustered up the courage to say, "Look, either you have deferred to me, and will allow me carry on this discussion, or you have not, and you yourself can continue".

Eventually, following the prior intervention of some the senior Northern ministers, politicians and Permanent Secretaries, Yakubu was selected and quietly sworn in late Saturday, July 30th, at Ikeja, as the new Head of State and Commander-in-Chief of the Armed Forces, but didn't address the nation until August the first".

"The way of the military and its normative code of hierarchy and order is perhaps sometimes difficult to justify and comprehend", Golu said pompously. "Yakubu was, initially, as you pointed out, with the establishment, trying to quell the coup, and could have arrested Muhammed and the other Northern officers involved, but here he is, being sworn in as the Commander-in- Chief, and people like Muhammed, Danjuma, and Martin, Garba, Pam, Tarfa and Yar'adua the vanguard of the coup just stand there on the sidelines?"

"Yes, but there were many other factors which the Northern politicians had to consider at that crucial moment, and, remember, Muhammed has already deferred the honor to Gowon as the most senior Northern Officer at the onset. But isn't it ironic that it was he, Muhammed that overthrew Gowon approximately nine years later!" He concluded with a smile.

"All the Northern officers and NCOs acted nobly", Aminu commented.

"At least some of the conspirators of the January 15th debacle have paid the ultimate price — with their blood and with their life, but believe me, there's more to come. We're not done yet", Golu finally ended his diatribe.

"You see", Professor Balarabe began, "the major grievance of the North was the of inequality that was felt as it related to the January 15th killings, where the crucial cadre, or cream, of the Northern leadership was wiped out clean, while the Eastern leadership remained effectively intact and unscathed".

"But isn't it the blessing of Providence that Nuhum, a Northerner was the one on duty when Ogbona's call came in?" Can you imagine what would have happened, had an Igbo officer been on duty at that critical hour?"

Aminu asked a contemplative question.

"I'm afraid the counter-coup would have failed, and all of the Northern Officers thus far involved would have been killed, as Danjuma aptly reminded Yakubu in their fascinating conversion earlier on — Muhammed,

Danjuma, Martin, Shelling, Garba, Dada, Yar'adua, Jega, Abacha, Buhari, Walbe, Hannaniya, Longboem, Useni, Jalo, Pam, Koleh, Maisamari, Paiko, Tarfa and a hosts of others. The loss would have been too great and tragic for the North to sustain and bear", Abba declared.

These sorry events, as you my readers, have no doubt already suspected, had dire consequences which would later lead to an all-out crisis and, following that, a civil war.

Chapter Seven
Araba/Aware-To separate- and the Aburi Accord

"The counter-coup", the Professor began, had unleashed pogroms against Igbos, especially in the North, but also against Northerners in the East. Many Igbo officers were killed, as well as civilians, throughout the North by Northern troops who seized on the opportunity to avenge the one-sided events of January 15. After the initial killings, it didn't take a miracle that things started to steamroller and got out of control, until the whole of the Northern public was participating wholesale. The flight of the Igbos to their ancestral homelands in the East (Northerners in the East were also forced to move to the North) was encouraged by the then-Military Governor, Ojukwu. But did you know that during the July coup, only Radio Cotonu reported the mass killings of Northerners in the Eastern state, which resulted in the subsequent mass movement northward by the Northerners? These and other factors precipitated the indiscriminate killings in the north. The catastrophic effects of these mass movements convinced Ojukwu and some Northern leaders , that since Igbos and Northerners couldn't find a guaranteed security in each others' region in the Nigerian state, the Igbos, Ojukwu and others argued, should break away and officially assert their independence by establishing a state of their own",

Prof. Balarabe paused briefly to clear his throat.

"I remember vividly, how, at this time, some Igbos, who had lived amongst us all their lives, with their families, wives and children, and had built careers or professions for themselves, were chased out of their homes and slaughtered in the streets like dogs. Some of them had started to wear *'baban riga* or *kaftan'* just so as to appear 'Northerner', but were easily betrayed by their accents in the mispronunciation of some Hausa words. I witnessed an incident in Kano where the following events took place. Several people were stopped in a dark alley and were asked these questions;

kace ruwa?; answer: *luwa; kace yarinya?*; answer: *yalinya/yayinya; kacefura?*; answer, *fula/pura*. The people were separated into two groups, those who pronounced these Hausa words, as they should be, without accents, were moved to the right, and those who pronounced them as *luwa,yalinya/yayinya* or *fula/pura* were moved to the left. Those on the right were let go of, but the fate of those on the left has remained a mystery because nobody seems to have heard any more about them. I understand that they were further screened and classified by the checking of their tribalmarkings, where an absence of mark, or a wrong one, coupled, indeed, with mispronunciation, even of a few select words, might constitute a flogging, torture or a death warrant",

Golu sadly observed.

"At the time of the *Araba or aware*" (a slogan meaning 'let's separate or dissolve', probably used first among the Bauchi rioters), Dr. Khan observed,

"I was a student at one of our prominent Institutions of higher learning in one of our most cosmopolitan cities, and remember seeing bodies strewn on the sidewalks, some burnt to ashes, and some evidently hacked with machetes. I vividly recall seeing people carrying kitchen-knives or butcher's knives, swords, machetes, and sticks, looking for someone who looked different from them somehow, in dress, hair-cut, tribal markings, or in the way they pronounced certain words. People burnt down stores that belonged to their neighbors, or even friends! This sorry state, in my view, reminds us all of mankind's regrettable inherent capacity for evil and violent retribution, whether justified or not. None of us is a paragon of morality or virtue, and under such extreme circumstances the moral compass of our humanity dissipates completely, regardless of our professed beliefs, as Christians, Muslims, or even atheists.

I still remember an Igbo gentleman who was brought to our town many years ago by the early missionaries. They brought him from the East to come help them maintain their garage and service their electric generators. He was skilled in his work and was loved by the whole community. His wife and children also adapted very quickly and were all fluent in both the local dialect and Hausa, especially the children. Many of their friends testified that the children didn't even spoke Igbo, because their parents hardly spoke it in their presence. They went to the local school with the other kids, and in everything they seemed just like any other children in the neighborhood. That was until January 15, 1966, when their world was turned upside down. I forget his name, but I think it was Jonathan, Josiah or Joseph. He was, however, simply referred to as 'Joe'. Nobody ever knew if he had a last name. Nobody cared, he was just Joe!

When the events of January 15 occurred, nobody in the town suspected anything, until rumors reached us that Igbos were being killed because of what they had done to our leaders. Neither Joe, nor the town elders ever saw this coming, let alone contemplated the possibility that he and his family would ever be in danger. Many considered him one of their families. So when the district head sent his people in the town to enquire if there were any Igbos around, the town mayor bravely hid the truth from them. He told them that there were none. However, as soon as the first batch of 'Igbo hunters' left, another group arrived in a decapitated jeep and went around the town looking. When they came to the garage and saw Joe, they immediately surmised that he had to be an Igbo; first of all because of his low hair-cut style and secondly because the locals at this time hadn't been exposed to cars, let alone the skills required to repair them. Having made up their mind about Joe's ethnicity, they just hung around long enough to watch him do his work or say some few words.

But Joe knew that would be his last day on the job. From stories and innuendos coming from the large urban centers of, for instance, Kano, Maiduguri, Jos, Bauchi, and elsewhere, the killings would appear as we've already mentioned often occurred during the night, after a day's visit, to ascertain ethnicity, by hair cut, style, dress or word diction. When it was time for Joe to go home, the jeep followed him for a distance and then veered off in the opposite direction. They were stalling him, and Joe knew it. At about sunset, with all the glimmers of yellow and brown light of the sun disappearing beyond the western horizon, some of the elders of the town came to Joe to advise him of the presence of the 'Igbo hunters' in town. Joe told them he knew; he'd spent most of the afternoon with them. For many that were the last time they would see or talk to him, his wife and children; because before ten that evening, Joe and his family were sneaked out of the town by his friends and the town mayor. Unfailingly the 'hunters' came around at midnight, and set the house on fire, and waited outside, expecting Joe and his family to try to escape. They waited and waited but nobody came out, nor did they hear any wailing coming from inside the conflagration. But most perplexing was that nobody even came out to help put out the fire, or just find out what the matter was with Joe's house. After waiting and nothing happening, they headed to the town mayor's house to enquire if *he* was hiding Joe and his family, but he informed them he had nothing to do with what was happening. They ransacked his dwelling but found nothing. Early in the morning, before dusk they left town for the next village; to continue their 'hunt' for Igbos. Joe and his family left because of his justified fear of potential harm, even death, coming from "outsiders".

This sequence of events was repeated ten, hundred, and a thousand fold, throughout the North, where Igbos had found sanctuaries and built a profession and a life for themselves and for their children. Nobody ever heard anything more about Joe and his family. Many people doubt that they made it to the East. "I'm afraid the whole family was very likely eliminated somewhere in the North", Dr Khan said, with bitterness in his voice.

"That's a sad story. Unfortunately, it happened in many places throughout the North, and possibly similar occurrences were experienced, at the time, by our people in the Eastern states as well", lamented Mallam Kaita and his wife AiShetu Bilkisu concurred.

"I had an Igbo personal friend, whose name, if I remember correctly, was either Nnebisi or Ekademe Jr. (a.k.a Junior), who was, at the time, attending an institution of higher learning in our then-federal capital, Lagos, but I'm afraid he was forced by the circumstances of the time to abandon his studies and flee to his ancestral homeland of Calabar", Dr. Khan observed laconically in a wavering voice.

"Ekademe's parents were brought from Calabar by Christian missionaries on their way to the North, and eventually settled in Garki my village. Most of the missionaries came from Pennsylvania, Indiana or Illinois, in America. They brought Ekademe Senior and "*Ma*"(up to her death, nobody in the town ever knew her maiden name, the locals, including her children, just called her "*Ma*") to help them run their hospital. Ekademe Senior was a hospital administrator. He was a short stout gentleman, with a medium-sized flat nose and fair light skin. Junior was a carbon copy of his parents, most especially his father, same head and nose, not to mention their general demeanor. He was short, stout and well-built, with modestly-light skin color and a small erect nose. His sister, Ame, was completely different from any of the rest of her family. Unlike either of her parents, she was very tall, beautiful, long-haired and attractive; with large bones and an artistic aquiline nose that stood out between her beautiful blue glistening penetrating eyes. Her long thick black hair was always tied in knots behind her, if not braided. Her sexy, broad-hipped, behind, and the way she wiggled it as she walked, was mesmerizing, and itself a beauty to behold! Looking at her, you would have never even guessed that *"Ma"* was her mother there was hardly any resemblance at all. For while, she had the smoothest and fairest skin I think I've ever seen, soft and clean to a fault. (*"Ma"* was quite the opposite, with dark, rough, grubby calloused laborer's hands). In short, Ame was the epitome of elegance, standing out as a unique creature of the most humble and pleasingly simple demeanor one might ever behold.

Ekademe Jr., Ame, and their parents lived in a relatively modern two bed- room house, a modest furnishing built for them by the missionaries. The house was surrounded with well-manicured *acasia* and *neem* trees. Right in front of the house was a very large, thick *nona* tree, which as children we would climb playing hide-and-seek in its branches. Also, not very far away, were *baobab t*rees, whose leaves were used as food, especially when they were fresh, when they were dry they would be pounded and ground into a very fine powdery substance called "*kuka*". During the *aviya*, rainy season, both the *baobab* and the *nona* trees yielded very sweet fruits that we would suck, like candy. Sometimes, we would soak the seeds of either of them and mesh them as juice.

The courtyard had beautiful, artistically-arranged evenly-spaced flower-pots of roses, carnations, sunflowers and African lilies; which *aviya*, rainy season, when they blossom cast off shadows of all the hues of the rainbow, when the sun sets on the western horizon, with its glare of red, orange, purple and yellow rays of light. Adjacent to the courtyard was a well-manicured all-season garden with a variety of tomatoes, carrots, radish, egg plant, spinach and cucumber. There were two or three rows of sweet-potato beds. The balcony of the house looked outward, facing the forest from across the only dirt road that passed through the town, and it too was adorned with flower-pots and plants. It was here that, at times, Ekadem and I would sit and watch the sun setting in all its beauty.

My grandma's house by contrast was a locally-thatched mud-house, surrounded with a *kadaka*, (a thatched corn-stalk fence), spruced with a few *nkwabihona*— a small tree with luxuriant wide leaves, which provide a year-round shade including *afaku,* dry season, against the sometimes unbearable sweltering tropical heat—intermittently spaced together with *iza*—similar to *nkwabihona* and providing tiny sweet fruit— around the *kadaka*. The front yard of our house, by contrast, was bare of flowers, with the exception of one very large luxuriant *nfur mbula*, (tamarind tree),which we would often climb to play hide-and-seek in its branches, or to pluck its sour bitter-tasting fruit. The fruit of the *mbula*, when dry, was used, together with *whada*, (peanuts), to make *kunu/mwadubu*. The tree also provided a very comfortable shade to women engaged in pottery-making and *daha*, (calabash decoration), especially during the *faku* (dry, sweltering tropical heat season). However everything changes *aviya* when the yard comes to life with the emergence of wild vegetables like *viranag, aleyfu, makdim* and vegetables purposely planted, like *tabwa, pinau*, corn and *kudikka*. Also commonly planted is *ngabi*, a lovely tall plant with sickle-like broad leaves, whose outer skin is used also for rope-making. These vegetables and shrubs are intertwined with grasses of all types and other undergrowth, such as *tarku thali*, a very bitter shrub plant used by the villagers in treatment of malaria.

In spite of our contrasting living conditions, Junior and I became inseparable buddies, friends, in fact. Even though he was older than me, and my house nothing but a ramshackle dump compared to his, he didn't mind it a bit. Their house servants, Hajara and Oscar Aliyu, always treated me with respect and dignity, as if I were one of the members of the family. When they went to the local market on a Tuesday they would always try to pick up some of my favorite things, such as *kose, waina* and *klishi*, (raw dry meat, thinly sliced and spiced with *kukuli* and hot peppers). We were always together, especially during the dull *harmattan* holiday season. We would go to the small man-made forest next door and hunt for squirrels, or eat some of the wild fruits that grew abundantly there *nturshu*, (cherry-like fruit) *fuma*, (thefruit oftheshea tree from which we get "shea butter"), *washina, kamda*, (figs), *dhaanyi* and *shika*, (similar to blackberries). I remember the time we killed a squirrel and some *izum*, (a big rat), and roasted them out there in the forest on a big pile of wood. We would go to the mountain behind our residenceto the East) and wander all day long, looking for fruit and hunting for rabbits or squirrels. All the time I would be bare-footed, whereas Junior might perhaps have on some old sandals, or just be plain bare-footed as well. At times, we would run into burning bushes, not minding at all the hot ashes left behind as we rushed on chasing the rabbits and squirrels. I remember one day we brought a baby monkey, *Ngozi*, home, after a hard chase by my hunting dog*Surna*, (my thing), despite a gashing wound from its side inflicted both by the alpha-male and the mother monkey. Ekademe kept little *Ngozi* tethered on their balcony with a rope loosely tied around its waist. *Surna* overcame her injuries, thanks to Ekademe Senior's help, with some ointment which we rubbed on the wound. I learnt later that the ointment was an antibiotic.

The day *Surna* died of old age, Junior helped me dig a grave on the edge of the forest and I 'buried' her, all the time crying, as if I had been burying a human being. It was a great loss, and even my grandmother missed her, especially when there was food left over. *Ngozi* was to all intents and purposes a member of my family and was a real treat, and fun, especially when the weather wouldn't allow us to go out into the yard. We spent a lot of time with her, teaching her tricks, like standing on her hind legs, or performing a somersaulting trick by flipping on all fours.

I was so close to the Ekademe family that, if I was not at home, my grandmother knew exactly where to look, or would just holler out my name, and Ame, Hajara or Oscar would rush to the balcony to fetch me. This was true with Ekademe's parents as well, except, in his case, his parents would send out one of the servants, usually Oscar, to come enquire whether we were back from our *kadha* (hiking). Ekademe Junior introduced me to such foreign exotica as Rosicrucian and Freemasonry magazines, which he got imported from India at that time; and other more mainstream magazines, such as *Newsweek, Time,* and a local magazine called *Drum*.

At times Junior could be a little weird with the exotic items he gets from overseas, and, at such times, my grandmother would warn me to be aware and be ever vigilant. For example, sometimes in the night, say, eight o'clock (eight o'clock in those days, in our town, was really late, especially for children!) Ekademe would ask me to walk with him into the forest, with some of the gadgets that he had recently obtained (say from India), a small black wand, a ring or bracelet, perhaps. We would go and just sit down, under a tree, with our legs folded up under us, in complete and absolute solitude and silence, after about five or ten minutes he would start reciting some passages from one of his Rosicrucian or masonry magazines or toyed with some of his special booty, like the rings or the wand.

One day, on a clear night, with stars twinkling in the opaque radiant blue tropical sky, Ame was suddenly informed by their father that she was being sent home to the East after her fifth grade (it was a boarding school for girls that she attended, about forty miles away, which was run strictly by the Church of the Brethern- Ekkleshiyar Yan Uwa missionaries.) She was shocked, and cried her heart out all day long that day but it didn't change the outcome. Ekademe Junior and I tried to console her, but she wouldn't stop sulking or crying. I felt it was unfair because this was the only town Ame had ever known, since arriving with her parents many, many years ago, when she was still a baby. Now she was going back home - but to whom? Everybody she'd ever known was right here. My conjecture at the time, and even today, was that her parents became hysterically obsessive and scared of a possible involvement with a local boy, Dallah; they definitely didn't want their daughter to marry in our town. However, deep in my mind, I'd always thought that Ame wasn't actually their true biological daughter, (I suspected they brought her with them as a house-helper), and this may well have exacerbated the whole situation and heightened their fear of having her marry, or even becoming seriously engaged with, a local boy. They knew that, at one point, there were way too many young local grown-up guys frequenting the residence other than Dallah under the pretence of visiting Ekademe Junior, but, in truth, they were just interested in seeing Ame — they needed not have worried about me, since I was only a child in the third grade, and much younger than both Junior and Ame. In this regard, they wanted to protect her, so that her real parents in the East wouldn't accuse them of letting their daughter run wild with a local boy from the North. All of us missed Ame when she had to leave, to go to a place where she was only vaguely aware of its culture and its language. No mention was ever made of her again in the family circle, or any visit arranged of any sorts. It was as if she'd never existed in the lives of the Ekademe family, and in the lives of those of us who had come to embrace, love and now regarded her as "one of us".

Just before the January 15 event, something catastrophic happened to Ekademe Junior, his father brutally murdered his mother! He cut off her head with a machete in the middle of the night and hacked her remaining body parts into tiny pieces. He tried hiding the pieces in bags and boxes, but there was too much blood smeared all over the property, and, in addition, "*Ma*"'s friends began worrying why she hadn't been seen in public for such a long time. This led some local gossips to spread the news about the "heinous crime" that might well have been committed by Ekademe Senior, which eventually led to his being found out. But, you know what? The district police from Hawule Headquarters came, made some inquires, took apparently, systematic and deliberate notes, but that was about it! I mean that was the end of the matter, case closed! Nothing ever happened to the senior Ekademe, until *after* January 15, when he disappeared on his own, probably to the East.

Two years before Ekademe Senior killed his wife, Junior had spent one full year at home, after completing his secondary school education at Gindiri Boys' College, and was waiting for his West African School Certificate Examination (WASC) results, administered by the West African Examination Council (WAEC) for all English-speaking West African countries. As soon as he got his results he applied, and got admitted, to one of our premier institutions of higher learning in the then-federal capital, Lagos, Advanced Teachers' College/University of Lagos. He learnt of his mother's painful murder when he came home for one of those short holidays.

The last time I saw Junior was our last holiday together a few months before the catastrophic event. At the time, I was in secondary school, form two or three, I don't remember, but all I recall is my parents sending me a message, instructing me to avoid any contact or association with Junior, at all costs. I must never visit the house again. For some reason, by this time, Junior himself had curtailed his coming home during the holidays drastically, if and whenever he came, he spent most of his hours indoors, never venturing outside in spite of concerted efforts and entreaties by few friends, including me of course, but in most instances we failed to convince him. Following the events of January 15, and with all the killings still going on in the cities and the outlying townships, the elder Ekademe packed up his things, with the assistance of several of his friends, and crept quietly away during the dark hours of the night. God knows if he ever made it to the East, because he didn't adapt to the local ways of life so easily as his son and wife. He still wore *dambara*, (tucked-in shorts or pants), wore a neck tie, or put on a safari "colonial" hat (the British pith-helmet-style hat, or its French version. On some days he would wear the African-safari version of the same helmet-style hat). He couldn't speak the local dialect with any fluency, neither could he speak Hausa. He still has that Eastern voice, diction and pronunciation. By all measures, he hadn't changed much from the time that he first arrived with the missionaries from the East, more than fifteen years ago, and took his first job as their hospital administrator.

"Burdened with these obvious characteristics, which by no means were his fault, I'm afraid he never made it pass the famous Makurdi bridge where life-and-death decisions were made based solely on the appropriateness of your dress or tribal marks, that you had or you didn't", Aluor Khan ended his account on a sorrowful note.

"As for my friend Junior, he never left me. I can still see the two of us sitting up in those tree branches in that small man-made forest, where we both grew up, with the sunlight flickering through the leaves onto his flat, broad nose. I can still see the two of us in tattered shorts sitting across from each other on the branches of either, *washina, nturshu* or *nona* trees, with our bare shoeless feet dangling freely and our pockets filled with *whada, g/nuts, ntalwa* or any one of several fruits, fresh-plucked from the trees, *shika, fuma, nturshu,* whatever. I see the two of us, and *Surna,* chasing after squirrels and rabbits in the forest with the rustle of the leaves under our bare feet, or peering between, and under, rocks for a squirrel or a baby monkey temporarily settled on an *nturshu* tree. I see us throwing *nturshu, shikka, and washina or fuma* fruits at each other, and running in the open savannah's empty spaces, until a boulder or a tree avails itself as a hideout. I see Junior leading *Ngozi* with a rope tethered around her waist with one hand and a hook-line in the other. I see him standing by the river bank with a hook-line in his left hand and an earthworm in the right, where he's struggling to attach it to the hook as a sinker, before swinging and flipping it over his head into the river, while *Surna, Ngozi* and I watch and hope for a good catch. The roles reversed after every one or two hours. I remember the two of us swimming in the river and playing a game of catch-up or hide-and-seek, where one person would dip his head into the water for as long as he could while the other one would try to find him. Meanwhile *Surna* would be busy trying to get our attention; that it too wanted a role to play, any role.

Even though I never found out what happened to my friend, it's my strong wish that he was able to remain incognito in the North. I hope he didn't respond to, or join the rebel leader's call. Finding him or knowing what actually happened to him is my enigma, my mystery, and I will work tirelessly to resolve it, one way or the other someday, *inshallah*", he concluded, choking on his words, broken down with emotion.

"I recall now your mentioning his name on several different occasions", his wife Veronica said, offering her support.

This session seemed to serve at the very least some therapeutic function, given the manner in which some of the older people in the company were moved and felt liberated, free to express their sentiments of the pre and post January 15. Alhaji Abba Habib volunteered that "there was a time when I went to the market in our town and came to a store where I knew the owner, and it was burning, and I observed some of his neighbors looting it!"

"I witnessed a similar thing during that period when I was a student at

Advanced Teachers' College (ATC) Kano, Golu continued, "but mine was at a bookstore called *'Zamani'* which, at that time, was the only bookstore in town where you could go to buy all of your advanced text books. The bookstore was burning but all everybody was interested in was just grabbing as much stuff as they could, books— on maths. Chemistry, physics, you name it—stationary, clothes. I entered, but instead of trying to put out the fire, I just joined in with the masses, helping myself to several mathematics and geography books; I felt guilty afterwards about my selfish inexcusable action, and still, up to this very moment, my conscience tortures me", he concluded in a sad subdued apologetic voice.

"It was indeed a great injustice, and to some extent pitiful, to stand-by and watch the *Zamani* bookstore burn down to ashes," Dr. Khan concurred.

There were numerous personal narratives every one of which evoked our individual sympathy especially as they related to events of that era. But as you, my readers, know, there are always at least two sides to a story. Action begets re-action. Time was when the same group that we see now as victims, were indeed in jubilation on the streets at the demise of the Northern fallen heroes.

"I've heard about the *'Aburi Accord'*, but have never really grasped what it is", Veronica declared; and Mallam Aminu Kaita concurred with her.

"Shall we discuss this the next time we meet? It seems it's getting late already", Professor Balarabe interjected.

"I think that's a good idea", Alhaji Wada concurred. "It seems I'm already thirty minutes late for a visit with my brother-in-law, Haliru, who was operated upon yesterday in the Tafawa Hospital. The doctors say he has prostate cancer, which must be removed before it metastasizes".

They all agreed that it was time to end the discussion for the day. As previously, they all in unison thanked *Mamu* and her husband for their generosity and hospitality in hosting the meetings. The women then departed to the women's section of the house and spent about twenty minutes gossiping about less momentous matters — the new couple who'd just moved in next door, the arrival of some new fashionable clothes in the Kingsway and Leventis stores. Kingsway and Leventis, as my readers know, are two of the high-end stores in town. Invariably anything you bought from either one of them would be considered fashionable, and would doubtless be expensive.

"The blouses and skirts (most were regular cut, in short and long styles and of all kinds of color; however few were in petite cut) in both stores are indeed right now, very much in vogue in America, especially New York, so I've learned", Fumilayo observed.

"They are not only in vogue in New York but in Paris and London as well!" both Francisca and Hajia Bilkisu added in unison, and Jamima nodded in the affirmative.

Finally, though, they all laughed and concurred that the clothes would be too expensive for them to afford at the moment anyway; maybe after six months when they go on sale they could afford them, because newer fashions would then have replaced them.

Professor Balarabe and the various other gentlemen — Golu, Abba, Aminu, Aluo and James — who were standing by the gate waiting for their wives to come out, tried hard to turn a deaf ear to these discussions about fashionable clothes in Kingsway and Leventis. They knew the two were the most expensive stores in town, and didn't want their wives to even dream or entertain the possibility of their going there for anything at any time soon.

After the ladies had finished their small-talk about fashion and lifestyles befitting the very rich and influential, Balarabe and *Mamu* saw their guests off and returned to the house. Balarabe went to his room first, but, some few minutes later, he decided to go see *Mamu* in the women's quarter of the house. As he approached, he heard he could hear his wife's voice. She was walking up and down talking angrily to Salamatu, who stood in the corner of the room crying.

"And you will stay there and stand in that corner all day! As a matter of fact, you will have all your meals there alone - and no toys!" She said this, not knowing how else she could adequately punish Salamatu.

"Oh, she's a truly disgusting girl!" *Mamu* said, turning to Professor Balarabe for conformation after she had noticed his presence.

"From where on earth does she get such wicked and abhorrent propensities?" she wondered out loud.

"Why? What has she done?" The professor asked, without much interest in the matter, because he had come in with the intention of asking her advice and opinion on some important issues regarding Salamatu's parents; but now it seemed he was going to be out of luck. Talking to Mamu when she was angry was not something you would want to do if you could avoid it.

"Zainab and she went into the garden over there and…. I can't really tell you what she did…"

She went on anyway, and narrated Salamatu's alleged "crimes" to her husband.

"But that proves nothing!" The professor said, after he'd heard the tortured tale of Zainab and Salamatu's crimes – Zainab and Salamatu had gone to the garden and ran over most of the vegetables while chasing after one another, carrots, onions, and cucumber—"it's not a question of evil propensities at all, it's simply a childish mischief".

"Anyway, what have you come here for? What's going on? You don't come over to this section of the house at such hours very often". Mamu queried her husband in a more subdued serene voice because he indeed never came to that section of the house without a purpose. She calmed down once her husband had, uncharacteristically, taken the time out to explain to her some of the idiosyncratic behavior typical of young adolescents. She became satisfied that Salamatu's behavior was then not so disgusting, that it did not rise to the level of aberrant "evil" or "wickedness".

From the tone of her voice Balarabe now felt he could ask her what he had originally meant to ask.

He went on and told her about his misgivings about Salihu, their elder son's recent decision to obtain a second wife. He explained to her that, religiously, he was entitled to up to four wives, that's what the Qur'an allowed him, if that's what he wanted, but with the global economy in torment and recession, and everything twirling in spirals and nose-dives everywhere, it did seem to him a bad idea for Salihu at this moment to choose to "add to his burdens". "Nobody knows what will happen in the country and nobody's job is safe", he said. "Unlike most developed countries, where there is a safety-net in the form of unemployment benefits if you lose your job, in this country, hard luck! There is nothing the Government will do to support you. You either turn to your parents for help, or you get swallowed up with debts and poverty; in short, you are on your own". He paused, and then went on to explain to her their finances and how meager his retirement money from the University was, and how they couldn't and shouldn't put too much burden on her confessedly small earnings. They already had four grand-children staying with them, two of whom were Salihu's children (one of these was Salamatu). Now, god forbid, but, if he lost his job, the three that were with them now would then have to come and stay with them until he got another job. And then there were three other married sons with a total of eight children, excluding Hassana, who seemed to be well-married and probably would not need their financial assistance, at least not in the foreseeable future.

Mariayamu said she understood and agreed with him completely and told him she was impressed with his analysis of the possibilities and consequences. But she advised him not to tell Salihu what their true feelings were with regard to the matter, lest he accuse them of controlling his life, or concluding that, "it's simply because I have two small kids living with you?" "Don't tell him any of this speculative stuff. Sometimes, apparently, you have to be suave and diplomatic, even play politics with your own children", she strongly advised him.

2nd Military Government

Professor Balarabe brought in some books today to share with the group, *The House Has Fallen* by Karl Maier, *The History of Nigeria*, by Toyin Falola, and *Nigeria: Struggle for Stability and Status* by Stephen Wright. But before he commenced his narrative about the events leading up to the brewing storm, he told them about Yakubu's August 1st broadcast to the nation, about the formation of a new National Military Government, and how he, Yakubu, brought the nation's attention to the upcoming conflagration gathering storm. However, on the very same day, the then-Governor of the Eastern group of provinces, Chukwuemeka, denounced Gowon, and called on all the traditional chiefs in the East, and all other civic leaders and groups, to advise him on the future status of Nigeria vis-à-vis the Igbos. As a matter of fact, for the first time, he made reference to the possibility of a break-up of the nation. Ojukwu also encouraged all Easterners to return to their homeland in the East, where he promised them protection from the savagery of the current Republic of Nigeria.

At the same time as has been alluded to earlier, there were reports from Radio Cotonou of Northerners being selectively and discriminately killed in the East, which necessitated the mass movement of Northerners in the East to the North, just as the Igbos were also moving to their homeland in the East.

"Why would he want to split Nigeria?" James asked naively.

"He did so for personal greed and for political power of course. He felt that, if he couldn't achieve his long-cherished ambition of ruling an independent Nigeria as a single entity, he would endeavor to rule a portion of its fragmentation, in the form of an independent "Biafra", Aminu replied

"I heard that, at the time, Chief O was in prison for treason, but that there was a concerted effort to have Gowon release him, so as to have the Yorubas with us", Golu commented in passing.

"Yes, and Gowon was a smart asshole because he did release Chief O immediately, earning the trust of the Western provinces", the Professor noted.

"Within days", he continued, "Gowon reversed Ironsi's decrees, including the abrogation of the ominous and notorious "Decree No. 34", and returned Nigeria to a federal structure, as it had previously been.

"By the way", Owoleye and Aminu inquired in tandem, "What exactly did decree No 34 say?"

"Oh, Oye, Decree No. 34", Professor Balarabe stated, matter-of-factly, "is the one, you remember that made Nigeria a Unitary State, with a unified public civil service. This meant all the regions were abolished, and, in their place, provinces were created, whereby any civil servant could be posted anywhere in the country, in all or any of the provinces, without regard to ethnicity, religion or language. Discussing the fall-out from this ominous "Decree No 34", Shagari has observed in his biography *Beckoned to Serve*", that, in the Northern view, the implication of the decree was seen in terms of distribution of power, allocation of public resources and amenities and of the prospect of Igbo and Southern domination — and, most importantly, the threat to mainstream Northern "ways of life", that is established norms were, in his view, absolutely "unmistakable". The next smart move Yakubu made was to create the Twelve States structure (established, May 5, 1967), with three of them carved out from the former Eastern State (Rivers State, South-Eastern State, and East-Central State). The non-Igbo South-Eastern and Rivers States, which had the oil reserves and access to the sea, were carved out in order to isolate the Igbo areas of East-Central State. Not surprisingly, Ojukwu evinced the strategy and immediately rejected it and officially seceded from the Federal Republic of Nigeria. He called his new country "The Republic of Biafra".

Gowon's strategy worked, because several of the ethnic minorities — such as the Ibibio, Efik, Ijaw, Annang and Oron to mention a few — refrained from offering their unconditional support to Ojukwu when the war broke out. As a matter of fact, many enlisted instead in the Nigerian army and fed the Federal Government with intelligence about the military activities of the Biafran operation(s), giving some details of their movements, including, in some instances, even their battle plans! There were a few amongst the minorities, however, who did side with Ojokwu and his clique, Aqwan, for instance, served as Secretary to the Ojukwu Government, Effoeng, served as Biafra's Chief of Defense Staff and a few others served in lesser roles", the Professor concluded.

At this point, they unanimously consented that it was once again time to break for the day, because several of them had significant errands to run. Jummai, Jamima and Fumilayo had planned to go to the recently-opened *Wasalamu* saloon, in the Lebanese quarter, to have their hair done, and wanted Pastor Owoleye to drop them off. Veronica had a previous engagement at her school and wanted her husband to accompany her. A girl at her school from a very good, respectable family was suspected of being four months pregnant and Veronica, as the Principal, had asked the parents to come in to discuss the girl's options. Golu also had to pick up his dry-cleaning at *Obewo Natural Cleaning* on Gusau and the corner of Lot Street, and to drop off his wife Francisca, at the General Hospital, on the way to the airport where she worked. She wanted, briefly, to see how one of her patients, who had excessive 'uterine fibroids' in her stomach removed the day before, was coping. Alhaji Habib and his wife AiShetu also had a naming ceremony of her cousin's to attend at the Gwarimpa quarters.

The Professor and his wife, after seeing all of their guests off, decided to stop by the *Dandaura* store next to Kaita Street to pick up few things for breakfast (eggs, bread, tea, promto, ovaltine, and milk).

"The last time we met", Professor Balarabe said, after clearing his throat, "Veronica had raised a question about the *Aburi Accord,* which we were not able to answer at the time, because time was against us. Today, however, if nobody objects, we'll open our discussion with that. By the way, are Owoleye, Aminu and Veronica here?

"Yes we're all here", was their chorus response.

"Alright, good, we'll then start", the Professor said.

"First of all, with regrets, the Alhaji cannot be with us today, he had to travel to the local village of Gaidam, to attend his cousin Abubakar's fourth wedding, therefore, we'll be missing his input and expertise".

"We'll be ok", Owoleye observed, and all present, including Dr. Kasimu agreed.

"The *Aburi Accord"*, the Professor began, "was a meeting that was convened in Ghana in 1967 by General Ankrah of Ghana, then the military head-of-state, who had been in the vanguard of encouraging the two sides to refrain from going to war, and to, instead, resolve their differences peaceably like brothers. Other prominent members of the vanguard— included Emperor Hailé Selassié of Ethiopia and Dr Martin Luther King Junior, of the civil right movement in the United States. These gentlemen stood shoulder to shoulder between the Federal Military Government and Ojukwu, in order to resolve the numerous thorny issues between them amicably. Aburi was chosen as a neutral ground, because, at that time, Ojukwu didn't trust his safety at the hand of the Nigerian State. The membership included the Head of State and some members of the Supreme Military Council (SMC) on the one hand, and Ojukwu and his minions on the other. *Aburi* was doomed to fail however, because, at the time, both the Federal Military Government and Ojukwu knew about the potential oil reserves that lay deep down awaiting some exploration. Thus, none of them were really bargaining in good faith. However, one of the main agreements that was said to have been agreed upon that day, but which Gowon denied later, was that of "decentralization and regional autonomy", which means, each region would, in some sense, be semi-independent, and control its own resources. This, of course, is something that the Northerners, in all good conscience, could not accept. However, from available records in the archives, it would seem wrong to make the assumption that it was Gowon who failed to implement *Aburi*; rather it was Ojukwu who, in a sense, misinterpreted the accord.

According to decree No. 8 which implemented the *AburiAccord*, provisions of section 86 of the Constitution stipulated that "no region shall exercise its power to impede or prejudice the Executive powers of the Federal government or endanger the continuance of the Federal Government of Nigeria". Furthermore, section 71 of the same constitution gave the Supreme Military Council (SMC) the power to take appropriate action against "any region which attempts to secede from the Federal Republic (of Nigeria)". It was this section of the constitution that Ojukwu objected to most strongly, and used as an excuse to abort the entire agreement. He then went on to accuse Gowon of acting in bad faith and declared a wholesale negation of all that had been discussed and agreed upon at *Aburi*. Gowon and his representatives, on the other hand, accused Ojukwu of massive distortions and half-truths. Somewhere I believe between these two views lays the real truth, which we may, unfortunately, never know.

"Well, but the Federal Government was surely right *not* to have allowed the Eastern Region to usurp a resource that belonged to *all* Nigerians. Up until now the country had subsisted mostly on Northern farm products, tin from Jos, cotton and ground nuts from other parts of the north and palm oil and cocoa from the Western region, as sources of foreign exchange earnings from which the entire nation had benefited. It would have been foolhardy of the Federal Government to allow the East to single-handedly inherit all the oil wealth, to simply throw up its hands and say, oh, it doesn't matter, you can have your oil", Aminu concluded precociously, and everybody applauded him recognizing it to be the correct analysis.

After a thorough discussion of the Accord and its implications, the group decided to break up early in order to go watch a football game between the Green Eagles and the Lions of Cameroon in the new Tafawa Balewa stadium.

"What are you doing?" Dr. Khan asked his wife, after he came back from the stadium, where he had gleefully witnessed the Green Eagles beat the Indomitable Lions of Cameroon Two-zip.

"Oh, I'm trying to reply Sarah's last letter. I've been busy…"

Dr. Khan wanted to say "doing what?", but he thought of the consequences of making such a provocative comment at a time when they both seem to be so happy and in such good harmony. It hadn't been like this all the time; so *Quieta non movere,*"don't rock the boat" when the sailing is going smoothly; in other words "let well enough alone", he quietly reminded himself.

"It's been more than five weeks now and I haven't written to thank her for the book that she sent us, *The Evolution of God* which you are now reading, not to mention the many kindnesses she does for Jimbala in New York on our behalf".

This is the complete transcription of the letter Veronica wrote her friend Sarah:

House No 93, Monte Sophia
March 15, 1968
My Dear Precious Sarah,

> *Your letter of the 20th gave me both joy and jitters. So you still love him, my dear poetic and romantic Sarah? Separation, of which you speak so ill, does not seem to have had the customary effect on you. Your complaints of loneliness pale in magnitude to nothing, compared with what one of*

my neighbors, Pamela is facing. Or indeed me, with all the children away from home, and Dr. K doing what he does best, that is silently reading and watching the sports on TV; I dare tell you that at times I feel almost as if I were a widower already! Oh! My dear Sarah, if it were not for the consolation I derive from my faith, I would be a very sad woman indeed!

Have you seen Jimbala lately? As usual, a fortnight ago, we received a letter from her, asking us to, again, replenish her account! Hey, whatever it is and she makes no mention of any crisis, we love her and are proud of her. Of late, she's begun showing some maturity even lady-like etiquette. She's decided on her major without discussing it with her father or me. You won't guess what your baby 'Ngwozi' (Jimbala's nickname) is up to! A cosmologist! She wants to be a cosmologist! She says she wants to contribute to our understanding of dark matter, dark energy, the Cosmic Microwave Background (the CMB), which is supposedly the radiation emitted four-hundred-thousand years after the Big Bang (estimated therefore to be something like 37.5 billion years old!), when our young universe started to cool down! Singularity, black holes, and the 'fate' of the universe!—an expansion or a crunch?! (What will it be?) Enough already about cosmology and Jimbala!

Why do you suppose that Nate shouldn't look with fondness on Rose? Now, don't you please interfere! I understand Rose is planning to attend Brown University next fall. I, for one, understand and sympathize with such feelings, —feelings that young people might naturally have for one another—and, if I cannot approve of them—never having experienced them—neither do I condemn them. I have always thought that Christian love, love for one's neighbor, love for one's enemy, love for one's community is worthier, smarter and finer than any feelings inspired by the beautiful eyes and the seductive ways of a young man on an impressionable and loving girl, like Rose. But that's our nature and our fate.

A thousand thanks for the book; The Evolution of God that you sent, which, as you well conceived, is hard to come by here. Sarah, I cannot promise you, but I will do my best to read it, even though, as you know, I have always believed that the reading of the Gospels and the Epistles is an activity far more enriching and beneficial to the mind than the perusal of some of these books, which, if not read with care or attended to carefully will distort and confuse and even poison your Christian faith.

Aluor has grabbed the book and is reading it now.

A few days ago I received a propitious letter from my brother Marc (the one on the St Martin Island) informing me that he and his wife Sharon will be paying us a visit at Monte Sophia! What a joy their visit will bring to us! I've reminded them to make sure they bring the new baby (Samuel) along with them!

My school (Queen Amina Gambo Sawaba College) did very well in this year's Joint Admissions Matriculation (JAM) and the University Matriculation Examination (UME) exams. All of my senior class everyone has been accepted to a university! Can you believe my joy and pride!

I don't want to bore you with life at Monte Sophia, but, recently, we organized a kind of neighborhood club, where we meet on weekends, to discuss some profound aspects of local or national history. At the moment we're discussing the events of January 15, 1966, which led to the Nigeria's civil war. You remember, don't' you?!

After we have exhausted this topic, we may even choose — I'll try to convince Aluor to support me in recommending it— as a topic of discussion, the history of the Islands! Won't that be fun!

Well, farewell, dear good friend. May you remain healthy!

Yours,
Veronica.
p.s.

Dr. K. and the Professor send you their best regards and love. Also a well endowed eligible bachelor, by name of Dr. Kasimu has recently settled in our quarter of Monte Sophia. He came from Canada where he'd lived and worked for over two decades. Sadly to say however, the gentleman lost his wife to cancer five years ago, and has since remained single.

With the time fast approaching for their regular discussion of the issues of January 15, James systematically prepared himself. He shaved, showered and then put on his kaftan and a hat, before appearing in the parlor, where his wife and their daughter-in-law, Adama Sanusi, were dutifully waiting for him. James was a stickler for social conventions and hated to be late on any occasion —"do unto others as you would want them to do unto you "was an axiom he held to, steadfastly.

"Are you coming with us?" He asked his daughter-in law.

"Yes Sir, Madam invited me to join you today", she answered, sweetly and politely.

"What are we discussing today anyway", Jamima asked her husband.

"I think the Alhaji is supposed to lead us in the discussion of the operation and execution of the civil war", James replied.

"Well it seems we should get ourselves prepared for a late, or very late, dinner tonight, because, as you know, the Alhaji seems to know *so* much and doesn't seem to know when to stop! It would of course be prudent for one of you guys to give him some kind of a signal when to stop!"

Jamima unambiguously expressed her opinion of the Alhaji with those few tart words to her husband.

"I'll defer that responsibility to the Professor, since we are all his guests", was James' response.

When James, Jamima and Adama arrived at the Professor's house for the day's discussion, James mentioned his discussions with his wife about the Altai's concept of time to the professor.

"Oh wow! This is amusing", Balarabe retorted, "*Mamu* had just made a similar observation. She asked me to intervene when I see her getting restless and fidgety because she has to run to the store next door very quickly later in the day in order to buy some foodstuffs, meat, yams and groundnut cooking oil for our dinner. I've promised her I'll keep my eyes wide open and focus more on her movements and signals". Both gentlemen laughed their hearts out and made a sincere pact to be more vigilant.

Chapter Eight
Declaration of Hostilities

When setting out on a long journey, or singularly changing their mode of life, men capable of reflection and introspection are apt to be in a serious frame of mind; and this was the case that day with Sergeant Adamu Abubakar. At such moments, one generally reviews the past and makes plan for the future. Sergeant Adam's face looked extremely pensive, but, at the same time, tender. With his hands clasped behind his back, he paced rapidly around the room, looking straight ahead of himself and thoughtfully shaking his head. Whether he had any qualms about going to war, or felt sad at the prospect of leaving his wife— his battalion has been called to report to the front— or perhaps both, we do not and perhaps will never know. However, we do know that he, evidently, did not wish to be seen in this mood, because, when he heard footsteps approaching from the outside, he made haste to un-clasp his hands and stand close to the dining-room table, stooping a little as if he were bending down and trying to tie up his boots.

When Hajiya Uwani, his wife walked in, she smiled and asked him, "Where on earth are you going at this late hour?"

"Ah, *I wanna go see Oga* (Boss)Lieutenant Gbor about the notice we received today commanding us to report to the war front", he replied quiet scared, clearly petrified. He walked out in the moonless night with his torch showing the way, and walked the alley leading to Lieutenant Gbor's quarters in utmost silence.

"The whole strategy from the beginning, as enunciated by Gowon in Gowon and Effiong, *The Nigerian Civil War And Its Aftermath: Views From Within*", Alhaji Wada began, when all were seated, "was to confine them the rebels to their estate, then progressively diminish their hold on the territory". Thus, federal troops were explicitly and specifically instructed to preserve civilian populations, as well as to protect public utilities.

They were ordered to try to act, as much as was possible, with discipline and decorum in the prosecution of the war, given the peculiar in-bred circumstances of the fighting your countrymen", Alhaji went on – "who, in some instances, may well be former colleagues, who have very likely shared drinks with you in the officers' mess hall, or have been together with you, perhaps, in the past on some important assignments. It's even possible that they've snuck into the same brothel as you, while, together, on some overseas courses. Hey, you never know!" Alhaji proposed this, smirking, but nobody laughed, everybody looked sheepishly the other way. His last joke about 'snuck into a brothel' missed its mark. Any reference to anything sexual, in a public place, even if only tangential, even in company amongst adult friends, was still taboo in our culture and was looked upon with embarrassment. Sexual matters were private matters and limited only to the participants and to the bedroom.

"All verbiage exchanges between the rebels and the federal government have now become part of the ashes of history, and what most of us had dreaded for so long, finally took place, center-stage in our national consciousness — the war began in earnest on July 6th, 1967".

Alhaji paused for comments.

"It was a war of necessity, as both sides would claim, I'm sure", Alhaji Abba observed. "However, in my opinion only the federal government had the right to make such a claim, because it had the responsibility of keeping the nation one".

The Civil War

"The civil war, and the first rifle assault therein", Alhaji Wada continued, "as we now know, started, at last, on or between May 29th and 30th, 1967, when the then- military-strongman of the East, Ojokwu declared Independence and proclaimed the erstwhile Eastern group of provinces "the Republic of Biafra". On those two days, there was a heightened defiance of federal authority by Ojukwu, especially with regard to the Twelve- State structure of the Republic, as previously announced by Gowon. With the declaration of the Republic of Biafra came incursions by the rebel forces into the border towns of the Federal Republic. At this juncture, many Nigerians didn't believe that Ojukwu would really want to go to war with the federal republic. If he did some conjectured, the Federal Government could easily wipe them out through a "mopping action" in as little as "four weeks". How wrong they were in making such presumptuous statements under-estimating the enemy. Convinced in their belief in a simple and brief one-month "mopping action", instead of an extended all-out war, the initial preparation by the planners at Supreme Headquarters and Military Headquarters was to divide the military into four areas of command. "1 Area" was designated the fighting force, "2 Area" was stationed in Ibadan for internal security, "3 Area" was assigned the defense of Lagos, and "4 Area" was stationed in Benin for the sole purpose of protecting the mid-west and any northward border-infiltration. After delineating the areas of command, because the Military Headquarters envisaged a short decisive war, they made a four-point strategic plan involving 21 and 22 Battalions. The main points were *first*, the capture of Nsukka and a southward mopping of the surrounds; *second*, the capture of Ogoja; *third*, the capture of Abakaliki, and *fourth*, the capture of Enugu, which, it was presumed, would force the rebels to surrender, thus ending the war. A simple axiom of war, however, is never under-estimate your enemy. The planners forgot, or over-looked, this simple rule of the thumb familiar to all military planners and scholars the world over.

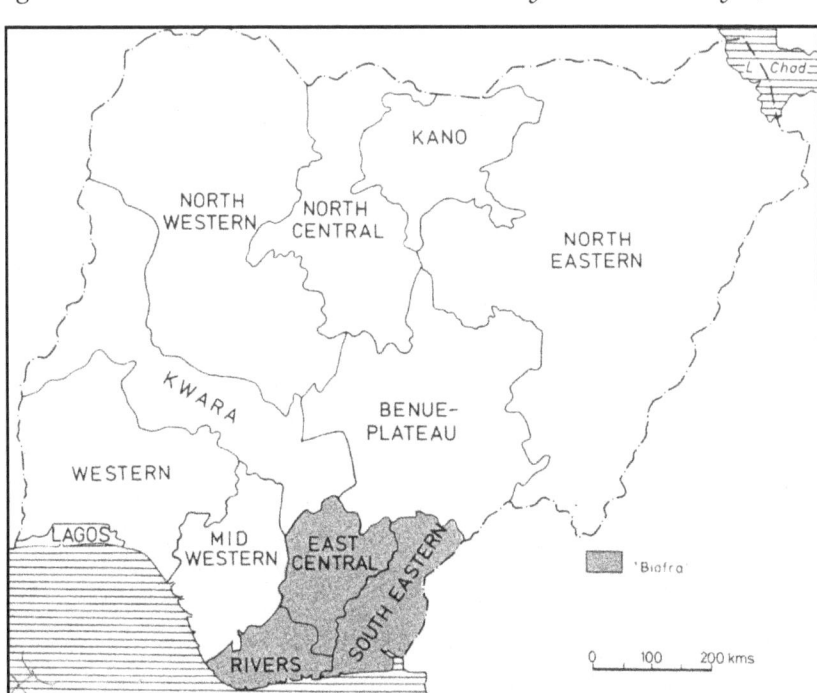

Fig.2: The Twelve-state structure announced by Gowon on May27, 1967

The rebel forces' increased incursions at many points along the common borders had finally reached a point of intolerability for the Federal Government. Out of patience, and wrongly assuming a short war, a police action — *Operation Unicord*— was instituted, in an attempt to help drive away the rebels. When these incursions doubled instead of petering out "1 Area" was given its operational directives on or about July 2nd 1967. Under the directives issued, 1 Brigade, made up of three battalions, would be in charge of the Ogugu-Ogurugu-Nsukka and the south front, and 2 Brigade, with the same number of battalions would be in charge of the Gakem-Obudu-Ogoja front. When *Operation Unicord* seemed to falter, a limited military action was proclaimed by Gowon on July 6, 1967. In the wee hours of that morning the civil war started in earnest with the first shots fired by the Federal troops at Gakem town, some thirty miles/ forty-nine kilometers from Ogoja by the First Division".

The Alhaji paused.

The First Division, under General Shuwa was the first to experience the brunt of the war. Despite menacing harassment by a B-26 piloted by a Pole/Czech nicknamed *"Kamikaze",* otherwiseknown as Brown? Wushishi and his men moved into Nsukka following an intensive fierce battle on both sides— Bukar, and his platoon leader Magoro, and the battalion RSM who has been designated to lead the entry having been seriously wounded earlier. The Federal troops made advances into Biafra through three axes; the Ogoja-Nsukka-Nkalagu sectors. Obudu, Garkem and Ogoja fell, less than two weeks after commencement of hostilities, after fierce fighting and with heavy casualties on both sides. The battle for Nsukka was one of the bloodiest of the whole contest, and was where both Tom Bigger, Ojukwu's half-brother, and the January 15 coup leader Major Kaduna were killed. The magnanimity of the Federal troops could not be anything other than praised. They gave Major Kaduna a burial befitting of his rank while a member of the Nigerian army, along with all appropriate military salutes and pageants.

From Nsukka, the southward movement of the First Division troop continued, with skirmishes here and there. The capture of Enugu was assigned to Danjuma, commanding the 1 Brigade and six battalions. The meticulous plan envisaged an exit from Nsukka to Nine-Mile Corner, led by 21 and 22 Battalions, with 5 Battalion between them. In addition to these fighting battalions, two thousand men were assigned as reinforcement for fatigue and casualties. The advance from Nsukka proved deadly for the federal troops, but after a prolonged intensive hand-to-hand battle they took Nine-Mile Corner and Eke. The battle was made worse for the gallant and brave federal troops, because this was the very first time they had come face-to-face with the killer, "Red Devils"—a pre-Second World War armored personnel carrier— which proved deadly for the federal troops, but also as it turned out to the Biafrans, because there was no way of escaping when it was hit. Everything inside would be incinerated. Minor villages, like Ikolo, Ogbede, and Ukehe were swallowed by the invincible federal troops on their way into Enugu, the most coveted price of all.

Also falling to the troops were Nine-Mile Corner and Millikin Hill. Thus, in less than three months from the commencement of intense and sustained hostilities, the well-defended rebel capital and its environs were liberated by the 20th 21st and 22nd Battalions, after extensive pounding, including also assistance from the 5th Battalion, and supported by Recce, artillery and corps of engineers - and this, despite the well-publicized propaganda slogan that "No power in Black Africa can withstand the rebel onslaught" — a slogan that now seemed to give credence to the truism of the saying "All mouth and no trousers".

Meantime Buhari and his men took the cement town of Nkalagu through the Ogoja sector, capturing a huge cache of ammunitions and batteries. Amongst those captured as prisoners-of-war as reported in the army gazette for that week were Ikem, Ezeliena, Amufu and Obollo."

Alhaji Wada stopped to take a sip of his *fanta* which had already begun to get warm because *Mamu* had brought it to him more than an hour before but so caught up in his discourse he never even touched it.

"Uzuakoli", Alhaji Wada continued, "was captured by Babangida, however because of an injury he sustained in battle, Vatsa took over the command and continued the advance onto Umuahia, later liberating it after fierce fighting. The First Division , with the active collaboration and strategic planning of the other Divisions, was at least in part responsible for the capture of such towns as Nsukka, Nkalagu, Enugu, Abakaliki, Okigwe and Umuahia (the struggle for that was one of the bloodiest!), an area including the non-Igbo town of Ogoja".

After the capture of Enugu, instead of pursuing the rebels, who were already in disarray, and which might have ended the war earlier, the 1st Division decided to reorganize and refit. In the new reorganization the brigades were re-designated sectors, thus 2 Sector, which formerly was the 2 Brigade, was assigned the task of capturing Abakaliki. The movement of their Divisional Headquarters from Makurdi to Enugu took a good six months, so by then, the rebel forces had had enough time to recoup, organize and stabilize their front.

"As you would guess", Alhaji Wada continued, after a short break, "events changed very quickly, though at first slowly, with the rebel forces staging a lightening blitzkrieg attack in the former Mid-western region, with the tacit support of Mid-West military officers of Igbo origin, who were supposed to be on the Federal side. The saying "blood is thicker than water" remains apt in this instance. The rebel adventure under Banjo into the Mid-West, I surmise, forced Yakubu to declare full military operations. He felt betrayed by the actions of the Federal troops in the region who had lent their loyalty to the other side. The incursion in the State was unexpected, because the State had declared its intention to remain neutral, and, as such had been somehow overlooked by the Supreme Headquarters in both their defensive *and* offensive plans. This was a very big and surprising miscalculation by the General Staff at Headquarters. In a war, as every veteran or a keen military strategist will tell you, you have to make plans for every contingency, both offensive *and* defensive. There is nothing like a "small war", a war is a war, and maximum preparation for both offensive *and* defensive plans are required at all times. The enemy, as the American General, General Colin Powell once memorably proclaimed, "must be hit with maximum force available, to ensure success and quick surrender". Hence, when it was learnt that the Mid-West had been attacked and taken, there was real pandemonium in Lagos, because the rebels were able to reach Ore in the Western region with almost no resistance or opposition, and were on their way to Lagos "unopposed" or so they imagined. In this instance, one would have expected heads to roll at the Supreme Military Headquarters, for negligence and abdication of duty, but nothing happened!

Araba Let's Separate

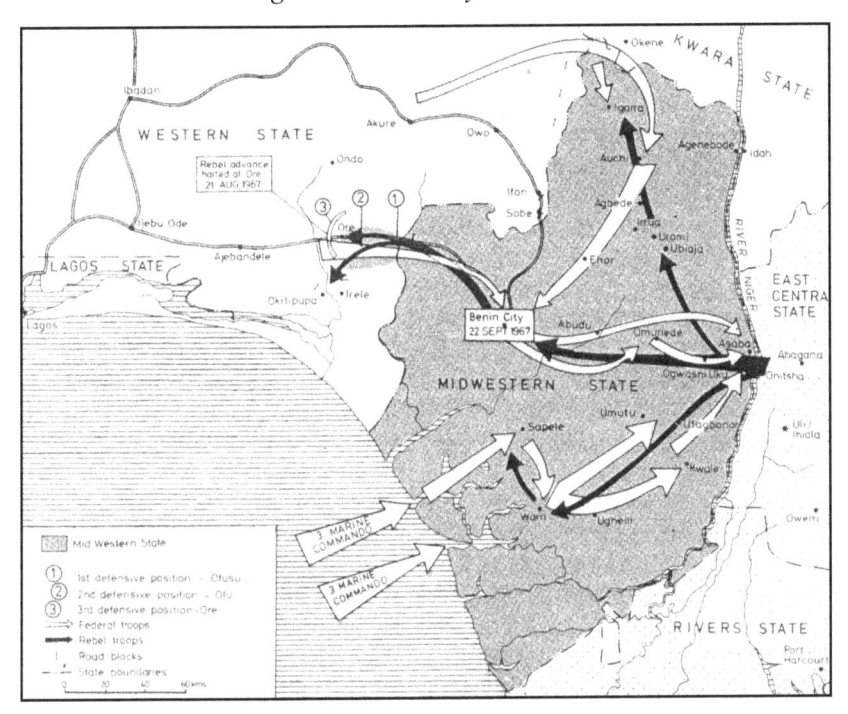

Fig. 3: Liberation of Mid-west

Adapted from Obasanjo, 1980

The criticisms of those at Headquarters became more vitriolic with the capture of the Mid-western state by the rebels. There were reports that meetings at the Military HQ went on and on, with no particular purpose, *adinfinitum, and ad nauseam*. Despite such criticisms they just pushed on unflinchingly, as if nothing had happened. However, the incursion led to the creation of a Second Division under the command of Muhammed (the July 29, 1966 coup leader, and later General, and Head of State). Muhammed, it was said, hurriedly formed the bulk of his fighting-force mainly from the then-Second Brigade in Lagos and Ibadan, and the rest comprised mostly of "stragglers, clerks, batmen, physical trainers, fishermen, parolees and pensioners. From its creation, many military theorists believed the Division lacked proper training, vehicles, and even sufficient military ammunition. However, what it lacked in military experience, training and hardware, was more than adequately made up for by youthful enthusiasm and exuberance and dynamism, under a most capable leader, Muhammed. The Division was made up of the 6 Brigade, under the command of Akinrinade, 8 Brigade, under Francis, and the 7 Brigade under the command of Ally. Ibadan was designated the rear of the Division under the command of Olu, later General and twice Head of state and commander in chief. The first thing Olu did as Rear Commander was to restore confidence between the 'Northern' soldiers and the 'Western' state soldiers, as well as the civilians in the West. Indiscipline was so rampant that a Northern soldier was more than likely inclined to report an incident to his northern brother-officer than to his immediate superior from another ethnic group. The same went with the Western soldiers.

There was for example one incident, where a northern soldier, an Angas, drove in a military vehicle all the way from Ibadan to Lagos to inform his 'brother' Gowon instead of his immediate superiors or commander. When Olu found out what had transpired, he reprimanded the soldier severely, having informed Gowon what had happened. This seemed to have nipped such behavior in the bud. News of the new resolve spread among the troops.

Olu also stopped the practice of Western soldiers discussing and talking only in Yoruba, as well as Northerners talking only in Hausa. He made English the official language amongst the soldiers, since English was the official language of the country. In most instances it seemed or sounded as if 'pidgin' English was indeed the official language, as most of the soldiers and the officers— even if their English wasn't necessarily good— communicated with each other under the new guidelines.

The route from Ore leading to Ibadan was fortified by none other than Olu, later a staunch third-termer proponent to the Presidency. He was the commander of the Ibadan Battalion at the time. Road-blocks were set up using trees, logs, broken vehicles and boulders to fortify other places, other than Ore, like Ifon, Irua, Sobe, Igbataro Irele and Okitipupa, to hinder, or at least slow down, the intended 'unopposed' march into Lagos by the rebels. The ambition of advancing to Lagos through Ibadan having been stalled, Banjo tried, through subterfuge, to entice Olu, by sending him an emissary whose name has yet to be revealed. The yet to be revealed emissary came in the middle of the night to broker a deal at any price, but he was rebuffed vehemently and instantly. "Surrender if you so wish, and I'll guarantee your safety, otherwise just face your fate as a soldier", was the terse response he received through his emissary.

With his dream of being a future head of state in dire jeopardy and Muhammed and his men on his heels pursuing him relentlessly, he had to abandon his pertinacious desire of holding onto the Mid-West. With the motley crew of the Second Division Troops, and the fortifications of the route to Ibadan, and Lagos blocked, Banjo's days were literally numbered and his ambitions along with it.

At the beginning of operation *hawainiya* (chameleon), it was first envisaged to have the 7 Brigade clear Ore in the Western state and advance to Benin, then, the 6 and 8 Brigades would move northward through the Western state to south of Okene and advance southward on to Benin. Under the 6 Brigade was the 63 Battalion, under the command of Jerodam, 61 Battalion was assigned the task of attacking Ososo, and the 11 battalion was to follow behind, mopping up of any remnant areas of resistance. Under this plan, 8 Brigade was to train for the crossing of the River Niger at the town of Ila.

With the convergence of these several prongs of movement by the federal troops, Asaba was captured, through the combined gallantry of the 7 and 6 Brigades, after an intense hand-to-hand battle. Also liberated after an intense and bloody battle was Ore - and with it, Benin. Thus, Benin was liberated by the Federal troops barely two, or two-and-a-half hours after the celebrated announcement of; "an Independent and Sovereign Republic of Benin" was made on Biafran radio. The so-called "Republic" lasted less than three hours! This was probably the shortest-lived Republic ever in history! After this victory, the citizens of Benin came out to the clamor and rapturous joy of being liberated; dancing and singing in the streets holding their right hand middle finger. The troops were initially surprised to see everybody raising one finger at them. At the time they didn't understand its meaning —in some cultures the raising of the middle finger implies an insult or a provocation meaning "fuck you"! —, until they asked, and were told that it stood for "one indivisible Nigeria". From this time on, the Division adopted the one-finger as its symbol, with a reproduction of the digit against a blue background.

Meantime, in Lagos, at headquarters, there was exhilaration and celebration by the General staff for the liberation of Benin. Their jobs had been saved by the dedicated forces under Muhammed. They were saved the ignominy of the pink slips.

Alhaji Wada suddenly paused because somebody had come asking for Mariyamu.

"Immediately after the recapitulation of the "Republic of Benin", Banjo, and his co-conspirators for the January 15, Ejefuana, Aleee and Sam, were hung by Ojukwu for their alleged coup plan to oust him and make Banjo the leader", the Alhaji said. "And do you know what? The executioner sternly expressed his opinion about Banjo after the fact in the following words": "From my conviction and impression, he was a man of the most despicable character, and frankly a coward. He was a calculating expedient schemer who was wedded to nothing other than plans for his own advancement and success. He made numerous egregious insinuations about the inability of others, and his sole ability to command, hardly giving his staffers any credit. He was not only an execrable coward, but the sum total and substance of all the different types of cowardice there are in the world that walk on two legs. He had the heart of a chicken. There were even innuendoes about his putative priapism, not to mention other sexual aberrations. When talking to me prior to his execution, he would always tremble for fear that I should kill him, though I never raised a finger or laid a hand on him. He fell at my feet and wept on numerous occasions, he literally kissed my boots, imploring me to grant a command or plead with the 'General' so he could be relieved of his sufferings". The executioner narrated these words to the presiding trial 'General', before Banjo and his co-conspirators were summarily court-martialed and executed without any fanfare less like humans, more like dogs.

"He's a sickly, chicken-hearted bastard full of ambitions, a feeble-minded epileptic whom any child could thrash", declared Lieutenant Nwachi Nicholas who was one of those who had witnessed the execution up close from the front row.

"The invasion of the Mid-West and the Western States, if anything", Alhaji Wada continued, "gave an indisputable credence to the suspicion of "Igbo domination" of the country among the Yorubas, and also turned the war national. Prior to the invasion, a good number of Western state citizens weren't sure which side to support, because there had been some background noises that said, if the East goes, the West must as well. However, the invasion changed everything and cast new perspectives on the war for the Western state citizens. From this time onward, most of our brethren in the West came to perceive the rebel leader for what he was, an arrogant, nakedly-ambitious and power-hungry human animal. These despicable personal characteristics made them want to tear every sinew in his body and throw him to the vultures scavenging and scourging around for feed" he said, stopping, posing for effect.

"The Division performed superbly, beyond anybody's wildest expectations", he paused and then continued "given its haphazard formation. Their success must be ascribed to the dogged determination and dynamism of its youthful commander. However, in spite of these successes, it was envisaged that tactics and strategies must be changed and improvised, if they were to do as well in predominantly Igbo areas, especially the planned crossing of the River Niger. Most armchair military analysts and pseudo-historians argued at the time that an opposed river-crossing of the Niger River from Asaba to Onitsha, code named Operation *giwa (elephant)* as was being considered by the Division, would be a military nightmare, if not an impossible feat to carry out successfully, especially without adequate equipment and a standard rigorous training for the crossing. In addition, the period allocated to the 8 Brigade for the training was seen as far too short and too haphazard to produce any meaningful possibility of real success.

Amongst other shortcomings, the 2 Division Commander faced the daunting task of commandeering a sufficient number of ferries or forcibly seizing them from fishermen under the order of a National Security Needs emergency, if it came to that. He instituted the training of the brigade earmarked for the operation with some simulations of the anticipated conditions, but, to his surprise, the Army Headquarters and Supreme Headquarters objected and advised against the plan. Instead, Headquarters proposed avoiding Asaba and taking instead an unopposed crossing at Idah, where the Division passed through 1 Division's secure position and then on to capture Onitsha.

"Heck", the commander was overheard quietly complaining "what do *they* (HQ) know about the situation facing us? They should be happy they have an office job; they should stop entreating us, the guys in the field, to do their will. Let them stick to their desk-jobs, do their desk-jobs well, and leave the decisions of the war to us, to do what we assess as the actions concomitant to the best chances of our success".

With comments such as these the dynamic commander of the 2 Division, who considered himself an unimpeachable student of military history, decided to break ranks, do it his own way with disastrous results, and consequences, of massive proportions, to his troops!

On the first attempt of Operation *giwa,* on Oct. 12th, under the stern and forceful leadership of the commander himself, they made a relatively successful landing, as far as battle river-crossing was concerned, and were able to set up a haphazard beach-head. However, the envisaged reinforcement of men and matériel never arrived, because a second ferry bringing the men had malfunctioned, broken into pieces, and had been thrown to the winds as a scape. This situation however might have been salvaged, if they had secured their hold on the bridge-head established, instead of rushing into Onitsha town, full throttle, for booties of war. In so doing, they exposed themselves to ambush and were over-run by the well-prepared rebel army.

Because life-preservation knows no bounds, many of those who were to have come with the second ferry that malfunctioned and broke into pieces jumped into the river, whether they could swim or not. A few who *could* swim survived through swimming their way through, however the majority who couldn't, perished. Many others were just massacred because of the disorder that ensued, some ran north toward Idah and survived, but some, unfortunately, ran southward toward the bosom of the enemy forces, and were just swallowed; skin and bones all. The only survivors were Officer Ejiga and a few others who escaped in a dug-out canoe.

Thus, the first attempt at the alternative crossing was a total fiasco. The second attempt, by Bassey, was a failure at its inception, and the third attempt, under Akinrinade, almost resulted into a mutiny, leading to chaos and gross disobedience by the troops and an open disagreement between Akinrinade and the Division Commander. Akinrinade became the fall-out guy, as the Officer assigned the task of crossing and was eventually moved out of the Division.

The Onitsha debacle was finally achieved, after three unsuccessful, brutal, and costly, attempts, by the Second Division of opposed-crossing at Ila from Asaba to Onitsha. This venture proved to be extremely difficult and costly, in human terms and in terms of materials, because of the inadequacy of the relevant equipment and the lack of any specialized training received by the troops for this kind of amphibious venture as against an unopposed river-crossing at Idah through the protective rear of the First Division. After the commander abandoned the idea of alternative river-crossing, he refurbished the Division in manpower and materials and then launched the operation *giwa* attack via the unopposed crossing at Idah, as first advised. After a well-executed platoon reconnaissance of the enemy by Shangev, WO 11, and armed with three battalions in the center, and the Recce and a mechanized battalion on the left flank, and an armored battalion and infantry on the right, the Federal troops moved with a ferocity and determination as never seen before.

The successful Niger crossing at Idah was led by 6 Brigade, under the able command of a youthful officer called Yar'Adua, who, together with Jallo, was originally from the 3 Marine commandos under the command of the Black Scorpion, but was re-deployed to the second Division for re-enforcement. Thus, marching gallantly through the rear and under the protection of the First Division, Operation *giwa* was accomplished, Onitsha was successfully captured.

"Move forward! Fire! Don't break the formation! Fire! Left! Center! Right and Left flanks move in Fire!" With these commands from a determined officer, after a fierce hand-to-hand bloody combat, the rebel forces were routed out and dispersed in disarray. Onitsha was secured six months after the initial attempt. Thus in less than a year of the rebel's foray into the Mid-Western State, they had been completely driven out, after the fall of Onitsha and a successful crossing of the bridge over the River Niger. The capture of Onitsha consolidated the Federal government's firm hold on the Mid-west", Alhaji Wada concluded.

But did it?!

"In view of the invasion of the Mid-West", Professor Balarabe begun, "Ochefu, of the Third Marine commandos, who, at the time, was at Escravos preparing to liberate Calabar, was ordered to clean up the Southern riverine rear and to link up with the second Division in Benin. After this was accomplished, the General Officer Commanding the Third Marine Division, The Black Scorpion, ordered his troops back to the task of capturing Calabar.

"Meanwhile", Professor Balarabe resumed, after all have been seated after their brief break; "the Black Scorpion (Adekunle) was busy planning and strategizing his next move. Amongst his targets, the first to fall would be Bonny, including the rescue of Mrs. Adekunle at Peterside Island from where she hailed. *Operation Tiger Claw,* as it was called, was designed to capture Calabar. The liberation of Calabar was to be led by Soroh, Ochefu and Hamman. Aliyu Abubakar was assigned for reserves and garrison duties. After the capture of Calabar, what remained for the Third Marine commandos was the further liberation of Uyo, Annang and Aba. Aliyu, with support from other units, had captured Obubra, after which an instruction was given to him by the General Officer Commanding (GOC) to push on into Port Harcourt. Port Harcourt eventually fell after a prolonged bloody and fierce battle; and just like the captures of Bonny, Enugu and Calabar, it left the world, especially the western supporters of the rebellion, in no uncertain terms, aware of the strength and the prowess of the Federal troops. The mercenaries had been bloodied bad, and ran away with their tails between their legs!"

The Professor declared this with a wide smile on his face.

"I have my own personal share of grief concerning the battle in the

Mid-west", Jamima volunteered. "I don't know whether it was for Benin or Onitsha, but I lost my elder brother, Ismailu Bhalami, who didn't even have the time to see us on his return from England where he had been attending the Royal Military Academy Officers course at Sandhurst. He was still in a hotel in Lagos, awaiting a formal posting, when the Scorpion dragged him off to his Division, and, within days, my brother was exposed to an ambush and killed!"

Jamima recalled this with venom and hatred in her voice and clearly unresolved enmity against her brother's murderer, the Scorpion.

"I have a letter here to share with you written to my mother by a friend in England at the time", she concluded, pulling out the crumpled letter from her handbag.

This is the letter Jamima shared with the discussion group:

June 28, 1967
My dear Deborah,

It would seem proper, from the view point of selfishness, to surmise that sorrow is our common lot, when the one we dearly love is surreptitiously snatched away from us in such an untimely manner, especially when he who is snatched has yet to have bloomed to his god-given potential, such as is the case with your beloved Ismaila. Your loss, my dear Debo,(a nick-name) is our loss as a society, but, most especially, a loss for the village, it is a loss which I can only explain as a special sign of the grace of God, who, in his love, is testing you and your most estimable, lovely daughter, sweet little Mima (also known as Jamima). Oh my Debo, religion and only religion, not necessarily comforts us, but, can save us from imminent despair, melancholy and despondency. Only religion, my dear, and faith, can sustain and explain to us why, and for what purpose, good and noble beings like our dear son, Ismail are called away to Our Creator, while wicked, good-for-nothing, mean-spirited and malign people are left to live and enjoy the benefits of His grace and love.

I know what you are going through, especially in regards to the role of fate in our lives, I asked similar questions when I lost my beloved sister-in-law, Lisa, to an untimely death in car accidentseveral, years ago. It has been what?, five years ago now, but, since that incident, even I, with my paltry intelligence, am beginning to understand why she had to die and in what way that death was but an infinite expression of the love and goodness of The Creator, whose every act, though hidden and beyond our human comprehension to fathom, is but surely a manifestation of His boundless love for us .Sometimes I'm still tempted to wonder why He should expose us to such pain such suffering if he really loves us. But, then again, these are things left to individual minds to ponder not matters of the heart which could or might be shared in the public square. Here am I reminded of the saying that we're all saved by His grace. What a love my dear!

At the time of my Lisa's loss I could not have foreseen the work of the glory of The Creator as I recognize it today, because I now know that she is "saved", she's in a place of comfort and grace which I dare not even hope for myself.

I write you all of this, my dear Debo, only to convince you of the Gospel of Truth, which has become the guiding principle of my life. I have the strongest belief that even a single hair on our heads doesn't fall without His will, if indeed there is anything like will! In this sense, anything that befalls us has been pre-determined by Him, the Omnipotent, who knows all.

Kindly, dear, express my sincere and heart-felt condolences to your dear husband, Mr. Balami, and to our dear Ismail's fiancée, Bata Yusef, who must indeed be under a tremendous spell of agony and pain and utter confusion. May our God, in His abundant mercy, comfort and be with her. I pray her love for Him will redeem her soul and give her the necessary will to live. It's not an easy matter to lose the one you dearly love, especially when that love is snatched from your prematurely, before you have officially tied the knot, sealing the bond of eternal commitment to one another through the God-ordained sacred institution of marriage.

You had asked me if I would be coming home this year for Christmas, but I can't; regretfully because, Annie's health is noticeably deteriorating, very fast, and we cannot now afford to travel anywhere without her.

Our family life goes on in its accustomed manner, except for my brother Andrew, who has put the death of his sweet Lisa behind him and is now studying in the United States for his doctoral degree in Mathematics. He has once more become himself, himself as I always knew him when growing up - kind, tender, and with a heart of gold, incapable of hurting a fly. I have not seen these qualities in any one—not even my husband Dr. Darwin!

I'm always amazed at the way rumors travel, or even get started!—from here in London to home in a matter of hours! This is especially true with regards to the rumor about my brother being engaged to little Veronica Lawrence. I have my doubts about whether Andrew will ever marry again—and time will tell—but certainly not her! I'll tell you why, firstly, because, even though he hardly mentions Lisa by name, his grief over her, has never left him; secondly, frankly, I don't think Veronica is the type of girl that would attract Andrew. I hope he doesn't choose her for a wife. I do not wish it for personal, selfish, reasons, which I can't fully explain to you in this letter.

Ah, I've written much too much already and will stop lest I also put you to sleep while reading this long, winding narrative. Good-bye, my dear friend. How I wish that someday we'll be together to reminisce about all that has befallen us in this ugly and selfish war. Suffice to say, may God, the Most Benevolent, comfort you, and grant you and your husband and little Jamima His most propitious mercy over the loss of your dear sweet boy, Ismaila. My husband sends you and your husband his sincere and heart-felt condolences. Remain in good health, my dear.

*Yours,
Emma.*

p/s: Send me kuka, banda (dried fish) and daddawa (cooking condiment) and anything else you deem I need when Melissa is coming back for her final year of studies at Oxford next month.

The group was silent for a long time after Jamima finished reading the letter to them.

"This is what true friendship is, what friends are there for" Pastor Owoleye remarked, and then continued,"to comfort you and give you words of encouragement in your time of sorrow and grief. At such moment we are at our lowest in terms of faith and need reminders to go on living". Everybody agreed and thought it was a very good, uplifting letter.

"The ambitious plan embarked next by the proud Scorpion", the Professor continued, "was called *OAU*, and it envisaged the simultaneous capture of Owerri, Aba and Umuahia. In implementing *Operation OAU*, Alabi and Utuk were charged with the capture of Owerri, Isemede and Shande were charged with the capture and liberation of Aba, and Majors Tuoyo and Aliyu were entrusted with the capture of Umuahia. Aba and Owerri fell to the Federal troops after, as usual, an intense defense by the enemy, especially from the infamous mercenary Rolf Steiner—he's been described as someone who likes beer, Benson&Hedges cigarettes, violence and very little else— who dominated foreign headlines during the war in the Congo now Democratic Republic of Congo, and his gang of "S commandos".

Professor Balarabe paused to answer knocking on the main gate.

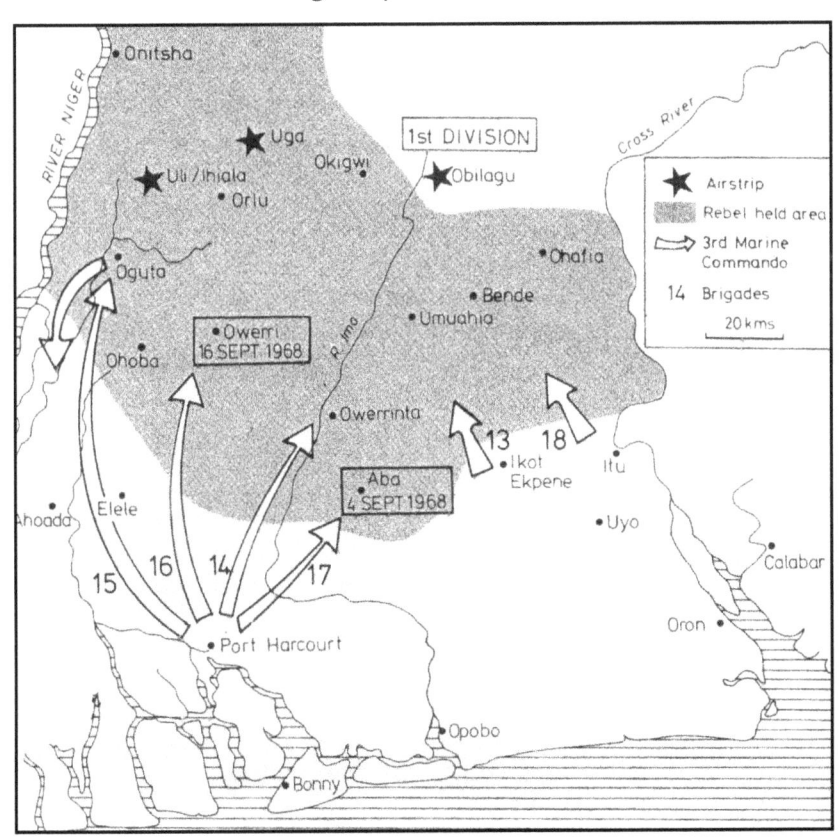

Fig.4: Operation OAU

Adapted from Obasanjo, 1980

"The movement or advancement on Umuahia proved formidable and a lot more difficult than first envisaged. This situation was rendered difficult because of sagging morale and insufficient material support from headquarters, and, to add insult to injury, the support rendered to Biafra by several countries, most specifically, the French – through their West African colonies — and, both the recapture of Owerri, with the support of the "S" Commandos Division, *and* the death of Major Hamma, Second-in-Command of the 16 Brigade, both of which caused a lot of significant malaise and a feeling of despondency among the Federal troops. These incidents shattered the sense of invincibility and the fighting prowess of the Third Marine commandos. Their morale had dipped to its lowest ebb. It was time for a change of leadership", Professor Balarabe concluded.

"The speed with which the southern rebel areas were liberated by the Third Marine commandos was amazing. Bonny was taken in a day, after being advertised as one of the most fortified Islands. Within a month, all adjacent towns had fallen. The Third Division also attacked the southern part of the Mid-west after the incursion of the rebel troops, in order to divert attention from Enugu. In less than two months, the Division had liberated Escravos, Warri, Sapele, Burutu and Forcados. Some think this surprising speed and the success of the Division was, in part, due to the co-operation of the intellectual community of the minority (Ibibio, Annang, Ijaw, Oron and Effik) ethnic groups. These minorities were now proud to have their own States, where they had the control of their destiny and resources, and they were, thus, highly supportive of the Federal troops. As a matter of fact, anytime an area was liberated, the youths enlisted in the Nigerian army *en-masse*. But that was all a long time ago, now there is an urgent need for a fresh leadership at the helm".

"Is it true that there were countries that recognized the Republic of Biafra at the expense of the Federal Republic of Nigeria?" James asked the Professor.

"Yes, indeed", the Professor responded; "the list included Gabon, Zambia, Tanzania, Cote d'Ivoire (Ivory Coast) and Haiti".

"I also heard that some mercenaries and international organizations were also actively involved in helping Biafra?" Francisca asked.

"Yes", again Professor Balarabe answered, "as a matter of fact, the mercenaries included the infamous German mercenary Rolf Steiner mentioned earlier who served in Katanga (now Shaba province in the Democratic Republic of the Congo - the DRC) and commanded the rebel special unit called the "S" Brigade. Some people think the "S" stands for "strike", but I like to think it stands for 'stupid'! This brigade made several unsuccessful attempts to recapture Enugu at any cost, but were always repulsed with impunity by the federal troops. Other mercenaries included those pilots who defied the Federal Government's order of a "no fly zone", and flew military 'supplies' plane through Sao Tome anyway. Some infantry mercenaries from the Katanga war were also recruited. In terms of international organizations, the International Committee of the Red Cross (ICRC) and some church organizations in Europe and the United States were both tacitly and directly involved in aiding the rebels by flying "mixed cargo" in the night, until, one day, a "mixed cargo" plane was shot down on June 5, 1969 revealing its contents as anything but harmless medicines. Its content consisted of medicines and food, yes, but also lethal weapons and indeed a huge amount of ammunitions. The ICRC claimed ownership of the plane where all the crew was killed. Dr. A. Lindt, the Director of ICRC in Nigeria was declared a persona non-grata by the Nigeria Government. Some European countries also served as conduit for supplies to Biafra, these included Portugal through Lisbon, and several of their Portuguese African colonies. The French also shipped arms indirectly through Abidjan and Libreville," he concluded in a distressing voice.

"Is it true that some countries actually *actively* sought to help Biafra in the civil war? Jummai asked of the Professor.

"The answer is yes", he said. " and, although there wasn't any direct or open United States Government involvement on either side", he continued, " the rebel propaganda was able to convince the United States Government to allow many Igbos to qualify as refugees of war and, as such, they were granted scholarships and residences in America. We view with regret the double-standards played by the United States Government, under the shroud of "humanitarian consideration", even though many of the Igbos didn't really seem to be properly fitting the category of "refugees". But to be fair to the United States, it did not recognize the rebel cause directly, other than with this tacit so-called "humanitarian' support". That goes for the British Government too. However, even though the British Government was supporting the Federal Republic of Nigeria, there were some individuals like Mr. Parker, the British Deputy High Commissioner in Enugu at the time, who were openly pro-Biafra. He encouraged the British Government's support of the rebel province which he portrayed in a cable subsequently released as a "viable sovereign state", "worthy" of British recognition.

It should however be made clear that, in their public statements, the United States and the British governments were incredibly one-hundred percent supportive of the Federal Government. But not necessarily morally or materially an example was the effort made by some members of the British foreign service to recognize Biafra as a viable state and as mentioned earlier with regard to the United States, the numerous "scholarships" afforded the Igbos under the cover of "humanitarianism" was symptomatic of such ambivalences. The story of the B-26 bomber remains as cloudy and shrouded in mystery as ever. Even though its origin was the United States, there was no direct evidence that it was supplied by the American Government. The official explanation was that it "had been declared obsolete and scrap by the US Air Force". As for the government of the Soviet Union (Russia), it was supporting the Federal Government from the beginning. I'm sure most of us know why they were eager to do so. It was their chance to get a foot-hold in Africa. As a matter of fact, we bought some Migs, 15 and 17, and also the Ilyushin IL 28 jet-fighter bombers that were used in the war, from them. At first, we didn't have anybody who could fly them, so we got some Egyptian pilots, supplementing them with mercenaries, to fly them for us, while we embarked on the intense training of our own pilots. The Russians even supplied us with Navy patrol boats, KA rifles and other military hardware. But, do you know how they were paid? They were paid with beans, ground-nuts, cotton, palm oil and a few other local products.

In complete contrast with the other governments, the Vatican saw the war strictly as a religious war, a contest between 'the blood-thirsty Moslem hounds' and the 'victimized children of the Pope', and, so, with limited understanding rendered the rebels unrestricted humanitarian and moral support, in addition to medicine - and military hardware! This support was sometimes delivered or sent, disguised through the humanitarian work of the ICRC.

As for the French, they were openly supporting the rebels both materially and morally, even though their foreign ministry had proclaimed neutrality. Their intelligence service was shipping mercenaries, doctors, journalists and arms to the rebels. At the end of the war in 1970, the core group of the French doctors and journalist who served in Biafra became the founding members of the *Doctors without Borders* or *Médecins-Sans Frontiéres* (MSF). At the time many Nigerians were baffled with the French double diplomacy, however, my guess is that they were doing this to show their disapproval of the British hegemony in Africa, and, most especially,

West Africa. At the end of the war, the French opened the borders of Cameroon for the Biafrans, even though Cameroon was buying arms on behalf of the Federal Government, but, to their shame and surprise, the 'Biafrans' remained in Nigeria, their "one indivisible country".

The Chinese seemed to have remained neutral, even after they endorsed the rebels' so-called 'self determination'.

Even neutral Switzerland sent arms to Biafra through Tanzania in East Africa. Mark-press in Geneva became the mouthpiece of the rebel propaganda in Europe, the United States, and, indeed, the whole world, spreading its misinformation with impunity, without any restraints whatsoever. Their propaganda was so effective that the Federal Government had to try to counter it by employing Galitzine, Chart, Russell and Burston and Mark-stellar Associates as its own salesmen in Europe and the United States respectively.

Israel was also involved in a clandestine activity of supplying arms to Biafra through such countries as Gabon and Tanzania, while giving lip service support to the Federal Government. I understand recently that Nyerere regretted his support and wished he hadn't acted so. But, hey, it's too late; it's like the saying 'closing the barn door after the sheep are stolen or closing the stable door after the horse has bolted! Israel at the time considered Biafrans the 'persecuted Jews' of Africa.

On the west coast of Africa, the Ivory Coast and Gabon provided the rebels with military training facilities, for all ranks. Most of our Northern Maghreb neighbors or States, with the exception of Mauritania, were supportive of the Federal Government, most especially Niger and Cameroon. These two countries were openly buying arms for the Federal Government from those countries who would not sell directly to the Federal Government", Professor Balarabe suddenly stopped because one of the house girls had signaled that lunch was ready.

Most of the women had brought in different dishes that day. Lunch this day consisted of a variety of dishes including *tuwon shinkafa*, fresh fish, rice and beans, pounded yam and *amala*, bush meat, chicken and *fura* as dessert. The men ate in their section as usual and the women joined *Mamu* in the women's section of the house.

After the meal the professor announced "I hope we've all enjoyed the different dishes served to us, and, if you all agree, we'll call it a day. I believe most of us would start to doze off if we were to continue, given what we've just consumed. I also believe all of you will agree that we've covered a lot today, and moreover, some of you, I know, have errands to run. So, if nobody objects, I suggest we stop here, and pick it up next week-end, even though some few have indicated they might be out of town then". The Professor stopped momentarily to pick his teeth.

Both Alhaji Abba and James voiced their concurrence, and all present deemed it the most appropriate thing to do, especially as regards to the fear of dozing off, because "I'm really just too full to simply sit up straight", James joked.

"Well friends, I'll see at least some of you next week-end then, *inshallah*".

And one-by-one the couples tripped outside, after expressing their gratitude to *Mamu* and shaking the hand of, or warmly hugging, the Professor.

Chapter Nine
Selected Battle Scenes

First Division: The battle for Enugu

Meanwhile the First Division under the Command of one of our most decorated and renowned General Commanding Officers (GOC's) at the time was under the authority of General Shuwa. The First Division was the first to experience the brutal brunt of the civil war. Shuwa was a medium-sized man very tough and demanding. He possessed a fair complexion, was very slender, but when it came to military science he had no equal, none could surpass him. He was a real military strategist of optimum repute.

The battle for Enugu was code named *Operation Lion's Paw,* and began, one fateful day, after an optimum military build-up and a continuous twenty-four-hour bombardment by 122mm artillery, coordinated by the First Division that succeeded in destroying most of the downtown section of the city, including the house of one of the city's renowned sons, Dr Nmadi Azikwe .The city's main town center leading to the vicinity of a town called Obiagu, some few miles to the metropolis of Enugu, or Enugwu (top of the hill), all experienced this barrage of an attack. Kayode Warrant 11 explained later to an interviewer that the purpose of such bombardment was to "soften the targets". Chief Warrant Officer Kayode turned to Lt. Colonel Bako entreating him to go back, as it was far too dangerous out there …."I implore you, sir, for God's sake!"He declared, and looked for support from the NCO who was standing next to him but who had noticeably turned away "There, you see!" He said, calling attention to the bullets non-stop whining, whistling and singing over their heads. The way he spoke, my reader, you would think that he had maybe some mystical protection from bullets and could not be killed by them.

As he spoke, he suddenly heard a gun crack and *poof!.. Poof!* Out came, a dense ball of smoke, which turned from violet to gray to milky-white and *boom! Boom! boom!...boom!,* the curtain of smoke that had concealed the luxuriant Emene/Uwani vale was slowly uncovered by a rising wind, as if by an unseen hand, from right to left, and the hidden hill now revealed the Biafran Artillery Squadron moving across it. Unbeknownst to the enemy they had been pinned down by the famous 20th, 21st and 22nd battalions, and caught in the middle by the 5th battalion, without much cover or re-enforcement of any sort. The valley had meanwhile turned into one enormous shouting and shooting gallery. All eyes involuntarily focused on some of the Biafran soldiers running down the hill in utter disarray, while a large number of vehicles, camouflaged in the swamp, advanced upon them. Once a while, a round would crack pass the Federal troops but nothing menacingly dangerous or fatal happened. They could see the Biafrans' shabby caps and could easily distinguish the officers from the men, and could also see the Biafran flag flapping against its staff, as some broke through and retreated for a safe haven in the forest.

"How splendidly they march as they retreat!" Someone among the ranks – vague remarked, sarcastically. Warrant Officer 11 Ningi was not only furiously angry but also aghast because his men had been unexpectedly banned from pursuing the rebel forces as they retreated. To nobody's surprise, early the next day, before they really knew what was going on, the rebel forces had reorganized and re-fitted themselves very well and the battle was engaged again with renewed determination and ferocity. There was a gun crack followed by *Tat-ta-tarat!Tat-ta-tarat...boom! Boom!* These exchanges went on for more than ten minutes, non-stop. And this was mingled with the sound of the big guns on both sides *boom!...boom!....boom!*

"... *Left!...Left!...Left!*" the commanding Officer Colonel Danjuma seemed to be telling himself and Lieutenant Bako Samari, at every inch of progress. And the wall of soldiers following his command, each with a stern face, each in its own way, echoed the mantra, marching onward and mentally repeating: "...*Left!...Left!...Left!...Left!...*" Awolabi, a very stout-looking Staff Sergeant, was huffing and puffing fell out of step and skirted to a bush of thick shrubs in the road., A soldier who had fallen behind looked dismayed at his defection, panting as he trotted along, trying to catch up with his comrades. Some bullets flew over Lieutenant Bello's head and landed just inches away. "*Allahhu akbar*", he reassured himself quietly.

"Close ranks!" The GOC, Shuwa, bellowed out. The soldiers moved in an arc but continued with the now-familiar movement of *…Left!…Left!…Left!* There seemed interspersed between the monotonous sound of their breathing and the uniform pounding of their feet on the ground, an occasional ominous silence, only to be broken by sounds of artillery and the big guns. After hours of intensive artillery-fire, the commanding officer, Colonel Danjuma moved, the 5th and 18th Battalions from the center to the right flank, to support the 21st, 22nd and 30th Battalions, where the fighting seemed most intense. This change brought about an immediate result, as things seemed to quiet down a bit and settle, at least temporarily. When Lieutenant Bako surveyed both the periphery and the heart of the battlefield, to his profound joy and amazement, he found that the enemy had retreated yet again and fled. He gleefully informed his commanding officer, Col. Danjuma, through his signal radio, informing him of the large cache of weaponry that they had discovered, including a sizable cache of Kalashnikov rifles that the rebels had left behind and a number of injured men abandoned in their hasty retreat. The ones that were trapped and had nowhere to go were waving white flags of surrender and seemed relieved they could finally surrender without any negative consequences or, the ultimate accusations of treason, punishable by firing-squad from the rebel high command.

There were losses on both sides, but the rebels seemed at first glance and it turned out to be so to have suffered more casualties, it looked like almost half of their fighting force was depleted and destroyed. This means thus the fortified capital of the rebel uprising had fallen to the Federal troops, under the apt command of Colonel Danjuma.

Later in the day, the GOC commended the Colonel in his private quarters, congratulating him on a job well done, and informing him that he would be most gratified and proud to praise his gallantry, and that of his men to the Commander-in Chief. The Colonel, however, deferred, relating the success of his campaign to the GOC's meticulous military planning and strategic acumen, and as such proposing that it was he who deserved the honor the most.

Shuwa's entry into Enugu and its environs was a brilliant military strategy which sent a signal to the rebels that they were fighting on the wrong side. The capture of the rich, and indeed incalculably wealthy, Biafran capital enabled the Federal troops to come into possession of a large and badly-needed cache of abandoned military supplies. Even more than this, it gave them an invaluable boost, a kind of breathing-space and a much-needed build-up of morale.

The rebel's army, even though only half-strength at this juncture, made several daring attempts to recapture their capital, just as with every other city they'd lost, including Onitsha, but to no avail. The Federal troops stood their ground. There were some at the moment of the capture of Enugu who thought or pontificated along those lines that the end of the war was near, but, boy, were they wrong! They underestimated the rabid determination, resourcefulness and ingenuity of the rebel forces. There were some who argued that the rebel leaders would be wise, and in an advantageous position at that moment, to seek for a peaceful solution and an end to the war, before the people experienced any further sufferings. On the contrary, the rebel leader used his power to choose the most foolish, unwise and ruinous options open to him, by attacking the Mid-Western State, which hitherto, as we have noted earlier, had declared its neutrality in the conflict. It is quite ridiculous, and unparalleled in the annals of civil war, for a state, which considers itself a part of the Federal Republic, to declare neutrality, when that Government is at war with one of the states comprising it. It is indeed amazing how the federal military-planners at Supreme HQ fell for this gimmick or cynical ploy, hook, line and sinker—but that are something perhaps best left to military historians.

After the capture of the rebel capital, Enugu, the GOC, with the commanding officer of the Battalion that captured it, Danjuma, at his side addressed the population:

You peaceable inhabitants of Enugu, artisan workmen and farmers, misfortune has driven you out of your city, but I advise you to come back now to your dwelling places and homes and you will be protected. Any violence perpetrated against you, by either soldier or civilian, will be punished with the maximum power that has been granted us, the GOC, under the powers of war. The Commander-in-Chief of the Federal Republic of Nigeria wants to assure you that, he wishes to put a quick end to your adversity and to your sufferings and to restore you to your homes and families and properties wherever they may be in the Federation. Farmers and workmen and all civil servants, come out of the forests where you have been hiding in terror for weeks, even months now, return to your huts and houses without fear, in absolute surety of protection by the Federal Government. The Commander-in-Chief of the Republic does not see any of you as enemies, except those who disobey his orders and take up arms against the Federal troops of the Republic…therefore lay down your arms and come out of hiding back to your houses and dwellings… As a sign of its generosity and commitment to justice and self-determination, the Federal Government has instructed me to announce to you the appointment of Mr. Anthony Askia as your Chief Administrator, with immediate effect. I'll be remiss of my duty as General Officer Commanding if I didn't also show my most profound appreciation and pride in the gallantry and bravery of our troops and its highly professional officer corps! Long live one indivisible united Nigeria…"

"*Hip Hip! Hoo-ray; Hip Hip! Hooray!*" The GOC proclaimed, and all the units responded even louder in unison, "*Hu-ra-a-ah!*" However, the loudest cheers seemed to be coming from the B Company, ("B" for Burma) of the 20th Battalion, who echoed with all the gusto, all the verve that they could muster. This was a particularly special moment for them because, in their last outing, they had been reprimanded by their commanding officer, Major Bohuk, for a lackluster performance. Now they were happy to have redeemed their honor by receiving special commendation from the GOC for their gallantry and their relentless assault on the retreating rebel forces.

Those captured or surrendered included Major Ezegbe, leader of the 54 battalion, Sergeant Okonkwu, a platoon leader, Izebo, Ezeumune, Nzegwo, and Chumeku WO 11. There were more than two-hundred enemy-corpses scattered over the battle-field. The Federal army lost three gallant officers including the highly-respected Major Dogonyaro, from the Bachama tribe, and a dozen or so of from other ranks, each of whose bodies were wrapped and adorned in the Nigerian flag, embossed with their units' logo-grams and soberly delivered to their parents in their home-towns or villages for a justified hero's burial. Brave patriotic officers like Major Dogonyaro in a better world should have been buried with full military honor, in a place of honor, like the Arlington national cemetery in Washington DC, which is reserved for national heroes, but of course nobody ever thought of honoring *our* national heroes in this manner. Instead, the country's heroes and icons, — deserving heads of state, paramount political and civic leaders, distinguished military officers et.al— are simply buried in their respective towns/ villages, and forgotten about after a short while, since there is no special resting place for their burial unlike in some countries, like the Arlington National Cemetery in the United States, nowhere which can evoke some strong patriotic sentiments on such important days as chosen "days of remembrance".

After the capture of Enugu, the Federal Government, as was stated in the GOC's address, appointed Mr. Anthony Ukpabi Asika, an Igbo, as an Administrator of, not only Enugu but, the whole of East-Central State. He continued in this position up until the end of the war, and the Federal Government thanked him for a job well-done. However, I'm still looking to find out if he has been awarded one of those National State honors, like Commander of the Order of the Niger (CON), Commander of the Order of the Federal Republic (CFR), or even, the lower ones, like Officer of the Order of the Niger (OON).

Before the battle of Nsukka started, Staff Sergeant Patrick S. Anande had approached his immediate Platoon Commanding Officer, Captain Jehuh, about a letter he had just received which was burning him up, churning his stomach inside-out, and making him nauseous. The letter was from his half-brother, Tando Anande, who had reported to him that his wife back in the village was disgracing, not only him, but, the whole clan, by indiscriminately sleeping with men. In fact, he alleged, she had been caught-in-the-act by one of their cousins, Ruben Zakkeh, who had dropped in unannounced to see how she was doing. The contents of the letter were very graphic detailing what had taken place. Ruben had challenged the gentleman to a duel and both had been subsequently taken in by the local police. "You're now the laughing stock of the whole town, as a cuckold!" Tando had written.

The graphic contents of the letter and its insistence and urgency seemed to demand his immediate attendance, since it involved marital infidelity and, quite possibly, the end of his marriage. This was why he decided to ask for a few days' off to go settle it because, as he put it, "it's affecting my readiness for the coming battle, *oga* it's gnawing my soul and conscience day and night". "You know what?" The Captain replied, without any amplification and, surprisingly unsympathetically "the best soldier is a bachelor because then the only thing he loses is his loneliness". While Anande was pondering the Captain's remark, Jehuh went straight to inform their Infantry Company Commanding Officer, Lieutenant Colonel Gbor, of his request. Much to the Captain's surprise, the Commanding Officer promptly responded to the request and granted Anande fifteen days to travel to Benue and settle his 'family problems' without having to inform their Battalion Commanding Officer, Colonel Wushishi. He was, however, ordered to return as soon as possible, for two reasons, firstly, that any requests for days-off beyond fifteen was above his pay grade, and, secondly, that all hands *must* be on board for the all-important battle for Nsukka— a reconnaissance advance team of Special Forces had confirmed the GOC's prognostications regarding the rebel forces' hectic and energetic planning .To Lt. Colonel Gbor however, the inclusion of the planned use and incorporation, for the first time, of the deadly 'S' brigade, which consisted of some of the most hated and hideous mercenaries on the planet, R.Steiner, J. Eramus, T. Williams, F. Alex, C. Leroy, I. Paddy and A. Iaranelli was a cause of urgent concern and of the greatest import.

"The family is a very important unit of support to a soldier at any time, but, most especially, at such critical times as war. He needs all the support it can muster and provide"; Lieutenant Colonel Gbor declared in passing, without any further elaboration, quietly reprimanding Jehuh as he inspected his engineering squadron's preparations.

Sergeant Anande took the only truck available, an eighteen-wheeler to the *harmattan*-covered North the following day, and, two days later, after going through numerous, mostly unnecessary and annoying, combined military and police checkpoints, he was in Makurdi, completely exhausted from hanging and holding onto the truck's metal frame, which was, at times, covered with a tarpaulin, because there weren't any seats inside of the truck. Anybody that has ever travelled in one of these trucks knows how suffocating and stinky it can be under those tarpaulins, especially when you have to share the precious available space with chickens and goats, and, at times, even pigs! From there, he took a *bolekaja*, a small bus-like motor vehicle with wooden structure similar to *KekeNapep* but much bigger and had four wheels,to his village, Akwaye Kogu. After a brief moment of rest, he confronted his wife about the letter that he had received regarding her alleged infidelity. "I know you were always on the wrong side of the tracks before I married you! But I naively thought you had changed, especially since I have provided for you all of the basic things you could ever want! You disgust me I am really disappointed". "Oh, I can't bear it, Anande! It's not true! Stop accusing me, you're hurting me", she tried to calm his nerves, by getting closer to him. But Anande would have none of it.

"Listen to me! I've put up with a lot of nonsense from you, because of your poor upbringing. I've often thought you weren't quite right in your head. I've excused you and never lifted my hand to you. But there's a straw that breaks the camel's back; and for me this is it". She paused, and then as if the words had been an evocation which called back imagined happiness of yester years, she blinked and immediately changed her facial expressions and stared fixedly at nothing! With a stubborn and bitterly resentful look on her face, she declared, "that's it you're nothing but a dope fiend"! With this, there followed a flurry of heated arguments and recriminations, to-and-fro, between the two of them. "Ha! I never knew that you would be such an irresponsible dirty bastard of a husband! Otherwise why on earth would I have consented to marry you? You fool! The only thing you know about is how to sleep with me, and even that you're not any good at! You don't love me!" She sighed and sobbed, with her hair matted and her face wet with a mixture of perspiration and tears. Finally, Jamila Raga had had enough. She sprung to her feet and rushed into her bedroom, still cursing and sobbing, grabbed a few items of clothing for her and her son, Atompera Ahimsa (absence of all harmful intent), stuffed them in her travel bag, and breezed off, after slamming the rickety door-frame hard behind her. She was lucky, because, as soon as she arrived at the local station, the last *bolekaja* to her parents' village for the night was just roaring, ready to go, like a jet plane preparing for a take off!

Anande roamed around that evening turning the past events in his mind, before finally going to bed. The following morning, he had discussions with Tando about the contents of the letter, and about his altercation with Raga the previous night. He said that when he had first got the letter he had gone into his bunker and cried and cried and cried, until he thought it was just a dream. "I sat up first, in utter surprise, until bewilderment set in, I started to feel as though my blood crept cold through my veins, and I started to cry again, but nothing changed. In my confusion I didn't know whom to turn to for help or advice. Eventually my mate, Corporal Kola walked in and calmed me", he narrated to Tando. That following morning was a Sunday and Anande and Tando his half brother went to church together to pray, but, most importantly, to see some of his old friends whom he hadn't seen in a long while, such as Amos, Kwande, and Ruben. After the service he decided to stay behind and discuss his problems with the Pastor of the Apostolic Trinity United Church of Christ in Nigeria (the ATUC), the Right Reverend Oche Otache.

Pastor Otache was a normally stout, thick-set, man of fifty-five or less of medium height, with a sallow face, and dark, gray, closely-cropped hair. By nature, this quiet middle-aged gentleman was taciturn and circumspect even detached. He struck me and not only me, but everyone else he encountered as looking extraordinarily pale and feeble of late. He seemed, to those who knew him, to have grown suddenly much thinner as if he were disappearing. On the pulpit, though, he was something else, an energetic giant, fluttering his hands in the air for effect and using his booming voice to maintain his congregants' rapt attention and commanding a completely hushed reverential silence. It was often said that in his church nobody had time to doze off because his preaching was so very engaging and, most importantly, non-accusatory in its delivery. He was one of the few liberal, or free-thinking preachers who didn't feel it their responsibility to condemn deeds they didn't think directly affected other people or perhaps curtails individual freedom of choice or free will- be it abortion or drinking. Being a Christian, for him excluded strict adherence to many of the things that the conservative preachers vociferously complain about and accuse their congregants' of doing, whilst privately doing themselves. Such things as perhaps once a while, taking a sip of some good wine, or admiring even lusting after the opposite sex but in their thoughts, not committing any actual infidelity. He hated false piousness and hypocrisy. The Bible, to him, was like a constitution, whose basic tenets or original intent was eternal, but whose interpretation must fit the needs of the time and needed to be grounded in personal experience. In short, for him, both the Bible *and* the constitution were evolving, as well as living documents, which were never meant to be static otherwise they lose their potency or purposes as guides to justice and morality.

You see, my readers, Patrick Anande was one of those pragmatists, just like, probably, some of you are presently reading the story, believed it didn't hurt to attend either a church or a mosque, just in case it turned out there was, indeed, a Supreme Being out there to pass judgment after death. Whichever of the two seemed nearest to him, he would attend, one or the other, with equal piety and fervor of devotion. He had been long exposed to both faiths and had no qualms with their demands and the rituals of their worship. Some of his aunts and cousins were Moslems and some were Christians. In short, Anande had placed a wager on life after death. After all, he felt, he wasn't losing anything by attending a mosque or church. As a matter of fact, if anything, he was gaining, if it turned out that the Pastor or Imam was right in their proclamations that there is an omniscient all-seeing God/ Allah. With regard to this bet about life-after-death Anande had hosts of travelling-companions, among whom is that great and justly famous French mathematician, Blaise Pascal, who once postulated the following assertion, familiarly known as *'Pascal's Wager'*: "*You'd better believe in God, because, if you are right, you stand to gain eternal bliss, and if you are wrong, it won't make any difference anyway! On the other hand, if you don't believe in God, and you turn out to be wrong, you get eternal damnation, whereas if you are right, it makes no difference"*. To improve his chances of getting the wager right, every time he prayed in a church he would always face East, just as Moslems do, because, according to his presumptuous belief, that "was where God was born and died on the cross". Moreover, Anande strongly believed that the cardinal teaching of every religion should be geared toward giving the ignorant and the misinformed, whose burden in this life was almost unbearable, hope, and an inkling of trust, sufficient enough to support them in their heaviest hours of need and desperation. He, furthermore, believed the life and potential of each individual personality is, fluid and in an incessant flux of births and re-births, in both its objective *and* subjective manifestations---*sui generis*.

As previously mentioned, after a general service of rich, uplifting, spiritual hymns and a powerful address upon the theme "*Christian Military Service in aPeriod of War…Changing World"* had concluded; Anande waited in the vestibule to see Pastor Otache alone. He sought his indulgence to make time for him for some candid Confessions. Anande implored Pastor Otache to grant him the opportunity to "cleanse his soul" from the "vile impulse" that was "gnawing him from inside". He told Pastor Otache how much he had enjoyed his message of Christian service during times of war and how relevant he felt this to be to his life. He thanked the Pastor for picking such an apt topic. After his continuous effusion of gratitude to the Pastor, they secluded themselves in the tiny inner sanctum of the church where the confessions usually took place. As soon as they were seated, he declared that he had "two things", that had been "eating at his soul", and, "since I'm on the battle front, where danger looms every second and the possibility of death is high and even expected at any moment", he wanted to die he said, "with a clear conscience "about his activities in the here and now.

"Christ is ever-present to receive our confessions, regardless of our state of sin", Pastor Otache said, looking at Anande straight in the face.

"Do you believe in the doctrines and teachings of the Apostolic Trinity United Church of Jesus Christ about salvation?" He asked.

Anande grinned and said, "I often have doubts, I've doubted. I doubt everything. I'm a skeptic", was Sergeant Anande's candid response.

"Don't you worry about a thing, doubt is natural, it has been part of the weakness of the human mind since creation, or evolution; it has been molded in our psyche, I believe by evolution, and continues to this day through natural selection", the Reverend replied.

Recently, a noted skeptic, Professor Richard Dawkins in his provocative, ambitious, book *The Greatest Show on Earth,* has defined natural selection as "the non-random survival of information that encodes embryological recipes for that survival". This, however, presumes that the repository of the information so encoded will reside in the individual bodies as a gene pool for its continuous survival.

Sergeant Anande reflected on what Pastor Otache had said, and reasoned within himself thus: "How can you possibly explain evolutionary products or procedures with creation? I thought the two are entirely antithetical. I certainly accept his postulation that the mind is the product of our evolution, the result of natural selection. But how can it also be a product of creation? I'm utterly confused with this form of argument or reasoning. I thought it was either creation *or* evolution - but not *both* in the same sentence! There seems to be a cognitive dissonance in such postulations", he surmised.

Not wishing to disturb the Pastor any further however, he kept such private thoughts about 'creation' and divinity to himself.

"But", the Pastor resumed, "we often have to pray to Him for strength and mercy. What are some of the things that you doubt, my son?" He asked, sternly.

"My chief sins or doubts, Pastor, are many, but the basic, most prevalent two are doubts about God and how He oversees the supposed 'institution' of marriage. It sometimes seems to me as if one is indeed in an institution, a mental institution!"

He said this in a flat, clearly dispirited, voice, revealing his obvious opposition, or at least confusion and regret regarding marriage.

Pastor Otache grinned provocatively, and wanted to say what a morbid nonsense! But instead he said in a calm reassuring voice;

"What is there to doubt about these two?" The Pastor asked, seeming to display a mild frustration, even anger, but he controlled his emotions, and continued with a detached calm;

"Remember, my son, doubt is natural, it has been part of our weak human minds since creation. But there is a possibility, according to the evolutionary biologist, Darwin, that this weakness comes to us, in part, from natural selection, whatever *that* means". Natural selection, Darwin postulated, " is implicated in endowing it to us", he said, reminding

Anande what he'd said earlier, about the mind being the product of both creation *and* evolution.

"As I said, I often find myself doubting the very existence of God! I'm at a loss whether to fully embrace evolution and natural selection, or a divine will, as a guide to my life, in short, whether to accept the theory of Creation as presented to us in the Old Testament by the revered Jewish patriarchs, or to go with Darwin. But, please, Reverend, don't perceive my statement as being pejorative of the work of those patriarch brothers, in any way. They did undoubtedly fill a knowledge-based vacuum in their time", he concluded looking even more perplexed than previously, if that were possible!

"But, my son, you're making no sense, you're eccentric, what sort of doubt can there be about the putative existence of God? When we see His manifestations all around us? He who has filled the heavenly firmaments with the stars and lights? Who has clothed the Earth with its elegant beauty and majesty?! Can evolution explain all of the beauty and the wonder that we see around us? "He said, looking imploringly at Anande.

Anande, for his part, just smirked and went on asking the Pastor numerous questions about creation, faith and the various theories of evolution.

"What do you think about Spinoza's conception of God as being synonymous with Nature", he asked rhetorically. "Isn't it a reasonable proposition, god is nature and nature is god? Isn't it also true that most of the things you mentioned above are natural and are the consequences of evolution and natural selection, and have little, if anything, to do with Creation or God? Doesn't the Big Bang explain everything, including the origin of the Universe, more cogently and rationally than the Hebrew story in the Old Testament, or the theory of Creation being postulated recently by some conservative Christians, the so-called "Creationists"?

Pastor Otache was aghast and getting irritated and frustrated, because, his understanding of the theory of Big Bang, and all that stuff about "singularity", "dark matter", "dark energy", "inflation", "cosmic radiation" and "density of energy" were all just limited and unconvincing explanatory formations of the (true) origins of the universe. For him, the Bible, and its story of creation, was the evolving word of God, as well as a book of faith. There were no "ifs" "ands" or "buts". He'd long been aware of all the misgivings and the inherent ignorance of the other theories out there about Creation, because, in his view, that's what they were, simply theories. In his life as a practicing Christian and as a pastor of a reputable church, he'd often prayed quietly and beseeched God for wisdom to help him explain to his congregants the true message of the Gospel and its ubiquitous promises of Salvation — and now to Anande! —but salvation from what, was a question that he had never thought to ask himself.

"But how do you explain the Big Bang without Creation?" The Reverend asked rhetorically, but then he immediately remembered coming across a book by Stephen Hawking titled *A Brief History of Time,* and another book by Paul Steinhardt and Neil Turok, entitled *The Endless Universe,*where the authors talked about the immense energy density at the Singularity, and the instant inflation/expansion, in nano-seconds, of the Universe, and that, for more than four hundred thousand years, as recently revealed by the Cosmic Microwave Background Radiation (CMBR), there was no light in the Universe, only perpetual darkness and expansion! Could this be where the story in the Book of Genesis picks up? He asked himself. As he read further, he discovered that these scientists claimed that the Universe is approximately thirteen billion years old - or was it fourteen billion? However, he surmised, if one accepted the story of creation as it is presented in the Bible, and did the math, it would only come out to about ten thousand years. He tried to resolve and reconcile these seemingly irreconcilable conflicting figures with archeological findings dating back millions of years, but decided not to worry or further speculate "about all of this metaphysical or theoretical stuff" because, after all, he wasn't "at a science seminar, but in a church", and in a confession, for goodness sakes!

In view of these latter thoughts, Pastor Otache swiftly addressed himself quietly;

"I don't know! I don't' have all the answers to these hypothetical mind-teasing questions". He wanted to add "devil take your pessimism. I feel low-spirited enough" with your way of reasoning; but again he constrained himself, and instead declared disgustedly;

"My! My! Where and how did he come up with such pernicious and ridiculous ideas?" He asked himself violently shaking his head.

"Don't you believe that all our sympathy, empathy, compassion, conscience, remorse, morality and a host of other qualities, are all and only the results of the vestiges of our organic history, in short, the fruits of evolution and natural selection?", Anande asked the Reverend, who by this time was getting really frustrated.

"My son, you don't believe, or know, that God created everything? Then what *do* you believe?" The Pastor quizzed him in an agitated, even, angry tone.

"I don't understand it at all", Anande replied. "I always assume we are such stuff as dreams are made on, and our little life is rounded with a sleep".

The reverend thought of being sarcastic himself by saying, no "we are such stuff as manure is made on…..!" But he reversed his layman's thought and immediately said in a strange objective tone;

"Well then, my son, pray to God and beseech him. But I want you to know that even Priests, even Pastors, and the Holy Fathers, have had at certain moments, their doubts. Have you heard about Mother Teresa and the constant doubt she had of God's existence or abiding presence? But she continued to the bitter end to devote herself to His services, ministering among the poor with prayer, always asking Him for strength and mercy".

"What are you going to tell your children when they ask you about all the wonderful things around them which they cannot explain? Are you going to tell them that "evolution" and "natural selection" have caused these beautiful and gorgeous things to happen"? "Or", he continued, "suppose your child asks you about 'what awaits' him in the life beyond the tomb? What will you say to him?" Don't you know that simple happiness, in this life, is irrelevant, and that what matters is the hereafter? He seemed to state his case with a super-human energetic finality. After having made his declaration, he convinced Anande to kneel down with him and pray to God to show him 'His light and mercy' and to cleanse him of his sins.

Inwardly Anande still pondered whether or not there was actually any 'Supreme Being' out there, who was listening to their prayers about his miniscule problems, compared to all else that was out there in the whole vast infinite Universe. Such happenstance, as the menacing birth of super massive "black holes", the death throes of stars many times the size of our sun, colliding and exploding stars, "gamma-ray-bursts" (GRBs) which herald the birth of black holes, and the phenomenal events taking place in our sun's magnetic field. And, most recently, the emergence of the discipline of quantum physics, with its bizarre hypothesis of the possibility of a particle being at two different locations or places, *simultaneously,* which has added greatly to our understanding of the many other hitherto unknown marvels in the Universe. Why would such a Being, whatever its name was, worry about him a tiny speck of a human, instead of all the phenomena listed above; or closer to home, why should such Being bother about him while there are raging wars taking place, with indiscriminate killing of the innocent by *al-Qaida, boko haram,* earthquakes, storms, tsunamis, floods - you name it!

"Now why do you have doubts about marriage as an institution"? The Reverend Otache asked him.

Anande had been married to Raga Jamila for five years now. He was somewhat happy, whenever they were together, but not in the manner that he had first envisaged. At every step throughout these years he had found his initial dreams thwarted and fading away fast, but, at the same time there were, new unexpected surprises. As a bachelor, he had watched his married friends and their wives feverishly involved with some petty cares or trifles, squabbles, jealousies, and, yes, even love! He had often smiled with contempt at such engagements. He had hoped his life to be different, but, lo behold, it didn't seem to have happened so far. He and his wife's life had become reduced entirely to the pettiest details, a victim of the very superficiality which he had so despised and abhorred in others.

That which he had despised had now, however, gained the most extraordinary overriding importance in his life, but he could do nothing about it, because doing anything would only infuriate or aggravate the situation, by making his wife more belligerent at a time he could not afford to be occupied by anything else, but war. Before marriage he had had the most exacting conception of domestic life, unconsciously, like all men, he had pictured it as the ultimate enjoyment of love and love's bounty, with nothing to hinder and no petty cares to distract from it. The most recent events in his life had, however, caused his doubts to inflame and burst out in the open, most particularly the confession by his wife of her infidelities while he was away fighting, "a senseless internecine war", as he puts it. Like most women as well as most men she had denied it until she was caught red-handed in the act. She hadn't expected him that day and coming in at that moment.

The first time he surprised her with another man in his house, his natural instinct urged him to take matters into his own hands either by challenging the lover directly, or by reactive behavior getting involved with another woman himself! And now this! The humiliation! An inner voice, however, cautioned him to take the higher ground and try to do everything in his power to forgive her, and prove to her his unswerving fidelity since the earliest days of their marriage, and of *her* in this case being wrong, more than once, with the sin of *in*-fidelity. But to prove her wrong would mean irritating her still more and making the rupture even greater.

These conflicting scenarios and consternation were the cause of so much of his mental agony and suffering. One insidious feeling impelled him to get rid of the conflict in his conscience and pass on the blame to her, another, stronger, one impelled him to, as quickly as possible, smooth over the schism, without letting it grow even greater. However, to remain under such clearly undeserved reproach were wretched, to say the least, and, most definitely he felt, not within his powers to effect any changes anytime soon! But he knew to make her suffer by justifying himself would be worse still. As a man, he tried to reconcile this conflict, and find some means of conjuring up help that might heal, or at least minimize the aching pain he felt inside him now, palliate it, bring it to a more bearable condition, and that's why he'd decided to see Pastor Otache.

"You see, Pastor", he began again, hesitantly, and then paused;

Anande sobbed and fought back more tears, but made finally a determination to refocus his thoughts and energy upon the matters at hand, but the situation still seemed too bizarre and grim to grasp at its rationality. He summoned all that he could muster from within, however, and then recollected, in a curt, but defiant, tone:

"My courtship period with her was short and sporadic because we lived in different towns due to my military training and constant postings, but due, in part, also, to a consideration of her job security. Also, I didn't know it at the time that she didn't have any humor, any heart, didn't really believe in anything, so to speak, other than maybe hedonism -seeking after pleasure. In fact, she was one of the most selfishly hedonistic, corrupt and vile women around, though nobody told me at the time. What happened was I came home for a brief visit and found out that Rachael Zikkeh, the girl my parents had betrothed for me since childhood, and whom I had always wanted to marry since our Elementary School days, was engaged and now no longer available. My father had seen her mother pregnant and jokingly said "If what you're carrying is a girl, she will be my son's wife". When her mother delivered a girl, my parents proudly took some tribal gifts of ankle-and wrist-bracelets, brass trinkets, five chickens and a ram, as a token of my betrothal to her. By this simple traditional act as you know she'd become my 'wife', in a manner of speaking.

At the end of my fourth grade, however, the family moved to another town because my father was a policeman and was constantly on the move, Gashua, Dambua, Kano, Daura, Malumfashi and many more. We moved around quite a lot. For many years I didn't see Rachael, my betrothed. We just corresponded, sporadically, through people travelling to the village from where my family happened to be at that time .Post offices at that time, didn't work, and things haven't changed much since Letters still take weeks to reach their destination! Days changed to weeks, and weeks to months, and months to years, in such quick succession, that, before anybody noticed, she'd grown into a blossoming beautiful young woman of an age to marry, but I was neither ready, nor available. By then, I had joined the army, and was either in training or on a constant transfer to one station or the other, and, eventually to the front. She'd waited for me for years, but, because of my service to my country, I didn't find the appropriate time to come. She had yearned for a formal engagement as a token of my continued commitment to the seriousness of our relationship, but I'd assumed too much and didn't respond to her wishes. By the time I found out and understood my folly, and rushed home, she had become betrothed to Jeremiah Woji, a teacher, who happened to be one of my childhood best friends.

It was in this setting that my friends introduced Raga Jamila to me, with a caveat that I should have listened to, but didn't. The caveat was that Raga's incontinence was undisputable! But that she was a wonderful person deep down inside. In this sense I'd always had an inkling of the wrong tracks she'd been trekking as a young woman, of her earlier infidelities with the man that she eloped with, but I tried to deceive myself thinking to spare her by hoping that when we got married she would leave her "evil ways behind". He paused once again already wet with tears streaming down his face. "We'd barely known each other for more than two weeks before we hastily got married, because I had to report to my unit on a specified date"; he concluded softly mouthing some curse words at himself for rushing into the marriage.

"My regret at ever having known her presently trumps any desire I might have for women. Bachelor life doesn't seem so bad after all", he dourly lamented

And to tell you the truth, my readers, he recalled a good many incidents from their past life together which seemed to suggest that there never was a real 'love connection', or love relationship, between them even early on in their marriage. They would sit together alone in a room but could not talk with each other for scarcely a minute without some form of argument or argumentative discourse poisoning their conversation. For this reason, most of the time they were together they just sat in risible solitude, whereby each delved into his or her own fantasy dreams and thoughts, isolated, watching precious time idly pass by.

"I made a mistake in linking my life to hers, but I guess there's nothing wrong in such a mistake, it's just that I can't now ever be happy—I will have nothing more to do with her, or, for the foreseeable future with, any woman. As far as I'm concerned, henceforth she doesn't exist..." he declared with a mixture of some venom and anger; with conviction and finality in his voice. However, he immediately remembered this line from Shakespeare during his secondary school days: "The fault, dear Brutus, is not in our stars, but in ourselves that we are underlings".

The Pastor listened intently and once again quietly prayed for divine intervention.

"My son", he began, "any attempts at instigating divorce would only lead to public scandal and recriminations, which would certainly be a godsend to your enemies, resulting in calumnious attacks on your character and repudiation of your achievements which would be impossible to defend in all manner of places. Instead, let us pray and ask God to give you the forbearance to forgive Jamila your wife of her shortcomings". Pastor Otache tried to remain calm.

Anande knew perfectly well that it would be incredibly disingenuous for him to try to exert any semblance of moral superiority or sanctimonious authority upon his wife, because such attempts, he instinctively knew, could lead to nothing but falsity. He knew that he too had some skeletons in his closet. When he was a bachelor he had attended wild parties with women of questionable repute. He might even have a child out there he didn't know about. Further-more, on more than one occasion he'd even peeped into a brothel. His "Trojan horse" was therefore equally dubiously hefty! Thus, he was scared to death to let open the base or vile "Pandora's box" of his misdeeds or maladies.

Though he never thought that he could find any motivation through religion that could support his inclination for giving his wife a "second chance", he was grateful Pastor Otache had shown him and passionately about principles of forgiveness, which were rooted in his faith –indeed all faiths! As he pondered the consequences of his actions, he argued with himself that there was really no reason why he couldn't perhaps still work out his differences with his wife, despite the immensity of the task. He didn't want to go back to the *front* still thinking about such problems. For the meantime they would just hush matters up, keep them "under the carpet", as the saying goes, if they couldn't agree on any reasonable resolution, until the end of the hostilities. "I'll deal with it all in good time, at my own convenience", he sadly muttered to himself in a changed tone, as if in contrition, nodding and flapping his hands in exasperation in the air.

"Yes time will pass and time heals", he thought to himself, "time will arrange everything, and I cannot be made unhappy forever through the mere fact that a contemptible woman, this wife of mine, has committed a crime of passion. I have only to take measured steps to find the best way out of the difficult and adverse situation that she has placed me in. There is a way out of this. I believe I'm neither the first man nor the last to be made a cuckold." He concluded tersely.

It is pertinent I intimate you with one more thing about Anande that will if he hasn't already awoken your sympathy. He could not bear to see a woman or child crying, or, for that matter, any human at all, without being disturbed and pretty much moved to tears himself! Given this weakness, many have wondered how he could possibly have functioned as an effective soldier. The sight of tears would throw him into a state of delirium and nervous agitation and a complete loss of rational reflection. On the front, he always hesitated, asking forgiveness from some higher power before disposing of the enemy. He showed extreme sensitivity even in the heat of the battle. His father always teased him that he had inherited this "effete emotional display" from his mother's side' of the gene pool!

After Anande made a commitment to Pastor Otache that he would consider forgiving his wife, they both, once again, knelt down and prayed fervently for God's guidance and mercy for both of them.

When Anande set out to return home after his confession, he still wasn't in his right mind; he was just as confused about the next step to take as he had been *before* the confessional! Despite his confessions and prayers he still harbored excruciating pain of shame at being a cuckold and wasn't at all certain of what he was going to do next. We know, or ought to know, that it is part of the great riddle of human consciousness for a normal person to feel and think about great conflicting matters, simultaneously, and yet still possess the power of thought to choose only one sequence of ideas, one path, one a course of action. A healthy person can break off even at a moment of intense contemplation to say "hi" to somebody without necessarily losing tracks of his thoughts, but not Anande tonight. He walked home along the, relatively empty, dark streets in complete solitude and hardly dared say anything to the few people he encountered, even those who knew him and tried to engage him in conversation.

His mordant thoughts were only interrupted at intervals by the chirping of birds contentedly perched in the *neem* and acacia trees along the street, and the croaking of frogs in the smelly fetid mass swamp of garbage or the stagnant ponds not too far from the main street, and a troubling sound of a barking dog in the distant darkness. The absence of garbage collection in this neighborhood, as in so many other neighborhoods in the townships, had led to the creation of these rotten-egg-like, putrid-smelling swamps, as the reservoir of breeding ground for mosquitoes, crickets and frogs, all over the town. In the not too far distance he could hear the persistent clucking of chickens and the braying of donkeys and the "moo" of cows. The thick blanket of darkness surrounding him served as a protective cover for his solemn and lonely trip home. With each heavy and measured step he took, there emerged a change in the constitution of his thoughts. At one moment his mind would be active, clear as to what he needed to do, and then, all of a sudden, everything would go blank, blurred and dark, he would lose his mental capacity and energy to think through the simplest sequence of thought.

"Yes", he said to himself, sitting on a chair in the semi-darkness in the corner of his room, "I need happiness and love, which all men and women are endowed with as an inalienable right. The happiness I need is one which, lies beyond material forces and outside the material and external influences of man. Isn't finding and owning it supposed to be within the grasp or power of every man, as ordained by God, or Nature, in the beginning of time, through our evolutionary heritage? For example, to love one's neighbor, to love one's enemy, to love everything that is divine — God/Nature and all his manifestations—was a critical part of man's evolutionary imperatives, surely? Aren't we all products of environmental determinism, and by implication evolution?

Divine, or Natural, love, they say, is the only love that cannot change, nothing, not even death, can destroy it, because it's rooted in our evolutionary past history. This is exemplified by all cultures persistent celebration of death, the anniversaries of our loved ones always ritually addressed with aplomb, untarnished reverence recollection and love.

Divine or Natural love, in short, is the essence of the soul, if you accept the possibility of the immortality and the indestructibility of the soul. "In my life I've probably hated a good many people" Anande mused, "but, at this moment, none of them I've hated quite like her".

All of a sudden his thoughts were stopped dead in their tracks. He was interrupted when he heard a soft voice whispering his name at the door. It was his cousin Catherine Dimkat.

"Oh, hi dear cousin", Catherine said, "I have come in person to comfort you and indulge you in your sorrow and pain. I urge you, beg you, not to give way to grief and melancholy. Your sorrow is a humungous one indeed, but it is not insurmountable. You must seek for consolation and peace from within. Nobody can grant it to you".

With a strange derisive smile, he responded, "Cousin Catherine, I'm crushed, broken, rubbished and annihilated", Anande said. "My situation is tragic and precarious, because I cannot find within me any strength to support, let alone console or pacify me".

"You'll find support, cousin. Seek it, not in me or from me, nor from any other, though I encourage you to believe in me, know that you have my unconditional support. My support is pure natural love, that love that comes from our evolutionary past. It will be your support and your succor merely for the taking"; she replied with garrulous familiarity.

"Oh Cousin Cathy for the love of God! I'm weak, I'm crushed and confused. I understand... Nothing!"

Without looking at him directly she said, "Your only recourse at this time, dear cousin, is forgiveness; we all need it and none more so than your wife at the moment".

Overwhelmed by shame which he tried to hide, he fumbled with his watch and said, "Cousin Cathy, you do not know my pains, my pains as a man. Even as a man, I have my limits, and I've reached them and surpassed them many times over", he declared emphatically.

"I understand, cousin", Catherine said, "I understand it all!"

"But how can you?" Anande shot back, "You are not a man!"

Cousin Cathy. I'm not angry with you, please don't pre-judge me. I cannot help myself. I can do nothing other than thank you".

"But, dear cousin, I beg of you don't give way to those feelings of despair and abandonment. Forgiveness is God's, or Nature's, attribute, as well as a Christian's, Moslem's or humanists' highest ideal and glory.

You should not thank me, but Him, and pray to Him for succor. In Him and Him alone are there peace, consolation and love". Catherine fervently declared her faith as she was getting up to go.

"Cousin Catherine you're sublime. I cannot help it, but, again, thank you for your wisdom, words of comfort, encouragement and promise of support" he said, getting up from the chair he was sitting to see her off.

She grasped both hands and pressed them gently and delicately against her chest before stepping out into the pitch dark outside. After seeing his aunt off, he retired to his dark bedroom, dark, except for a flicker from a kerosene lamp in the middle of his small brown rickety table. A shadow of vague guilt crossed his face as his eyes fixed on the blank gray wall facing the small table; he sat down to write a letter to his wife. At this moment, his mind was in a flux and stirred by the events of the day which, to say the least, had not been glamorous, and was not, of course, something that he had been proud of.

This is the letter Anande wrote to his wife, before he went back to the front:

August 12, 1969
Dear Raga Jamila,

As regards our last conversation, where I promise to communicate to you my decision with respect to the abhorrent topic of our earlier discussion/conversation, I have decided as follows: Having had the privilege of considering everything with the utmost quietude, permitting deliberate and conscientious reflection, I have decided that, whatever your conduct may be, I do not consider myself sufficiently justified in judging you, let alone officially breaking the ties of which we were tied as husband and wife. It would be foolhardy and disingenuous of me to even try to claim that superior moral rectitude.

Love, especially love between man and woman, is both a divine as well as evolutionary mystery. This means we neither have the right nor the moral justification to break up the family, which is a sacred bond or unit of social organization by any whims, caprice - or even by the sin of infidelity. Neither by both or one of us, as the case may be. This means, in my view, our life has to go on as it has been in the past, with the abiding commitment these out-of-control actions will never happen again. This is important for me as well as for Atompera, our son.

It's my ardent hope and persuasion that you will have repented of this heinous societal transgression. I also hope you will work with me to eradicate, or ameliorate the causes of our estrangement and forget the mistakes of the past. Let's start a new life afresh, a new beginning. I hope we'll have the opportunity to discuss all I have said in this letter face-to-face, if time permits, because I've got to go back to the front as soon as is possible. I therefore implore your indulgence to return to your matrimonial home as swiftly as possible, before I depart for the front, this coming Thursday August 15. I beg you to observe the singular importance I attach to your compliance to my request.
Greet your parents for me.

Yours
Anande

p/s. Enclosed is some money for your transport.

Anande read and re-read the letter through, several times, and felt completely satisfied with it. It was palpably conciliatory, he surmised, there were no harsh, condemnatory or accusatory words, no reproach or undue indulgence in the letter. In his mind he'd obviated, at least he hoped he had, the worst, and, hopefully, had succeeded in bridging a little the gaping chasm between them.

He folded up the letter and called Ayodele Gwar, his cousin, to go hand-deliver it to Raga Jamila, in the village. After about an hour-and-a-half of rough-riding in the only *bolekaja* that served the two small villages, Ayodele arrived at a small, out-of-the-way house, hidden and surrounded by neem and acacia trees, but, instead of going in to deliver the letter in person , he gave it to Lammey, a young boy of about ten, standing around in a brownish tattered shirt and old jeans that had lost their factory color to farm dust and now clearly visible were dried porridge, mango juice and cattle and sheep wastes.

It was about half past six in the evening when the letter was delivered to her. Dusk was gathering in the living room, an early dusk due to the thick *harmattan* outside which had blanketed the whole region. When Raga(Pleasure) was handed the letter by her mother, Ngwakat, who had received it from Lammey, she went into her bedroom leaving the family quarters where she had been with her father, Mara —which, in Buddhist scripture, means the arch-tempter— mother, sister Rati(Desire), son Atompera and Indo, a young female house-help. She locked the door gently and delicately behind her, and, once she was ensconced on her hard wooden bed, opened the envelope with extreme care and slowly started reading it, from the bottom up. The first thing she saw therefore was the ps., "Enclosed is some money for your transport", and a line above that that read; "I attach importance to your compliance to my request". "What an arrogant bastard!" She declared after briefly perusing the letter. This letter, in her mind was a mixed blessing of menu, but more awful than what she had expected.

"He's right!" she said sardonically, "He's always right, he's a Christian, or at least that's what he purports to be, or tries to convey to outsiders! He's generous! Yes, but a vile and base creature! No one understands him like I do, and no one will even try, and yet, I can't explain it! I know he's now laughing for hauling the ashes and throwing that dog-shit at me in this letter! They say he's religious and highly principled, so upright, so clever, so smart, but they don't see what I've seen or had to go through. I've never been a bride, in the true sense of the word. Oh, I'm so sick and tired of pretending this is a home; I never felt it was my home. Everything was done in the cheapest way. Immediately, the morning after our wedding, he was off to his station, there was no talk of going on honeymoon, of just sharing a moment or two together.

People don't know how his constant absence from home has crushed my once-youthful life, crushed everything feminine and physical in me! They don't know how at every step of our journey through this marriage he's humiliated me, has shown no respect and has only been pleased with himself. They don't know that he's nothing but a fucking bag of shit! He's nothing but an execrable libido full of himself. I think him as everything that is amicable and worthy, I greatly esteem him, but I'm tired of his self indulgence and lack of consideration for my feelings in matters that affect this marriage. He'd been content to sit back like a lazy lunk and sponge for the rest of his life until he joined the service...

Nobody knows what I know about him. Nobody knows that he enjoyed gallivanting around with other women of dubious morals while I, his wife, remained lonely, unsatisfied, here at home! Didn't I strive to give meaning to this life of solitude? To find something that give meaning to this marriage other than a child? I struggled to love him, as a wife ought, or should, didn't I love him as a husband? So how then that it's my fault when *he's* the one that left *me* to fend for myself and his son? I know there were periods in my life that people thought I was on the wrong side of tracks, but that's in my past; my skeletons. Isn't it true with everyone when their past lives are scrutinized? Am I not entitled to love just like any woman, despite my past? I know he's doing just what's typical of him and his mean character, taking the high ground. Don't I as a woman deserve love? I have heard it said that women love men even for their vices, but I hate him for his virtues. I know I don't have virtues, am not refined, don't have noble qualities, but I love 'strongly, exclusively and steadfastly'. I'm resilient, I'll put up with a lot. But no! I can no longer live with him". I can no longer cheat myself that I am alive. I am *not* to blame. God has made me, so I must love and live. I know him, he's just trying to do what he always does, keep himself in the right, so people can sympathize with him and praise him, while I remain in ruin! He's always sneering at someone else, always looking for the worst weakness in everyone. Yes, yes, I've lied and flirted before but no more! I can't take it anymore!"

Jamila cringed at the thought of her past lies and dishonesty, sobbed, and wiped her face with the back of her hand, before she continued mumbling guiltily, without resentment;

"I was telling lies all the time against my honor — or what was left of it— and my conscience, but who doesn't? All I wanted was to save this marriage and him, because, even though he hated and despised me, I loved him, so very much - we had a child together! I hate him for his self-professed generosity which was no generosity; there was nothing there for me but....oh god! How many times have I read the judgment in his eyes? "But you came to me yourself..." He hated me. He didn't love me, but married me for cheap, easy sex. He married me for his own greedy selfish ends and for instant purely selfish gratification. He never understood why I married him, and — this is unnerving to me — is capable only of suspecting the basest of motives. I know his obsequiousness and servility are nothing but a mask, and anyway had all but disappeared early on in the relationship and all that remained was this sarcastic and malicious cynic, this twisted sensuality. The spiritual side of his character had been obliterated, while his appetite for life on his terms was quite extraordinary. As a result, he sees nothing now in life but sensual or carnal pleasure. He knows nothing of a husband's responsibilities or a father's responsibilities or the spiritual duties of a man entrusted with a family, as a matter of fact, he laughs at them, if they are (ever) called to his attention! His only philosophy is 'Let the whole world perish in conflagration, I don't care, so long as I'm alright'!"

It is appropriate at this time to save you from the boredom of continual listening to my further narration or transcribing everything she said. Henceforth I'll refrain from further reporting of her analysis verbatim. Suffice to say, I'll leave it to you, my readers, to arrive at your own conclusions about the state of her mind, especially with regards to this long lonesome syllogistic soliloquy.

Suddenly there was a weak rapping on the door. It was her two-year old son Atompera, who was crying. Raga quickly rubbed his face with a handkerchief and pulled herself together, as if everything was quite normal. She opened the door slowly and gently, to attend to her son. She put her arms around Atompera's shoulders with a fond of solicitude which at the same time seemed remote. Her mother, Ngwakat, also peeped in nervously to see why Raga had been inside, alone, for such a long time. She asked her in a casual fluttered tone about the letter and who had sent it to her. Her face contorted with stubborn denial, she told her mother that it was from her husband, Anande. She further told her mother that he was very solicitous in demanding that she "return immediately, the next day".

Jamilla never told her parents the truth about why she had come to them in the first place. She told them instead some story about "the child needing some herbal medicine for his distended stomach which was not readily available in the city".

That evening, after Jamila Raga had put Atompera, her son, to bed, she drew out her dark brown travelling bag, pulling it by its long strap, unzipped it, and retrieved a round blue bottle the size of a small Bayer aspirin bottle or morphine, and taking out four pink pills the size of water-melon seeds swallowed them with a glass of water, and instantly fell asleep.

In her sleep, she dreamt of being in a high-rise building, somewhere in a big city in an unfamiliar country with several other families around her, but, even when she tried especially hard to locate it, she couldn't tell exactly which city or country. In her dream, she saw Anande, her husband, crouched upon his knees genuflecting, asking her, feverishly, for forgiveness. In his hand was a tome, but she couldn't tell — even when she tried by waking in the dream, 'forcing her eyes to open' — whether it was the Holy Bible or the Koran. "Anande, Anande!" She cried, but nothing changed, everything remained quiet and uncannily silent. She rose up in bed and bent forward and yawned, at first, surprise, and then bewilderment came over her, and then as she later put it "my blood crept cold through my veins". Fairly quickly she gained consciousness and found herself drenched in sweat and perched up on the edge of her bed. She had expected to see her husband by her side, his actual physical presence. She couldn't believe that the figure that had been imploring her only a few moments ago was just a mere product of the dream-world, a phantom of her dream-mind.

"On waking, a gleam dazzled my eyes. I thought…oh its daylight, but I was mistaken, it was only the kerosene lamplight flickering very low", she recalled, speaking to Naomi Barau, a friend of hers, a few days later.

She wanted to believe that it was true that he had begged forgiveness of her, and, indeed, convinced herself that it was so, but everything remained the same, until she started to recall some of the more memorable, happier, moments that they had had together, like the time that he took her to *Albarkacinku*, a store on Ahmadu Bello Way and told her to pick anything that she fancied, and that he would settle the bill. At first, she had expressed her objections, furtively whispering in his ear, because the attendants were watching, but he had insisted. Despite considerable resistance she was persuaded finally, and she picked three relatively expensive samples of lace materials one white, one red and one maroon, two pairs of genuine English wax *attampa zannuwa* —wrap-around— and a pair of moderately expensive black shoes, and he had paid for the whole thing without the slightest grudge. She also recalled the time she had had her baby. He had been outside in the waiting room for more than five hours because he wasn't allowed in the delivery room with her, and, as she remembered it, her water wouldn't break that easily. She was then, and, indeed, still was, proud of his resolve to wait, because most of her friends' husbands didn't even bother to go to the hospital when the time came for their wives to give birth. Most of them visited hours after the delivery, and never stayed for the event itself but were merely shown their babies for a few moments by the caring but always overly-zealous nurses. She remembered that not all of the men went back after the two or three days of rest and recuperation to bring their wives and their baby infant home. He, by contrast, had waited patiently to see his infant child *before* he went away! And he was there all the time for the two days that she was in the hospital and thoughtfully took her and their new son home by himself; instead of sending a friend or a driver. She also recalled that he personally gave her, her first warm bath when she arrived home. This was an extraordinary thing for him to do, because Nigerian society didn't expect a man to bathe his wife, no matter what the circumstances. In the instance of a childbirth, either the woman's or the man's mother would, traditionally, be around to perform such functions. In her view, these sporadic and limited but truly happy moments when he showed her genuine affection trumped every shortcoming that he might indeed have. Consequently, she decided, without any further reservations that she was going to return and try to give their marriage a second chance.

A day before Anande's return to the war front and hours before Raga came back; his aunt Susan Uchafu visited him to find out what had actually happen and to offer him her support.

"Dear nephew", she said "you ought not to give way or continue to grieve for what has happened. Your sorrow is, indeed, a great one, but you ought to find some consolation and forgive her".

"I know, I know, he replied, but, as *you* know, a man's strength has its limits and I've reached my limits, what else can I do?"

"You must thank Him, call on Him, in Him alone we find peace, consolation, salvation, and, yes, love", she replied, standing up, ready to leave.

"Susan, I'm very, very grateful to you for coming here and offering your words of comfort", he said.

"Early disillusionment, early betrayal and fall, the treachery of her lover who jilted her, then poverty and the curse of all that, might, perhaps, have turned her into a bitter woman, filled with a morbid grudge and hate towards not only individuals but society as a whole", Susan speculated.

Anande didn't quite understand all of what Susan said, but thanked her anyway.

Raga returned to her husband that evening and they made up surprisingly quickly, and shared their intimate love and future aspirations together, amicably. Neither of them brought up the subject of her infidelity or his ever again. Not even the pained letter that he had written to her was ever further discussed. They both summoned up their inner courage and vowed to comfort each other lovingly, and promised each to the other that they would try to avoid any repetition of such occurrences in the future. They further promised a 'new beginning' in their marriage. But would it be? Could they actually sustain it?

The following morning, Anande took off and headed back to his to sector, a happy and renewed man, full of spirit and hope.

He arrived just forty eight hours before the strategically significant Battle of Nsukka.

He thanked his GOC for giving him the time off to go settle some of his most urgent family problems, promising to give him his all now in the forthcoming battle. Prior to resumption of battle he presented the GOC with a letter. "Sah", I may not survive the coming battle", he said, "may you please hand-deliver this letter to my mother in case…and tell her that I love her, but that I love my country even more…. To my wife just tell her, that I've forgiven her all that has happened". But has Anande truthfully forgiven his wife at end of the war?

Anande survived the battle with little more than a few minor injuries on his legs. He was hit on the left leg and the shinbone was crushed. Three days after the battle and two days after his broken leg was put in a cast, he retrieved the letter he had handed over to his commanding officer without ever divulging its contents. As we shall see later, Anande went on to distinguish himself in the battle for Nsukka and proved both to himself and to others, including his immediate commanding battalion officer, Major Bohuk that he was no push-over. Anande's gallant performance exceeded anybody's expectations, including his own, and he was given a field promotion to the rank of Sergeant Major (WO11) as well as a gold medal for "gallantry which exceeds the call of duty". It was only appropriate and deservingly so, that, years later, after the war, Lieutenant-Colonel Patrick S. Anande was awarded the National Honor of the Officer of the Order of the Federal Republic (OFR) by then President Shehu.

Disposition for the battle for Nsukka

On returning from a full inspection of the disposition of the battle, drawn up by himself (GOC Shuwa) and his two battalion commanders, Wushishi, the commander of the 21 Battalion and Bukar, the commander of the 22 Battalion. Lieutenant Unateze was assigned the 234 company to lead the initial reconnaissance and attack. The plan, as conceived by the GOC and his two most senior commanders, was a model of perfection. They had assigned three mechanized companies at the center, two Racce companies, from the 22 Battalion, on the right flank, and three armored and infantry companies on the left. The disposition of these forces for the battle of Nsukka, code-named, *Operation Kunama (scorpion)*, was more than satisfying for the GOC.

Reassured, Shuwa returned to his quarters and ordered some orange juice. The following day he sent for the guardsman, Lieutenant Batatunde, and began talking to him about certain changes in the battle plans to be implemented.

Uncharacteristic of the GOC, that day, of all days, he showed some lingering interest in trifles and jested with Batatunde about his wife's passion for travel overseas and shopping and how expensive it was to maintain her lifestyle, what with the salary he was receiving! He chatted casually as if he were a celebrated, self-assured and practiced surgeon. "I have everything under control", he mused, referring to the war plan. "It's all precise in my head. When the hour comes to implement it, I shall perform as no one else could ever have done. But, right now, I can jest, because, the more I jest, the calmer, more serene and confident I become. I presume such confidence ought to be one constituent of genius", he concluded on a somber yet assured note. The Lieutenant accepted his GOC's views without any reservations and assured him of his complete and unconditional confidence in his military genius.

After this exchange, the GOC went in to rest before the gargantuan task which awaited him next day. He was so preoccupied with what lay ahead that notwithstanding his assurances of a deep serenity to the Lieutenant, he was unable to sleep, even after taking a strong anti-colds potion or preparation as a treatment for a cold which had been exacerbated by the humid weather and the evening damp, he just tossed and turned in bed.

He got up at about three in the morning and hastily got dressed and ran out to his barely-lit porch where a single kerosene lamp was left on the porch for security reasons, loudly belched and blew his nose. Outside, it was fresh and dewy. A bright clear day, he thought. The sun had just burst from behind a cloud that had obscured it, and its rays refracted through rifts in the clouds, splashing over the leaves of the surrounding foliage, over the dewy-flecked dust of the dirt road. The noise of the big guns sounded more distinct and threatening now than ever.

The adjutant on duty that evening was Captain Sule Kambari and he came in to the quarters and asked the GOC if he needed anything, but the GOC replied that he was fine.

"Do you think we shall succeed today?" he asked Sule Kambari.

"Yes sir, without any doubt!" The adjutant answered, standing straight up like a silhouette of him.

The General stared at his adjutant, and then said,

"Our boys have always done what is asked of them with distinction, but I'm afraid they are tired, especially after the battles at Enugu and the scattered villages around it", he mentioned some lesser encounters at places like, Obudu, Garkem, Ogoja, Akpugo, Abakpa and Obiagu. "We have diminished a little but the armored and the Recce regiments are still fully intact are they not?"

"Yes, sir", Kambari responded, in not-quite-so reassuring voice which the General quite clearly noticed but chose to ignore.

The General sat down calmly and took something from his side pocket and put it in his mouth, grabbing a glass of water, he sipped. But none of this did any good. He was not still sleepy, and the morning was still a long way off, and there were no other orders he could give just for the sake of "passing time". All the important orders that could be given to ensure success had been issued with apt precision and all nuances considered and amended where, and if, necessary, and it was all being, or had been, executed with the outmost diligence and attention.

"Has all the ammunition been distributed to all units—infantry, armored…?" he enquired.

"Yes, Sah!"

"It is imperative that all hands are on board and ready to perform to and beyond the call of duty".

"Yes Sir, the orders and battle dispositions are crystal clear to every Officer, NCOs and the rank and file", the Captain explained.

"Excellent", the GOC replied.

"I can neither taste nor smell", he confided to his adjutant, sniffing at the glass placed on his small side-table. "I'm sick with cold. They talk of… medicine…What's the good of these "medicines" any way? They prescribe them to you, you take them, following the prescription-instructions methodically, but they can't even cure a simple common cold! Lieutenant Colonel Aluo (Division Physician) gave me these useless tablets which were supposed to relieve the nasal congestion but, kaput, nothing! What can they cure?—nothing! Our body, you know, is a teleological friggin' living machine. It's organized for it, that's its nature. Let life go on unhindered, let it protect itself. It will do so much more by itself than if you paralyze it by glutting it with remedies. Don't you know that our body is like a clock, meant to go on for certain time? The maker (if there is one) cannot open it; he can only fumble with it as if masked in a blindfold. Our life is a teleological machine for living, as well - that's all". The General stops suddenly after positing his inane philosophy of life and biology and its minutiae idiosyncrasies to his adjutant the morning of an important battle that will make or break the backbone of the rebel revolt.

"I guess it is part of our fallible human nature to meditate with deep thoughts and concern about events whose outcomes are not certain to us", alhaji Abba observed and James concurred.

"Yes this seems to be an apt observation because this General was one of our greatest, but still showed some palpable concern, his fallibility, by not being able to sleep, and by jokes to help divert his attention from the all-important impending battle that awaited him", Golu observed and was seconded in his thoughts by Owoleye and *Mamu*, respectively.

"Do you know", the General began again, "what military science or art consists of?" He asked his adjutant. Before the adjutant could answer, he said "it's the art of being stronger and smarter than your enemy at any given moment, and that's all".

Adjutant Kambari nodded, almost reverentially, but said nothing.

"Tomorrow, we shall have the rebel boys to mow down like stalks of green corn in the field. We shall give them hell, a hell they will never forget!"

He whispered loud enough for Kambari to hear.

He glanced at his watch and also looked at the clock on the wall. It was only four o'clock. He still felt no desire to sleep, the juice was finished, and there was nothing left to do. He got up and paced to-and-fro', around the room, and then put on his military hat, and went out again to the porch and looked up at the clear open sky with the moon up above at its zenith. Nearby, he could see the outline and the camp fires of his Division units. All seemed to be quiet and still, but for the rustle and the deft maneuvering tap of his soldiers, who were already moving in forward formations, which was clearly audible to him.

The General paced up-and-down on his porch, continuing to survey the fires and listening to the shuffle of random feet; then he went in and dressed in his military combat uniform. When he emerged, in his splendid medal-bedecked war uniform, he passed Corporal Dogonyaro, a tall six-foot shaggy guardsman, who had relieved Captain Kambari on duty, near his quarters. The Corporal drew himself up straight, like a black wooden pillar and saluted, "Sah!"

The General glanced at the guardsman with an affectation of military bluff and studied geniality but, not looking at him directly, asked, "What year did you join the service, Corporal?" The guardsman was confused, because he didn't expect the General would have any interest in him as a person, but composed himself, stood erect as dead wood, and answered him in a firm voice.

"Ah! An old campaigner! Served in Congo? Burma?"

"Congo and Sierra Leone and Liberia, Sah!" He answered, in a firm but respectful tone, again commensurate with an old soldier used to receiving orders. The General moved on without a further comment or glance. The guardsman sighed and let his guard down momentarily and resumed his diligent watch.

On the first day of battle, the 22 Battalion Commander, Bukar; his mortar platoon Commander, Muhammad Magoro and the Regimental Sergeant Major (RSM), Oyedele Balagun, were all wounded, when a shell mortar was dropped on their headquarters. Significant though each of these men were, these commanding vacancies were immediately filled up with capable officers from the Division.

By the evening of the second day, the troops had assembled in their assigned places, and, during the night, had even made some modest advanced movements. It was the rainy season and the night was pitch-black but there was no rain. Though the ground was damp, it was not muddy, and the troops moved noiselessly, except for the occasional faint clanking of artillery. The men, as is often the tradition of the military were forbidden to talk aloud, to smoke, or strike a match. By early morning, the big guns were pounding the city, and artillery fire was even said to have hit the house of Dr. Nnamdi Azikiwe, one of the famous politicians at the time, but, of course, he wasn't inside, nobody was inside, it had been vacated days previously. To be precise, it had been evacuated exactly three days before. By daytime, most of the residents, including the rebel forces had packed and retreated into the bushes for safety. Many were said to have packed only few things, in a hurry, because they didn't believe the Federal troops had the where-withal to capture the city. And certainly in not such a short space of time! The Federal troops had swiftly and successfully surrounded the city and occupied many key points including most of the Government buildings in the environs outside the city proper.

The General nodded in satisfaction to his Brigade commander, Wushishi, and sauntered, or rather ambled off to his vehicle, with the measured and deliberate steps of a successful and elated military commander. Still conscious though of the final battle to take and occupy the city, and all of its environs.

Three days later, the sun had just burst forth from behind a cloud that had obscured it. Its rays, refracted through rifts in the clouds, spread generously over the distant huts, far deep into the thick forest, and over the dew-flecked dust of the roads and the roadside-grasses and leaves. It was exactly five a.m. and the General drove off to the next battle scene in his adorned military jungle combat regalia; in short all his military finery. He had always had a morbid interest and obsession with how his uniform looked, crisp and straight. The battle took less than three hours of furious exchanges, after which the rebel forces, as before, scattered in utter disarray, into the forest, after suffering heavy losses in manpower and materials.

"Well done lads!" Lieutenant Colonel Unateze barked to his armored battalion.

The final onslaught came five days later, when the General, again, stood in his vehicle and barked out commands for the resumption of battle to his Brigade commander, who passed them on to the other subordinate commanding officers and RMSs. The final battle skirmish with the still-determined enemy took place in the vicinities of Obodo Ururu and Ajamee Uno and the surrounding areas. As he drove out he could hear artillery shots booming on the right (in the direction of Oruku and Amagunze,) which would die away momentarily in a temporary prevailing silence. Several minutes passed before he heard a second, followed rapidly by a third, a fourth then a fifth, all in rapid succession. The first shots- *poof!* - *Poof!* - had not yet ceased vibrating, when the others followed, in unison *boom!—boom!—boom!* Mingling with the big guns and overtaking one another. *The boom!—boom!—boom!* Of artillery and the *tarat-ta-tat!-tarat-ta-tat,* of the rifles sounded more distinctly now.

After a heroic encounter with the remnant of the rebel forces and the maintenance throughout of strategic intelligence from the General and his unit commanders, Wushishi and his men entered Nsukka, where they were rapturously received. The rebels had been routed with heavy casualties, and

Araba Let's Separate

the prisoners were brought down from the field, among them a few rebel officers—Colonel Okwenze and Major Effee and their men, who were surrounded by the proud and gallant Federal troops. The artillery and Recee regiments on this occasion performed extraordinarily, and deserve a special mention.

As the General went around visiting the prisoners, he recognized several officers from "the good old days" who he had served with in the Congo and had shared jokes with in the mess hall (Colonel Njokwu, Colonel Effeogwu, Lieutenant Colonel Akwapwu, Major Francis, Major Mbanifu, Lieutenant Ezeku, and others, but there were also many he didn't know. At the end of the line, next to the trench, was a young rebel officer, still slumped over, twitching and wriggling, but nobody bothered to prop him up or relieve him of his suffering. He must have been crazed with thirst and bewildered by the sheer amount of gun-fire ricocheting back-and- forth across the ground around him before he expired. Later, he was identified as a Major - I think Efujuna was the name, if my memory serves me right, one of the prime January 15 plotters. No, that Major was one of several hanged by Ojukwu for planning a coup against him, together with Major Banjo also a participant in the January 15 debacle. The name was Major *Kaduna*, the coup leader of January 15. Next to the Major was a corpse that was later identified as being that of Tom Bigger, Ojukwu's half brother. There were other senior rebel officers killed as well; and some were found, can you believe it? With their rations of the day's *gari* and three cubes of sugarstill in their pouches untouched!

Later, it was revealed that the leader of the coup plotters, Major Kaduna, had indeed been killed by the men of the 21 Battalion when he tried to ambush them, by sneaking out on a night reconnaissance mission with the rebels. From what was later reported after the war, he was buried with full-scale military honors! Can you imagine? Military honors for a guy who was planning on killing as many Federal troops as he could? How do you explain the sort of capricious and muddled logic, that prevailed in granting him a full-scale ceremonial military burial, this, after all the havoc that he had already caused to the country! It does indeed boggle the mind, and every ordinary Nigerian's sensitivity.

After the capture of Enugu the GOC, Shuwa had addressed the population *inter alia*, and he repeated the same address, with minor modifications, after the fall of Nsukka:

You peaceable inhabitants of Nsukka, artisan workmen and

farmers, misfortune has driven you out of your beloved city, but I advise you now to come back to your dwellings and you will be protected. Any violence perpetrated against you will be punished with the maximum power granted the GOC under powers of war by the Supreme Military Council. The Commander-in-Chief, General Yakubu Gowon, wants me to assure you that he wants to put a quick end to your adversity and restore to you your homes and families and anything else you might have lost in any part of this great country of ours.

Farmers and workmen and all civil servants, come out of the forests where you have been hiding in fear and terror, return to your huts and houses without fear, in absolute surety of absolute and guaranteed protection by the Federal Government; whoever you are and wherever you are, hand in your guns and ammunition to your Administrator, Mr. Asika, who has been appointed by the Commander-in-Chief, Gowon. Direct all of your complaints and requests to him. The Commander-in-Chief does not see you as enemies, except those of you who disobey his orders, by refusing to accept the twelve-state Federal structure of our Republic, and, in so doing, plunge our country into this cruel and senseless war. Even then, if they should denounce their arrogance and accept the twelve- state Federal structure, will be summarily forgiven. Even though in their arrogance and in a blind grab for power, they decided to take up arms against the Federal troops of the Republic… I implore you, once again, to lay down your arms and come out of hiding from your houses and dwellings… Long live one indivisible Nigeria…"

Strange to say, all these assurances, which were in no way deceitful promises, had no apparent effect upon the hearts of the populace, just as had been the case in the Enugu petitioning.

One of the locals, by the name of Mr. Ezek, was appointed an overseer by Mr. Asika, the Chief Administrator of the state, through consultation with the Federal Government, to run the local affairs of the city and its environs.

There was one interesting event that happened during this time which I deem it appropriate to acquaint you my readers to it. There was a dog which Captain Zang found loitering between Chime Avenue and Emene

Road during one of his normal evening patrols. The dog probably belonged to somebody who had run out of the city in a hurry, fearing the ferocious attacks and continuous bombardment of the Federal troops. The dog had no name, so Captain Zang and his colleagues just called it "Floppy", others just called it "Gray" because of its most salient color. The fact that it belonged to nobody and didn't have a name, or any distinguishable color, did not seem to trouble the dog in the least. Its floppy tail stood up erect. Its bandy legs served it so well that, often, as though disdaining to use all four, it would gracefully lift one hind leg and quickly and nimbly run along on the remaining three! Everything was a source of complete satisfaction to it. Sometimes it would roll on its back with its four legs lifted up high in the air, yapping with unbridled delight, at other times, it would bask in the sun, thoughtfully as if it were concentrating on getting a sun tan, or it would play around with a chip of wood, or a piece of a pebble, like a human infant. There were times where it attempted wild somersaults, as if it were a frisky cat. It was, indeed, something to behold! Sergeant Adamu wanted to take it along with them, as a kind of mascot, perhaps, but he was persuaded not to. After the war, it was alleged, and later confirmed, that Mr. Anthony Asika, the Administrator of the East-Central State, had adopted it, naming it "Floppy". Many of the soldiers spoke of this with, hilarity, laughter and amusement after the war.

At this time, the GOC of the First Division, M.Shuwa experienced the utmost privation that man can ever endure. Its causes could have been two-fold: either because of the loss of one of his trusted, gallant, and reliable Majors, Major Waltinafa, or, it could have been perhaps due to , less specific influences of "war fatigue syndrome". But thanks to his good health and strong physical constitution, of which he had hardly been aware up until then, and still could not believe he hadn't mercifully, hit rock bottom. The deprivation came upon him gradually, so gradually that it was impossible to say precisely when it began. However, most who knew of his relationships with the fallen Major say, with assurance and some conviction that it occurred almost immediately after his death. By this time he seemed to have attained that serenity and inner bliss for which he had so long been vainly striving. In the course of his adventurous life he had sought, in various ways, that inner peace of mind, that inner harmony, which had so impressed him in the soldiers when they march side-by-side, in lock-step, a scene he had first witnessed as a youngster growing up in the suburbs of Kano city. Now, without so much as a struggle, he had found transcendence, possibly through the horror of the death of a dear colleague and friend.

His friends and those close to him tried in vain to find a succor to mitigate his melancholia but without success. He would sit in his quarters alone, for hours on end, without seeing anyone or uttering a single word to his staff. All that occupied his mind at those times were the war's senseless deaths, the sufferings, the brutal executions. These meditations and numerous more on like subjects had, as it were, washed forever from his imagination and memory the thoughts and feelings that had formerly seemed of paramount importance to him. He now sought, and agonized in, solitude and isolation, and nothing seemed to matter to him anymore.

The GOC's own personal feeling of self-justification regarding all that he had done - successfully - in the persecution of the war, including all of its moral implications, was aptly reinforced by the opinion his fellow soldiers, and, for that matter, the opinion that the general public, formed of him after any of his numerous exploits. His gentleness to his officers and the ranks, and his great physical strength, which he demonstrated to his troops on numerous occasions, endeared and earned him their respect, to the point of them becoming almostreverential.

The following is a sample letter the GOC received in this period of deep and abiding sorrow:

May 28, 1969
To The First Division GOC,

Sorrow, it seems is our beneficent lot in this senseless and vain war we've been fighting. Your loss, and indeed the loss of many able-bodied and brave soldiers, is so terrible and painful a thing that I can only explain it, through my own experience, as a sign of the grace of Him who created us or from the place where we evolved, if one accepts that theory of evolution. On January 15, 1967 I lost a dear childhood friend - la illaha il Allah, Muhammad u rasul ullah, (there is no God but Allah and Muhammad is His messenger) - to the war on the Calabar front. This young man was fresh from an artillery officers' course in India and wasn't even officially assigned to a "Theatre/Sector" or Division yet, when "the Black Scorpion" snatched him from the balcony of a Lagos hotel and exposed him immediately without riposte to a fatal ambush by the enemy, the following day. He died, instantly, without ever having had the opportunity to see his parents or fiancée, and after having been away for almost two years. What a loss! What a tragedy! I was one of those who accompanied his body home. You should have seen the agony and the anger on the faces of the villagers. They all mourned him and fulminated against a war that didn't seem to have an end in sight. A war that, we were told earlier by some of our Northern leaders, wouldn't be lasting supposedly more than forty-eight hours!

In view of everything going on around us, it is pertinent to assert that religion - I hope that you still believe in Allah, in spite of the killings and all the sufferings that you see around you! -Religion alone, at this time of suffering and reflection, is our lone, our one solace - inshallah. In my humble opinion, only religion can help explain to us what, without its help, men cannot possibly comprehend the fullness of, or dimensions of, limited in our scope as mere mortals. For instance, why, and for what purpose, do good and noble people so often die early? Or often, are unable to find happiness in this purely temporal life? From my skewed observation and experience, such noble souls, I've noticed are usually people who have not only, never harmed anybody of their own volition or instincts, but who are also indeed necessary to the happiness of others. Such are the ones called away to Allah - innalallahi wa inna illaihirraji un (from Allah we are and we are going back to him) *- especially at such critical moments of national catastrophe and forbearance, to keep this our beloved country as one and indivisible. This is why the wicked, the greedy, the mean and the malign amongst us are left to live and even left to prosper!*

The first death I saw in this war made an indelible mark on my conscience, reawakening me as to the futility and utterly barbarous nature of this friggin' war; of all fuc'n wars!

I urge you, as a colleague and a friend, to put this loss, gross as it is, behind you, and just immerse yourself in devotional prayer (if you still believe that there is someone out there listening) with the hope and joy that you would both mentally and spiritually be relieved of the burdens and wickedness of this blasphemous world through Allah's saving power, inshallah.

Ranka shi dade oga,

Wa salam,
Colonel Sadique Haliru; (5 battalion, 2nd Div.)

The Second Theatre/Division

"The GOC of the Second Division, General Muhammed", Alhaji said, "was a tall giant of a man, light in complexion, very friendly and affable in his private life, but a heck of a disciplinarian and very scrupulous to details. He was a "stickler", what we might call "a soldier's soldier"'. As a commander, he was very stern and completely results-oriented, but very humorous, humane and easy-going with his subordinates. He did his best to accommodate them their needs, fears and concerns. And they reciprocated by giving him their all in battle, fighting even beyond the call of duty.

The military theatre of operation of the 2nd Division included the former Mid-Western region (constituting of the present Delta, Imo, Bendel and Bayelsa, States). As alluded to earlier in the story, the Division was haphazardly created, after the incursion into the Mid-West by the rebel troops. It comprised of the 6 Brigade, under the command of Akinrinade, 8 Brigade, commanded by Francis, and 7 Brigade under the command of Ally. Ibadan was designated the rear, under the command of Olu. The bulk of the fighting force at Lagos and Ibadan comprised of the Second Brigade. The rest were clerks, cooks, stragglers and pensioners", Alhaji Wada paused.

"The initial Military Operational Directives specified that: 7 Brigade would clear Ore and advance to Benin, while the 6 and 7 Brigades moved northwards through the Western state, south of Okene, and advanced southwards on Benin. The two axes would converge on Benin. The 63 battalion of the 6 Brigade, under the capable command of Joradam, was to form the main thrust, followed closely by the 61 and 11 Battalions. However, the movement of the 7 Brigade was seriously hampered by the destruction of the bridges on the Owena River, between Ore and Ofusu. They were unable to make any further advance until the arrival of the rest of the second Division force in Benin, whereupon the rebels were rounded and dealt a harsh and critical blow".

The Alhaji paused to answer a question from one of the members.

"In a sense, the real war, other than minor skirmishes, actually started in the former Mid-West, as the Biafran rebels began harassing the many towns and villages, like Agbor, Ozoro, and so forth, along their common borders, to the point of sheer intolerability. The Division was created to give support to the police action already ordered and taking place around such border towns as Gakem and Nsukka.

The following is the GOC's address, given to all of his Staff officers, Battalion Commanders, NCOs and soldiers before *Operation Kan Giwa* (Operation Elephant's Head),that developed into the battle of Benin/Ore, April, 196---. The GOC, Muhammed, paused to clear his throat, adjusted his side arms and read the following address to the group with great passion and conviction:

"Soldiers! The Biafran army is advancing against you to avenge their most recent heavy losses. But you should know that these are the same battalions that you have already defeated and inflicted immense casualties upon, and which, ever since, you have been pursuing, up to this point. Our position on the hill is a stronger and impregnable one. If they try to advance to our right flank, they will expose their left flank to our indomitable Recce battalion soldiers, and if they try to penetrate from the right flank, our ferocious artillery will annihilate them, before they make any advance at all. Furthermore, our centre is well guarded by the formidable Burma Infantry Battalion, under Major Yakasai.

Colonel Zakari will lead you. I, meanwhile, will keep out of the range of fire and if you, with your customary decisive valor, bring about disorder and confusion among the enemy ranks, I won't have to join in. However, if victory seems oblique and in any way in doubt, even for an instant, you will see me your Commanding General expose myself to the first provocations and blows of the enemy; for there must never… be any uncertainty of victory!"

He paused to wipe, with his handkerchief, the sweat that was now profusely dripping down his face as a result of the stifling heat and humidity, and then continued:

"Do not break ranks with the custom of retrieving the wounded or the dead. Let every man be imbued thoroughly with the thought that we must defeat these rugged Biafran rebels! It would be unfortunately remiss on my account, and a shirking of my professional command responsibility, if I didn't remind you of the oath you all took when this war began, (It's a select part of the US Army Ranger's creed, which in part says).

"Never shall I fail my comrades. I will always keep myself mentally alert, physically strong, and morally straight, and I will shoulder my share of the task,

whatever it may be, one hundred percent, and then some. Gallantly will I show the world that I am a specially selected and well trained soldier. My courtesy to superior officers, neatness of dress, and care of equipment shall set the example for others to follow. Energetically will I meet the enemies of my country. I shall defeat them on the field of battle for I am better trained and will fight with all my might. Surrender is not a Ranger word. I will never leave a fallen comrade to fall into the hands of the enemy and under no circumstances will I ever embarrass my country......" and so help me the most benevolent.

He then continued; "this victory today may not conclude this war, but will go a long way in ending hostilities on the other fronts, and, of course, after this, they will never want to face us again! Only following such decisive victory will we conclude an armistice that properly deserves of your heroism, gallantry and of the heroism and gallantry of the peoples of the Federal Republic. Long live the Federal Republic! Forward ever in Unity for Indivisible One Nigeria! Hip! Hip…"!

And the undiminished rapturous response which echoed through the surrounds was an emphatic *Hurrah... Horay!... Horay!*

"That was an inspiring motivational speech", Aminu commented.

"Indeed it was, especially since it was delivered before an important battle, upon which a lot depended", Professor Balarabe agreed.

"Alright, let's continue, it's getting late", the Alhaji declared and resumed his narrative.

Operation Kan Giwa(Operation Elephant's Head), was one of the first important battles fought to deny the rebels an advance into Ibadan, and, most likely, Lagos. The battle of Ore was fought within a confined area between the towns of Onitsha and Edo hill. It was in a thick valley, where the Federal troops had positioned themselves on a hilly area and the rebel forces below in the dip of the valley however, it was open enough for both sides to see each other.

The wind had subsided, and black storm clouds hung low over the Benin/Ore/Onitsha front, merging with a light rain on the horizon. Darkness was falling, and in at least two places located on an escarpment the glow of conflagration grew more and more distinct. The patrol, led by Major Gadzama, stopped for a moment to analyze the situation before them, and then decided to continue, no matter what the consequences to their persons.

The previous night the GOC had taken out a thick black notebook from his desk, while in his quarters with his most senior officers, and sketched a plan for the deposition of the troops for *Operation Kan Giwa*. In two places he made notes of points that he intended mentioning to Lieutenant Alagali. First, he proposed concentrating all the artillery company under Major Gadzama in the center, and, secondly, to withdraw the mechanized battalion to the other side of the ravine".

The Alhaji stopped suddenly, because Owoleye had stood up to go. He had to leave to prepare for his sermon, the following Sunday, at the Evangelical EbenezaTrinity Church of the Savior, where he was the senior Pastor.

And it seemed that he was not the only person there who had some errands to run. Jamima and Jummai also indicated they had to rush to the market before it closed. In view of this they all, unanimously, decided to stop right then and to resume the following weekend. Meanwhile, Dr. Khan and his wife, Veronica, distributed the recently-printed-up wedding-invitation cards to their cousin's marriage that was scheduled to take place in a fortnight's time in the village of Awume-Logos in Ohimini Local Government some two hundred miles away.

"The military plan for the capture of Benin involved the participation of the 3 Battalion marine commandos", the professor resumed. "Lieutenant Colonel Obia Ochefu was ordered by the marine GOC to clear the riverine areas of the Mid-West with the 6, 31, and 32 Battalions, and to link up with the 2nd division in Benin, instead of the planned operation of the 3 Battalion marine commandos advancing on to Calabar. The GOC joined the link-up in person at Benin", Professor Balarabe added, before they all departed.

"Meantime the 6 and 7 Brigades had had a hand-to-hand battle with rebel forces *before* their capture of Asaba", James added as a note of information and a final observation.

When they resumed the following week, after some exchange of gossip, pleasantries and highly-private scoops — such as the conviction of the Chairman of the Konshiha Local Government and the installation of the Emirs of Viu, Iyaya and Kwande — garnered over the week-end; the Alhaji cleared his throat, belched, thanked everybody for sharing their personal week-end experiences, and then continued:

"The battle began on both sides with fierce artillery-fire exchanges. With the entire valley immersed in smoke, two of our battalions advanced on the rebels, Major Akpam's armored company approached from the right that is, viewed from the troops' perspective) and Lieutenant Colonel Barau's Recce's battalion, from the left. The idea was to encircle them and get a quick surrender. But it wasn't to be. The rebels had their own strategic plan which they had hoped likewise execute with stunning precision and thus bring deadly results for the Federal troops.

The main thrust of the rebel army was about five miles away, in a valley at the bottom of a small hill from where the GOC was stationed, half way up in the mid-section of the Aureko hill. The town of Mosogai was about ten miles to the South, as the crow flies, consequently the General could not see what was happening there, especially since the smoke, mingling with soft rain, hid the whole area from his view. The rebel soldiers were visible only when they tried to maneuver around the hill in an attempt to gain higher ground. However, they weren't given the opportunity to gain higher ground; they were pinned down in the ravine and met with guns and heavy-armor pounding. The smoke from these bombardments obscured the entire slope on the farther side where the rebels were attempting their ascent, but were denied.

Through the smoke it was, at times, possible to catch an occasional glimpse of something black moving, probably men, or just possibly, the glint of guns. But whether they were moving or stationary, whether Federal troops or rebel soldiers, nobody could tell from where the GOC was stationed, and this greatly frustrated the General, causing him to curse and complain thus under his breath; "Shit! What a terrible thing war is! I pray that one day mankind will find a sensible way of settling disputes and manage to avoid it at all costs! The politicians mustn't be allowed to expose our young men and women to an ugly and early death through their folly, arrogance and selfish irrational, myopic and, execrable ambitions! They must be forced to learn to sublimate their personal greed for power and glory or history for living and life!"

The rising tropical sun burst with vengeance from the clouds above, with immense brightness, and shone straight into the General's eyes, even though he tried to shade them with his free hand, while hugging his side-arms with the other. The smoke from the ravine hung over them constantly. At times it looked like as if it were only the smoke moving, at other times it looked as if it were the troops that were moving. From time to time, a shot would ring out in rapid succession until the entire ravine was engulfed and became killing-field. But, it was impossible to know precisely who was being shot at! It was even more confusing to know who had the upper hand. In short nobody knew what was going on down there!

Standing on the hill he looked down with his binoculars into the ravine, where he discerned men, sometimes his men, sometimes opposition, rebel, troops. He descended to a knoll on the hill and began pacing up-and-down, listening to more sounds of the ominous heavy artillery coming from the smoke-filled and clouded battlefield.

What worried the General was the fact that it was impossible to know exactly what was happening down there, especially from his vantage-point. For a period of several hours amid incessant artillery and gun-fire power, one could, at times, see a Federal soldier alone, at times a rebel soldier alone, now an infantry, now an armored vehicle; each force fighting for a vantage position where eventually the two forces met with such ferocity of force, at times scarcely not knowing what to do with one another because of their proximity.

From the Battlefield Adjutants and Staff Officers that the General had sent out; would constantly come reports of the progress of the battle; but all were questionable and probably false because it was really impossible to know what was going on in the heat of the battle, in part because of poor communication. In addition the situations or positions were very fluid and changeable within minutes.

Another reason was that many of the Adjutants did not go to the actual area of intense action for fear of being shot, but merely repeated what they had heard others say or reports from people who had been injured and who had left the battlefield an hour or so previously. As a matter of fact, by the time the Adjutants reached where the GOC was stationed, circumstances had changed dramatically and the news delivered to him was no longer relevant or valid. For instance, an Adjutant came running-and-puffing in, claiming that Major Oporoma of the rebel's Third Infantry Company had been captured and was now in Federal hands, but before he could turn his back to go, another Adjutant contradicted him, saying that it wasn't so, that, in fact, they said Major had escaped! Another came, running almost, pale and distraught, to report that the rebels were having an upper hand, after which the General ordered his Adjutants and Staff Officers to get ready and join him on the battlefield. But it also turned out he didn't have the correct assessment of the most current situation on the battle-field!

However, what *was* true, at this point, was that the federal troops had broken into the rebel center and were beginning to cause real deadly havoc and military victory. The General was consequently advised not to join. "It's almost over!" shouted his Staff Officer, Jalo contradicting an earlier officer.

Eventually, after one of the most intense battles of the entire campaign, the insatiable ambitions of the rebel forces were stalled, if only temporary. A large portion of Benin was liberated, but the rebel forces were still active in several isolated sectors.

It is no secret to those under his command that General Muhammed always liked to visualize the entire picture of the impending course of his military operations in his mind, in its broad outline, the evening before "the big dance", as he called it. He would always imagine large-scale possibilities, speculating as follows: "If the enemy launches an attack on the right flank, the Recce will hold their positions until the armored company in the center pounce with deadly force to finish them up! In the event that they lay attack on the center, we shall release and advance the mechanized Corps, from the left flank, and annihilate them!"

As he pondered these battle-plans for Ore/Onitsha, some of the officers and the NCOs in the adjacent tent were whispering among themselves about the next day's up-coming battle.

"No, Sah", Captain Guar heard Corporal Libbeh declare "I say that if it were possible to know for certain what is beyond death, none of us would be afraid. That's so, my friend".

"Afraid or not, there's no escaping it", countered Captain Guar.

"But isn't one always afraid? Oh, you most learned men!" Major Alack rejoined addressing both Libbeh and Guar

"Of course, you artillery men are very clever, you can take everything along with you", Captain Zakkah said jokingly.

An infantry NCO standing close by burst out laughing.

"Yes, one is always friggin' scared."Corporal Libbeh jumped in,

"One is always scared of the unknown" the corporal continued, "that's what it is. It is part of our evolutionary history to fear the unknown, that's the initial motivation for the mysterious rise of the worship of, first, the inanimate forces of nature, including thick forests, clouds moving across the sky obscuring the moon, ancestral spirits, the sun, *Shamanism*, and, only later, "'god or gods". No matter what one may say about the soul going to some place, call it what you may, it's my personal conviction and belief that there is neither a "heaven" nor a "hell", there's only atmosphere and stars up there, the warm sun being one of them", he concluded with some strong personal conviction or possibly a lack of it.

The Corporal had barely finished his sermonizing about the origins and the development of the 'god/gods' concepts and the immortality of the soul and the hereafter, when all-of-a-sudden they all heard, what they, at first, thought was just some inane whistling-sound, bursting out from nowhere, in the thick evening air. At first, the instinct of preservation sent them rushing for cover, but then the hard fact dawned on them that, in this situation, inaction wasn't an option and they immediately ventured outside the tent to survey their surround.

"It has begun! Here it is! All hands on board! It's awesome and joyous!" The face of every officer, NCO and soldier seemed to say.

"All hands on board! *Operation kan Giwa resumes* and is on!"

Major Gadzama shouted out the order of engagement.

After an intense and bloody five hours of fire-power and tactical military maneuvers and skirmishes, the center seemed quieted somewhat and the rebel forces were seemingly in disarray and retreating.

"Sergeant, I'm hit ", moaned one of the Major's men to NCO Bakari who was stooping over him.

"Forward", Major Gadzama commanded, even as he noticed the blood-soaked shirt of Private Shitu Katagum and observed that he had indeed been hit in both his upper leg and his torso. Private Shitu lay helplessly with hands cupped under his stomach, writhing and moaning in pain.

It had grown so dark that one could not distinguish the soldiers' uniforms from ten paces off. But, just as it had started, the firing suddenly stopped. Then, just when they thought they were out of danger, in a nearby valley, a volley of shots rang out and cries were heard. The shots flashed in the darkness revealing the direction that they were coming from—the town of Oghara. This was another attempt by the Biafran soldiers to lure the federal troops away from the target of crossing the bridge over the River Niger, near the village of Okquaebo/Mbaise, an outskirt of Oghara and just a few miles from Abraka. There were hours of intense and sustained fire-power and maneuvers which the federal troops executed without missing a beat. When the shooting began to die down, the rebel soldiers were noticed hastily retreating and leaving behind them a large cache of weaponry, and, of course, their injured and the dead. The Federal soldiers in contrast were animated with conversations and exhilarated, and, even though completely exhausted and wasted — like a hunting dog — they streamed into the city of Benin, after an intense five-hour exchange of deadly and ferocious fire on both sides. The battle for Benin had been won, Benin was completely liberated! There were instantaneous shouts of "*Hip! Hip! Huh-a-ra-aah! Hip! Hip! Huh-a-ra-aah! Hip!Hip! Huh-a-ra-aah*"! After which came the rapturous acclaim and adulation of the common citizens of Benin, who poured into the streets *enmasse* dancing and spontaneously raising the middle finger as a gesture in acknowledgement of their liberation

"Not hurt, Dale?" Private Adamu asked, stooping on the butt of his rifle.

"We gave it to them hot today, *broda*. They won't mess around with us again!" said another Private.

"I hope you're right, but I don't think this is the last time we'll encounter these daring fuckin' rebels", one of the older NCO's sitting down cleaning and shining his rifle observed.

The Biafrans had been repulsed, for the second time, so, thank goodness, the city still remained under the Federal control and was safely secured. The rebels had scattered in complete disarray so Major Gadzama's men sobered and rested their guns. The rebels had no idea how fast the ground was shifting, or sinking, beneath their feet. It would later hit them, like a ton of bricks into their "psychic solar plexus".

For the first time the soldiers noticed that the people who came out to welcome them were raising their middle finger at them. At the time they didn't quite know what it meant until it was explained to them it meant "One indivisible Nigeria". From that moment on, the image and emblem of the Second Division came to be symbolized by the middle finger against a blue background. This was later changed by Haruna who took over the command of the Division, for a brief time, from Muhammed.

Chapter Ten
Bugile Wallace Gwor and Marianne Rabi Sambo Wedding

This is an account of Bugile, Dr. Khan's cousin and Marianne's wedding, which took place about two-hundred miles away in the town (the place is actually a village but the residents refer to, or regard, it as a town) of Awume-Logos, about five miles from the local government headquarters of Ohimini, and was attended by their cousin and his wife, Dr & Mrs. Veronica Khan, and several other members of the *Monte Sophia Historical Society* discussion group. Those from the group who were able to attend included James and his wife Jamima, Golu and his wife Francisca, Abba Habib and his wife Jummai, the Professor and his wife Mamu and Dr. Ahua Kasimu, a new addition to the group. Owoleye and his wife Femilayo, and Aminu and his wife AiShetu, had prior commitments and were unable to attend.

Immediately upon their arrival, Dr. Khan had observed that the structure of the church where the marriage was to take place seemed boxier from the outside than he had remembered. This might have been because it had been more than a decade since he had attended any services in the church or any Church for that matter; or maybe in the intervening years a major renovation has been done on it. The last time he had attended was when a friend, Ayua Atoh had physically dragged him there, when they had visited the village for a respected elder's death, Suwuan Tofi. From his present perspective, it seemed that the vertical columns and the triangular pyramid-shaped supports all obscured the massive circular dome with the spire rising high up in the sky on it. As a matter of fact it looks more than just renovation", as he looked up and read the bold inscription on the entrance:

Awume-Logos Apostolic Evangelical United Church

A crowd had gathered in small pockets inside, whilst many others had spilled outside into the corridor of the Awume-Logos Apostolic Evangelical United Church (A-LAEUC) after the regular service which had been led by the Most Reverend Pastor, Noah Dachu Muri. With extreme brevity he had concluded the service in expectation of the formalities of the wedding that would follow. The congregation was comprised mostly of women and children, who were milling around the church, which had been effusively lit up for the wedding.

"We are lucky, praise the Lord, today we have few men amongst us", observed Jimbala.

"Yes, but you know it's only because of the wedding, otherwise, do you think that they'd come? I bet you they won't be here next week", Quatir enjoined.

"Our men think attending church service is the responsibility of women and children only. Fools! They'll see what happens to them when they leave this world to join their ancestors in the after-life. I won't share a drop with any of them, not even my husband Suwang (also known as Kyerma), not even a single drop of water on my finger-tip, as was said of… whom in the Bible?.. Oh, I think the name was *Laizurus*", Jimbala said, jokingly, and all the women laughed.

The few men in attendance could be seen standing in small clusters whispering and chatting amongst themselves about the weather and the year's crops, isolated and separate from the women. Among them were a few soldiers who were on leave from the front. They could easily be identified because invariably almost all of them were wearing their camouflage jungle-dress fatigues with heavy boots. They too exchanged with each other news from their various fronts. One of them lamented the recent death of Ismaila G Bhalami as unnecessary and declared that it "would seem a violation of military justice, because he was never assigned to the sector officially". But the one amongst them who was wearing a sergeant's uniform reminded him that, in times of emergency, or war, officers can grab any soldier they deem fit, even if he is not assigned to their sector. The others kept numb, because they weren't particularly knowledgeable or conversant with military law of any kind, and, most especially, with that pertaining to war and the concept of "forced conscription".

After waiting outside for say twenty minutes, the congregation went back inside the church and sat down. Those of them who did not succeed in getting inside the main church crowded about the low window-openings, pushing and peeping through the small shades.

The invited guests included Dr. Khan and his wife Veronica; the beautiful Drs. Hadijatu Apollo and her sister Quamtin Bhala of the Bukar Abba Ibrahim (BAI) University of Damaturu, Yobe; Salisu Mangga, Veronica Khan's brother and his esteemed lawyer wife, Rose Elinor. All had been given prominent seats in the front row, and were enjoying the attention of the villagers. Also among the invited guests were the Registrars of some our prestigious Universities: ABU Zaria, the new Mirnga International University, Kaduna (MIU) and Maiduguri University. Representing ABU was the beautiful and elegant Drs. Helen Uchefu Ambe; and the charming but stern Drs Uwani Shehu Boni represented Unimaid; MIU was represented by its VC, Professor Muhammad G. Hassan.

Salisu Mangga and his wife never thought they were going to make it on time, firstly because the distance they had to travel, from Kwagh-Hir Bam township to Awume-Logos, in their old brown 1960 Opel Record, was quite substantial, and secondly, because of the dangerous journey— there had been recent reports of fatal armed robberies in the area — not to mention, the poor pot-holed nature of the road.

The third reason why Mangga and his wife thought they were never going to make it on time was because they came across two secondary-school boys, Jobs Mischell and Pette McCoy, who had been expelled, or, more probably suspended for four weeks — the outcome depending upon a hearing after the four weeks — from their school, for alleged drinking and malfeasance against one of the new young male teachers, who had shown an unfortunate propensity for admiring one of the boy's friend's female friends.

When Mangga saw them trekking along on foot, in the middle of the pitch-dark night, he instinctively stopped and asked them to clamber into the car. It was only when they were safely inside that they told him of their expulsion, or suspension, in as very few words as possible, and that they planned to go on to Pette's cousin in the next village to spend the reminder of the time there. Jobs told him and his wife that they had spent the first two weeks with his aunt, and now they planned to spend the remaining two with Pette's cousin .They confided to them that the cousin, Boyd Libbeh, was the headmaster of the local school. As they were driving along the deserted dirt road, Mangga revealed to the boys that, Wadai, Pette's older sibling, had been his best man, during his marriage, some five years ago. They had been college mates and very good friends, but hadn't heard from each other since the wedding. He asked Pette where and what his brother might be doing now?

Pette told him that his older brother, Wadai, had retired and was, now involved in local politics, representing Obagaji village in the state's House of Assembly. "Oh my goodness, I didn't know that Wadai had any knack for politics?" "None of us saw it coming either, but he's doing just fine" Pette said, with some pride. Elinor tried to get a little more detail about what actually happened with their suspension, but the boys proved a bit circumspect and unwilling to go beyond the little that they'd already revealed. After several attempts without success, Elinor gave up and just dozed off for the remainder of the journey. After one-and-a-half hours of driving on a lonely village dirt road full of pot-holes and fallen trees blocking the road, they finally sighted the village, through the uninhibited bright shining moon, strung atop a luxuriant lavish slope, but just then the road abruptly came to an end. In front of them was a deep dark valley, a part of the famous Lake *Tae'hla*. "I'm sorry", Mangga said, "As you see there is a valley and it seems the road ends here. I can't go beyond this point". The boys thanked him and said, "We understand".

However, before Mangga could complete reversing the car onto the narrow road, two men appeared from the bottom of the Taéhla valley. One of them was an elderly man with a thin gray receding hairline and a very sparsely graying goatee. He was wearing a tattered and unkempt traditional white *baban Riga*, with a worn-out *Zanna dipcharima* (hat), and heavy bi-focal glasses. He was dragging his left leg, limping as he walked, making a wide obtuse arc, which made one wonder how come he had never tipped over on his sides? He also had a knife stuck to his waist. The other gentleman looked much younger, with a clean-cut and lush goatee wearing a long dark-blue *kaftan*, shining from over ironing, with a blue and red *zanna dipcharima* to match.

"*Sala mala ikum*", the men greeted Mangga, "*mala ikum salaam*" Mangga and the boys answered in unison. The older gentleman introduced himself as Alhaji Tanimu Lamido, the village head of Akweya, and the younger one as Mallam Ibrahim Usman, the assistant headmaster of the local school. They said that they had been sent by the headmaster, Mr. Boyd Libbeh. They explained that this was what the headmaster did all the time, sending out someone to help his guests, every time they sighted a car approaching. This was because, most of the time, people who came in a small car or a jeep or land rover were either district officials visiting the school or a contractor. Mr. Libbeh, they said, was "always conscious of offering hospitality to the district school officials" because "that was the best way to be in their good books when they make their presentation at headquarters". More than this, they expected it, this personal service, as a right, to have the locals come carry their bags to the village proper.

The assistant headmaster, Mallam Usman told Mangga that the headmaster had been expecting visitors from the district headquarters for the past week so when he saw the flicking lights of the car approaching, he concluded it must be his visitors. And as was his usual practice he had sent them to help the visitors to the village. After this brief interlocution; Pette told the men that the headmaster was his cousin and Jobs, his friend. Both had come to spend one or two weeks with him, and, if it was convenient, to help in the school, by "relieving some of his teachers, when we're around", as he put it. "*Inshallah*! Say what? Of course, the only difficulty was going to be which teacher, but I guess it was going to be Mrs. Comfort Ukpan, because she was pregnant and expecting very soon, and doubtless would need all the help she could get", Mallam Usman retorted excitedly.

Alhaji Tanimu Lamido enjoined by saying to Pette, "*dan uwanka, heamister mutumin kirki ne kwarai, iyana da imani da jin tsoron Allah*", (your cousin is a good and God-fearing man). The younger gentleman said, "*Inshallah,* at least we didn't make a futile trip, let's go", and they grabbed the boys duffle bags, tossed them onto their shoulders and said, *salaam*, to Mangga, who responded *salaam*, then, started his engine, stepping on the gas, as the old Opel farted its way along on the dirt road, thumping and whining, as loudly as a jet taking off at JFK in New York. Both Mangga and his wife Elinor were sleepy and dog-tired, but they stuck it out, they persisted arriving at four that morning, and here they were now in the church at eleven o'clock.

What Pette and Jobs didn't tell Mangga and his wife was that the Missionary boarding school they had attended and had been suspended from, was run by a very strict and mean Principal, Bob Hasse — a five-foot-ten, tall, hairy, well-built American, from Pennsylvania with a ruddy complexion and an impish face whose glare was enough to induce fear in your heart, especially with young boys and girls of that boarding school age.

Mr. Hasse had instituted draconian rules and had outlawed any local dialects being spoken by the students on the campus as well as drawn up rules about what to drink, tap water, and sometimes on week-ends, *fanta*.

If a student was caught speaking any dialect other than English he or she would be punished severely, right in front of the whole student body, as a deterrent for others. Jobs had had such an experience a few months before his present suspension, when Mr. Hasse himself had caught him saying *"asir mana"*, (please come), to Inqui, one of the girls in his class. His punishment had been to dig out a boulder, buried in the ground, using only a hoe, shovel and pick-axe. Looked at it on the surface, the boulder looked fairly small (Mr. Hasse knew the sizes and how deep the rocks were buried because he had supervised the clearing of the land ten years earlier), but it took Jobs three weeks of all-day digging, without attending classes to get that boulder out.

By the end of the third week the palms of his hands were bruised and bleeding and calloused like day laborers. Jobs had been cursing quietly and lamenting the fact that nowhere else would Hasse have got away with this "child abuse". "He's just damn lucky that child abuse, or corporal punishment, is not a crime in our country, otherwise he would have been disciplined", he told me in 1972 almost sobbing after a sociology lecture at ABU. He said he remembered at one time "shedding tears mixed with sweat on my dark and dirty face and wiping it with the back of my dirty, bruised and swollen palms. And this is merely for speaking! Speaking your local god-given birth-right, dialect"! He remonstrated."Language", he continued, "is an instrument of cultural and morés transmission and shouldn't be canned and censored in the name of alleged progress! If you should be caught drinking anything other than water or *fanta,* say *burkutu* or *pitau,* thetwo most commonlocal brews available to students, you will have earned yourself a month or two's suspension, after your parents have been forced to come and apologize to the disciplinary committee and debase themselves on your behalf", he concluded.

Pette, Jobs and his co-ed classmates had been sent to the village of Schaffa as teacher-interns and were very excited, indeed ecstatic, to be away from the school's stifling environment and being under the constant stare of the watchful and vengeful eagle-eyed Bob Hasse. Another reason for their excitement, and which had actually a greater import for them, was the fact that they got the chance to use some of the cardinal principles of learning and classroom-management that they had studied and to observe experienced teachers, teaching, giving them the chance to use what had hitherto been a theoretical thing for them. Last, but of equal import, they presumed, was the opportunity it gave them to flirt with the local girls as well as their female colleagues, as freely as they wished, as well as the freedom, outside of the school's harassing and stifling environment to speak and converse in their local dialects.

Every day they stayed at the local elementary school until it was late in the evening, always claiming that they were working on their lesson-plans for the next day, whereas the truth was, in some instances, they were not working at all but flirting with their female class mates —who were just as excited of their freedom as the boys — in any conceivable place; on top of the small school desks, or on the relatively large table in the Headmaster's office —Principals were in charge of secondary schools and Headmasters/Headmistresses, elementary schools.

Typical of adolescent behavior in all societies, the girls, like the boys were equally happy and willing partners in this wild libido exploration. There was never any intimate intercourse involved at any time. However, as the students would learn later, in a hard way, too much freedom without caution could beget all sorts of other by-products, which you never initially planned for and hoped would never happen.

One clear, sunny Saturday-afternoon, after completing their lessons for the following Monday, and bored, not knowing what do next, some of the student interns decided to visit one of the local *burkutu* and *pitau* (both burkutu and pitau are locally brewed beer, but whereas burkutu is thicker and 'heavier', pitau is lighter but more potent and intoxicating) parlors in the village, just around the corner from the school, across the only dirt road that passes through the town. Whilst they were there in the parlor drinking, they ordered *balango*, (roasted beef/goat-meat), and *tsire*, (kebab) to go with the drinks. After two, or maybe three, hours of such gluttony and self-indulgence, some students clearly had had more-than-enough, and began acting or anyway, seemed, drunk. A few had already puked in the parlor's open latrine. Recognizing that things were quickly getting out of hand, the owner— an elderly gentleman, Samuel Idakoji, originally from Gboko, who had a congenital paralysis of his lower facial muscles, and limped because of a twisted atrophied left leg that had only sallow skin over bones as thin as paper clips — asked them to leave.

Watching Mr. Idakoji walk, swinging his scraggy left leg in arc, one wonders how he never toppled over. Mr. Idakoji confided to friends that he was born as normal as anyone else, but was hit by a bullet, that passed through his spine, during the Great War, World War II. In addition to his paralysis, he has lost all of his front teeth and could barely chew. His hair had also thinned and turned gray with age. He told friends that he kept the drinking parlor to supplement the meager and unreliable benefits he got as a pension for his injury and services from the Government.

"Please," he begged the interns "you have to leave because it's almost closing time". After a very long interval, one of them finally got up and said "let's go ". When the students came out of the *burkutu* parlor, they all began to sing some incomplete verses from Haruna Uji's *Balarabe* song in Hausa.

>Ni Haruna Uji mai Waka,
>A Kano city aka yi ni
>A Hadeja akayi min Sarki….
>Balarabe ya Balarabe, Haruna Balarabe
>Balarabe jikan mata……(repeated three times)
>Translated to English it means
>I'm Haruna Uji
>Born in Kano city
>And crowned at Hadeja…
>Balarabe Oh Balarabe, Haruna's Balarabe
>Balarabe the queen of all women……

At the conclusion of this song and its rousing chorus, the students engaged in general local obscene curses and name-calling, which was addressed to no one in particular, or rather, everyone, as they marched along on the road oblivious of others or the trucks. People had gathered to witness what was happening and a few trucks had stopped because of the crowd.

It so happens that, at this juncture that, Mr. Ndako Wakawah, a five-foot-three tall gentleman appeared on the scene, looking tired and exhausted. Ndako was one of the young African teachers who had been recently employed after the completion of his secondary school education at Gindiri to teach at the secondary school which was one of the two Missionary's post-primary schools in the area. The other was a Teacher Training school where the interns were attending at the time. He had gone to Tiraku, a small village next to Debroh and five miles south-east of Schaffa to see his parents, and was returning on his new motor-cycle humming contentedly (at this time, all the Missionary proprietors of the School were able to give to the indigenous African teachers as a perk, or an inducement, to join the two schools they ran, as staff members, was an advanced loan, enough only to buy a Honda motor cycle, ninety, or one-seventy-five— this explained the ubiquitousness of parked Hondas in every staff quarter at the time!). Now when Ndako came to the village and saw the curious crowd milling around on the dirt road, he stopped to see what was going on—it was, after all, the only street in town!

All of a sudden, almost out of nowhere, Alex Soubong, one of the patently drunken interns, jumped out and went straight to Mr. Wakawah, and said something to him which made some of the interns and a section of the crowd cackle in unison. Not about to take any insults from a student, Ndako said something back, to the effect of "how dare you guys disgrace the school in this manner, in the village. You were sent here to teach and not to act like drunkards and vagabonds. Your behavior is atrocious, revolting and utterly unacceptable". Alex, who was face to face with Ndako, repeated what he had just said, mocking him, in a whining voice, which everybody thought was hilarious. The female interns who had also come out to see what was going on, also, giggled. This reaction further aggravated Ndako and made him say contemptuous and condescending words to Alex, like "You're nothing but a piece of fuckin'shit! But worse of all you're just a bastard full of yourself…" To make matters even worse after Mr. Wakawah's insults, Alex challenged him to a fight, saying that he was so "small, weak and ugly" that he could beat him with "one hand tied behind his back". Ndako got really angry and tried leaving, but Alex grabbed his motorcycle and blocked him until Adamu Bwalah, one of the villagers, intervened. Adamu was a five-foot-six gentleman about forty years old. On this occasion he was wearing a brown *kaftan*, (a long gown) with thinning silver-gray hair combed back from his gutted forehead, and tufts of white and gray bushy eye-brows and a goatee. On getting closer to him you couldn't help but smell the tobacco he chewed to help relieve him of a pain from decayed teeth — one of the cumulative results of all the *burkutu* which he'd consumed over the years. He got between Alex and Ndako and pleaded with Alex to "please calm down" and "allow your teacher to leave".

"*Kamnyar nga zannuwa*, because of you sir, I won't disrespect you as an elder" Alex said, and slowly let grip of the handles of the motor cycle allowing Ndako to leave.

Mr. Wakawah had barely left the scene, as the dust raised by his motor cycle was still visible, when the sexy, slim-hipped, full-breasted female classmate, Diacca Zokka, for whom Alex had put on his gutsy but foolish display of affection, appeared. What happened is that Alex had heard rumors, and believed, or suspected it to be true that Ndako, had, surreptitiously, invited Miss Zokka and her friend Hallyma Zhoka back to his quarters on campus, thinking perhaps that he was interested in her? Even though Alex didn't have any concrete evidence that it was true, he accepted the innuendos and gossips as fact, as a result becoming incensed with jealousy and misguided notions of revenge.

That evening when Ndako reached the campus he went straight to Bob Hasse's office, before going up the hill to his quarters, and reported the incident to him. Bob Hasse became incensed and wasted no time, and immediately summoned the school's Board of Governors—the Board membership consisted of two indigenous headmasters selected by the Missionary proprietors from amongst their pool of headmasters, and three pastors and one church elder, also nominated by the Missionary proprietors, the Missionary's Schools' Superintendent and the two principals of the two schools under the Missionary proprietorship. All of them, the full board were summoned to come to the school for an urgent meeting of the greatest import. "This is what they're doing, getting drunk, instead of doing what they're there for!" He had shouted in his office in frustration - and to no one in particular, after Mr. Wakawah had left the office. In his rush and fervent desire to get the students suspended as soon as was possible, he didn't even bother to call the students in, in order to find out *their* side of the story.

In short, he didn't care what the facts were, or what the other students, who weren't involved, would wish to tell him as eye-witnesses. Consequently, the first evening the students returned to the campus, the Board of Governors of the school met and decided on the disciplinary action to be taken, without one of them raising the issue, morally or legally, of suspending this number of students without hearing from them directly or from one of their classmates, or even of having a representative of any parent present. Instead, and in spite of everything, at the end of their very brief deliberations, Bob Hasse went to the dining hall that evening and announced the names of all the students that Ndako had given him as being at the center of the incident in the village. In his usual deep and hoarse authoritarian voice he had declared that, as from that evening, all of the students whose names he had just called out were to be suspended and wouldn't be allowed to stay in the dorms that night. All the five students suspended, including Pette and Jobs, were consequently forced out of the dorms, and they each went their separate ways- and that's why the two were seen on that lonely village dirt road that dark night.

Now, back to the church, where Mangga and his wife along with the rest of the congregation were well ensconced, after a treacherous all-night drive. They waited patiently for their cousin's marriage to commence. The list of invitees along with the local church attendees, had been waiting for a prolonged time, about an hour for the ceremony to begin but it had not begun yet. Every time the crowd inside heard the creek of the door opening, the conversation inside died away instantly and everybody turned and looked around, expecting to see the bride and the groom come in. The door had now opened more than ten times already, but, each time; it was either opened for a belated guest, an usher, or somebody going out to relieve him or herself!

The Most Reverend Pastor Muri was a tall, spared man, with long thin legs hidden inside his wide trousers. He had extraordinarily long, thin, pale fingers, a closely-shaven face, demurely short hair, and thin lips which seemed, from time to time, twisted into something between a sneer and a smile. He looked about fifty, but he could have been older. His face would have been pleasant, were it not for his eyes, which were tiny like beads and inexpressive, and set so close together that the only thing that divided them was his thick, flat nose. Indeed, in my judgment, his face had something 'curiously birdlike' about it, commented Amoke Denem, one of the Church members attending the wedding. "This was just my first impression of him", Amoke concluded. However, the Reverend was an educated and humane person, who had a good practical knowledge of his calling and harbored some of the most progressive ideas of our days, including the right to abortion and a respect for, even support of, same-sex marriage. He was however, rather vain but was fortunately not overly-concerned about that, and not overly-concerned about his career. "When I shook his hand", Dr. Khan later confided to a friend, "I found him to have a powerful iron-clutch grip, strong and manly". The main concern of his life at this time was to be recognized as a man of advanced views and illustrious moral principles. Besides, he had perhaps the real reason for his station, good political connections and a considerable independent fortune, which he had inherited from his late father, the famous business tycoon, Dr. Jangura Woji (the doctorate had been conferred on him by Gwagwalawal University for his philanthropic work among the poor, especially the homeless and the ostracized. He also built several clinics all over the state that catered to all, regardless of one's ability to pay. Among the many were Gaidam, Buratai and Konshishe clinics. His generous donation to Gwagwalawal University among others was well known; and deservingly the medical school was named after him; *J Woji Medical School*).

At first most people assumed the bride and the bridegroom had arrived early; and few attached any significance at all to their being late in coming inside for the program to start. The delay however began, after a while, to be positively discomforting, and people, although still looking as if they were actively involved in the wedding became engrossed, rather in intimate personal conversations, about the rains, farming, the war, what to do about the burned down local market. The church fell hushed with expectation every time someone walked in, many in the congregation now thinking that it might be the bearer of some bad news, regarding the groom. Dr. Khan had apologized to his guests numerous times already, including to the most beautiful woman in the room, Hajiya Bintu of Garki University's Department of Pharmacology, (she preferred to be called "Hajiya" instead of "Professor"), whose entry had caused such a sensation and dead silence to fall on the church, as everybody turned to admire her elegance, grace, and style. She eventually sat down with a most nonchalant but at the same time knowing air of superiority and intelligence. Dr. Khan and Mr. William Angwe, Bugile Wallace's brother had pleaded with them to be patient because, "this is the way villagers operate, no sense of time at all"! He remarked.

Pastor Dachu Muri had also started fidgeting and seemed worried.

"It really *is* strange!"A lady with a shrill voice shouted from the middle right pew in the corner of the church and everybody turned to see who she was and began loudly voicing their support for her observation, and their amazement and dissatisfaction over such an extraordinary delay. N'Quabila for it was, kept on muttering and murmuring loudly and was completely beside herself, needless to say regardless of the consequences. Though she and the rest of the congregation were restless and agitated, this wasn't, it should be pointed out, the first time that they had experienced this happening, it had happened several times before. N'Quabila decided to approach the dais with a light, noiseless step, swaying slightly, as plump women sometimes do, but before she was able to go too far, she was stopped in her tracks by one of the ushers, a Junior Pastor named Jatau Kashim. She gazed and sneered at him, looking neither to the left nor to the right, but he stood his grounds. This behavior didn't endear her to the congregation, especially the bride's mother, who had shown her disgust for such behavior sometime already that evening by icily staring at her. But she didn't seem to care. There was no doubt in anybody's mind that she was trouble or a trouble-maker. She left a very disagreeable impression on everyone, even though many who knew her claimed that she came from a very 'respectable' Christian family. This knowledge didn't deter many, and certainly not the bride's mother from casting contemptuous and despicable glances upon her.

"The marriage ceremony is quite broken off" declared an elderly woman, Fati Ogoli, standing aloof, almost by herself, and facing Hannah, her childhood schoolmate.

"I'm in a position to prove my allegations, an insuperable impediment to this marriage exists", she continued.

"What proof do you have in support of such a gross allegation? This is a Christian ceremony and a holy one", Hannah concluded smirking and stressing the word "holy".

"A child already exists between these two, her name is Etty", the first woman said, with a crazed but awesome finality. Upon hearing this, Hannah and everybody else in the vicinity went silent, edging themselves away adroitly from the "disturbed" Fati.

When informed of this allegation, the bride's aunt, Pamela Bhuk's face turned colorless, like a rock, and her eyes were both spark and flint, but she too said nothing, walking away in a hurry also.

"Women! Oh women! Whenever two or more are gathered together, there must always be some unwanted gossip!" she was heard murmuring under her breath, as she walked away briskly.

On seeing what was going on and how restless the congregation was becoming, one of the bridegroom's men went out to find out what was happening. He found the bride outside still nestled in the car that had brought her, and she too, extremely worried whether or not the bridegroom had developed "cold feet" and had decided to cancel the whole thing, without even bothering to notify her. "It wouldn't be the first time", she said quietly to herself "it has happened once before, except in that instance it was the bride that changed *her* mind, at the last minute, while people waited patiently in the church". In that instance, the groom and his friends and invited guests, were kept on waiting in the Church, only to be informed, after a long fruitless wait, that the bride had changed her mind, had taken off her wedding gown, and that the wedding was off! Dead silence fell on the congregation and everybody was shocked, but there was nothing they could do. In the old days, before the movement for feminine equal protection, she would have been forced to have had to go through with the marriage and then petitioned for divorce there-after, but things had changed - a lot! The groom in that case was stealthily and surreptitiously smuggled out of the church by the best man, and other relatives and friends, and driven to the nearest town where he boarded a truck/bus to Kano, or was it Jos? He was never heard of or showed his face again in the village for the next twenty years, even though he eventually got married to a girl from that very same village (the girl was delivered to him after all traditional and local formalities were completed by his relatives).

In the present story, this is what actually happened to the bridegroom and his best man. The car that was supposed to bring them to the church had a flat tire about a mile away; and they worked hard to replace it with the spare one. Unfortunately, to their dismay, the spare was no good either. Completely panic-stricken, flabbergasted and confused, they asked the people that had gathered around them watching, if there was perhaps, a place nearby that they could have their tires fixed, but they were told there was none. The nearest tire-fix shade/shop was more than three miles away in the opposite direction. So, given the predicament that they found themselves in, and the limited options available to them, they decided to rent, if it were possible, two bicycles and just leave the car there. By the time the bicycles were brought to them, it had begun to drizzle softly however, but they had no other choice other than dare the rain, "come rain, come shine", and ride the next remaining mile to the church.

"Hey they've come! Here he is!" Iyaya Gbeja sighted them, about a quarter of a mile away, peddling and looking completely exhausted, all soaked up wet and dripping all over.

"Oh my dear, he looks more dead than alive", one of the bridesmaids remarked, as soon as she caught a glimpse of them.

"I was beginning to think that you had meant to run away!" the bride said to the groom, only half-jokingly after they arrived.

"It's stupid, but I can't explain to you what actually happened to us right now, because there is no time, but it's my fate, or "bad karma",if you will", he said, in an apparently calm voice, given his present situation, as he maneuvered and tried to lead his bride through the masses already thronging toward the entrance of the church.

"Look at your suit, especially your shirt and tie, in fact your whole attire!" The bride observed stunned and disapprovingly.

"Yes, yes, but what do you expect?! Let's just go through with the fuckin' shit"!

The bride was understandably shocked and took a step backward, because he had never used these obscene words in her presence, and most especially, to be hearing them now on this their special day.

"So this is just a "fucking shitty"thing to you uh? She repeated what had tumbled out of his lips unconsciously.

"Oh please dear, forgive me, forget what I just said, Can't you see that I'm frustrated and tired to my bones? You know that I don't feel that way at all, my dear, I'm sorry." She melted on hearing his apology.

"Oh dear, I'm yours, take me away anywhere you please", she responded holding and cuddling him and gazing at him with sincerity and passionate love from the heart.

"Aren't you frightened?" an aunt commented looking at the bride.

"Aren't you cold? You look pale," an old lady standing by said, directly addressing Bugile.

"No I'm fine", he answered, surprisingly politely given his angst and his turmoil at the moment, as he continued briskly toward the doorway on their way inside of the church.

"Take the bride's hand and lead her up the pew", one of the ushers advised him. He didn't seem to understand or hear, so the best man moved closer, tugged at his shirt and whispered the instructions into his ear. Bugile was utterly confused and didn't seem conscious at all as to where he was or what it was that was dutifully expected of him.

One of the senior Pastors of the Church, Pastor Moses Mbela, who was dressed in the same customary black robes with white under-shirt as The Right Reverend Noah Dachu Muri, the Senior Pastor, came and joined them marching down the aisle, maintaining only some few respectable paces in front. The crowd of friends, relatives and ordinary on-lookers were mesmerized and moved closer to the aisle in an effort to get a good glimpse at what was going on, especially to get a look at the bride's cascading petite white wedding gown and a sleek matching globes and ear-rings. An elderly lady pushed through the throng of the crowd and pulled, or more appropriately tugged on the bride's flowing gown, slowing down the graceful flow of the august, seemingly flawless, procession.

Pastor Noah Muri was immaculately dressed in his ecclesiastical robes of black and a white under-shirt and a white handkerchief in his breast pocket to match his black robes. He stood solemnly erect at the front of the church, right in the middle of the two pews facing the marching party as they moved, gracefully but at a snail's pace, toward him. The procession was unnecessarily slow because of unusual and persistent interruptions from the curious on-lookers. There were some occasional *yerali* (ululations) emanating from the female relatives and friends who had pushed themselves to the forefront, onto the nearest pews. Meanwhile Pastor Dachu was nervously waiting and fumbling with his Bible in his left hand, and the white kerchief in his right hand, dabbing the sweat on his forehead. He had his reading half-reading glasses perched on the bridge of his pointed nose, precarious, as if it might fall at any moment. Around his massive neck was a gold chain depicting Jesus on the Cross of crucifixion. He looked on, with weary and melancholic eyes, at both the bride and the groom, as if he wanted to say, "You've wasted a lot of our time already, hurry up", but, instead, he just let out a deep sigh, which, unbeknownst to him, was loud enough for people in the nearest front pews to hear.

When the wedding party finally came to a stop in front of Pastor Muri, he pulled out his right hand from under his robe and made an obeisance toward the bride and groom. He then raised his right hand with the solemnity required on such occasions, and said, in a gruff but reverential voice, "Blessed be the name of our Lord God, from the beginning, is now and ever shall be". The whole congregation responded in unison, "Blessed be the Holy Sacrament of the Cross, now and forever, Amen". The Pastor then raised his hands again, bowed, and blessed the bride, the bridegroom and all the people in attendance, especially the official invited guests and relatives who had come from far and wide. He then crossed himself, and touched the foreheads of the couple, and said "In the name of the …… the… and the …..Spirit." To which the congregation answered, in unison, "Amen!"

Meantime Bugile was thinking, "This is it, but is it true?" He glanced at his bride and saw her face in profile, and from the way she appeared he knew she was fully aware of his eyes upon her, and probably asking the very same question. All the fuss about his dress, about being late, all the talk of friends and relations, their annoyances, had suddenly all evaporated and been filled with joy, ecstasy and admiration.

"Blessed be the name of our Lord God, from the beginning, is now, and ever shall be", Pastor Noah Dachu had intoned again, and the whole congregation responded again in unison: "Now and forever blessed be the

Holy Sacrament of theCross". The choir stood up and sang with gusto and their voices echoed throughout the whole church, spreading even to the outside. This was followed by the Lord's Prayer led by Pastor Moses Mbela, one of the senior priests and recited by the whole congregation.

"…. O Lord we beseech thee…" Rev. Muri prayed, and the congregation responded, "Blessed is the name of the Lord, now and forever".

"How do they know, or surmise anyway, that it is help that is what we want?" Bugile asked himself.

"…..Eternal God that joins together in love them that were separate…", the old Priest continued, peeping through or, rather, over his glasses , "Whosoever has ordained the union of Holy wedlock that cannot be set asunder…" And he paused.

"It is amazing to me how he *knows* that it is ordained by God; people can't just fall in love? And how did he know it is "holy", what does he *mean* exactly by "holy"?" Bugile amused himself with these cynical clearly inappropriate meditations.

"Thou, our Lord who didst bless Holy matrimony through the ages, according to Thy Holy Covenant, bless thy servants, Bugile and Marianne in the name of the Father, the Son and the Holy Ghost, now and ever shall be".

"Amen," the congregation responded again in animated unison.

"…Joins together in love them that were separate?", again Bugile asked himself, "What deep meaning there is in those words!" He paused, sneaked a look at Marianne, his bride. "Is she feeling the same as I am?" he wondered.

Pastor Dachu asked the bridegroom to put the ring on his bride's finger and likewise instructed her to do the same.

"Do you, Bugile Dashu Gwor, take Marianne Rabi Sambo to be your legal wedded wife and to love and cherish her in plenty or need until your last breath here on Earth",

"I do", Bugile contentedly responded, but not fully aware of what he was responding to, because his mind wasn't really there at all. He was thinking about the car, how he was going to get it repaired. He had exhausted all his finances for the wedding and had nothing to fix the car with. His only hope, he surmised, was to either ask his cousin, Dr. Khan and his wife, or his brother, for help. "But Dr Khan and his wife have already taken on the responsibility for sponsorship of the entire entertainment costs of the wedding, and my brother and his wife helped me pay for the dowry, and, besides, it was their indulgence and generosity and incomparable kindness that paid for my wife's beautiful wedding gown. How can I ask them for more?

Several sobs were heard coming from the middle section of the women's section — women always sit separately from the men. N'Quabila was again seen being restrained, by her elder aunt, because she had gotten so emotional, on the verge of hysteria, and had made threats of joining the bride and bridegroom, up front! A good number of the women were to be observed holding their palms up to their faces and wiping away a free flow a trickle of tears. The men, some of them, likewise, had some sort of handkerchiefs to their faces, not willing to publicly display the fragility of their emotions for all to see, lest it be construed as a sign of weakness.

"Do you Marianne Rabi Sambo take Bugile Dashu Gwor to be your legally wedded husband and to love and cherish him in time of abundant plenty or dire need until your last breath here on planet Earth",

"I do", was her response also.

But she reflected upon the phrase 'last breath….', and thought, inwardly, "I have no intuition of dying with him… he may depend on that", and then she immediately flushed and became self-conscious wondering if her thoughts had been overheard by anyone. She smirked idly at the priest. Some amongst the congregation noticed slight differences in the wedding citations and the manner the newly-weds responded to in their pledge; but after all who cared? The old man was doing his best, what most of the people wanted, at this hour, after such a long delay, was for the "friggin thing" to be over!

"Thou, O Lord, who didst, from the beginning create male and female", the priest read, after the exchanging of the rings, "From thee woman was given to man to be a helpmate to him, and for the procreation of children. O Lord, our God, who has poured down the blessings of thy Truth according to thy Holy Covenant upon thy chosen servants, our fathers from generation to generations, bless thy servants, Marianne and Bugile, and make their troth fast in faith, and union of hearts, and truth, and love…"And the response was "Amen now and forever be the blessed Holy Sacrament of the Cross…"

Bugile was more perplexed now than ever in his life, "so Marianne is just a helpmate? I thought we each had equal at stake in this union, I didn't know that she is just to be seen as an appendage". Marianne also was bothered by some of the things that the pastor had said. For example, that marriage was "for the procreation of children", but she convinced herself that the old priest was just following precedent, and didn't really mean to say that she was just a helpmate who was expected to merely procreate, to bring forth children, and not an equal partner in this relationship.

While these thoughts were percolating in their minds, they heard the priest take out a piece of paper from his coat pocket and read the following:

"Do either of you, or anyone in the congregation, know any impediment why these two people may not lawfully be joined together in matrimony, if so ye do now confess it, for be ye well assured that so many as are coupled together otherwise than God's word doth allow, are not joined together by God, neither is their matrimony lawful.. .". He paused, waited and then continued, "If there is, speak now, or forever hold thy peace". The church was hushed in silence, like a graveyard, until a young man in one of the middle left pews abruptly stood up, stared with a blank expression at the gray walls of the church's interior and then left, without uttering a word. Everybody sighed, as all eyes turned to him until he reached the exit door. Apparently, he had received an urgent message which he had to respond to immediately. There was a simultaneous sigh of relief emanating from all four corners of the church when this young man walked out, solemnly and without further ado. The anxiety expressed by the waiting congregation was fully plausible, because the young man who got up had been rumored to have displayed some sort of coquetry and romantic sentiments toward Marianne as little as two years ago.

When nobody publicly declared any impediment to the marriage, the priest intoned "In that case…" he paused, again, flexing his neck muscles, clearing his throat and emphatically declaring:

"By the power vested in me by the Logos Apostolic Evangelic United Church of Jesus the Nazarene in Africa, I pronounce you husband and wife. You may now kiss your bride". There was, at first, a dead silence, followed by rapturous applause, the clapping of hands and *yerali* (ululation) as everybody in the church rose to their feet, some clambering upon the earthen bench-like seats to witness this Western-style, vivid visual display of affection.

Immediately the newly-weds stepped out of the church, their two-year-old daughter, Etty, came running out and grabbed the end of her mother's gown with smiles and a look of profound joy spread all over her tiny face.

Bugile picked her up and kissed her on the cheeks, before gently putting her down. As the congregation began to file out, it was announced, in a loud booming and clear voice by Sage Waltinafa, the master of ceremony (MC) for the occasion, that there was going to be some entertainment at the local town club house, where food and drinks would be served (the club house had, in part, been built by money provided by donations received from the eminent sons and daughters of the village, but the bulk of the financing came from one of the senior military officers who hailed from the village, the ever-popular, and indomitable, Colonel Sujuwan Aphar (Retired), formerly of the Federal Marine Guards). In addition to food and drinks, the MC announced, there would be both traditional dance and *gulum* or *hadtha* (gulum is stringed instrument like the banjo; and hadtha is a sentimental grinding performed by young women) as well as, he added, Western dance and music for the young people, if they so desired.

Dr. Khan and his wife led their friends to the VIP reception area, where they ate the sumptuous sweet lamb-meat that had been prepared, as well as some rice and beans, fried plantains, and a choice of several kinds of beverages. In another section far removed from the main hall was a small group of elders talking in whispers and drinking local brews of burkutu and pitau out of calabash bowls. Dr Khan and his friends retired to their lodging after indulging themselves for an early and the onerously long journey back to their homes at Monte Sophia.

For those readers who are not familiar with the Logos Apostolic Evangelical United Church (LAEUC) of Jesus the Nazarene in Nigeria; it is a kind of a mainstream Church, in most of its services and liturgy, when compared to its next door neighbor, The Christ Emissary Living Church (also known as E-Living Church or simply E-LC), which is quite extraordinarily different in many respects. Some have compared the E-Living Church with the Church of Scientology, but, indeed, there are many differences, both salient and subtle, between the two. The E-LC under its adorable and dynamic leader, the Most Reverend Jeremiah Kris, looks like a cross between the 15th Century Order of Martin Verga, and the Catholic institution of *Opus Dei* (which some news media has referred to as "God's Mafia" or "the cult of Christ") which was started, by SaintRosemarie Scribal, on October 2, 1928, in Spain. Recently the *Opus Dei* has been accused of diverging from its original mission of "helping people turn their work and daily activities into occasions for growing closer to God through serving others".

Once a week—-usually from around twelve midnight until the early-morning hours, say five a.m.,the Church has, what they call "early vigil ", where any individual member in attendance is required to kneel down and confess all his or her faults or sins he or she may have committed within the past week (a similar event takes place at the end of each month, however, the monthly vigil or "reawakening", lasts for, at least, three days). Besides the open confession which is accepted every week, the monthly reawakening incorporates '*la couple'* (which is a French derivation from the Latin word *culpa*, meaning guilty). To perform *la couple*, one prostrates oneself and remains in that position until the Chief Bishop *We're*, or in rare instances, the *Mere*, indicate by clapping their hands thrice, the signal that the sinner might raise onto his or her feet. This act of penitence is applied to, as minor and insignificant things as, breaking a glass, talking behind a church member, or mere tardiness for a meeting, forcing members to wait, to major stuff, such as outright lying, or mental, or actual mental infidelity. During both the early vigil and the reawakening periods, fervent and frantic prayers, involving dancing and glossolalia ('speaking in tongues') are offered, and requests are made for an early revelation of The Coming, or at least for a sign of the coming Rapture. The series of books, *Left Behind*, are obligatory readings for each member.

The members of the E-Living Church are always required to speak in low voices and to walk with bowed heads. The faces of their female members' are always covered, from-head-to-toe, with black cloth which they refer to as –*lullipi-adilchi* or*Sanctee*, the sacred, with only small slots for the eyes, which are often the only visible part. Both male and female members are required to always dress in white. Each member is required to make a prayer of atonement, once a day, for all the sins of the world, (including all disorders, errors, volcanic eruptions, tsunamis, violations, crimes and commission committed – both human and natural disasters). There is at least one person in the inner sanctorum of the church at all times, praying for the sins of the world. This they call the "Perpetual Adoration of the Lamb of God". It's been noticeable that many members have unsightly yellowing teeth, since they are discouraged from using a brush and tooth paste. Instead they chew a fresh tender neem twig to help clean their teeth, at specific hours of the day, but nothing else. They are always encouraged to refrain from saying the words, "mine" or "my" instead, they say "our" or "ours'". The members own nothing of value and cherish nothing. None of the members are allowed any place or room of their own. Spartan living is expected, with the most minimum of modern conveniences. However, people who are close to the membership say that the Chief Bishop — who is affectionately addressed as *Pe're*(Pa) and his wife as *Me're,* (Ma), by the members of the Church — is the only person allowed some lee-way with luxury. This sanctimonious behavior or hypocrisy has not gone unnoticed by the lay members!

Anytime a member feels that he or she is beginning to get overly attached or cherish something of value he or she would be directed by a bishop or priest, whose directives are absolute, to give it up to the Church, to hand it over to the *Pe're* or *Me're* who would so the tradition goes give it over to the poor. This is an inordinate expansion of the doctrines set up between 1567 and 1571 by St. Theresa. Most members live together and are not allowed to shut their doors or lock themselves in a room; all doors must remain completely open at all times. They have a few old cars, which they use for going to and from their community farms or to the market, but these are always left open with the keys inside for anybody who would wish to use it.

When two members meet, especially at, or during, their weekly "early vigil" or monthly "re-awakenings", their regular greeting is always "Praise and worship to the Holy Sacrament of the Altar", and to this, the other member will answer, "Amen", or "Forever", no handshakes, or hugs (this is long before anyone knew anything about the H1N1 virus!). Their church bell rings every hour and, as a member, if you hear it, no matter where you are, or what you are doing, you must stop and silently recite "At this hour", say nine, "and all hours praise, worship and adoration to the Holy Sacrament of the Altar", then you can continue with your business. This custom, they argue, is designed to check the flow of one's thoughts at any moment of the day, making certain that your thoughts are directed solely back to God. The Chief Bishop, Bishops, and Priests (there are no female priests in the Church yet, like the Universal church its doctrinal teachings prohibits female priesthood) must take a vow of poverty and austerity and chastity and complete unadulterated obedience to the Church doctrines and teachings.

To be a deacon in the E-Living Church; you must take a vow of poverty and austerity and fast every Friday in remembrance of the Crucifixion. Also every member is expected to fast for the whole duration of Lent and other days special to themselves, throughout the calendar year.

To become a 'Priest' or 'Junior Pe're" (JP) or "Junior Me're" (JM) is more arduous than becoming a Deacon. The probation period lasts at

Araba Let's Separate

least three years and a novitiate lasts another five. It is indeed an exception for one to become a JP or a JM any time before the age of thirty. The ceremony of the final vows of the "novitiate" is very elaborate and unique. The "novitiate" is often dressed in a white garment (sometimes black is accepted) covering all of the body from head to toe. The "novitiate/postulant" then lies down prostrate on a specially-spun cloth before the Chief Bishop.

During the ceremony the members would form a circle around the novitiate, lying down and moving around him, clapping, and singing at the top of their voices, and dancing to the beat of drums. As they do so, all are expected to chant "Our brother, our sister is dead" to which the other half would respond "Alive in Christ Jesus our Lord and the Virgin Mary, our Spiritual First Beloved Mother". After they have excited themselves to the point of euphoria —for instance by constantly and in unison declaring God, Elohim, El Shaddai, Jehovah, Adonai send Fire! Fire! To anoint and bath your servant with your Holy blood and Spirit! —-and begun "talking in tongues", the Chief Bishop would tap the head of the novitiate with his right hand three times. That was a sign for him to get up, that he'd been *resurrected*. The "novitiate" himself would join the dancing and singing and start speaking in tongues". Only when he'd revealed a 'gift of the tongue' would the ceremony be considered successful and over. At this juncture, the Bishop would give a sign, with both hands raised, and the congregation would go back to their seats. A fervent prayer would be said by the novitiate to show that he had, indeed, been received and possessed by the Holy Spirit; and that his ability to speak in tongues was guided by the power of that Holy Spirit.

Observers have noted, by surreptitiously attending the services of the group, that the prayers of the postulants were terrifying, and those of the novices were worse still, and those of the other members, worst of all. "Nothing being said makes any sense at all, that speaking in tongues stuff is all gibberish" commented one of those who had attended the service out of mere curiosity.

As alluded to earlier members were encouraged to live a Spartan life, with the most basic minimum of modern conveniences. All the senior members of the Church including the Chief Bishop, Bishops, Deacons and Priests and "JP" and "JM" are required to always "purge their souls from sins" they may have committed by self-flagellating, lashing themselves at the end of each day, with what they refer to as the *bulala*. This act to them serves as a perpetual reminder of Christ's sufferings. The *bulala* is specially made and similar to the "spiked cilice" of the *Opus Dei*. The members of the E-LC like to refer to themselves proudly as the people of "the Living Way", and sincerely believe that they are God's instrument for change in the world.

To outsiders, however, it seems obvious that the Bishops have manipulated the doctrine, because their life-style is anything but austere, and the members sometimes complained about it. But every time a member broached the matter, he would be reminded of the Church doctrine and teaching that says, "All believers must obey the Apostles that have been chosen and ordained as God's representatives in this Church".

Nobody knows for certain how this form of church liturgy came to be established in Nigeria, let alone in this remote village, but church historians believe something akin to it was originally practiced by the Benedictine-Bernardine Order of Martin Verga in Spain in the fifteenth century. Certainly, numerous changes have been introduced in its liturgy and doctrinal teachings since its inception in this corner of the country by a Missionary group, early in the twentieth century.

At the next meeting of the Local Historical Society Study Group (LHSSG), following the wedding, those who attended were very fascinated and eager to share their experiences with their colleagues who had not been able to make it due to some previous commitments. The Professor was most profuse in his praise of the process, it being his first time attending a Christian wedding. The Moslem wedding he declared is so much simpler and briefer, without so much of the "I do" stuff.

"I'm pleased and privileged to introduce to you our new member, Doctor Ahua J. Kasimu", the Professor announced.

"The privilege and honor is mine", Doctor Kasimu responded.

"Will the doctor care to tell us a little bit about himself?" The Professor asked, in a dignified voice.

"Well, there is little to know about me, other than that I'm a Nigerian like all of you, and I came from Canada, where I've been living for the last three-and- a-half decades. I'm a banker by profession, but now I'm retired and single. Many of you would wonder how come I'm still single at this age. Well, in truth, I'm a widower. I lost my wife to cancer some few years ago", he concluded in a somber voice.

"Well, we extend our heart-felt condolences to the good doctor and to his family. But maybe our good doctor won't mind being introduced to few of our most affable and beautiful women", Pastor Owoleye said jokingly trying to break the silence that had suddenly built up after the doctor's use of the word 'cancer'. The expression on his spotted face was solemn and devoid of any sign of its usual joyfulness and simplicity.

"I thank the good Pastor, but I beg to decline the offer of being introduced. However, I wholeheartedly accept his offer of condolence on behalf of all of you. For your information, I live in house number 5 between Broad Street and Row Avenue, and look forward to receiving some of you soon. I joined the Society because of my avid interest in history. At the time the events under purview took place, I was studying in Canada, and didn't have all the information I needed in order to appreciate the consequences for the foreseeable future".

"One more thing, I'm a staunch advocate for the eradication of cancer— all types and forms of it — I vow to do all I can to help in eradicating it off the face of the planet and will pursue you, or to say it less mildly, cudgel your brains and shame your sense of humanity until some of, or all of, you become involved with WORCEC" he announced.

"What's that?" James enquired sheepishly.

"Yes, what does the acronym stand for?" Jummai asked politely.

"Oh, I'm sorry it stands for World Organization for Research, Cure and Eradication of Cancer. It's a worldwide association of dedicated philanthropists and other individuals who have committed themselves to the eradication of cancer, all types of cancer".

"This is one profound difference between the Western developed countries and us here. They can organize for a noble cause and mean it, here if you try to organize, nobody will join with you, because everybody is afraid their money will end up in somebody else's pockets, (or be used for an extra wife or house!) No trust at all", Golu said, emphatically.

"Do you blame them? How many times have we seen reports of such frauds committed against innocent individuals, and the perpetrators, still free, going about their business, as if nothing has happened?"

Habib declared with equal fervor in support of what Golu had said.

"Ok, enough already, let's move on to better things than quarrelling about the endemic corruption which is snuffing the air out of the lives of hard-working citizens of this country', the Professor advised them.

"Anyway Doc, that's a noble cause that I for one, won't mind associating myself with", the Professor sturdily proclaimed.

"I wholeheartedly applaud your dedication and commitment to such a high ideal, and I too associate myself with it, and consider it an obligation to join, because I too have experienced an unpleasant encounter with the ugly and deadly disease of cancer. I lost my elder sister and father to this terrible, obnoxious disease", Alhaji Wada revealed this information to the members for the first time.

He had never talked about it because of the helplessness that he felt, since in this culture, nobody talked about such matters in public. However, now he had somebody he could relate his sordid experiences to speak of the devastating effects of cancer on the dying and the survivors. Without an exception, all members present agreed to become WORCEC members as soon as the doctor could get formal applications for them. They all pledged to join.

"Well, where do we begin?" Alhaji Wada finally asked.

"We are supposed to be discussing the battle of Onitsha", Jummai reminded him.

The following letter was anonymously written and sent to General Muhammed during lull over the battle of Onitsha.

June 18, 1969
Dear GOC, Muhammed,

Sah, I cannot find words enough to express to you my displeasure with what I hear that the Minister is proposing on doing. I presume, sah, the Minister has already been in touch with you, or with your second-in-command, regarding the importance of the seizure and control of the Onitsha Bridge. I heard he was advocating a retreat to a safer zone, to either regroup, or surrender it up to the rebels, wholesale. It is painful, deplorable - as a matter truth, it stinks! - and not myself alone but the whole army is in despair to hear of such foolish misplaced advice regarding such an important and monumental target, central to our cause. I, personally, on my own, entreated him most urgently, both in person and by letter, to desist, immediately, and withdraw this heinous, and maybe even traitorous, recommendation to you, but nothing it seems will persuade him.

What does hefrickin' know about the science and prosecution of war? I strongly advised him to stick to his frickin' desk policy job, and leave the prosecution of the war to commanders like yourself and your officer corps (NCOs and the gallant other ranks). Our troops have fought, and are still fighting, gallantly and heroically, as never before. If the Minister thinks we are temporarily bogged down and have suffered some losses, "that's war", but, more than that, the rebels have suffered a hundred times more, incalculable, losses.

There is even a rumor floating about out there that he's talking about peace negotiations. God forbid that you and I should succumb to, or even contemplate, such an absurdity such insanity of purpose! I've learnt from powerful sources that he was even talking of him signing an armistice! He has no right whatsoever to arrange armistice talks without you! He is causing you to lose the fruits of a whole campaign. Order him to break the armistice talks, at once! What a treasonous act to behold! To make "peace", after all the sacrifices that have been made all the investments made in blood and ammunition is insane! And not only that, but it means my children and yours will have to fight them again in the future, because, I guarantee you, this will not be the end of their diabolical plans for the Republic.

General, forgive me, sah, for writing so boldly but, frankly, I'm beside myself with exasperation at such a thought coming from a senior Minister of the Federal Republic. The Minister may be alright in his Ministry, but as a General he is not merely bad, he is execrable… yet the fate of the Republic has been entrusted to such as him… It is a fearsome proposition indeed!

It is obvious to me, sah, that whoever advises the concluding of peace at this stage in the war, and especially this foolishness of entrusting the Minister to speak on behalf of the army, does not truly love our Republic.

As a Regimental sergeant, sah, I will obey his command in certain matters, even though I am his elder, but this capitulation is painful, painful for me to bear for the love of this country. Tell me, sah, for God's sake, what will our children and grand children say about such cowardice?! And why we should abandon our good and brave soldiers and country to the whims of the few in suits and ties or baban riga (gowns), or, for that matter, military uniforms in the headquarters, or ministry pencil-pushers sitting in air-conditioned offices, with their feet high on the table, studying or doing their part-time law school work, in preparation for life after the military. These scandalous men, sah, it seems to me, are intent on planting hatred and division amongst our fighting men! But who are they? And what is there to fear? In every war there is always a period of a stalemate. Who then are we afraid of? - Ourselves?

It is neither my fault nor yours, sah, that the aforesaid Minister is irresolute, cowardly, dense, dilatory possessing all of the worst qualities. The whole army, and most especially the Second Division, bewails it, and curses him bitterly, on behalf of all the fighting men and us— true Nigerians!
Wasalam oga Sah,

Faithfully yours,

RSM .....; (12*th* Division Home Front).

*The Battle for Onitsha *

"The first battle for Onitsha of opposed river-crossing obviously didn't accomplish its objectives as conceived by the Colonel and his commanding officers. That is, there were failures and set-backs in his aim of leading his army according to the order he prescribed in his war disposition to Major Galatasa Doso and his general staff. The commander's conception of opposed crossings of the river proved disastrous and, in fact, fatal. Neither the objective of taking Banjo alive as a prisoner, nor the objective of destroying the enemy army, relegating them to a non-fighting force, was accomplished. Instead, the Federal troops suffered heavy losses and were beaten back.

The second attempt didn't yield any better, or different, results either. It was a fiasco. Once again, these grim and painful failures were due to faulty strategic decisions by the Colonel, his decision to attack the enemy from a frontal position, by crossing the Niger River, thereby surrounding and decimating them. The logistics and nuances of this plan didn't work however because, at the time, the Colonel's Mechanized Division didn't have the amphibian capability of river-crossing. As a matter of fact, the soldiers were not trained for river-crossing warfare at all! Consequently, their military exercises for such crossings were haphazardly carried out, using a *kolekole* (a small boat), recently procured - or, in most instances, just commandeered - from the locals and fishermen, with the simple explanation of "war-emergency needs". It is, therefore, not surprising that the heroic troops of the Second Division suffered a disappointing retreat with massive loss of life and materiel's, including the waste of huge amounts of ammunition. The third attempt of opposed river-crossing for the capture of Onitsha almost ended in mutiny because of the losses incurred.

The reception of the anonymous letter by the so called Regimental Major angered but, at the same time, inspired the GOC to share its contents out loud with his officer corps, and he encouraged them to share its import further with their NCOs and with the other ranks. The letter boosted their morale and determination, giving them a strong impetus for success, for the third and final onslaught on the Onitsha Bridge. Some strategic decisions and changes were put in place in the battle deposition plan that had not been considered in the previous plans.

It was decided that the Final attack of unopposed river-crossing would go through Asaba —as first recommended by Supreme Military Headquarters (SMHQ) — in the rear of the Third Marine Division, for the necessary support which would be required if the rebels tried their now-ubiquitous and all-too-familiar craft of an ambush. The battle disposition and all other repositories were implemented to perfection, and the result was a resounding success which was appreciated and praised by all those concerned Nigerians who were following the prosecution of the war on a daily basis. It was considered a stroke of genius, a memorable event in the annals of the art of warfare. It was quite clear that the final battle was successful, (in spite of the incongruities of going through the rear of the Third Marine Commandos,) because of the impetus the soldiers received from the Corporal's letter, but, above all, the protection thus provided by the Marines. This, undoubtedly, was what was wanted at that stage of the campaign. (It would, as you would imagine, my dear readers, indeed, be difficult, if not utterly impossible, to envisage any other outcome more expedient at the time than the outcome obtained). This was so because, at the time as was revealed in the anonymous letter from the Home Front, there were rumors floating about in the ministries, market places, and important military quarters, of a peace deal.

The final, unopposed, crossing, through the rear of the 1 Division, was one of the most important events of the whole campaign because, not only did it forestall the rebels' dreams of advancing through the West - through Ibadan - and making a run through to Lagos, but, at least temporarily, it shut out the voices of the early propagandists for appeasement . The transition from retreat to advance by the Federal troops meant that the weakness of the Biafran forces was exposed and the shock administered was exactly what was needed to exert pressure on the rebel forces for a quick termination of hostilities, rather than just continued flight and retreat".

The following is a brief recounting of the plan and disposition of forces for the Onitsha battle, which was given the code name *Operation Zaki*(lion).

The GOC had called his officers to his residence to discuss the disposition, and other nuances of the fighting forces, for next day. He did this always. The 6 Brigade, under Yar'Adua, would lead the main force, he told them. In his mind he knew what he wanted to do, but, at the same time he knew that the prosecution of war requires additional input and participation by the officers and the NCOs. The plan was to use the Recce and the armored Battalions in the center, while the infantry and the mechanized Battalions covered the right flank. The left flank was assigned to the indomitable *force eliminate* of the Marines, who would also cover their rear. After the completion of the plan and the disposition of the forces, he asked his officers if there were any further comments or adjustments that they would perhaps like to suggest. When they all indicated their consensus to the present disposition, he thanked them and wished them a fond "good night", but reminded them that he reserved the right to change his mind in the morning, if he perceived any shifting in the plan, the emergence of any possible weakness. He also told them he would like to address the troops and the officers *before* the commencement of hostilities or engagement.

The following, *inter alia*, is the address the GOC gave his officer corps, NCOs and the ranks, in the wee hours prior to the battle of Onitsha.

Soldiers! The rag-tag Biafran army is advancing against you, determined to avenge and re-arrange their most recent humiliating losses at Benin and Ore. But remember these are the remnants of the same battalions you have already defeated and decimated at Benin and Ore, and which you have, ever since, been pursuing, right up to this point. Be prepared to inflict an even more devastating and humiliating defeat on them than on the previous encounter.

This time, there should be nothing short of complete surrender. This encounter must yield the ultimate results we expect —– unconditional surrender——– and nothing less.

Our present positions, on the upper bank of the river, and with the Third Marine Commandos at our rear, and the lower bank for support and protection, are stronger vantage points., If they try to advance to our right flank; they will expose their left flank to the thick, marshy febrile riverine and to our Recce Battalion soldiers as well as the fierce and indomitable 'force eliminate' Battalion of the Marine Commandos.

I myself will lead you, with the help of Lieutenant Colonel Barau Apollo. I will, meanwhile, be at the rear following every implementation of our battle plan and giving additional orders and directives, only if deemed necessary, otherwise I entrust the command to our gallant Lieutenant Colonel, and Majors Angwe and Lamurde, , with the assistance of our brave and invincible NCOs, to lead in the disposition of the battle plan, as planned. I'm confident that, with your customary valor and heroism, you will bring about fear, disorder and confusion among the enemy ranks, in an instant!

However, if victory seems, in any way, oblique or in any doubt, even for a nano-second, you will see me, your Commanding General expose myself to the first blows of the enemy for there must never be any uncertainty whatsoever about total victory, at all costs, this time!

Don't break ranks! Don't stop to care for, or carry away, the injured! Finally, I would be remiss if I didn't mention the call I received last night from the Commander-in-Chief of the Federation, wishing you, and the whole nation, a great and well-deserved victory!

Forward, gallant and brave men of the Second Division! May this day be etched in gold and blood when the history of all wars this country ever faced is recounted by generations to come! Long live the bravery of the fighting force of the Second Division! Long live one indivisible Nigeria!

The darkness had fallen along the zone of conflict and was complimented by the somber flow of the River Niger in an easterly direction, punctuated with the fearsome sound of nocturnal predators. Above the general rumble of troop-movement and the clanging of guns and artillery, arose the voices and moans of the few wounded by half-hearted ambush, their cries, more distinct than any other sound in the darkness of the night. They seemed to fill the gloom enveloping the Recce Company of the Second

Division, which had been the very first to come under rebel fire, as they had approached the river from the center.

The convergence of the moaning and the darkness united became indistinguishable, until it seemed as if they were one and the same thing.

"Forward and fire!" Major Angwe commanded. "Right flank! Move forward! Fire and attack!" He continued

"Break through their center!" Major Lamurde commanded Warrant Officer 111, Zikkeh.

"Poof!" And this was followed by another succession of *"Poof-poof!"* Suddenly around them dense smoke was forming that seemed, temporarily, to blur their vision. Then, the sound of the big guns was heard from the distance, *boom-boom!* Seconds later, they were engulfed in another cloud of smoke, this time thicker and harsh against their faces, making their eyes burn, but they pressed on.

"Poof-poof!" two clouds of smoke arose, colliding and merging with one another, boom-*boom!* The deafening sounds of the big guns confirming what their eyes had experienced and seen.

The Colonel, who was following the movement of his troops, looked at the first puff of smoke, which, only an instant before had been a round compact ball, and now, in its place, he saw balloons of smoke drifting away to one side and then.. *poof!*... a pause... then, three more, then a fourth appeared, each one answered at identical intervals by a firm, precise majestic *boom!*... *boom-boom!* At one moment, the cloud seemed to scud across the sky, at the next, to remain fixed, while the woods along the banks and fields glittered with sparks from the big guns. From the left, over the fields and bushes, these great balls of fire and smoke were continually appearing, followed by their solemn unnerving reverberations. Whilst, nearer still, in the thick bushes around the river banks and the fields, burst little puffs of rifle-smoke that hardly formed into balls at all, but, instead, formed glitters of sparks, or embers, that died out in an instant. *Trak-ta-ta-tak!* The less-threatening, but, all the same, deadly, rapid successions of uneven cracks from the rifles sounded a little bit feeble, in comparison with the rhythmic and majestic roars of the big guns in the distance.

The Colonel wanted to be there in the midst of all the smoke and the glitter and sparks, but he merely blushed, smiled, and raised his hands to the heavens, because he knew that, this time, the center of the enemy forces really had been broken into, and that the rebel troops were in disarray, and were now firmly on the run. And run they did! The Federal troops streamed over the Onitsha Bridge across the River Niger, and Onitsha was liberated and the bridge secured, after an intense eight-hour battle, with heavy losses in lives and of materials on both sides. The local citizens poured into the streets, dancing on the bridge and rejoicing, some adorned the troops with garlands of flowers and with fine clothes.

"*Huh-ra-rah! Huh-ra-rah! Huh-ra-rah!*", Majors Angwe and Lamurde led their other officers, NCOs and the ranks in a rapturous response brimming with joy on the bridge.

Suddenly Private Lanem asked, "What did he say? Where to now? Are we going to halt?"

"No, there are still pockets of skirmishes and resistance outside the city proper, in the vicinity of the near-by villages that *Oga* (the boss) wants us to go to and mop off and secure", answered Warrant Officer Zikkeh.

There were several anxious questions that the soldiers would have liked to have asked after the ambush, as the Recce Battalion of the Second Division, under Second Lieutenant Owolowe, triumphantly marched forward, seemingly in unison. But none dared ask. Then, an order was passed along in whispers among the forward armored battalion that they were being ordered to halt. All came to attention where they were, right in the middle of the muddy narrow path. The talk grew louder and more intense amongst the men, once they stopped, not knowing *why* they had been ordered to stop. The answer that they had been squabbling to find out came to them when they learned that Lieutenant Bello Shehu had ordered Sergeant Woji to go fetch the Physician, Colonel Lamba, to come and treat the injured, because it was becoming increasingly difficult to carry them along. As a matter of fact, one of the injured men, Corporal Jajom, was shivering feverishly from pain, and from the cold and the damp surroundings. He was overcome by drowsiness and was restrained from any meaningful movement or action, due to the excruciating pain in his thigh and his arms from which he could find no comfort. He kept closing his eyes even as he lay down, and opening them again to look at his injured arm and the battered thigh caused by the enemy shrapnel from when they had fought back the ambush, only moments ago. Corporal Jajom had actually complained bitterly that he needed a vehicle, something, to convey him to one of the mobile clinics.

However, because of the GOC's original instruction, that they should not break ranks to cater for the injured or sick, and the tenuous nature of the terrain around the villages on the banks, it was viewed most impracticable to have Colonel Lamba come over to treat the wounded at this time. At one point Corporal Jazom had complained to his regimental sergeant major, Awume that they wanted him to "die like a dog".

"You don't mind, *Sah*?" Corporal Jajom asked Lieutenant Yohanna. But before the Lieutenant could answer, he volunteered:

"I got separated from my Company, *Sah*, I don't even know where the fuck I am!... frickin' bad luck, eh?!"

"What *does* you mean, you pick it up? Younoh, you no go get away with dat!" shouted one of the soldiers angrily. Meantime, another, slender and lean, soldier, with what looked like a soaked and blood-stained bandage wrapped around his head, came up to Sergeant Major Baddeh, and demanded, in an angry voice to see the Physician.

"They don't send for one *owlridy*", was his terse answer.

"Must one die like a dog?" Corporal Jazom suddenly blurted out again in a fit of furious and irrational anger ".

Not far from the Artillery Corps camp, in a quarter that had been prepared for him, Muhammed sat at a dinner table with his unit commanders, discussing the prosecution of the battle so far, and the war in general, especially the most recent victory— the battle for Onitsha and its surrounds.

Among those sitting around the dinner table was one of the Armored Battalion commanders, Lieutenant Colonel Umoru who was busy chewing on a chicken leg and wasn't really listening to the on-going conversation —he was an officer who had served, irreproachably for fifteen years, with distinction. In a corner of the quarters, stood a flag captured from the Biafran army. Surveying the room with an eager and naïve curiosity, reflected in both his eyes, Major Shelleng was feeling shell-shocked and fatalistic, and he shook his head vigorously, in perplexity, perhaps because the flag really interested him, or perhaps, because it was difficult for him to conceive of the flag of a mortal enemy, *affronting* him, even as he tried to enjoy a sumptuous meal, the likes of which he hadn't eaten in a very long time.

The Biafran officers captured in the battle for Onitsha and its surrounds and the bridge, included five Colonels, ten Lieutenant Colonels, ten Majors, eight Captains, and an untold number of NCOs and private soldiers. A whole camp was set up and securely guarded by the capable and noble heroic Federal soldiers to accommodate the prisoners. Some of the Federal troops who were more than eager to see instant unmitigated "jungle-justice" and old-fashioned vengeance meted out, in its crudest and most primitive forms, on the captured rebels, were reprimanded and denied access to the camp. General Muhammed gave directives to that effect, and it was rigorously obeyed, to the letter.

Meanwhile the GOC was thanking the individual unit commanders and querying them about the details of their engagements and losses in the battle that many hoped and prayed might well spell out or at least usher in, the end of hostilities, by the renunciation of any further aggression and an acceptance of the Federal structure and Federal authority by the rebels. A senseless war imposed on the Federal Government by the intransigence of few megalomaniac Igbo officers and some 'wise' politicians, leading to a brutal chapter in the nation. Finally, it would be over.

"When I saw, sir, that their first Battalion was disorganized", Lieutenant Colonel Umoru said, "I stood up straight and said to myself: I'll let them get through and then meet and massacre them with the fire of my whole battalion… -and that's just what I did!" The Colonel animatedly shared his successful military strategy with his GOC and comrades, and then continued,

"In addition, I must also report, sir, that Private John Jide, who was reduced to the ranks, took a Biafran officer prisoner before my very own eyes, and particularly distinguished himself".

"Where is this Private that you refer to?" The GOC asked.

"Sah, Private Jide is outside", Lieutenant Colonel Umoru replied.

"Bring him in", the GOC ordered.

Private Jide walked in, looking straight ahead, and saluted, with all the energy he could garner, and stood to attention, as if he had been some statue.

"Private Jide", the GOC began. "I was made aware of your heroic gallantry on the battlefield today",

"Thank you, *Sah, but* it's my duty, *Sah*", Jide responded, straightening up and in firm attention with a mixture of humility and pride, his eyes facing straight ahead of him, as if he were only a silhouette of himself and was expecting or waiting for some intervention or miracles to occur.

"In view of your heroism and gallantry in the heat of battle, you've, as far as I'm concerned, redeemed yourself, and, as your GOC, I am restoring you to your full rank of, Captain Jide!" There was a hush and complete silence in the room, which was followed by rapturous and explosive applause and military salutes. Private Jide now back to being Captain Jide could hardly believe what he had just heard. He fought back tears and reflected through his tortured life-story in silence and recognizing that he could hardly remember anything so great or so magnificent ever happening to him. He was, to begin with, sullen and speechless, but when he finally processed and understood just what had happened, he stood firm, erect, fighting back the tears, and saluted his GOC, turning and saluting to his unit commander, Lt. Colonel Umoru as well. "Thank you, Sirs"! He turned to the GOC again with tears now streaming freely down his cheeks.

Each officer of the Second Division gave account of his unit's commendable performance at the Battle of Onitsha to the General and to a sort of 'Council of War' cabinet.

"I thank you all, gentlemen, all units fought and behaved heroically, infantry, armored, artillery and our mechanized battalions". The happy, victorious and proud GOC concluded.

"Sir, I'll… if you permit me to express my opinion",

Second Lieutenant Gatasa observed.

"We chiefly owe our success to the genius of the GOC, and his salient experience and strategic insights into the science of war".

Everybody stood up, clapped and saluted the GOC.

"In the artillery Squadron the heroic endurance of Corporal Bukar Biu was exceptional and outstanding", 2nd Lieutenant Gatasa declared, recognizing the bravery of one of his favorite corporals.

"Congratulate him on my behalf, and tell him that I've heard how he distinguished himself under fire. And congratulate Bukar, Warrant Officer 11 on behalf of the Division as well", the GOC said with joviality and finality.

"Warrant Officer, Sir?!" Lieutenant Gatasa asked, with utmost surprise and flushed, almost blushing.

"Thank you *sah*, I will convey the news to Warrant Officer Bukar Biu, he will be really, really excited and grateful", he said, standing up straight to attention, and fervently saluting the attending GOC.

"Yes, Sir, he would be highly exalted to hear that you recognized and applauded his performance, but what will excite him most especially will be the promotion and the perks that go with it!"

Araba Let's Separate

"Bring the *Dokta* to him quickly", Warrant officer 11Bello commanded another soldier who was standing close by next to him.

At the conclusion of their meal and discussion, the officers of the Second Division again thanked their GOC, Muhammed, especially for the intimate and frank war-planning sessions, without which, success might easily have eluded them, or not even been achievable at all. However, for many of them, the meal was especially memorable, not because of Muhammed, though they *were* very grateful to him, but, because most hadn't had this sort of proper sustenance in a very long time!

After the capture of Onitsha, there was a long period of doldrums and a lull which the soldiers found unbearably frustrating. It wasn't because they didn't want to organize, refit and fight, but was due more prosaically to a lack of equipment and military materials, which, their officers felt, was prolonging and retarding the effective prosecution and ultimate completion of the war. It was at this time that, at his wits end and getting no satisfaction, the GOC, Muhmmad decided to journey to Lagos, to find out for him-self what was going on.

When the staff officers in Lagos saw him they got scared, and more than a little worried. "This is the officer who toppled the last regime that brought in the Commander-in-Chief", they observed,

"I hope he's not up to anything similar at this crucial moment", one of them added, jokingly, to his friend at the airport where they had gone to await and receive him.

"Something really bad *must* be going on, otherwise how could such a distinguished and proud officer leave his Division unannounced and without proper orders or protocol?" Lieutenant Habib Kyari, presciently, wondered.

After the GOC had settled and rested for the night in his posh Ikoyi hotel, he went down to the Supreme Military Headquarters, the following morning, and in front of all the officers, dressed them down very eloquently, not mincing words, using all the obscene military jargon he could remember that might adequately express his feelings at such moments. In essence, he accused them all, including the Commander-in-Chief, of treachery and a deliberate and purposeful effort to starve and malign him and his troops, willfully withholding from his division necessary equipment and military materials. He also accused them of deliberately trying to prolong the war. He said he was "pissed off" with the attitude of some of them at SHQ, because, while Commanders like him and other officers, and the rank-and-file were paying with their blood and lives the price of keeping the country one, many of them were just loafing around, biding their time, taking law-degree courses part-time at the University of Lagos in preparation for their future lives in *babban riga* (civilian dress), as soon as they'd hung up their khakis!

The officers were damned, silent, wishing he could just vanish, but he made sure he got his points and feelings across in a clear and unequivocal fashion, as befits a successful Nigerian war hero.

Muhammed was accused of indiscipline and insubordination by the Supreme Headquarters, especially after his direct attack on the Commander-in-Chief. When word came to him that the officers were conspiring to find a way that theycould discipline him, he said, "All of you! Fuck you! You think I give a damn with the Commander-in-Chief!? A man that I was instrumental in making a Head of State!? You can all go fuck your selves", and he sauntered out.

The decorated hero of the last *putsch* and the conqueror of Onitsha and Benin lulled around for days to see what the Supreme Headquarters would do in terms of disciplining him for insubordination and reckless dereliction of duty, but nothing happened. While he was waiting and nothing was happening, he became bored, bored to the bone, and decided to become pro-active asking for his own discharge from the military.

"I'm fed up with incompetence and indecision with regard to the war he said to himself, I'm out of here". With these parting words, he also attached his application for his terminal leave and off he went, taking a holiday overseas to England, without waiting for the response.

There were rumors in Lagos and other parts of the country that the GOC had indeed confided to friends that, from day one, he had seen in the Commander-in-Chief's eyes that he lacked the courage and acumen of an effective leader.

You see, my readers; the 2 Division's GOC, Muhammed, was one of those fundamentalist religious types who believed that things happen because of a divine will or solely through divine intervention! Viewed from this perspective he didn't appear to give his fighting men the proper accolades that they deserved, as a result of their gallantry and sheer determination of purpose. He strongly and sincerely believed that the Biafrans were defeated through the will of Allah, forgetting that the rebel forces had also prayed for victory to the same God or Allah! If one accepts his belief in divine intervention, what belief did the Federal troops have that the Biafrans lacked? Why would God grant *them* victory and not the rebel forces, who had similar hopes and aspirations and prayed just as intensely as the Federal troops? To ask a rhetorical question, where was the divine in the first three attempts of opposed river-crossing where they suffered the agony of retreat? What did they do differently to please the divine that they didn't do in those three battles? What I'm trying to say here, my readers, is that we should, and the GOC should, give due credit to the efforts of the troops, rather than reposing their well-deserved success to the omniscient intervention of a divine Being. The rebel forces also depended on the same divinity, and so why were they let down? The Federal troops deserved and earned their victory and success through superior military strategic plans and laser-like execution, period!

It was at this juncture; after the show-down in Lagos and the Second Division's GOC's sudden departure to England, that Haruna, a staff officer in Lagos, was appointed as the GOC of the Second Division. Haroun wasn't all that effective with the Division, as had been expected, because he abstained from making the hard and necessary substantial changes and decisions that were paramount in order for it to regain its confidence as a fighting force. He didn't hide his unhappiness and frustration with regard to the situation. It was marked all over his face, shown in his actions, even recognizable in the way he wore and buttoned his uniform! It was evident for anyone, who wanted to, to see. He didn't have to worry that long anyway, because, after fifteen months, or there about he was relieved of his command. The New Operational Instructions were announced, together with changes in command for all Divisions.

"I understand that there were countries that recognized the new Republic at the expense of the Republic of Nigeria", Abba asked perfunctorily.

"Indeed", the Professor answered in the affirmative, "Gabon, Zambia, Tanganyika, Cote d'Ivoire (the Ivory Coast) and Haiti", all did recognize Biafra.

"Also I heard that some mercenaries and International Organizations were engaged to help the projected Republic of Biafra", asked Francisca.

"Yes", again the Professor reluctantly responded in the affirmative—reluctantly because he believed they had discussed the mercenary menace before— "as we discussed earlier the mercenaries included the infamous German mercenary, Rolf Steiner, who also fought in Katanga (Shaba Province) in the Democratic Republic of the Congo (DRC) in the 1960s. He commanded the Biafran "S" special unit ("S" here stands for "Strike"). Others who had also fought in the Congo as mercenaries joined the rebel cause as infantry, these included John Erasmus, Taffy Williams, Alex Edmund , Armand Iaranelli, and Paddy Leroy (the mercenaries often didn't give their full real names, which means the lists may vary from one area or country of operation to another) . The "S" brigade made several futile attempts to recapture Enugu, but to no avail. Other mercenaries included pilots who defied the Federal Government's "no fly zone", flying in military supply through Sao Tome, Also supporting the Biafran adventure was the International Committee of the Red Cross (ICRC) and several church organizations in both Europe and the Americas. They were directly involved in aiding and abetting the rebels by flying in 'mixed cargo' during the night. 'Mixed cargo', as you may know, means medicine, food, weapons and ammunitions", he concluded distressingly.

"It should be made clear, though, that the Governments of the United States, the British, and the Soviet Union (Russia), gave their unflinching and uncompromising support to the Federal Government of the Republic of Nigeria", he added.

Chapter Eleven
The Southern theatre

"Prior to the issuance of the New Operational Instruction (NOI) that directed changes in the command positions for the military", Alhaji Wada resumed, "Adekunle, (a.k.a "Black Scorpion") was in command of the 3 Marines Commando Division, which were formerly the Lagos Garrison Organization (LGO). The Garrison initially had the 6 Battalion, but later, to the 6, the 7 Battalion was added. The bulk of the fighting force, were, non-Igbos. The first successful landing of the Garrison was at Bonny, after a fierce battle at sea that also involved the Nigerian navy. At almost the same time, the troop captured Peterside, and Mrs. Adekunle was rescued. She hailed from the island and was captured and interned by the rebel forces until her rescue. The Shell BP manager at Bonny didn't fare much better, as he too was captured and asked to pay a substantial ransom royalties. He also was rescued by the federal forces after their capture of Bonny.

Following the rebels adventure, or infiltration, into the Mid-West state the LGO was ordered to move to Escravos, to render help to the Second Division. The 6 and 8 Battalions, under the command of Ochefu, headed for Escravos, while the 7 Battalion remained in Bonny, under the command of Abubakar. With the apparent dissipation of his forces, the Scorpion went to Lagos to lodge his complaints to SHQ. But, also, to twist some arms — it was at this time that he seized Lieutenant Ismailu in a hotel in Lagos after his return from the Royal Military Academy Officers' course at Sandhurst, England, and dragged him to the front, whereby, within three weeks, exposed to battle without proper orientation, still considerably confused and traumatized, he was swiftly killed by rebel ambush.

The Scorpion was successful in his requests, because the LGO became the 3 Infantry Division — even though he did all he could to get it named 2 Division because, according to *his* logic, the LGO was the second formation to enter the war proper — and was boosted to Brigade status, with troops from Kaduna, Zaria and Lagos. Two Battalions were formed, the 31st and 32nd, under the respective commands of Aliyu and Hamman. According to eye-witness accounts, Ochefu, who cleared Warri, once remarked that the three Battalions under him, 6, 7, and 8, didn't have to fire their guns, as the locals were able to flush out the rebel forces amongst them, capturing a cache of weapons.

With the 3 Infantry Division now headquartered at Warri, the Scorpion embarked on a prodigious planning. His plan envisaged the 3 Infantry formation advancing north to Umutu, Utagabunor, Uronighe Kwale and Ughelli in the riverine areas and linking up there with the second Division troops.

Once more the Scorpion went off to Lagos to plead for his formation to be designated 3 Marine Commandos Division. As with the last time, he pretty much got what he wanted, and they did indeed become the 3 Marine Commando Division. From Warri, the newly-minted 3 Marine Division moved on, once more, to Bonny where he launched *Operation Tiger Claw* to capture Calabar. He had expected an easy and quick victory, but it wasn't to be. Phillip was designated the General Staff Officer for the operation. It was at this time, in Warri, that the one-thousand ill-disciplined, hurriedly-trained militia volunteer indigenes under Boro I Adaka joined the 3 Marines. Half of the Boro men were left at Bonny while the other half including Boro himself joined the Calabar landing-force, under the command of Abubakar, but most died in the intense battles that ensued, including such patriots as the Mathematician, Bodman Nyanayo, Historian, George Amangala and Nottingham Dick. The quick and easy victory didn't materialize, as the rebel 9 Battalion and their navy put on a heroic battle and gave hell to the Federal army.

The Federals' battle plan consisted of 6 Battalions including the hardened and battle-tested 8 Battalion, under the command of Ochefu, and the 33 battalion, under the command of Hamman. At the resumption of action, the experienced 31 Battalion, under Aliyu, joined the fiasco, in addition to the relatively untested 34, 35, 36 and 37 Battalions. After an intensive and bloody battle, lasting hours, the cement factory finally fell to Ochefu and his men of the 8 Battalion. By this time the rebels had become encircled, by the 37 battalion, under Abubakar, the 33 battalion under Hamman, and the 34 battalion, under the GOC himself, who sealed off the southern-most escape route around Calabar. The 33 battalion and one of the three other battalions mopped up the encircled rebels and pummeled them from the rear, whereupon they were eliminated, by the 8Battalion, in a merciless military fashion.

The capture of Calabar led to a rapturous celebration amongst the local population. They streamed out into the streets, from their hide-outs in the forests, swamps, hills and every patch of the riverine, dancing and beating drums. The capture of Calabar, which came close on the heels of the capture of Enugu by the 1st Division, gave the Federal troops an unsurpassed confidence and a very helpful boost in morale. Biafra, at this time, was sealed from the sea and their only means of communication with the outside world was Port Harcourt. It was at this time that the cry of genocide was loudly heard all over the world, a propaganda spread by the "Voice of Biafra" radio, and by the so-called 'friends of Biafra' ensconsed in the Western capitals.

The rebels made concerted and dare-devil efforts to retake Bonny from the Federal forces, but their determination and efforts were repelled and met with fierce defense by the Federal troops, who also suffered losses and injuries, including that of Bello, who was shot and had to be evacuated to Lagos for treatment. It was at this time that the "B 26 menace and harassment"—the harassment consisted of the rebel's ability to hit some northern cities and airports at will because the Federal Government didn't have interceptor fighter planes to challenge it— reached its peak. Beside the B26 menace, the rebel "red devil"— rebel battalion formed exclusively of mercenaries—inflicted the most casualties amongst the Federal troops. At one time — can you believe it? —the rebels and the Federal forces were just one hundred yards apart, facing each other, but neither had the strength to inflict any damage on the other, nor make the first attempt at attack, because of fatigue and exhaustion. The two forces just lay sprawled out, looking at one another across the battle line, each expecting the other to make the first move. After what seemed an eternity, the 15 Brigade, under Akinrinade, drove the rebels out of Bonny for good.

What the Black Scorpion had on his plate at this time was the capture of Uyo, Annang and Aba. The capture of Port Harcourt and Owerri was initially assigned to the 2 Division, but after the capture of Obubra, the Scorpion ordered his men to advance on Port Harcourt. In spite of the rebels' best efforts to hold on to Uyo and Annang, the dynamism of the Federal forces could not be deterred. Uyo was taken with untold losses in both human and materiél terms to the rebels. At Ikot Ekpene, it was said, the rebel forces abandoned their formation in utter disarray, snatching any civilian clothes that they could lay their hands on from the local population and running into the bushes. Some were dressed in skirts and blouses!

The Boro's Sea School Boys as mentioned earlier were some one-thousand ill-disciplined, ill-trained, Rivers State militia which Isaac Boro hurriedly collected and had join the 3 Marine Brigade at Bonny. The Boro Boys proved indispensible within the ri-ve-rine areas. Their knowledge of the ri-ve-rine lakes, swamps, ponds, and their ability to leave off the land was a lesson in forest management and primal survival; this, beside their adept fluency with the local dialects. These qualities endeared them, especially in areas like Opobo, Andoni, Opolom, Oranga and Buguma. The unrelenting push toward Port Harcourt even astonished the Federals themselves, and resulted in among other things an utter confusion among the rebels lodged in Port Harcourt and Umuahia.

However, the death of Boro in a hand-to-hand combat at this time, led to the dissolution of the 19 Brigade. Immediately after his death, the 3 Marine Brigade commandos entered Port Harcourt and, to their complete amazement, found the Biafran defenders in absolute disarray. One didn't need to look too far to see now that the tables had turned squarely against the rebels, especially with the sequential fall of Port Harcourt, Bonny, Enugu and Calabar. The mercenaries began to pack their back-packs, looking for a way of escape. They wanted to get as far away as possible from defeat and disaster. As for the Federal forces, not even the Scorpion could stop them from enjoying the spoils of war.

The next mother-of-all grand plans, envisaged by the ambitious and rambunctious 3 Marine Brigade GOC was nicknamed *Operation OAU*, that is, the simultaneous capture of Owerri, Aba and Umuahia.

Prior to launching *Operation OAU* the riverine areas had to be mopped up completely by the 15 Brigade and the remnant of the dissolved 19 Brigade, while the Division was reorganized into sectors. Under the mother-of-all plans, the capture of Owerri was assigned to 15 and 16 Brigades under the commands of Alabi and Utuk respectively, and Aba was assigned the 12 and 17 Brigades, under the respective commands of Isemeda and Shanade. The capture of Umuahia was assigned to the 13 and 18 Brigades, under the commands of Tuoyo and Aliyu, respectively. The link between Owerri and Aba was to be accomplished by the 14 Brigade under Innih. The mortal mortar attack on Aba was to be led by the 105 Battalion of the 17 Brigade, and that on Owerri by the 33 Battalion of the 16 Brigade.

Swiftly the battle was engaged, and with fierce exchanges of mortal fire, sometimes with hand-to-hand combat the backbone of the enemy was broken and the 16 Brigade were successful, Owerri they could happily declare had fallen. This deadly defeat followed a calamitous fall of Aba, a fortnight earlier; it was over-run by the 17 Brigade", the Professor paused to answer a question from his granddaughter, Etty/Salamatu who had come in running and breathing hard.

"You see", he continued, "The Scorpion was always looking for a way to make *his* commandos the best fighting force in the entire enterprise. As such, he immediately embarked on another re-organization of the Division without even informing the Supreme Headquarters until after. The Division was re-organized into four sectors as follows: sector one, comprised of the 15 and 16 Brigades under the command of Ally, sector two comprised of the 14 and 17 Brigades, under the command of Akinrinade, sector three was comprised of the 12, 13 and 18 Brigades, under the command of Alabi Isama, and the fourth sector was administrative and was based in Calabar, under the command of Ariyo.

The push to Umuahia by the third sector proved very daunting and gave considerable concern to the GOC and to Supreme Headquarters as well. The 2 Division in Onitsha was bogged down and wasn't moving at all, while 1 Division was making a mere snail's crawl toward their target after the disposition of Okigwe.

After desperate international outcry and accusations of "genocide" and evocations of "pogroms" by the rebels, some countries, like the French and Tanzania, resumed their support both morally and militarily. These actions boosted the morale and fighting efforts of the rebel forces that launched a dare-devil do-or-die kamikaze suicidal attack on the Federal troops, with the determined intention of recapturing Owerri and Aba. At first their efforts were repelled by the vigilant and equally determined 105 Battalion of the 17 Brigade and the 33Battalion of the 16Brigade; but a more megalomaniac attack by the rebels 14 Division, a fortnight later, involving the now-desperate mercenaries and the "S" division proved devastating and fatal to the Federals. They were encircled, and food had to be dropped in, from the air. There were numerous occasions when drops — food, medicine and ammunition! — actually fell in the rebel territory and was seized and celebrated. This often occurred because of the inaccuracies of the drop-offs, which were caused in part; by a mortal and understandable perhaps fear of being finding oneself shot-down by the rebel Battery, or else due to the low level of pilot visibility of the area. On such occasions, the rebels feasted all day and all night gleefully on sumptuous unexpected delicious meals and the re-stocking and refurbishment of their stock of guns and weapons. The federal troops were dying, not only of injuries but starvation, and hunger as well. It was a dire situation, the sick and the dead lying side by side, and the living, barely a notch better. Night and day the living was surrounded by sordid moans and squeaking cries of hunger and death.

Eventually, desperate for survival and continued living, the federal forces withdrew in the pitch dark night, quietly, by a disused road, as the unsuspecting rebel forces feasted on more of the misguided drop-offs of food that had come their way two days earlier, along with some palm wine, which they had been given by Okozeh, a farmer. In spite of the difficulty of their escape and the uncertainty of any success it might portend, the faithful soldiers, just like the US Rangers' could not leave behind the body of Major Hamman, their tough and loving second-in command who had died during the siege. He was buried with full military honors later that month in his town, far from the battlefield.

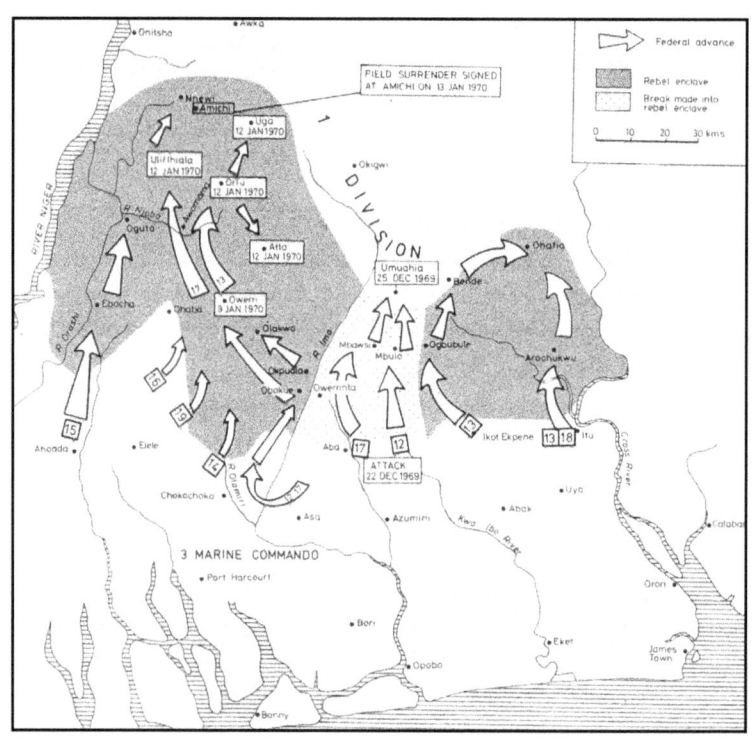

Fig. 5: Retreat

Adapted from Obasanjo, 1980

The withdrawal from the siege as narrated above, took place under the pitch-dark nocturnal clouds of the tropics using a disused escape route. Certainly the death at this time of one of the most celebrated commanders in the southern Sector, had created panic, despondency, even a morbid melancholy, among the soldiers, and had also shattered with irreparable stain the myth of the invincibility of the Division's GOC and the unstoppability of his soldiers. An importune change was required and urgently. Before changes were made however, the 1 Division maintained their pressure on Umuahia and Bende. The two towns were captured only days apart, and prior to the announcement of the new operational military instruction.

The new kids on the block were as follows: 1 Division was assigned to Bisalla; 2 Division, under the command of Jallo, and the 3 Marine commandos Brigade under the command of Olu. The change of command implied change in a robust strategy and with execution. The new and robust changes were as follows:

A
- 1 Division, under Bisalla was to take over from 2 Division in the Onitsha area.
- Advance to Nnewi and beyond yonder
- Capture Orlu and continue forward movement in order to exploit the remaining surrounds.

B
- 2 Division under the command of Jallo has the primary function of the defense and protection of the Mid-West
- To hold and enhance defensive positions along the River Niger to prevent border incursion and infiltration by the rebels.

C
- The 3 Marine commandos under the command of Olu was charged with stabilizing and maintaining defensive lines of attack
- Assigned the daunting task of recapturing and holding on to Owerri and exploiting the surrounds beyond.
- The recapture and holding onto Oguta and its surrounds.

With these changes the stage was set for our new generation of commanders, the Professor concluded his talk, recognizing, by glancing at the clock, that it was their lunch time.

Chapter Twelve
Light at the End of the Tunnel
The Marine Commandos

At this point, let me digress, momentarily, to discuss the role of a Divisional Commander. Those versed in military matters know that a Divisional Commander is always in the midst of a series of "shifting events", and consequently can never, at any one moment, be in a position to consider the import of *all* of the decisions or events swirling around him, simultaneously. At every moment, events always shift rapidly events, about which he has little or no control. According to General Muhammed, he remains always at the center of the most complex play of "intrigues, worries, contingencies, authorities … councils, threats and deceptions" imagined or real, which he is continually obligated to respond to, and evaluate, or countless number of conflicting questions, addressed to him, without the benefit of time to really mull the issues over in a deliberative manner.

In most cases, the commander has before him, and especially at critical moments in battle, not less than half-a-dozen projects and recommendations all seemingly based on sound rules and principles of strategy and tactics and often diametrically contradictory to one another. It is, thus, his responsibility to winnow out the good ones from the chaff, those practicable and most likely to yield the most-desired results. People who forget, or are not even aware of these intricate conditions that a commander works through, can and must be excused. The decisions of life-and-death that commanders must make under the most stressful conditions would challenge any of the brightest faculties in any of us! And yet these are the situations all commanders find themselves in, including the commander of the 3 Marine Commandos, Colonel Oloye Olu (later, General Oloye Olu).

"So how did the war end?" Both Abba and Dr. Kasimu asked simultaneously.

"I see that you're putting the cart before the horse, but, before we discuss it at length, the replacement of the Black Scorpion with Commander Olu as the GOC of the Third Marine Commandos was a turning point in the war. When Olu took over the command of the Marines, the Federal soldiers had begun to suffer what is known as 'war fatigue' and their morale was low. But this was also true of the rebel forces. Many professed, with surprising conviction, that with the apparent dissipation of the fighting spirit of the rebel soldiers, their surrender was imminent.

But boy were they wrong! - Big-time!

Even though the surrender article was finally arranged by the GOC of the Third Marine Commandos, General Olu, and Effiong, (coming from an Ibibio minority) and, representing the rebel leadership - I'm not very sure if I am pronouncing the name correctly— there were still long protracted periods of tense and fierce battle before that occurred.

"Do we have any information on how the different sectors or fronts prosecuted the war after the appointments of the new General Commanding Officers?' James and Francisca asked.

"Yes", Professor Balarabe answered, "There are several books written after the war that address this, but, you know, most of our people depend on what our fighting men told them when they returned home, after the war. Some of the stories, as you know, may be a little bit exaggerated, but all the same, I will narrate some of these tales told at the time".

Typical battle scene, plan and disposition
The Third Division of the Marines under the Scorpion

One would have thought it impossible for a man to stand any more rigidly to attention than Captain Samuel Oche had stood when being reprimanded by the GOC of the Third Marine Commandos Division, Colonel Adekunle (also known as The Black Scorpion) for the shocking infringement of an unpolished epaulette. The moment he was addressed, he drew himself up until he looked as though he could not possibly have sustained the posture had the GOC continued to look at him much longer. The Black Scorpion, a tall heavy-set, officer, understanding the Captain's position and wishing him nothing but good, quickly turned away, and a barely perceptible smile flitted over his puffy face, which was mildly disfigured with several tiny smallpox scars. The GOC sauntered to some of the other units under his command for inspection.

The third Recce Company, commanded by Colonel Zibeh was the last to fall out of the parade line, and the Black Scorpion, apparently trying to recollect something *important,* stood alone self-contained in his thoughts. Then Major Apollo approached him, saluted and said,

"Sah, you instructed me to remind you of the reduced officer, Bokot".

"Ah! So where is this Bokot"? The Black Scorpion barked.

Bokot had been reduced in rank; he'd been demoted from a Major to a 2nd Lieutenant. This was because; he had gone out with his platoon without permission and attacked Mbaise, a village hidden in the thick riverine forest area. Unfortunately, he had lost some few men; consequently he was now dressed in a 2nd Lieutenant's combat dress instead of a Major's.

"Bokot", the Major shouted his name.

Instead of answering, Bokot, a thin trim figure with a bald head; a jutting-out chin and wide open eyes, just stepped right out of the line. He walked up to the GOC and saluted.

"Ah, so I hope this will be a lesson to you!" The GOC said. "Do your duty and follow orders, the Head of State and C in C is merciful, and he might well restore you on appeal. I shan't forget you; if you merit it, I will make the appropriate recommendations to him", he concluded with an air of finality and authority, as he did in many ways over life and death issues.

Before the GOC departed after he'd addressed the Bokot affair; Bokot declared in his firm and raging voice, "One thing I ask of you, Sah… that I be given an opportunity to expiate my guilt and prove my devotion to the Head of State and the Commander- in- Chief, and the flag of the Federal Republic…"

"Tell me", the GOC said to Major Apollo, "I've been meaning to ask you about him… is he behaving himself? In general, is he…"

"As far as the services are conceived, he is most punctilious…but his character Sir…"the Colonel broke off dismissively.

"What about his character?" the GOC asked.

"It's different on different days", replied Colonel Zibeh, "One day he's sensible, intelligent and good-natured, and the next day, he's a wild beast, a monster. As a matter of fact, I have recently entertained the idea, correct or not, that he suffers from what the psychiatrists call a "bipolar personality". In fact, sir, if you please, recently, he became enraged and nearly killed an old stooping-down civilian in the town of Okigwe, near Oguta, because the man wouldn't let him use the roof of his house for a reconnaissance position. Forgive me, sir, but such are the symptoms of bipolar personality, or it might be what they now call "traumatic battle-field syndrome". Major Apollo nodded in the affirmative to everything the Colonel had said about Bokot.

"Well, well" said the GOC, "Still, one must have pity on a young man in trouble, he has important connections, you know… so you just…"

"Yes, sir", said the Colonel, showing by his smile that he understood the GOC's wishes and prerogatives.

"Ah, yes".

"Major Apollo", the Colonel spoke, "you've heard what the GOC said with regard to Bokot?"

"Yes *sah!*" Major Apollo answered saluting the Colonel in a strict military fashion.

Among his fellow-officers on the Scorpion's staff, and in the army in general, Major (now 2nd Lieutenant) Bokot had an outstanding reputation as a gambler and a so-cial-izer, he was known as the "party animal" just as he had had been in Oturkpo, before joining the army, some years ago. The story circulating around about his life before he joined the services was that of a man always gallivanting with women, while his beautiful wife, Maud, was left tragically at home to fend for herself and their two children. Hence, although a minority of the officers regarded him as being different from themselves and everyone else — some even expected great things of him because he was witty and smart, some listened to him, even admired him and imitated some of his antics. With them he was 'natural', agreeable and pleasant— a majority of them, however, disliked him and considered him cold, conceited, disagreeable, manipulative, and thought that he deserved the mess that he got himself into. A minuscule number thought he has an imposing attitude and personality that made him worthy of respect, even reverence as a leader.

Colonel Zibeh emerged from the Scorpion's room with papers in his hand, and his friend, Adjutant Captain Omotosho, who, standing at the door, asked,

"Well Nas (a nick name) how did it go?"

"I've been asked to write a memorandum on the reasons why we are not advancing as rapidly as we should, or had been expected".

"So we aren't, are we"? Omotosho asked

Colonel Zibeh only shrugged his shoulders and said nothing.

As they stood there trying to figure out why they weren't advancing to Bonny after camping forty-five miles away, suddenly a five-foot eight gentleman dressed in a camouflage jungle outfit breezed in with a red handkerchief around his neck, and irrepressible curiosity.

"Commander Scorpion?" he inquired, in a hurry, hardly slowing down, and speaking in a clear Hausa accent, and looking from side to side as he advanced, without pausing, straight to the door of the Scorpion's private ante-room.

"The Commander is engaged, Sir", Omotosho said, hurriedly going up to the unknown visitor and blocking his way, standing rigid at attention as if he were standing on a parade ground. The visitor's face clouded temporarily, his lips twitched and quivered. He then quickly took out a notebook from his inside pocket and rapidly scribbled something in pencil, tore out the leaf and handed it to Omotosho, then went to the window where he flung himself into a chair and looked up at the audience of officers, as if to say; "I'm surprise you don't know who I am?, so my false appearance has worked. But why are you staring at me?" Then he lifted his head, and cracked his neck as if he were about to say something, and, with affected indifference began humming a song in Hausa (*Ta'aziyar Ahmadu Bello* by *Dan Maraya* of Jos) under his breath, producing a strange sound for the ear indeed.

The door to the private ante-room of the Black Scorpion opened and the Scorpion appeared. "A note, Sir" Omotosho said, and handed him the note from the visitor still waiting outside. When the Scorpion saw the note and looked at the name at the bottom, he just darted out, without bothering to read the rest of the contents of the note, and called out

"General Shuwa! What a surprise, Come on in! Why did they keep you waiting?'

"Excuse us sah, we…"

"There is absolutely no excuse; I need an explanation … later".

He ushered in his visitor to his private suite and they began chatting about the progress of the war on the different fronts.

Meantime Captain Omotosho was shaking in his boots outside. "How is it I didn't recognize him?! I've seen his photos literally thousands of times, but had never met the audacious and, frankly, somewhat enigmatic general ever before in person"! - Until now!

Adjutant Captain Omotosho should have known, because this was one of our most successful sector Commanders, his accomplishments were legendary, just like those of the Scorpion's! In physical stature, the General was of a medium height, about 5ft. 6 or 7 inches tall, very slender, with a light complexion and normally very affable. To tell you the truth, he didn't really look like those pictures of him we see on the covers of the *New Nigerian* or the *Daily Times*. He was a much better-looking and more-unassuming gentleman.

"I owe the General a thousand apologies for my seeming inopportune conduct" Omotosho remonstrated quietly with himself, wondering how he was going to explain his inordinate unbecoming conduct and his seeming stupidity to the Scorpion.

Four hours after his arrival to see the Black Scorpion, the stranger walked out hand in hand with his host and quietly disappeared into the shadows, and was heard humming another Hausa song, *Yaki ya ci Ahmadu* by Dan Kwairo.

As a digression, I want to remind my readers that the life of a nation is not dependent on the lives or judgments of just a few men. In the life of a nation, whatever event may occur, whoever may stand at the helm of that event, theory can always claim that such-and-such an individual took the lead, but only because of the collective will of the people. Whenever an event occurs, a man, or men — here, it should be taken as axiomatic that women are included in this term man/men —appears, by whose will the event seems to have taken place, in an instant, it is obvious who these men are. But it's not our proclivity or interest at this time to go back and attempt to revise History by apportioning blame or platitudes to striking individuals.

On the other hand, reason shows that the expression of man's will—that is his words and actions—are only part of the general activity that are expressed in an event, be it a war or revolution. It is almost inconceivable but reluctantly necessary to accept the fact that words was the source or vehicle of the mass movement and engagement of millions of men and women on different fronts during the War, with the consequential results of suffering, untold deaths and lives taken before they even have the chance to flower.

Such was the death of a friend's son, Ismailu Bhalami, who had just returned from the Royal Military Academy, Sandhurst England, from his military training. This young budding officer hadn't even had the privilege of seeing or meeting his parents, when the Black Scorpion fetishly intercepted him in a hotel in our capital and asked him what front he belonged to? The young man, so naïve of the powers of GOC during war, told him he hadn't been assigned any yet, because he'd just finished his course overseas and was yet to be deployed.

The Black Scorpion cut him off abruptly "then fuck you, you're a Northerner, Hausa, isn't that so?"

"Northerner, yes sir, but not Hausa" was the young man's answer.

"What's the difference? Now your frickin'ass belongs to me; pack up your stuff and come with me".

The young man did as he was ordered and, a few days later, news came to his parents in the village that he had died a hero's' death; that they should be proud of him because he had died for his country. His parents were devastated and inconsolable for years, following this, the death of this lone son. And so, yes words and actions *do* have consequences and sometimes even catastrophic and hideous ones.

"I need an explanation in writing in the next two hours", the Scorpion belched out an order to Omotosho.

"Yes, *Sah*", Omotosho responded, standing up erect.

Squadron Commander, Aondakka, was a sanguine, thick-set middle-aged Lieutenant-Colonel, with grizzled eyebrows and whiskers. He was broad from chest to back then across the shoulders. He wore a brand new uniform, still creased where it had been folded. On the uniform were thick military epaulettes, which he had earned from his missions in Katanga-Congo and Liberia. The epaulettes seemed to stand up on their own, not even requiring the weight of his corpulent shoulders.

Viewing the parade with his GOC, Colonel Aondakka walked with arched back and a somewhat a quivering body; however it was not difficult to see that, with every step he took, there was an air of a happy man performing one of his life's most sacred duties. Believe me, it wasn't difficult for those watching to see that the Squadron commander was admired and was justifiably proud of his men.

Beaming with smile he approached Second Lieutenant Wambai, one of his platoon commanders, and said,

"We certainly had our hands full last night. However, they aren't the worst squadron… eh?"

"No, Sah", the platoon leader answered, with his whole body straightened, in full attention.

"Thank God, not even one infantryman or officer was upbraided today for his appearance, shabby uniform, absence of attention, or unpolished insignia", the Lt. Colonel Aondakka noted.

Major Abagana having reached the furthest point of the right flank of the Second Armored Company of the Third Division, began walking downhill toward the towns of Mbieri in the East, and Mbano to the South, where the gunfire was heard, but, actually, nothing could be seen, on account of smoke, and because of the mists and thick undergrowth and the vast swamps. The nearer he and his Platoon leader, Second Lieutenant Garba, got to the bottom of the hill, the more they felt the premonition of the discovery of the central battle field. They encountered several wounded soldiers, one of whom had a bleeding head and had lost his protective cap. He was wheezing and spitting-out blood. A bullet had evidently hit him in the mouth, or the throat. Another soldier, with a wounded arm from which blood poured over his combat dress, was groaning. He was, for all intent and purposes, expressing more groans of fear than groans of pain. After crossing a shallow stream between the towns of Orsu and Isu, they descended a steep incline, on which they saw several men lying on the ground, some of whom had been wounded and were awaiting rescue. There were also some who were merely exhausted and had passed out.

The Major and his Platoon leader continued to ascend the hill, breathing heavily. However, despite noticing Lieutenant Colonel Dimkat, giving orders to the left flank, they didn't stop, they just saluted him briefly, and continued, whispering to each other about the fallen brothers, fallen soldiers they had just encountered. Suddenly they came across a group of retreating soldiers who had been ordered to go back, but were reluctant, for fear of an ambush. The whole area between Orsu vale and Oron was completely permeated with smoke and all the faces of the soldiers were blackened. Some were firing blindly, at random, because of the smoke which the wind didn't lift, and others with no method and with no focus, out of the fear of death.

Corporal Ekpene Botte approached the Major and informed him that his company had been ambushed and attacked by a bunch of tattered Biafran soldiers, and that though the attack had been repulsed he had lost a few men. In telling the Major that the attack had been "repulsed", Corporal Ekpene Botte was merely applying a military term to what had happened, but, in fact, he did not himself know *what* had happened, during that half hour or so, to the soldiers entrusted to him. To tell the truth, he could not say, with certainty, whether the attack had been repulsed or whether his men had been routed and had just run away, in disarray. This incident was just one of hundreds that happened during the civil war– similar confusion could be seen on both sides of the conflict.

By evening of the fourth day, the troops of the Third Division had assembled at their designated places, and, during the night, had even made some subtle advances. It was the dry *harmattan* season in the Northern part of the country, but on this front there were thick clouds in the sky, thou it hadn't started to rain yet. Though the ground was damp in the area, it wasn't particularly muddy, and the troops moved noiselessly, except for the occasional faint clanking of artillery and vehicles. Talking aloud was forbidden, lest the enemy be forewarned, as well as smoking or striking a match.

It is plausible to assume that the secrecy of the enterprise heightened its allure and magnificence. But in spite of everything, the soldiers marched with pride, buoyancy and cockiness, as befitting a confident army. Several of the units, supposing they had reached their destination, halted and rested their guns as they settled down on the wet damp ground, others however, marched all night, reaching places beyond their area of operations.

As you may surmise, the Scorpion was livid when he found out about this blunder of mixed signals and confused orders. He immediately sent signals out for those who stopped before their assigned destinations commanding them to "double-up", and be in their right places before battle ensued, "otherwise…well, you know what!"

Only Lieutenant Gwor and his Recce Company reached the right operational vicinity of Mbano and Orlu. His detachment halted at a thick and swampy forest of the outskirts of Mbano, on a path leading to the village of Ogbia, and waited for the other Battalions. Toward dawn, Lieutenant Gwor, having dozed off, woke up, and sat down at the edge of his camp bed. What woke the Lieutenant was a clamor about the presence of a Biafran dissenter from Major Okigwe Effiong battalion. Corporal Ezakiel Ezeumune explained to the crowd of Federal soldiers around him that he had deserted because he had been slighted in the service of the rebel cause. He said he ought to have been an officer because he was

Araba Let's Separate

braver than any of those that had been promoted. He deemed this as an ethnic discrimination, because he was from the *Calabari* ethnic group and not an Igbo. He said that he had left with the intention of getting back at them. He said that Major Effiong's Battalion was spending the night near the town of Amassoma, less than ten miles away from where they were. He pleaded with them to give him a unit of about hundred or so soldiers, which he would lead, in order to capture Major Effiong. Lieutenant Gwor and his NCOs looked at each other with suspicion, but finally agreed to consult and debate about this dicey situation. This offer, they felt, were just too good to be true and at the same time could not be easily turned down, it could work to their advantage but they were not sure if it was a set up. The rebels had used such ancient war-strategies, thousands of times in the past, to lure the troops and then ambush them.

Lieutenant Gwor, therefore, decided to contact his superior, Major U. Uchedu, who had a direct line with GOC, the Scorpion. When Major Uchedu contacted the GOC and relayed to him the situation, both men remembered the story of the albatross, where it is said that "you're damned if you do, and damned if you don't". However, after a lengthy discussion and several arguments involving some of the senior commanders, it was decided to assign at least three Battalions (armored, artillery and the Recce) with sufficient fire-power to accompany the corporal, and it was decided that all three Battalions should be under the command of a Colonel.

"Now, listen good", Colonel Martin Adzira told Corporal Ezeumune, "If you lied to the GOC and me, I'll have you hung like a dog, with your head and balls down and your feet up, but if what you say is true, you will be a free man and will indeed be given the option of joining the Federal army as a Captain. That is a promise from the GOC",

Corporal Ezeumune made no further comments, but resolved more than ever to lead the way.

The unit, under the command of Lieutenant Colonel Bamaiyi and the Corporal, disappeared into the forest, while Colonel Adzira, two other officers (Adjutant Major Chonge and Lieutenant Kyari) and a reconnaissance Platoon, under the command of Lieutenant Kompur, went ahead. Colonel Adzira was shivering in the cool early dawn, and excited by this adventure, or *mis*-adventure, you might say. They were soon out of the forest, and Colonel Adzira reminisced that the troops ought to have begun appearing on the open area directly to the right. He looked in the direction of the towns of Orlu and Amassoma, but, though the troops should have been visible there was nothing in sight. It seemed to him, at this moment, that there was some sort of foul play at work. Among the advanced units, things were beginning to stir, and this observation was confirmed by his sharp-eyed Adjutant, Major Chonge.

"Oh it's too late!" Colonel Adzira declared, in his booming voice, after gazing at the rebel camp in the near distance through his high-resolution binoculars.

As often happens when someone you have trusted is no longer before your eyes and out of your reach, and they never told you where they were going, suspicion sets in and takes over your thoughts about that person. Likewise, it suddenly seemed absolutely clear and obvious to Colonel Adzira that Corporal Ezeumune had been an imposter all along, that he had told them a pack of lies! "Why didn't I, or anybody else, see it coming?" He lamented. Corporal Ezeumune had snickered back to the rebel camp after obtaining permission to relieve himself!

"I can't believe it!" Major Chonge puffed out, in frustration and anger.

"Of course, all along I'd suspected that the rogue was lying", Lieutenant Kompur declared

"Our men should be called back", Lieutenant Kyari, recommended to nobody in particular.

"Hey! Really…what do you guys think? Shall we let them go on or not?" Colonel Adzira sought the opinion of his senior officers.

"Do you want them to turn back, Sah?"

"Yes! Get them back, and get them back urgently! I can't sacrifice those brave soldiers, not without the other Battalions, especially the armored',

Colonel Adzira ordered and justified his order.

The Adjutant, Major Chonge, quickly sent a signal to Lieutenant Colonel Bamaiyi to return, informing him that all had been a set-up and that he didn't have enough fire-power or men to face the enemy. When Colonel Bamaiyi received the signal he called his staff officer, Lieutenant Waltinata and other senior officers under his command, including few NCOs, and discussed the situation and the prospect of their retreat. The provisional war-council unanimously agreed that there was no return, that if it was their fate, they would face it squarely as men; and leaves their decisions for posterity to judge, but, as for them, the dice was cast. They'd decided to push forward and attack, no matter the consequences to their very lives!

"Battle and attack formation", Lieutenant Colonel Bamaiyi barked out the order to his Staff officer, Captain Hassan Katagum.

"Forward! Attack! Long live the Federal Republic of Nigeria!" They all shouted back in unison, and charged with ferocity that hadn't been seen before in the history of this war.

"*Hu-a ra-a-aah*"! They all proclaimed, with alacrity, which reverberated through the thick air of the forest, as the men charged forward with impunity and determination rarely seen before, with the armor and the Recce companies leading the attack with devilish ferocity of purpose.

This is what happened. Even though Corporal Ezeumune had slipped back to the rebels and told them that the Federal troops had been hoodwinked and fallen for his trick, they didn't believe him, and were not willing to oblige his claims. However, when one of the rebel officers looked outside and saw the whole forest infested with federal troops and further observed that it was as if the whole forest were on a menacing move of its own. He ran frantically to alert Major Effieong who at the time was in the bathroom, but immediately dressed himself and gave orders before he emerged to take immediate command of the preparedness for battle. Some of his men were still half-dressed, some half-asleep, as they ran in all directions, abandoning their armor and weapons. There was a complete break-down of discipline and the issuance of disarray, characteristic of an ill-prepared and ill-disciplined army. The best way to describe the situation perhaps might be through the saying 'everyone to him or her own self'. They ran in all directions cursing and looking for a cover. Had the Federal troops pursued them without the fear of being ambushed by the few who might have been left behind hiding, or the fear of a sudden re-emergence of previously-concealed re-enforcements, they would have captured Major Effieong.

The NCOs insisted on pursuing the rebel army in order to capture the infamous Major Effieong. But Lieutenant Colonel Baimaiyi stopped them conscious of the danger of being ambushed (The Colonel was unmistakably aware that sabotage, ambush and trickery had been used as weapons of war with effective consequences just as potent as artillery and hostilities with small arms). He proudly and profusely congratulated his men for their gallantry in trouncing the rebels and capturing more than one hundred prisoners; and a cache of weaponry, including valuable artillery pieces, in spite of the fact that they hadn't had all the support units they needed.

The rebels who had escaped tried to re-group, but they didn't have enough men or weaponry to mount any meaningful counter-attack. This gallantry from the men of the Third Marine Commandos Division was actually the beginning of the end of the rebel resistance in this theatre of war. The gory body of Corporal Ezeumune was found among the dead in a deep dry gorge in the forest, thus saving him from a more ignominious death by hanging with his balls dangling or stuffed in his mouth for all to see!

Change of Command: The indomitable GOC at the helm

"We are now going to shift our attention and focus on the pivotal role played by the Third Marine Commandos under the indomitable Olu, through whom the Article of Surrender was negotiated and accepted, after the defeat and surrender of the rebel forces", the Professor said, setting the tone for the next line of discussion.

"Anybody familiar with the prosecution of the war at the time under the Scorpian, who was not surprised with the speed at which the Third Marines were moving and wondered why they could continue at that rate, must be very dishonest of his faculty. Such mendacity is pardonable because it's not very often that we encounter such phenomenon as it pertains to war," the Professor observed.

But critics of the then GOC who knew the geography and social networking of the ethnic groups of that area (Calabari, Ijaws, Ibibios et al) argued that the Balck Scorpion was able to make such rapid advances because he was operating in a theatre 'among friends'. Such sinister argument was abetted and reinforced by the fact that minorities in the area such as the Ibibio or Effiks were clearly excited to have their own State and control of their common local political destinations and independence. The critics cited the difficulty the marines suffered when they moved to the 'hostile territories of the Igbos'. They were bogged down.

It has been said that 'change is the spice of life', and if this old adage is accepted as a truism, then the replacement of the Divisional GOCs was a smart and timely move, because some of the marines had been at the front for two years without relief, and were beginning to experience *war fatigue syndrome* which may be tantamount to loss of command-enthusiasm and discipline and low morale.

Given the stalemate in some fronts, the Supreme Headquarters and the Army Headquarters made the decision to replace Muhammed of the Second Division with Haruna; Shuwa of the First Division was replaced by Bisalla and the Black Scorpion of Third Marine Commandos was replaced by Olu. Some of these changes, as was mentioned earlier, were because of stalemate on the front, but, also, because of the recognition that the assistance Biafra was receiving from the international community helped to bolster its image thereby making it more daring, especially with the recapture of Owerri. There were some countries who were it became clear playing a double-standard, for example, the Republic of Dahomey, Sierra Lione, West Germany (now just Germany), Spain, Portugal, Switzerland and Sweden, who were tacitly giving support to the rebels. The despondency and low morale existing, most especially among the Third Marine Commandos brought about by the recapture of Owerri and the death of Hamman, one of their most able second-in-commands, with its consequent moratorium on the capture of Umuahia, all demanded urgent solution through a new GOC.

"First however, I must introduce to you the new no-nonsense Third Marine GOC. Commander Matheu A.Olu was a forty-year old barrel-chested of a man with soft patty-like features. He wore the Colonel's uniform with pride and flair of his own creation. His men called him the "Pa Grizzly". Commander Olu was not a man who deliberately thought-out his plans or schemes, and still less did he even think of harming anyone in order to gain his own ends. He was simply a man of the world who got along with almost anybody out of habit and through a simple law of survival that he had learned from his parents when growing up in the tough neighborhood village of Owu- Abeokuta in the Western region (now Ogun State). There were numerous schemes and plans he had acquiesced to but which he never rightly accounted to himself, or ever considered means to an end, but which have constituted and continue to constitute his whole interest in life and existence.

But make no mistake, when it comes to war, he's stubbornly meticulous and unyielding to higher powers when he's convinced of his plans, strategy and the philosophy behind his movements. He always pays scrupulous attention to his plans or schemes, whatever they are, when they are made. He has never tried to endear himself to others for his own personal gain or aggrandizement, as a military officer. His integrity and honesty have never been questioned or in doubt. However, many keen observers of the time shook their heads at the rapidity of his complete turn-around, when he left the military and became a civilian. Whether in politics or business encounters, they surmised, he came to embrace these later qualities (means to an end, power-grab, greed and personal aggrandizement) as if they were in-born instincts to his survival.

The effects of *'war fatigue syndrome'* created a level of mis-trust between those commanders in the field and those at the Supreme Headquarters and at Army Headquarters as well. Those in the field had a feeling those at the

Headquarters were deliberately starving their Division of ammunitions, and even of ordinary supplies. A case in point was the reported rift that developed between Muhammed, the GOC of the Second Division, and the Commander-in-Chief, where it was alleged that Muhammed, who never had much respect for the C in C, threatened to leave the Army. Those in the know of the events surrounding this incident, further allege that the staff at Dodon Barak was all in shivers when the threat reached them; because they remembered the role the Second Division GOC played in the last coup that brought the Commander-in-Chief to power. Thus, everything, including appeasement, was done to accommodate the Second Division Commander and the rift was eventually amicably resolved through the intervention of some senior Northern leaders and Emirs, especially that of Kano.

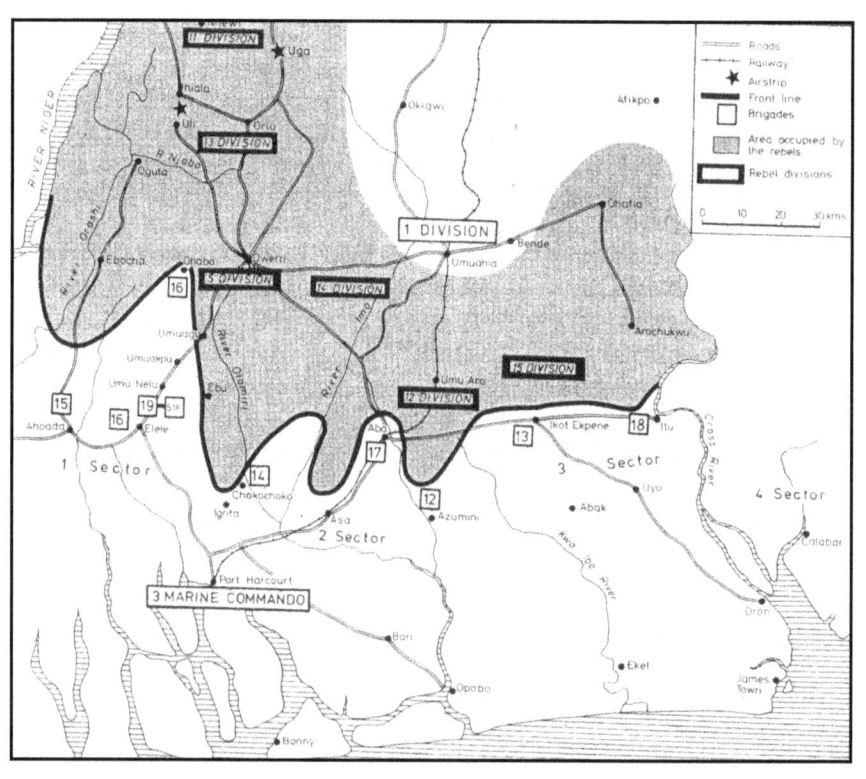

Fig. 6: Front line in Mid-1969

Adapted from Obasanjo, 1980

Olu Implemented new changes

Consequently with the change of leadership in all three Divisions, the Third Marine Commandos underwent some profound changes under their new indomitable and stubborn GOC, with the sole purpose of raising the Marines' sagging morale, discipline and fighting spirit. The whole Division was reorganized to reflect the new GOC's philosophy of shared responsibilities, as well as for ease of command or operational control and facilitation of communication, as he was overheard boasting. Under the new structural innovation of the GOC, the Sector Commander post was abolished and eliminated. This was because there were many Battalion commanders who claimed to have never seen or even know who their Sector commanders were because these commanders limited themselves with the Brigade commanders. In the new set-up the flow of information was from Divisional Headquarters/GOC- Brigade commanders-Battalion commanders…", the Professor stopped to answer a question.

"I heard at the time of the war that the Third Marine had what was referred to as "commandos girls", what were their roles in the new command structure as introduced by the new GOC?" Owoleye asked this with a wan smile spreading all over his rough-pitted puckered face that as a small child, he had almost died, from smallpox which had left its pocked marks on his face. There was silence for a moment, because most of the discussants had felt that the question was improper coming from a man of the cloth.

"Oh that's neither peculiar nor limited to that Division, but theirs became public because of the changes implemented by the new GOC", the Professor declared. "In the first instance, the "girls" were recruited as soldiers, with regular identification numbers and wore the uniform of their rank - all were Private. However, one of the problems that this created was in the line-of -command and following orders, and what they did after their 'official' hours. They were very intimate with the rank-and file, but, most especially, the officers many of whom ended up marrying them. For example, there was an incident where an NCO wanted to discipline a "girl" for insubordination and sent her to the guardroom as was common practice. But do you know what she said to him? "Sergeant, you are frickin' wasting your time because I won't be in here for more than ten, tenminutes; start counting!"She declared with sarcasm spread all over her snickering face. And, lo and behold, after only seven minutes the news had reached a Major who dispatched another officer to immediately have the "girl" released, without any explanations. After her release she winked and gave the NCO a middle finger, mimicking words with her lips as if saying 'I told you so', before walking straight to the Major's quarters with her head held high where it was rumored she spent the next three to four days, "recuperating" and "nursing" his sensitivities and libidinal proclivities.

Thus, to avoid these kinds of outright disciplinary problems the new GOC asked all of the girls to resign and to reapply as civilians who would continue to do the same 'chores', whatever that meant! This was intended to take care of the discipline problem, because now whatever happened they would be disciplined and treated as civilians and not as soldiers. Some of the girls argued that they joined the army for the uniform and were not willing to accept the present arrangements and therefore left, but most complied. In a way however, the presence of "the girls" in either the army, or as civilians (they maintained their residences within the camps), promoted ethnic inter-marriages as many of the Northern officers ended up bringing them up North with as their wives. Those officers who were either already married, or, for religious reasons, did not dare bring them up North as their wives; settled them in other parts of the country or in a different state other than their own.

Many of such women and their children today live in our big cities — Abuja, Kano, Kaduna, Jos to name a few— and townships without the knowledge of the man's relatives or his other wife. These become real issues when the man passes away and his properties have to be shared amongst his children"; Professor Balarabe stopped because Mariayamu had signaled him that lunch was ready.

The women went to the women's section of the house where Mariayamu had also set up their lunch. The lunch consisted of rice and beans with fresh fish. For dessert a dish of *fura* was served.

After lunch, they all decided it was time to call it a day. Some had chores and errands to run. For example, Dr. Khan and his wife needed to go to the airport to receive Veronica's brother and his wife and child. Balarabe had to travel to the village the next day to buy some foodstuff and some few live chickens, and, if the price was right, buy a ram for the forthcoming *Eid Sallah*. James and his wife Jamima were planning on attending a marriage ceremony in their village which required a day's journey by car, and wanted to start early in the morning. AiShetu and her husband had planned to visit her brother, whose second wife, Amina, had just given birth to his sixth child, and her second. Dr. Kasimu had a business meeting at the Headquarters of the Canadian consortium financial firm, where he worked, as a consultant. In view of these personal or familial commitments, they all agreed to meet the week after the *Eid Sallah* festivities because some of them would not be in town over the holidays.

During the *Eid*—the celebration of the end of the holy month of Ramadan, when Moslems fast, from dawn to dusk— Moslems of stripes, rich or poor, try their best to provide the best in terms of what to eat, what to wear, or how to behave to their families, relatives, friends, neighbors, and indeed just about everybody; the festivities last for three days. People hug and kiss and greet each other with the words *barka da sallah,* that is, "happy *Eid*". Often children will wear their best attire and go to relatives' or family friends' houses, or just any house in the neighborhood, asking for *barka da sallah* where they are given candy, *goro,*— kola nuts, or money, similar to what kids do during the Halloween season in the West. In some families, gifts are wrapped for each member and opened with joy and hugging and the words *barka da sallah,* just as Christians do during Christmas, but with less of the deceit of Santa coming down the chimney to deliver your gifts. During the *Eid* celebration, your gifts come from your parents, relatives or friends. It seems Santa hasn't figured out quite how to introduce himself during this season, as yet. "When I was a young girl", Jummai said," I used to go out with my elder sister to our Aunt, Binta, and say to her *barka da sallah,* Aunt, may we all see next year together, and she would respond *inshallah-(*God willing). She would then give us a lot of stuff like new clothes which she had bought early in the year and hidden in her *adudu,* (specially woven box-like container) candy and money, it used to be my happiest day of the year. I always look forward to *Eid*. But now that I'm a grown-up woman I sure do miss the *barka da sallah* part of growing up. When I went to boarding school, I found fasting difficult, because usually you do not get to eat good meals after you break the fast at dusk, and also because it was often difficult for me to wake up and line up for the early meals. So I ended up not eating anything at all often for days", she concluded coyly and laughing.

"I hope everybody had a good break and rest during the *Eid* week, and have had time to recuperate and be ready to start anew", Aminu made these remarks after their return from the *Eid Sallah* holidays.

All of them answered in the affirmative and expressed the wish that there would be more such holidays, because it was invigorating bringing families and friends together to share their blessings for the year.

"Now we're looking forward to Christmas", Owoleye observed with the measured calm of the man of the cloak.

"Yes, but that's months away!" Jamima reminded them.

"Ok where were we?" Professor Balarabe asked.

"We were discussing the changes that the new 3 Marine Commandos GOC introduced in his Division", Abba said.

"Well, excellent!" Professor Balarabe nodded in affirmation.

"Another change introduced by Olu was the contract procedures, and the amount of money the contractors were charging the Division. Can you believe it? He had time during war to bargain with the contractors who were intransigent at the beginning, but came around when he told them that, if they didn't like his offer, they could go to hell, he would find new buyers? 'There are thousands out there who would be more than happy to supply the Division', he was quoted as saying. All the contractors acquiesced and reduced their bidding, in some cases by fifty percent, saving the Division thousands of naira. The next major change he dealt with was infiltrations of the Battalions by the rebel forces — spying. It became really bad that if you farted anywhere within the Marine Division area, the whole rebel army would be laughing in the next five minutes, because, somehow, somebody had already relayed the incident to them. Such leaks were hugely inimical to successful war-planning and execution. A vetting system was introduced for people working in the Divisional Headquarters, Brigade, Battalions and every conceivable place of high security.

The next other significant change he had to deal with was that of *'self-injury'* where soldiers would, on purpose, shoot themselves or mutilate some parts of their body, which was not going to be fatal but would grant at least some ten or fourteen days' rest. This was because some of them had been at the front for more than fifteen or twenty-four months, without replacement or proper leave. Apparently, in those days, there was no surge! In fact, some of these pernicious practices were encouraged by some of the junior officers and NCOs of different Battalions or companies to the men, as a form of relief. The change introduced also involved the creation of a nice recreational mess with a full staff — women were recruited to *"attend to"* the *"needs"* of those at the mess. A Colonel was put in charge of running the mess. Now, instead of those who inflicted on themselves deliberate self-injury, each Battalion could dispatch ten to fourteen soldiers, at a time, who had distinguished themselves in battle, or in other duties, to simply go and relax. This strategy became, as you would, guess, very popular, and helped to reduce the incidence of 'self-inflicted-injuries'to a minimum. In addition, he commanded the Divisional Physician to report to him directly if he suspected, or observed, any cases of such self injury.

Area command tour and Operation Tailwind

After these changes were developed and in place, a plan was developed for an offensive attack, but not before the GOC toured every Brigade, battalion and the soldiers in his Division. Some of the soldiers he met were in the trenches. But, of course, the rebels had a plan of their own to welcome the new GOC. They launched an unexpected attack for the re-capture of Abba, after they learned of the war plan which had been developed, but not implemented because of the GOC's tour. At first, they succeeded with heavy casualties on both sides, but, after a Divisional reinforcement of men and ammunition, and an intensive five-day battle of sheer determination and cunning by the new GOC and his men, they were able to re-take every piece lost under the command of the most able Tumoye and Akinrinade. Thus, the rebels' plan of establishing a roadblock on the Port Harcourt-Abba road, with the ambition of capturing Abba, was stalled, and denied for good. However, after this experience, the vetting process became even more urgent and stringent, and was tightened a notch above in hiring and assignments.

The Third Marine Commandos continued its restructuring and organization for *Operation Tail Wind*— the final onslaught on the rebels in consonant and strategic planning with the other Divisional GOCs of the First Division, Bisalla and the Second Division, Jallo. As a matter of fact, the Third Marine Commandos GOC visited Enugu himself for discussion of the final push but the GOC was away from his headquarters, but his GSO 1, Danjuma, who we met during the July 29 *putsch*, was present and appraised the plan presented to him by the Third Marine GOC, and was very sympathetic regarding it, but could not say much because he knew his GOC had a different plan and he dared not make any commitments of support on his behalf. However, he pledged to brief his GOC about the substance of the visit when he returned and this he did. The GOC of the First Division thought it was a brilliant and impeccable plan but he had already committed to an operation in the Awka-Onitsha and Okigwe sectors.

"There was at this time a high morale and a strong fighting spirit, after the demoralizing Owerri debacle. The high morale of the thirteenth Brigade of the Third Division was expected to catapult to Umuahia and Bende, regardless of the rebel forces defenses. For *Operation Tail Wind* to succeed, it was envisaged all the troops of the Division must be deployed strategically, in order to meet the target of securing the axes of Owerrinta, Okpuala, Olakwo, Owerri, Awomama, Uli, Ihiala, Atta, Orlu, and to link up with the First Division", the Professor paused to take a sip of his tea.

All the same, the Third Marine GOC went on ahead with *Operation Tail Wind*. However, before the final push, Olu gave a pep talk to his commanders and the rank-and-file. In part, he wanted to lift up their spirits and to praise them on the coming holidays of Christmas and *Id-El-Fetri*, and to wish them well.

"We soldiers, at this time should remember that the future of this country and that of generations yet unborn depends on us. If, therefore, we are able to preserve unity and oneness of purpose… we would have left an important and worthy legacy for posterity to emulate…We're the 3 Marine Commandos! We have fought, and will continue to fight, gallantly for the unity of this country. We cannot afford to relent until the rebellion is successfully crushed and Nigerian unity preserved, and until brotherly love reigns supreme amongst our different ethnic groupings!….The way is not long but the task, at this final state, is indeed arduous, and demands the best in all of us. We cannot fail. We must guarantee ourselves victory at all costs! We must keep up the good work with renewed determination and sacrifice. The end is in sight…"

Gentlemen, our cause is noble and virtuous so that God/Allah will not forsake us, he will guide us to crush this rebellion caused by none other than the miscreant tyrant of our time—I don't need to call his name! We must expiate the blood of our fallen brothers and gallant heroes. What did the rebels promise their people? Nothing, all were but empty and calculated deceits. And that that they promised, they won't even deliver to their people!

We in the 3 Marine Commandos have fought, and are fighting, gallantly…. we can't rest on our laurels for the unity of the country depends on us…The way isn't long but the task…..and..it… demands the best fortitude in us. We can't fail…. All eyes are on us. We must keep on the good work we started the end is in sight and within our grasp!

The disposition for tomorrow, or rather for today, for its past midnight, cannot be altered now", he said. "*You have heard it, studied it, and we shall all do our noble duty for the Republic of Nigeria. And before battle, there is nothing more important*", he paused for effect, then declared after the pause, "*a good night's sleep*". Bravo comrades!

After this pep talk, the plan for the final onslaught was finalized, and the seventeenth and twelfth Brigades, which were designated as frontal forces, equipped with heavy artillery and fire-power, launched their ferocious attack against a lackluster defense by the rebels to reach Owerrinta with the intention of linking up with Umuahia and Bende. Among the rebel soldiers captured were farmers and mere school children— some only of the age of about sixteen.

"Was there any infringement of the Geneva Convention in this instance, pertaining to the illegal use of 'child soldiers'?" Dr. Kasimu asked. The professor paused and said;

"At least no one raised the issue at the time, it seems, at that time, the International Court of Justice (ICJ) wasn't functional or aware of its powers, limitless powers, especially as it portends to the Third World countries. If this had happened in the 'eighties or 'nineties maybe somebody would have rifted an eye-brow just as happened to the former President of Liberia, Charles Taylor" he paused again before continuing his narrative.

"One of the soldiers captured was found to have a piece of boiled cassava in his pocket, which he said had been a portion of his meal for two whole days. By the time the rebel leadership could organize a real attack force, the Marines were at the gates of Umuahia. As a matter of fact, the GOC of the Third Marine Battalion had to send a warning signal to his First Division colleague of the imminent presence of his force in their backyard in the Umuahia location, thereby linking up Abba with Umuahia. Twenty four hours later, to the amazement of HQ, (Both Supreme and Army), and the many following the progress of the war, the Third Marine Commandos were shaking hands with their colleagues of the First Division outside the trenches around Umuahia.

"What was happening at this time on the diplomatic front"? Golu asked the Professor.

"At this time can you imagine? Ghana was on the verge of recognizing the republic of Biafra, until they were told to save themselves the embarrassment of making such a gesture at a time when the so-called republic was in its last throes of defeat and the war on the verge of coming to a natural ending soon? They did listen good and saved themselves an international embarrassment", Professor Balarabe said and paused again.

"Well, let's finish *Operation Tail Wind*", Aminu reminded the Professor.

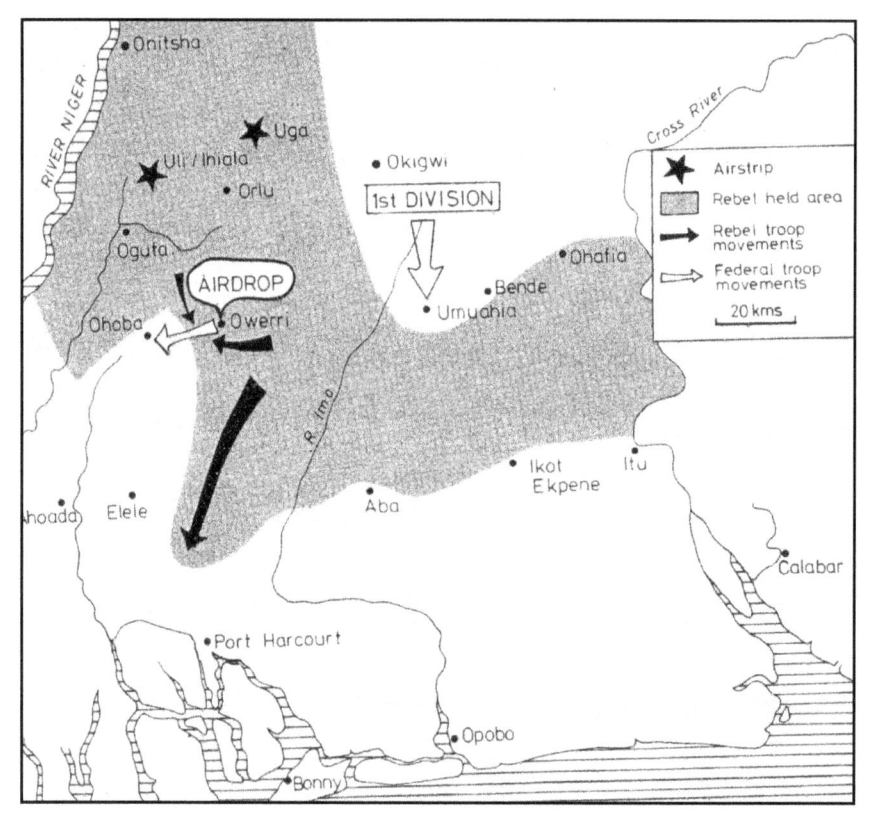

Fig. 7: Final Offensive

Adapted from Obasanjo, 1980

"After Umuahia was liberated, Owerri came under the grip of the Federal troops again, after an intense battle with high casualties on both sides, and, less than twenty four hours later, was liberated. The speed and mass movement of the Third Marine Commandos into Owerri not only scared the rebels but threw them into pandemonium and utter disarray and confusion. The Uli-Ihiala air strip came under incessant barrage of attack by 122mm artillery shells, and, by night-time on the same day of the fall of Owerri, had also fallen to Federal troops.

Araba Let's Separate

It is a well established fact that by the time the Federals' 13 Brigade made their unstoppable movement into Awomama and Owerri on a colossal course of an ultimate rendezvous with the rebels at Uli-Ihiala and Atta-Orlu airstrips, the rebel leader had finalized his escape to Abidjan. The GOC commanding the 3 Marine Brigades had given stern instructions to his officers not to harm Ojukwu, under any circumstances he was to be protected, at all costs, because he was worth more alive than dead. He told them he didn't want Ojukwu to die as a martyr because that would make him a venerated folk hero, which might even have prolonged the war. The myth of his assassination would become a legend which he, personally, thought (and believed) Ojukwju didn't deserve. But he also revealed to them his inner thoughts and belief that Ojukwu wasn't really the type to commit suicide for a cause such as shame and defeat in war because "he loves life too much". Little did the GOC, or anybody else, other than the inner circle of the erstwhile rebel General know, that he was already planning his escape into safety, which was duly camouflaged, of course, as his final attempt in search of a peaceful resolution of the war.

Late in the darkness of the night, a rumor spread amongst the scared population still under the control of the rebels, but was not yet ascertained, that the Uli airstrip had been put out of action by the ruthless Federal planes. In view of this fact, the General's earlier planned journey had to be amended with most urgency. It was first planned that he was to leave the following day, two days after his wife, children and paramount chiefs and important figures in Nnewi had been flown out of the country. But now, the rumor was that he was leaving that night, before all the airstrips were out of commission. There was argument amongst senior members of the government who were concerned about the General's departure without even giving some notification, a broadcast to his poor people. All this fell on deaf ears, Major General P.Effiong would have to improvise, and deal with the situation *after* his abscondment, to Abidjan, Ivory Coast.

Eventually the helpless people around acquiesced, and an intricate retinue was formed and directed to take the only relatively-safe escape route that went around Uga. Some of the people in the entourage were skeptical and not fully aware of what was going. Apparently, that route was chosen for two reasons, firstly, in order to give the General's dispensable scouting agents enough time to ascertain the truth about the Uli airstrip by snooping around in the bushes, and secondly, as a maneuver to avoid any encounter with the hostile Federal troops. Throughout the journey, as reported by those involved and who were eye witnesses, there were often and sudden unexplained stops, at time lasting more than half-an-hour, where the agents went about scouting the bushes in case of any ambush. Meantime, the General, and his august European friends and officials, waited in the pitch darkness in his Peugeot 404 station-wagon, with all the headlights off (Rumor had it at the time that one of those European friends was R Steiner, who in the course of the war had risen to the rank of Lieutenant Commander of the 4th Commando Brigade; later becoming a chief military consultant. However, most recent information seemed to show that Steiner resigned from his services following several confrontations with his colleagues, was arrested and expelled in hand cuffs).

When, eventually, the retinue reached the Uli airstrip, there was some confusion as to who would escape with the General. His family and several other officials had left in a different plane the previous night. There was hustling and dealing as to who was to travel in this huge cargo-plane, and who should travel in the French Red Cross plane, parked on the other side of the airstrip. Finally, it was sorted out, but that took time, and time, at this moment, was a precious commodity that they couldn't afford to waste. When all the passengers of the cargo-plane had entered, they discovered that there were now only four seats left in the entire plane, all available spaces were taken over had been taken over by personal effects. Other than the General, and a European friend, who has so far remained a phantom and unnamed, and two other high-ranking 'government officials in exile', all the rest of the passengers sat either on their personal luggage or on the floor.

After five hours of taking off from the Uhiala airstrip, the contingent eventually arrived at Abidjan, landing on a pre-arranged military airstrip.

It was after their self-congratulatory and celebrated arrival of; 'We've made it *oga*' that the now-infamous and disingenuous address to the people of 'Biafra' was made, by the now-well-ensconced and runaway General-in-exile. The broadcast was carried by 'Radio Biafra', while artillery shots were hurtling by and scraping the bushes around it, and bombs were falling from the air onto its fragile structure, and as the Federal troops raced to capture it and to close it down. To be fair to the runaway General, there were two contrasting conjectures made with regard to his broadcast, one that the broadcast was allegedly made *before* he escaped to Abidjan and that the tape was played when he was well-ensconced in his new country, the other, that he made the broadcast directly from Abidjan. Whichever proposition holds more water is immaterial at present, what matters was the fact that he made the broadcast at all. The broadcast, in part, read as follows:

"Proud and heroic Biafrans, gallant fellow countrymen and women.... My Government has been reviewing the progress of... war since the beginning of hostilities...., what we are fighting to safeguard.... determined to continue to defend ourselves... I would personally go anywhere to search for peace and security for my people. I shall be satisfied that this venture... yielded fruit.

As I go on this noble search for peace, I've arranged for Effiong to administer the Republic in my absence together with what is left of the....

I know that your prayers go with me, as I go overseas in search of an honorable peace and an end to the inhuman suffering of our people..... Nigerian Government.... I shall soon be back among you...

I, once more, pay tribute to the Biafran Armed forces.....Proud and courageous Biafrans....Biafra shall live forever...God bless you...

With this terse but informative message delivered, the rebel soldiers started looking for Federal troops to surrender to outright, or at least to discuss their terms of surrender and protection.

The mass abandonment of fighting meant that, by early January 1970, Oguta, Uli- Ihiala air-strips, Atta, Orlu, Okigwe and Uga had been captured (the rebel leader had fled his newly-minted "Republic of Biafra" for Abidjan Ivory Coast, forty-eight hours earlier, before the doomsday). It is, therefore, not surprising that, a few hours later, the Third Marine Commandos linked up with the First Division, at the Onitsha/Awka sector, effectively bringing the senseless megalomaniac war to a sorry but merciful end. Tumoye had wanted to push for "the kill", but, by the evening of the twelve of January, a Capitulation Order was sent out to the disarrayed and tattered rebel troops by their substitute administrative head, Major General P. Effiong, and the rebel minions that were still around. The unfortunate and misguided rebellion has been duly crushed! Colonel Olu received the battlefield Article of Surrender from Effiong, after he broadcast what amounted to an unconditional surrender to the people of the East and to whoever was left of his troops. *Interalia*, this is what he said:

Fellow countrymen and patriots... as you are aware, I took over the reign of our Government two nights ago....as our leader went to search for a belated peace...I take this opportunity to congratulate the armed forces of Biafra, and you civilians for your endurance and remarkable support, in spite of seemingly all odds to the contrary.

However, I'm now convinced, beyond any doubts that the unnecessary shedding of innocent blood must now stop.

The odds are stacked against us! Our people are completely disillusioned as to why we should continue this course which, in no uncertain terms, leads only to our humiliation and destruction......I've, therefore, instructed our brave and gallant armed forces to call for an orderly disengagement, wherever they may be. I've already dispatched a few of our talented officers to contact the Nigerian commanders in our townships and villages - Onitsha, Owerri, Awka, Enugu and Calabar, and so on. We now recognize that our differences with the Nigerians should have been dealt with in the political sphere. We have been misguided and misconstrued.

We now pledge our allegiance to the green-white-green flag of the Nigerian Republic and accept the twelve-state structure of the Federal Government of Nigeria!

Wherever you are, gallant and proud Biafrans, hand over your weapons and ammunitions to the nearest Nigerian military garrison or Nigerian police station. I have a guarantee that all of us will be protected. Obey all police instructions, and adhere to your sense of respect for law and order.

Once again, on behalf of our noble cause and our peoples' sacrifices, and our international friends and supporters, I ask all of you to succumb to, and obey, the orderly hand-over of your weapons and the maintenance of peace and order. May the Almighty be with all us!

Immediately after the speech, the 3 Marine Commandos sent out a brief statement to his field commanders. In part, the terse message read:

".. Unicord.... Effiong today issued what amounts to unconditional surrender. Tactical movement will continue until every inch of 'Biafra' is physically occupied and all rebels... disarmed. Troops will not open fire, unless....fired at. No change from ops order on treatment of POW and refugees".

This crisp and concise, but paramount historical message was sent out to all commanders in all sectors for their immediate implementation. The GOC had maintained a classic code of ethics which had guided the behavior of *all* the Federal forces during this senseless internecine war.

Amongst those conventions were these "bullet-points":

- Under no circumstance must pregnant women be ill-treated or killed.
- Children won't be molested or get killed; they will instead be fully protected.
- Hospitals, hospital staff and patients should not be tampered with or molested.
- Soldiers who surrender should not be killed; instead they should be disarmed and treated as prisoners of war…. Honor.
- No property… should be destroyed maliciously.
- No looting of any kind admittedly (tough to obey after you've just escaped, precariously, with your life).
- Churches and Mosques mustn't be desecrated.
- Women will be protected with honor against rape or indeed any indecent assault.
- All military and civilian wounded will be accorded treatment, regardless.
- Foreign nationals on legitimate business will not be molested or maltreated (this, of course, excludes mercenaries).

Uppity has no place in a war that pitted brother against brother, father against son*et. al.*; no matter how justly it ends. From the beginning the Federal troops were instructed to fight a "clean" and "decent" war! A "clean" and "decent" war seems however a misnomer, something of an impossibility, something that exists merely in the minds not the practice of men and women all over!

Subsequent to Effiong's speech, the indefatigable Third Marine GOC and the remnants of the rebel authority met and agreed on the futility of continuing on with this farcical war at this critical stage. The proud and victorious GOC had to break the ice first by approaching the rebel leaders and giving each one of them a physical hug! (His favorite was the gripping bear-hug). Some of the rebel leaders were, of course, in tears by this time, even as he (the GOC) tried to put them at ease with his infectious laugh and jokes. The rebel leaders were indeed shocked to see the grizzly and exuberant GOC warmly hugging and happily shaking hands with them, as if they had just met years later at a civil-war convention, or at an officers' mess, and not on a real battle field where they were the vanquished; this including Gbulie (Effiong's Chief of Staff) who was amongst the January 15 plotters, and who had served with the GOC at Kaduna.

The 3 Marine Commandos made it clear to General Effiong that the address he had made didn't go far enough; a real Article of Surrender would have to be worked out. "What else do you want from us? We're a defeated people", was the General's meek and perhaps understandable response.

The scene of events during this solemn and tense period was captured on a borrowed camera by Captain Shuaibu Barau, and is now in the military national war archives in the Federal Capital.

After the broadcast by Effiong urging what was left of his 'troops' to lay down their arms and stop fighting immediately, without conditions, and to deliver all of their weapons to the nearest police or Federal military command post, the Third Marine GOC decided to visit the vocal, and popular, rebel radio station, known as "The Voice of Biafra" for himself. He was stunned to his core when he was taken to the enclave, deep in the thick forest. There was really nothing that, in any true sense of the word, could be called a 'building'.

The infamous mobile 'Voice of 'Biafra' Radio Station at Obodo Ukwu

Adapted from Obasanjo, plate 8, 1980

Araba Let's Separate

The whole structure of the infamous and inflammatory "Voice of Biafra" shortwave radio station consisted of a collection of ramshackle rickety bamboos, tree trunks and leaves which could be moved and relocated at an instant. It was camouflaged within the dense forest by all manner of leaves, rags, blankets and plastics and had only knee-high stools as part of its décor —and nothing else. There were no chairs to speak of. Inside the structure were scattered four huge batteries, which the radio operated on, and miles and miles of cable wires criss-crossing every available space within the ramshackle central location and connecting to *this* battery or *that* speaker, or something! The GOC sat down quietly and searched for some explanation from deep within his soul: "If the bloody frickin' smart Igbos can do this for an apparent meaningless war, why can't they employ or showcase this innovative technical expertise in the Federal Government's service? Nigeria would go a long way technologically, if they would employ these skills for the good of the Republic". Before he could complete his line of deep inner contemplation and marvel at the absolute creative technological ingenuity and appreciation of the Igbos, someone Chukwumaja Eze, (aka Igbo Kwenu) said, "*Sah*, we dey ready". The GOC was going to broadcast *his* message to the Easterners on the "Voice of Biafra" radio. He was taken inside this ramshackle structure, where he had to bend down, almost to his knees, before he could enter. When he entered, he was presented with a stool which his relatively huge butt (the GOC had an uncharacteristically big behind when he was young, which somehow forced him to swagger when he walked) could not fit on properly, so he merely managed to squat as he taped his maiden broadcast. Later, he was mesmerized when the speech was played to the world, after Effiong's speech. To his utter amazement the broadcast was distinctive, crystal clear, and well-distributed. It was heard all over the world!" The Professor remarked.

In part, this is what the proud and victorious GOC of the 3 Marines Brigade, Olu said over the familiar "Voice of Biafra" shortwave radio enclave to the people of the East, and indeed, to the entire world :

"*I, Colonel Olu…. General Officer Commanding the 3rdMarine Commando Division, Nigerian Army, having accomplished the task given to me by the Head of State and Commander-in-Chief of the Armed Forces of Nigeria wish to make this appeal to all our brothers and sisters in the Eastern States who are in hiding to come out of hiding and settle in their respective normal places of abode.*

All soldiers who fought on the 'Biafran' side should immediately surrender themselves and their weapons to the nearest Federal Troops location or…police station. The Commander-in-Chief has given a solemn guarantee to the safety of all law-abiding citizens of the Eastern States.

I've, through the powers vested in me by the Federal Republic of Nigeria, ordered all tactical movement of our troops stopped. Henceforth the Nigerian police will maintain law and order throughout the Eastern states. Any abuse by any soldiers will be summarily dealt with, through the war emergency channels of misconduct. All troops are garrisoned and confined, throughout the Eastern States, to their barracks.

All officers and warriors of the 3rd Marine Commandos send their regards to Commander-in-Chief for his generous encouragement in our……task. We also thank…… Nigeria for their…. support and steadfastness….make particular mention of the co-operation and … support ….all the people of the Eastern States.

I hope that the magnanimity which had been shown by the Commander-in-Chief and all our people since the beginning of this "unnecessary and wanton war" will be strengthened by the ready and willing co-operation shown by the people of the Eastern States. Thank you all, and long live one united Nigeria".

(Owerri, January 14, 1970)

After the battlefield proclamation of surrender, the party flew to Lagos in the same plane arranged by the Third Marine GOC for the formal acceptance of the Articles of Surrender by the Commander-in-Chief of the Armed forces of Nigeria.

Before the formal surrender ceremony could take place at *Dodan* Barracks in Lagos, however, some of the rebel civilian representatives, for example Mbanefo and Njoku, still seemed be having a few problems with the terms and conditions, especially the reference to the Twelve States structure. They were still trying to deny acceptance of the twelve state structure of the republic. "Have you forgotten where and why you are here? It's because you surrendered", one of the officers present reminded the rebels' representatives. At one time, the GOC of the Marines, who had accepted an article of surrender from the rebels on the field, became angry and told them, 'You know what? There is a plane outside in the near-by field, and, I promise to give you all the weapons and ammunition you will need from my Divisional stock, so let's go back and finish it finally, once-and-for-all, on the battlefield, as men of honor'.

There was complete silence, this stern and invidious provocative comment didn't fall on idle ears with the assembled rebel representatives. After this outburst of anger by the victorious GOC, it was said that the representatives fell into a stupor and cowered like children who had been told by their parents to go to bed or to eat their vegetables! They immediately digested its implication and quietly in unison cursed their maker for their present predicament, but promptly perceived reality and acquiesced, after what seemed like interminable consultation with each other, to the Articles of Surrender, as presented by the Federal Government, including the Twelve-State Federal structure, without further adieu. The terms and conditions of surrender were read by Effiong on behalf of the rebel representatives, *inter alia*, as follows:

"I Major General Phillip Effiong, Officer administering the Government of the Republic of 'Biafra' now wish to make the following declaration:

a. *That the Republic of 'Biafra' hereby renounces session and therefore ceases to exist;*

b. *That we peoples of the Eastern region affirm we are loyal Nigerian citizens and accept the authority of the Federal Military Government of Nigeria unconditionally;*

c. *That we accept the existing twelve-state structure of the Federation of Nigeria without any rancor or reservation;*

d. *That any future Constitutional arrangement will be worked out by the representatives of all the people of the Federal Republic of Nigeria.*

With these curt but solemn and powerful words the short-lived "Republic of Biafra" went into oblivion and into the dustbin of history. In short it became a mere asterisk and ashes in the dustbin to the glorious history of the Republic.

"At the surrender-signing ceremony there were other rebel leaders, such as Amahi, Ogunewae, Anuwunanah, Mbanifo, Njokwa, Mba, and Okeki", Alhaji Wada paused for effect, and then continued.

"On January 15, 1970 at *Dodan* Barracks in Lagos the Armistice was signed; exactly four years after the coup d'état that killed the Northern Premier, Sir Ahmadu Bello, the Sardauna of Sokoto and other eminent northerners including among others, the Prime Minister Sir Abubakar Tafawa Balewa and was the source of the civil-war. Immediately after the signing, a general amnesty was announced by Gowon to "all rebel leaders and their proxies", Alhaji declared smirking with satisfaction that the war had come to an end.

This was naturally followed by the victorious Commander-in-Chiefs' acceptance of the Articles of Surrender, and the promise of the beginning of reconciliation, reconstruction and rehabilitation. *Inter alia*, this is what was said at the time— which can be found, together with the Articles of Surrender read by Effiong, in the National archives of Military War and Antiquity in the nation's capital:

"...Fellow countrymen, congratulation, the civil war is truly over!..... Today, at Dodan Barracks, the erstwhile rebels, through their spokesman, Effiong, and in the presence of their representatives, capitulated and accepted the articles of surrender and denounced secession, in short, the republic of Biafra has officially ceased to exist. It's as if it never happened. They have accepted the authority of the Federal Military Government and the present political structure of twelve states, as we have demanded it from the beginning. The so called "Rising sun of Biafra" is set for ever. We honor and pay homage to the fallen heroes, and those still living. The armed forces deserve the greatest praise for their valor in battle, their loyalty and dedication, and for their resourcefulness in overcoming the formidable obstacles placed in our way.... The penultimate sacrifice they have made in blood, and, yes, even death can never be repaid! We owe them our fraternal gratitude. We have overcome a lot over the past four years.

Now we must embark on the tasks of healing, national reconciliation, rehabilitation and reconstruction. The Federal Government guarantees political freedom and security of life and property to all law-abiding citizens of Nigeria. All former civil servants and public corporation officials will be reinstated as soon as is feasible.

The Federal Government will accept donations from genuine and germane foreign governments, but not "blood money" from those who helped to prolong this war to the peril of our people and the loss of lives by tacitly aiding the secession. We thank the Organization of African Unity for the positive role it has played in this, our dire time of need. Our international relations and obligations with all foreign governments will continue in spite of some misgivings and dubious double-standards by some few. They know who they are!

Finally, I must once again congratulate the gallantry of our fighting forces, officers and all ranks. Our victory for national unity was earned on a platter of blood and sacrifice and for these we shall for ever remain indebted to our armed forces.

I have the ultimate confidence that our Republic will forever remain a great and united Nation. So help us God/Allah. Long live the Federal Republic of Nigeria!"

"This is very enlightening. I didn't know about these facts, especially about the Aburi accord and the general prosecution of the war, but, most especially, the Articles of Surrender, entered into by the rebel representatives", Aminu commented and was supported in his remarks by James and Veronica.

"Immediately after the surrender ceremony and the announcement of a general offer of amnesty by the Commander-in-Chief to those soldiers who fought on the Biafran side, reconciliation started in earnest. Soldiers in many Divisions and formations began to, willingly; volunteer their rations of food, transport and medicine, and even money, to their fellow "Biafran" soldiers who were in dire need. The Nigerian Army immediately formed the vanguard for helping those in desperate need of shelter, food, and immediate medical attention. There was anurgent need and safe return of all Nigerian children, who had been flown out of the country by the rebels through their French sympathizers; to places like Gabon and Ivory Coast. This mission rested squarely on the shoulders of the Nigerian armed forces. And they didn't fail. The National Commission, responsible for rehabilitation, observed this much in July, 1970, about the important role of the army, "The 'humanitarian' and welfare service provided by the army in terms of value was quite substantial". The Professor paused letting this conclusion sinks in and then continued.

"A large number of those who fought with Biafra but were members of the Nigerian armed forces began to report to their last postings before the war, and were, in most cases, gladly or reservedly welcomed by their colleagues. Of course, many didn't remain in the army; they chose to retire with their benefits. The fact that they didn't resign or retire *en masse* was seen to some degree as due to the success of the dictum "no victors!"

Many of those who answered the rebel leaders' call at the time and left their businesses behind, came back to either reclaim, sell or form partnerships with the person now running the business if it was still there. There were many instances where amicable arrangements were entered into. For example, Eziekwe Oke was a tailor and had a small stall in the Kaduna Central Market before the war. After the war, he returned and was paid back the value of the store and everything in it when he had left. The current occupant was more than willing to relinquish full ownership or to enter into partnership with him, but he made the decision that he wanted to move to another city. Mallam Haroun Katam was more than accommodating and paid everything in full. Mr. Francis Effeh owned a small printing press before the war on Ahmadu Bello Way in Kaduna and, on his return after the war, he entered a partnership with the current owner Alhaji Alheri Baidu, who had expanded the business to include a book-publishing division (Alheri Publishing Inc, or simply, AP Inc.), including import and export divisions, which are still thriving today, and have made it one of the largest publishing-houses in our capital city. They worked it out amicably, whereby each now owns fifty percent of this profitable venture.

There are many such instances of cooperation, all over the country. In Kano for instance, Mr. Wachikwu Eze used to own a *Total* gas station in Wudil, a town on the Kano-Dutsen Ma road, but left, during those hectic days, without any proper arrangement of ownership. A few of his former workers however took up the challenge and successfully managed the business, with a lot of innovative skills. Such innovations included diversifying into the liquid-gas business and thus growing, as one of the largest suppliers of cooking-gas cylinders in Kano, and its environs. They also built stores and restaurants near each of their numerous filling stations where their customers could rest comfortably and eat or buy some kind of snacks. Upon his return they were glad and excited to see him back alive, and laudably relinquished the business, handing it back to him. He was so impressed with their entrepreneurial ability and honesty that he asked each one of them to join him as partners, thus forming a very strong partnership, which continues and is known today as *Kano Dutsen Ma Partners Ltd.*

By the end of the war, the strength of the Nigerian armed forces has risen from about ten-thousand in 1967, and organized into 2 Infantry Brigades; Lagos Garrison Organization (LGO) and Arms and Services, to two-hundred-fifty- thousand in 1970, organized into 3 Infantry Divisions, LGO ,and huge sizes of Arms and Services sections. This massive peace-time military build-up definitely wasn't going to be sustainable by the economy, especially at a time when many Reconstruction work was required all over the country, but most especially in the Eastern States. A way must be improvised to reduce the number to a more manageable size without letting loose too many angry and well-trained fighters on the streets frustrated looking for something to do to fill their long, boring and idle daily hours.

The scheme envisaged was to loan a large number of them some money, sufficient money to entice them to go out and start a new business, preferably in the agricultural sector. Hundreds of thousands were given six-months training as horticulturists, poultry farmers, mechanics, tailors, haberdashers and other types of businesses such as pottery and barbers and braiding. Many were given lands around the big cities where they could easily find a market for their products. One of the most successful of these enterprises was *Fatan Arewa* (North's Hope) Farm founded by Sergeant Alack J. Bakari, along the Kaduna-Zaria road where corn, rice, yams, cassava and potatoes were produced and processed in large quantities. A business that now employs more than two people. *Fatan Arewa* farm processes cassava into *gari*, the yams are processed and sold in plastic packets as "pounded yam or *amala*", and different kinds of chips are made from the potatoes. These products can be found in markets or *shago* all over the country. The farm supplies some of our textile industries, including the ones in Kaduna and Kano, with fine processed cotton.

Fatan Arewa farm even exports eggs to several West African countries, such as Ghana and Liberia. It is one of the more successful ventures that started with loaned money to entice soldiers to leave the army. But needless to say many others have regrettably fallen by the wayside and in those cases the loans have been written off. The few that are still thriving are a living legacy of the war and its aftermath. *Fatan Arewa* farm became *Bakari & Co Partners, Ltd* with a change of ownership in 2000.

Among "the 3R's", enunciated by the then Commander-in-Chief at the time, "Reconstruction" was the one that seems to have so far taken a back seat. There are still many areas in the former Eastern State that could benefit from reconstruction. Rehabilitation and Reconciliation have been achieved at an un-precedent step, which the people of the country can be proud of. The Igbos has been fully integrated in the nation's life and aspirations.

There is a house on Maitama whose gate is always locked and to get in you must be announced. On one dusty, *harmattan* day, with very low visibility, a lady approached the security-guard at the gate, and introduced herself, as Riga Jamila. From her looks, it was easy to see why she was unkempt and 'dirty', covered in dense *harmattan* dust. She had been on a *bolekaja* (a rickety wooden-bus) for three nights straight, with occasional stops to pick up passengers waiting along the dusty, single-lane, road. These buses have a nickname, *akwatin mutuwa*, (death-box!); because of the frequency of their fatal accidents: collisions, somersaulting off the road due to speed, breakdowns, and so on, and so forth, as they ply the country's single lane roads, day and night. She had introduced herself as Raga Jamila, but nobody seemed to know who she was!

When the *maigida*, (head of the household) was later informed of Raga's presence at the gates, he, at first, sighed then exhaled, before explaining to Uche, his wife of eight years now, that, during his youthful exuberance, he had to confess, "unofficially gotten married" to 'this lady' —as he explained it —, as the tradition of his clan demanded when pregnancy resulted in an out-of-wedlock relationship. Such tribal traditional marriages, he further explained, are consummated to give the child a father and to protect the woman's dignity, but it's never construed as a legitimate marriage. The couple didn't have to stay together after the birth of the child; they could each go their own way. With this explanation, he assured Uche that *she* was his legitimate spouse, since their marriage was conducted, according to the Christian faith, as well as traditional moresand blessing from his clan chief. Seeing that Uche understood and completely appeared to accept his explanation for his "youthful mishaps or indiscretion and bad-boy exuberance" with "that woman at the gate", he called over one of the female helpers and gave her some money to take it to the 'lady at the gate', suggesting that it would be sufficient for her fare back to the village.

Major Patrick Anande had met Uche Okonkwo at the war front, after the capture of Owerri, where he had displayed an uncommon valor and personal responsibility, beyond the call of duty, and was given a field promotion to Captain. Miss Okonkwo had enrolled in the Biafran army as a spy and *agent saboteur*, but, after the fall of Owerri, she was one of those captured and held as prisoners-of-war. Somehow Anande was able to convince her of the futility of continuing to believe in any future for Biafra. Uche was a smart woman who left her University education to answer Ojukwu's "home land call". She immediately seized the opportunity and ran with it, by becoming a military informant and saboteur agent working against the rebels for the Federal Government. They continued to see each other at any opportunity that presented itself, at first, sparingly, in the shadows, but later, openly, and more frequently, until their relationship blossomed into a serious love affair, and they eventually ended up tying the knot, just before the recapture of Owerri and Aba. This is one of the numerous marriages that took place almost on the eve of the end of the war, between some of the Northern officer corps and Biafran women who had served in various capacities in the Biafran army. Miss Okonkwo, thus, was one of many young beautiful Igbo women who ended up marrying either their former field-boss or their capturer.

Major Anande had never mentioned his relationship with Raga to Miss Okonkwo *before* their marriage. He had kept it a secret, even to himself, until now. He and his wife now had three children, two boys and a girl, Bohuk, Angwe and Lamy, respectively. Atompera, his son with Raga Jamila, had gradually been introduced to the other Anande kids as a sibling and spent a part of his holidays with them in Abuja, away from his mother and step-father in the Kabba State capital.

Patrick Anande's mercurial rise from the-ranks had remained a mystery to many, including him-self! Major Anande had distinguished himself in many of the battles he participated in, and had earned a field promotion as the highest non-commissioned officer, first, as Regimental Sergeant Major (RSM), and then, in the battle for Owerri, proving to be a one-man-dominating-force, in his Battalion, so much so that his Battalion commanding officer, Lieutenant Colonel Buakar, had no choice but to forward his name to the GOC for another field promotion. In the battle for the recapture of Owerri, he again proved indomitable, and excelled in valor beyond an individual soldier's call of duty; by holding off a platoon of the enemy by himself until help arrived; and for this he was given the field promotion to Major.

Doso Jazom's house was just a block away from Major Anande's because he too had done very well for himself ,and had earned a field-promotion as a Captain; after at one point complaining to his superiors that they wanted him to "die as a dog".

Anande and Jazom came from the same state and had gone to the same secondary school. They had obtained their West Africa Examination Certificate (WAEC) in 1966, but delayed going on to obtain their Higher School Certificate (HSC) so they could join the army, because of the needs of the time. For this reason, their conversion to the higher, more remunerative officer's ranks became relatively easier after the war. They both attended the officers' conversion courses at the Nigeria Defense Academy (NDA) and the Infantry School at Jaji, Kaduna to have their field-promotion ranks become substantive and recognized as legitimate. Major Anande's ambition has spurred him to aim higher, and he's now taking law-school courses, part-time, at Gwagwalawa University. At the same time, he's put in an application for the leadership course at Nigeria Institute for Policy and Strategic Studies (NIPSS), Jos.

"Well I think we have covered a lot of the history of the war today, and, because I understand some of you, including Mamu and I, have errands to run, I suggest we stop here and pick it up next week-end, even though some few have indicated they might unfortunately be out of town"; the Professor stopped and thanked everybody present for their attendance, daring to brave the bad *harmattan* weather.

Chapter Thirteen
Lessons of the War

The subject of history and warfare in the structure of power amongst the life of a nation is as indispensible as the people who constitute that nation. To describe the life of a nation by the single act of an individual is at times a misleading proposition, a misnomer, but not an implausible or inopportune one. There are plenty of examples in history of the lasting influence on a nation through the single act of a transformational individual e.g. Abraham Lincoln in the United States, Marx and Lenin in the USSR (now Russia) or in more recent times, Nelson Mandela in South Africa.

There are those who have always posed the question of how such individuals acquired the power to impose their will on their nations? And where did such people get the will to do so? In the early centuries, both answers were given in terms of "destiny" or "fate" or even "divine will". However, in the present dispensation, it may be more appropriate to answer the two questions in terms of historical happenstance and strong democratic principles or values in terms of what the transformational leader and the people perceived as the 'right' thing to do at that particular time and in that particular place. Democratic principles are what allow leaders to impose their agenda or programs, on their nations and the same values endow such leaders with the power to do so. It is, indeed, unfortunate that Nigeria has yet to have a transformational leader; most of our leaders were and are ethnic or regional. The one exception, in my estimate, might have been Muhammed, but he died too early and too young before he could blossom as a full transformational leader.

It is therefore instructional to look at the events that led to the civil war in Nigeria, to help us fore-stall such events from ever re-occurring. We can continue to ask whether it is due to the effect of one individual person or event, or a composite of many different events. The historical perspectives of the time indicated that democratic values were not particularly in vogue at the time, since the country was under the rule of a dictatorial military regime; many people, at the time, including, of course, politicians, were in a state of helplessness, which, in itself, is a disease. The behavior of the prior political leadership left a lot to be desired, and was ostensibly repudiated by some few, with little or no effect at all, leading to the coup and then the counter-coup. Some at the time actually came to the reluctant contemplation of the possible direct participation of a deity in the affairs of the state. This tacit acceptance of the role of a divine power in governance, this passivity no doubt, became one of the ingredients in the recipe for war.

What is needed from all of us, at present, in order to avoid a recurrence of the 1960s', and a re-occurrence of the unspeakable atrocities of the civil war is to make democratic values the corner-stone of our political life. But, of course, this is easier said than done or practiced. Just as it is in marriage, so it is with politics, politicians must be truthful and transparent to the electorate and to those they govern.

In spite of misgivings by the pessimists, the country *must* accept the infallible fact that its survival as an entity must be endowed in firm democratic principles, which are not only to be pronounced but must be visible, as the ubiquitous *neem* trees that adorn and line the streets of many of our cities and townships. It is only through true democratic participation that a leader worthy of the trust of the people can emerge with the power to impose, or hope to implement, his programs, for which the public freely and fairly have the opportunity to endorse through the free exercise of their cherished civil liberties at the ballot box. Military or selective 'qualified candidates', selected by one or few powerful members of a board of directors, through backroom channel intrigues and corrupt political swaps, is simply not good enough, and surely un-democratic. Candidates must be chosen by the people, through open and fair primaries, and not by party-bosses, sequestered in a dark smoke-filled room. The country can't afford the politics of "do or die". It doesn't have to, and should never be conceived as such.

The effective use of the power of political liberation was one of the reasons that minorities in the then-Eastern Nigeria threw their unqualified support and resources behind Federal efforts in the civil war. The simple act of giving them their own states, in short respect for their autonomy, with the consequent result of grass-roots-level participation in the choice over their governance proved far too tempting to ignore or refuse and was clearly "the right thing to do". Self-determination, in terms of national, state, or even city, developments is always an enticing innocuous political strategy that politicians can sometimes exploit for the betterment of (or sometimes, as in the case of the *agent provocateur*, to stir up) their people. If the rebel leadership had listened to some of the Igbo '*wise politicians*' advice at the time, they might have realized that they could have won more concessions for their people through negotiations than through the senseless war that resulted because of their intransigence.

In terms of foreign policy, the Government of the day should be proactive, instead of waiting for events to happen. One instance, from the civil war, was, if we look at the enormous propaganda campaign mounted by the rebels and their *agent provocateur* assistants; calling for a proactive, sustainable and vigorous foreign policy isn't just an option, but a paramount necessity. The propaganda, mounted by the likes of Marpress, on behalf of the rebels was immensely powerful and evoked deep sympathies in Europe and the Americas, especially those presentations of images of starving children. These images touched the consciences of everyone around the world, leading one young American to draw attention to it in New York in front of the United Nations Headquarters by setting fire to himself! The Federal Government had no immediate response to those "starving images" or the young American on fire, until months later when they hired their own public relations agents of Galitzine, Chart, Russel & Burston and Markstellar Associates to counter the Biafran propaganda machine.

It is now a common knowledge that some of the humanitarian contributions by churches and industrial establishments meant for the "starving Biafran children" went, instead, to the purchase of ammunition and weapons, thereby prolonging the suffering and death of the Nigerians which the contributions was intended to relieve. As a matter of fact, some of these donations went into private hands and never saw the light of day for the purpose for which it was intended. There were some countries which prolonged the war inadvertently, by playing a double-standard. Proclaiming neutrality by day and sending weapons by night to the rebels. At the end of the war, as a matter of fact, when such countries attempted to donate money to help in the reconstruction, the then-head-of-state, Gowon, refused. In refusing he stated bluntly to such countries that Nigeria didn't need their "*blood money*". The fact is, of course, that, in foreign policy, there are no permanent enemies; out of self-interest some of those same countries are now Nigeria's staunchest friends. These include also some international agencies and organizations.

"So, what lessons have we learnt from the civil war, and how do we ensure that it doesn't ever happen again? Abba asked the Professor.

"That's a good question, which I suggest we put on hold and discuss next week. Meantime I think we have achieved quite a lot today, and so, it may be appropriate to call it a day, if there are no objections. I've noticed that some of you, including *Mamu* and myself have some pressing errands to attend to, before it gets dark or before the stores close!" He declared with a glint in his eye, and most of the company got the joke.

All of the attendees to this historic form of self-education consented that it was indeed time to call the day's productive session over, and to pick it up next time after a long period of fasting.

"I think the lesson of the civil war, definitely, is that it doesn't take a huge conflagration to start a war, a small spark can result in dire consequences for a nation, or among nations. Most wars start like this, that is with something relatively minor, or seemingly unimportant, that could be settled, if only rationality was allowed to prevail in public discourse, and resolution. The event may start as a minuscule spark, but, if not approached with right equipment and determination, it could grow and engulf a whole village, town, state, nation or nations. In terms of what happened, I think it was, in large part, due to a lack of intelligent and creative problem-solving skills, on both sides of the divide. There was a lot of personal greed, ambitions and self-aggrandizement on display. The principals set themselves up on a high pedestal, and were not willing or considerate enough, of the effects of their decisions on the masses" the Professor observed, pausing for comments.

"Now that the war is behind us and reduced to a mere ugly blip — a footnote — on our history", he resumed, "there must be a concerted effort at equity distribution in *all* spheres of our society, in terms of educational, political, and economic developments. Nigerian elites and intellectuals must eschew self-aggrandizement, tribal exploitation and religious fanaticism. The patronage system must desist, and meritocracy must be adapted as a national supreme metric of achievement; the only true and fair measure of success in both political and civil service appointments. The concept of *federal character* sounds all very laudable and ideal indeed, but you don't fill positions with people who might not be capable of fulfilling the role expected of them because they're not either qualified or have merely paid some highly placed civil servants for such positions, just so it can look suitably *federal*. What does it matter to a farmer in Kabba, Kano, Ondo,

Lagos, or Enugu states, as to *who* built that road that he can now use to get his crops to the market? Or the clean water that he now has? Or the stable and reliable electricity that he can now access, without having to spend the meager money he earns from selling his farm products, buying and maintaining a generator.

The Nigerian elite and its intellectuals must propagate and disseminate the virtues of tolerance instead of fear, scare-mongering, suspicions, discrimination and retribution. The Government of the day has a responsibility to ensure that no geographical entity of the Federation either has the right to monopolize, or, to be left out of the national "cake". Those entrusted with the public trust have the responsibility and obligation to perform without bias or favoritism. There must be true patriotic governance and less personal vendettas, less greed and wealth accumulation at the expense of the public good. There is nothing noble, prestigious or inspiring in the notoriety of being known as one of the most, if not the outright most, corrupt countries on the planet. It not only brings *de facto* disrepute to the country, it also hinders internal investments, business and trade. Businesses need to open up and develop to help absorb the huge unemployment among the youth of the country. There are too many young people parading around the ministries for contracts who, when given them didn't have the means,or expertise to carry them out". Again, Professor Balarabe paused to entertain any questions or comments, but so far, there were none.

Suddenly Dr. Khan informed them of his efforts to trace the where about of his childhood friend, Ekademe. Unfortunately so far his travels to the South East, specifically to Calabar and the other cities have not yielded any positive results, in spite of his buying several advertising spots in the local newspapers and radio stations specifically asking for anybody who has any knowledge of one 'Ekademe Bassi' to contact him. He had sat by his phone patiently and fearfully fidgeting with his fingers whenever there was blink, but the phone remained mute, no calls came in. He had read every advertisement page of the local papers to see if anybody would respond to him through that medium, but again nothing came either. His only consolation was that he didn't find any record indicating that he's dead. This he said "continues to give me the impetus to keep on looking for my friend. I believe one day I'll find him, even in very old age", then he stopped and cleared his throat.

"It seems", the Professor surmised, "this brings us to the last discussion of the Araba Era and its consequent calamitous civil war. When it comes to the survival of Nigeria we're all stockholders; and let nobody tells us otherwise. Are there suggestions about what we need to discuss the next time we meet? If there is none at this moment, I want each one of us to go home and think over such areas of interests, of course not exclusive and limited to; Pre-independence Struggle and Colonial London Conferences; The Merits and Demerits of Regional Governments; The preferred system of Government for Nigeria or the Colonial settlement of the West Indies nations..", he paused and James said,

"I would also be indulged, and no doubt flabbergasted - as I know many of you would be too, - if Dr. Kasimu could be persuaded to consider or agree to lead us into a discussion of the 2007-2009 Collapse of the Major Financial Systems of the World. It may be instructive to our Bankers in the future", he quipped.

Abba and Veronica thought all the suggested topics were worthy of the group's considerations, but advised the group ponder and mull over all of thembefore making their selection after the long *Eid sallah* and Christmas celebrations. All the members present assented to Abba and Veronica's suggestion.

The professor then stood up, shook his neighbors' hands warmly, and wished all of them "good luck" and "good night", but most particularly to Dr. Khan in his search for his friend. *Mamu* came and stood by his side, as both of them watched their friends departing in the shadows, each to their respective houses.

Ten years later the members of the Local Historical Society Study group that had remained at the *Monte Sophia* quarters—Alhaji Abba, James and Owoleye and their wives, Hajiya Jummai Bukar, Jamima Idakoji and Fumilayo Afolabi —decided to attend the Peoples' Democratic Quest (PDQ) party primary rally being held in the Ahmadu Bello Square, adjacent to the old market. By the time they arrived, humungous African drums were being played, *algeta*, (a wind instrument similar to a trumpet) was also being played, in addition to numerous other entertaining instruments, *garaya*, (a percussion instrument, similar a banjo), *shola*, (flute), *stianza*, (xylophone), et.al. The high Table had been set on a velvet carpet and lavishly decorated, each seat adorned and labeled with the name of its distinguished occupier and his spouse. The whole stadium was in pandemonium and also a state of wild excitement and hilarity. Of the luminaries attending the party, and of some of the invited guests, some of the names that immediately jumped at all of them out of the whole lot were those of people they were already intimate or familiar with.

These included: His Excellency (H.E) Prof. Balarabe Musa Yousef, distinguished Ambassador to Saudi Arabia, Dr. Aluor S. Khan, the Foreign Secretary of the Federal Republic of Nigeria, Alhaji Musa Wada, Federal Minister of Defense, H.E Mr. Golu Bunzu, the Ambassador to South Africa; Dr. Jimbala Ngwozi, the first female African astronaut in space, Dr. Etty Bugile Gwor, the world-renowned evolutionary biologist from Oxford University, H.E Alhaji Salihu Balarabe, Governor of Kudu State, H.E Dr. Ahua J. Kasimu, Deputy Governor Central Bank of Nigeria, and, last but not the least. H.E, Retired Lieutenant Colonel Patrick G. Anande, Ambassador to the Royal Court, United Kingdom.

"We should all thank His Grace for the present dispensation; it would seem we're all in capable hands!" James shouted, over the noise, to Pastor Owoleye, with a marvelous look of surprise in his twinkling eyes (He wears glasses now, but one could still make out the expression of gratitude and surprise in his eyes), and Pastor Owoleye shouted back in agreement.

After they had finished exchanging intimate thoughts to each other about the current political environment; then a young, beautiful, elegant lady from the department of law, Mirnga International American University (MIAU) got up and signaled the boisterous out-of-control crowd to "quieted down".

"His Excellency", she shouted trying to block out the bursting and disturbing noise, "the Governor, distinguished Ambassadors and Government Ministers, Ladies and Gentlemen", the chairwoman of the department of law atMIAU, Dr. Hadizatu Hayatu paused to regain her normal sweet voice and even breathe.

"I have the enviable privilege of introducing to you our main speaker for this august party gathering tonight. He's not a stranger to most of you; ladies and gentlemen I present to you our new crop of politicians and public servant, the most distinguished Honorable President of the Senate of the Federal Republic of Nigeria, the one and only Doctor Atompera S. Anande".

The whole gathering erupted in euphoria, jubilation, and shouts of: "Power to PDQ! Power to PDQ! And long live Nigeria "could be heard well beyond the confines and walls of the huge stadium.

Glistening tears could be easily observed welling in H.E Patrick Anande's eyes. He sobbed openly and quietly. When Uche his wife saw the specter of her husband sobbing openly in public, she pulled out a beautiful white kerchief from her gold purse and handed it to him gently to wipe his face with.

"Ladies and gentlemen", Dr. Atompera thundered above the drowning noise of the crowd and the huge drums, "the insidious politics of "do or die" is behind……." Somebody interrupted him by shouting "Power to PDQ!"

He cleared his throat and resumed "Moreover, the doctrine of rotating the Presidency between the Northern Muslims and Southern Christians, as advocated and purloined by some parties, is dead and a non-starter for us in PDQ! Such a nefarious doctrine, if adopted, or allowed to take roots, as some of the parties would have us believe, (I won't name names because you already know them!), will forever consign some of our citizens to a second-class citizenry and stifle the aspirations of a Northern Christian youth of ever becoming a President, *vis-a-vis* a young Southerner who happens to be a Muslim!" He paused in expectation of applause, and also to wipe his face, which was drenched in sweat from the sweltering tropical heat. However, to his utter amazement, nobody seemed to hear, or was indeed paying any attention to, what he was saying at all, all eyes were turned and fixated on the elderly woman hissing and murmuring loudly….

When Dr. Atompera looked to his right in the direction where the attention of the crowd was turned and looked some few seats away from the top table where he stood, he recognized the familiar face of the lady drawing the attention of the crowd, and solemnly acknowledged her by half genuflecting toward her and blowing her kisses. But, of course, neither the lady nor the man sitting next to her noticed. The woman continued to sob feverishly and continuously. Her face had been completely immersed in golden sparkling tears of joy, and she refused to be comforted. People sitting close to the couple could see the lady's ashen shrunken face and, of course, hear her loud murmur and whisper. She was heard saying under her breath, "God is great! God is great!" She was completely immersed in euphoric ecstasy and epiphany.

References

1. *Charlotte Brontë; Jane Eyre; Introduction and notes by Susan O. Weisser, Barnes &Noble Classics, NY, 2003*
2. *Dostoyevsky; The Brother Karamazov, vol.2. Translated by David Magarshack, 1958*
3. *Hawking, Stephen and Leonard Mlodinow; The Grand Design, 2010*
4. *John N. Paden; Ahmadu Bello, Sardauna of Sokoto, 1986*
5. *Leo Tolstoy; War and Peace, Translated by Ann Dunnigan, 1968*
6. *Nowa Omoigui; Citizens for Nigeria: Northern Nigeria military counter-Rebellion July 1966; www.citizensfornigeria.com, 2009*
7. *Olusegun Obasanjo; My Command; An account of the Nigerian civil war, 1967-1970; 1980*
8. *Paul J. Steinhardt and Neil Turok; The Endless Universe: Beyond the Big Bang, 2007*
9. *Richard Dawkins; The Greatest Show on Earth; 2009*
10. *Robert Wright, The Evolution of God; 2009*